A HO 2016 NOVEL
AN Ea NOVEL

Margaret Graham has been writing for thirty years. Her first novel was published in 1986 and she is now working on her sixteenth. As a bestselling author her novels have been published in the UK, Europe and the USA.

Margaret has written two plays and numerous short stories and features, and has co-researched a television documentary, which grew out of *Canopy of Silence*. She is Contributing Editor for *Frost Magazine*, and is also a writing tutor and speaker. She founded the Yeovil Literary Prize and now that she lives in High Wycombe she has launched and runs the charity www.wordsforthewounded.co.uk. WforW raises funds for the recovery of wounded troops by donations, literary festivals and the Independent Author Book Award writing prize.

She has 'he who must be disobeyed', four children and three grandchildren who think OAP stands for Old Ancient Person. They have yet to understand the politics of pocket money. Margaret is a member of the WI, her local U3A. She does Tai Chi, and eats too much.

For more information about Margaret Graham, visit her website at www.margaret-graham.com and www.wordsforthewounded.co.uk

Margaret GRAHAM

A HOUSE DIVIDED

AN *Easterleigh Hall* NOVEL

arrow books

3 5 7 9 10 8 6 4 2

Arrow Books
20 Vauxhall Bridge Road
London SW1V 2SA

Arrow Books is part of the Penguin Random House group of companies
whose addresses can be found at global.penguinrandomhouse.com.

Penguin
Random House
UK

First published in Great Britain by Arrow Books in 2016

www.penguin.co.uk

A CIP catalogue record for this book is available from the British Library

ISBN 9781784751043

Typeset in 11.5/14.5 pt Palatino
Jouve (UK), Milton Keynes
Printed and bound in Great Britain by Clays Ltd, St Ives Plc

MIX
Paper from
responsible sources
FSC
www.fsc.org   FSC® C016897

Penguin Random House is committed to a
sustainable future for our business, our readers
and our planet. This book is made from Forest
Stewardship Council® certified paper.

*For fellow writers: Pat – born to dance and Michael –
forever Ambridge.
They lead me astray – yes, it is that way round.*

Chapter One

Easterleigh Hall, May 1936

At eleven on the day of Jack Forbes' wedding, Evie Brampton, part owner of Easterleigh Hall hotel, head cook and wife of the Honourable Auberon Brampton, roared with laughter and chased Lady Veronica Williams down the yard steps, heading for the kitchen.

'Nearly got you,' Evie called as they entered the boot hall, but Ver darted ahead into the kitchen, laughing too.

Behind them, Mrs Moore manoeuvred her way down the steps, shouting, 'You're in your forties, not a couple of bairns, you daft pair, and this is no way to sort out the final preparations for your brother's wedding buffet, Evie. And you, Bridie Brampton, for the love of God, come away from the stables; your mam needs to test your canapés. That horse can do without your strokes for now.'

Evie and Ver raised their eyebrows, laughing so hard they had to hang on to one another as they leaned against the nearest range. It was still warm from the cooking of quiches. Ver whispered, 'Has she finished bossing?'

1

Evie shook her head and the laughter continued as Mrs Moore heaved herself down the last of the steps, still issuing a stream of orders. Finally, they heard her call, 'Bridie, pet, come *now*. Evie might be your mam but she's still your boss. And everyone remember to wash your hands before you touch anything, if you don't mind. By, it would all go to pot if I wasn't here.'

Evie and Ver pulled themselves together, straightening their pastel-coloured silk outfits. Evie set her wedding hat more firmly on her head and skirted the huge kitchen table, heading for the apron hooks against the end wall. Ver said, following her, 'Crikey, eighty and still in full voice, bless her cotton socks.'

Evie laughed again as she threw an apron to the woman who was her best friend, hotel partner and sister-in-law. 'How will we get ourselves from A to B if she ever *does* properly retire? It truly doesn't bear thinking about. I just love her so much.'

She shouted, knowing that Mrs Moore would hear because she'd be entering the boot hall by now. 'The forties aren't old, so very there, but those in their eighties are ancient.'

The two women heard Mrs Moore's great booming laugh, and rushed into the scullery to wash their hands, thrilled that Jack and Gracie were married at last. They headed into the cool pantry set alongside the scullery, and within seconds they were putting the desperately extravagant gift of Russian caviar onto the pastry bases, set on wire trays, that Bridie had baked at five this morning. The job done, Evie saw her anxious daughter hovering in the doorway and picked up a couple of the pastries.

Ver nudged her. 'Come on, then, Evie, let's taste 'em.' The two women grinned at each other, then held their noses as they ate the canapés. They grimaced. 'Mam,' Bridie whispered, her hazel eyes wide as she stared at Evie. 'Are they really that bad?'

Mrs Moore appeared and put her arm around Bridie's shoulders. 'No, pet. If they were, your mam would be thinking of a nice way of telling you. That daft expression means the canapés are nigh on perfect. They're just being silly, because they're heady that your Uncle Jack and Auntie Gracie have regularised things.'

She steered Bridie to the huge pine table, above which hung the gleaming copper pans that had been in use since before even Mrs Moore had joined Easterleigh Hall. Evie followed, smiling. Mrs Moore and Bridie, the young and the old, stood together at the far end. The old had experienced so much, before and during the awful war when they were a hospital, and the years after when Easterleigh Hall had become a hotel. The young, fresh and eager, was soaking up the handed-down knowledge like a sponge.

Behind them, at the end of the ranges set along the left-hand wall, the furnace gurgled. Evie had stoked it up before they left for the blessing in the church, and that should see it through for a few more hours. Over everything hung the heavy smell of baked potatoes, which were keeping warm in the end range, and would be served with the buffet.

Evie gazed around, and waved to the kitchen and laundry staff taking a break in the staff hall before putting on their finery. First, though, they would take some buffet treats across to the Neave Wing Convalescent Centre, which as usual had its fair share of patients recovering from injuries, though not war induced any more. They would then join in the fun.

'Our very own Easterleigh Hall hotel. Seventeen wonderful and peaceful years,' Evie murmured, overcome with emotion. Ver slipped her arm through hers, saying, 'They have been, haven't they?'

During that time the hotel had grown, only stalling slightly during the years of economic depression. The Neave Wing had continued its care of the injured, and Jack and Mart had been able to keep most of their men employed at the pits they managed for Auberon. They were hoping that they might open yet more seams, but the problem was selling the coal at a viable rate in these parlous times.

Of course the hotel had to be cautious, but, following on from the war, the kitchen staff were experts at making something excellent out of very little. Many returning guests were ex-patients, whom Evie loved, and who had eventually eased themselves out of the darkness of their wounds and their memories into the sunlight.

At the thought of war and darkness, she faltered. Were such times returning again? There had been trouble between the communists and the fascists in Hawton last week, and similar outbreaks had occurred in many major towns. There was still nationwide unemployment, the Nazis were in charge in Germany and had taken back the Rhineland. There were strikes and anarchy in regions of Spain.

It was too concerning to contemplate, and she concentrated on Mrs Moore and Bridie, who were heading for the wedding cake. It stood on three tiers at the end of the pine table, hidden from view beneath swathes of muslin to await, as promised by Bridie, the great unveiling.

Evie murmured, 'I just hope that everything improves, Ver. Not just in the world, but here, in our family.' Ver said nothing, just tightened her mouth and reached forward, touching the table for luck. Evie did the same, for she could feel her joy sliding away.

Damn Millie. Jack's wife had run off with a German prisoner of war based near Easterleigh Hall, but eighteen months ago she had written to him out of the blue, offering him a divorce which would enable him to marry Gracie. They had all celebrated that the woman was finally giving Jack his freedom after all these years. These celebrations, though, had been cut short when Millie had begun writing to her son, Tim, whom Jack and Gracie had brought up in the face of her abandonment. Not just writing but inviting him over to Germany, and so it had started.

Evie whispered to Ver, for what seemed like the millionth time, 'Good grief, Ver, we now have a member of our family who is a fascist. It doesn't seem possible.'

Ver nodded. 'I know.'

Evie glanced at the clock. Eleven twenty. They'd have to report for the photographs when the bridal party returned from the church. What on earth was keeping them? Bridie and Mrs Moore weren't ready either, it seemed, for they were still deep in conversation.

Evie moved closer to the table and the lists she had made last week, which were laid out in two piles. She leafed through them, checking them off again in her mind: the quiches in the cool pantry, the chicken legs, the ham, the potato salad, the forced lettuce, the . . .

Ver cut in, leaning close to Evie so that the others couldn't hear. 'Of course, Millie will be encouraging Tim in his politics, bloody woman. She always was a poisonous baggage. Think of the trouble she and that POW caused before they scarpered, destroying Harry Travers' hives, blowing up the cedar tree, stealing the silver. Now she wants her son back, body and soul, probably because he's too old to be dependent on her.'

Evie gripped her friend's hand. 'We don't know that, she might have changed,' she whispered.

Ver's smothered laugh was harsh. 'Don't be ridiculous. More than half the pleasure of her reunion with

6

her son will be the pain his conversion gives Jack and Grace, not to mention the rest of us. But don't forget, Tim's in his early twenties, Evie darling. There's still time for him to get himself sorted out.'

At the other end of the table, Bridie was grinning at something Mrs Moore had said and looking for her notebook. Evie took it from the pile next to the lists and scooted it down the table. The pencil was on a string and dragged along behind. 'Thanks, Mam.'

Bridie wrote something down.

Evie whispered to Ver, holding up one of the lists as though they were discussing it. 'But it's as Jack and Gracie say, the lad has every right to make his own choices, and they don't want the family condemning him for his decisions.'

Now Bridie and Mrs Moore were running through their own lists for the desserts. Evie continued, 'The trouble is, I'm not at all sure that Bridie accepts that. I find I'm really on edge when they're together in case she says something unforgivable, but he does taunt her so. Have you noticed? It's a nasty type of bullying when all three cousins have always been so close.'

Ver slipped her arm around her friend. 'Bridie's a chip off the old block, so she'll still be standing when the rest of us are flat on our backs.'

The pair of them smiled at one another. Evie said, 'Anyway, Millie hasn't taken him over completely yet, Ver. The lad's still working and living in

Newcastle, so I suppose the time to despair will be if he moves to Berlin.'

Ver said flatly, 'We're not even going to think about that.'

The women fell silent, watching Bridie and Mrs Moore and trying not to look at the clock, because if there was something very wrong with the cake, they'd need a few moments to sort it out. Another five minutes passed and Evie wondered if she could hurry them up, but then, glory be, Bridie and Mrs Moore began to untuck the muslin that covered the wedding cake. Evie called, 'Your da is so proud of you, Bridie, and can't wait to see it.'

Ver said, 'As are we all.' She whispered to Evie, 'She does like her moments of drama, doesn't she, bless her.'

Now she said loudly, 'Bridie wouldn't discuss the cake at all, you know, Evie, but said I had to wait. Do you know, I think she could even outshine your cooking, my girl, in time, and with Aub's blonde hair the boys will be like bees round a honeypot.'

'Oh, Aunt Ver,' groaned Bridie, adjusting her grip on the muslin.

'Over my dead body,' Evie murmured, knowing that Aub would be beating them back even before she got off the starting block.

'Over your dead body can be arranged,' Ver countered.

Evie laughed gently. 'Aye, no doubt it can, and I can see that the reputation of Easterleigh's secure with Bridie, because, my dear Ver, one day we will be old and decrepit.'

Mrs Moore swung round. 'Who's old and decrepit? I'll show you. Ready, Bridie? Let's do it, pet.'

Evie watched the young and the old as they lifted the muslin with a flourish, revealing the cake. As the muslin floated back down, Bridie scrunched it into a bundle. She faced her mother, flushed with excitement, standing there in her powder-blue silk dress with a darker blue jacket, and her small feathered matching hat. She looked more beautiful than Evie could remember, and the cake was supreme.

For a moment there was silence until Evie eventually found her voice. 'It's quite the best I've ever seen, truly it is.'

Mrs Moore patted Bridie. 'Aye, we work well together. She has the most nimble of fingers.'

'Yet another triumph, both of you. It is absolutely grand.' Evie moved to Bridie, loving this child, loving Mrs Moore, and cross with herself for twisting and turning in Millie's breeze.

'What do you think, Mam?' Bridie asked.

'I'm just trying to remember when I've seen such workmanship, and I can't. Jack and Gracie will be so pleased.' Her heart lightened. It was her brother's wedding, it was a day of joy, and her daughter had helped to produce not just a magnificent cake, but excellent canapés, and desserts, which was something that Evie would not have been able to do when *she* was fifteen.

Ver was circling the table, looking in awe at the wedding cake, which would need to be carried out to the marquee. Kevin, who had been the bootboy way back before the war but was now on the front of house team, would organise that.

Bridie slipped to Evie's side. 'Mrs Moore let me do quite a bit of the icing, Mam. She's such a canny cook, isn't she, even with her poor swollen hands and all. Do cooks always get arthritis?'

Evie replied, 'I haven't, so no, and yes, she is clever. She taught me all I know.'

Just then they heard the revving of a car as it drew into the garage yard. A moment later there was the slamming of a door. Someone came rushing down the steps. Evie hugged her daughter, and now they were both laughing.

Evie said, 'If I'm not mistaken, that's the sound of James' tippy-toes, and before he comes, remind me to make sure you have a glass of champagne this afternoon. You deserve it, though you're a little too young.'

'I'm nearly sixteen, Mam.' Bridie sounded irritated.

Evie laughed. 'Of course you are, quite the old woman.'

James Williams, Ver and Richard's son, clattered into the kitchen, his suit creased and his tie askew. He tossed his hat onto the table, and Mrs Moore bawled, 'Off, off.'

He put it on one of the stools instead, hurrying

across to Evie and Bridie by the dresser, his face hot and sweaty.

'Aunt Evie, I've finally delivered Uncle Jack, Aunt Grace and Tim to the photographer following the church blessing. I had to get strict with everyone at the church, as they were just milling about and wouldn't get a move on. It's like herding cats. The vicar is following on his bike. I do wish he wouldn't, he's not safe wobbling all over the place. Honestly, he's halfway to heaven already, with his head stuck so high up in the clouds.'

His mother, Lady Veronica, didn't turn, but continued to pace around the table, her eyes on the three magnificent tiers. 'Draw a breath, James. Yes, I think we gather that you're back, but you must come and admire this work of art. Honestly, Mrs Moore, and you, Bridie, I'm not surprised Easterleigh Hall hotel is being asked to hold so many wedding receptions.' She swept back to her son, kissing him, then moving on to Evie, Bridie, and finally Mrs Moore, kissing them all.

James shouted in his frustration, 'Do listen, everyone. I've just said I've dropped the bride, groom and Tim with the photographer, but Uncle Jack's being difficult, saying he doesn't want the photos on the steps, but in front of the cedar tree. Tim's getting in a state because the photographer's arguing, so he's sent me to tell you and Aunt Evie, so you can sort it out.'

Evie grinned at the boy, and tilted her head at Ver.

Mrs Moore was tutting and making her way past the table. Evie and Ver caught up with her. All three linked arms, and they set off. 'Calm down, James, we're on our way,' Evie said. They marched through the door, Evie calling over her shoulder, 'Jack's right, everyone was fond of the old cedar tree. It gave people comfort in the war, and just see how tall the replacement has grown. James, make sure Bridie doesn't slide off to fret in the dessert pantry. The crèmes brûlées are perfect and she should be proud. Bridie, cover the cake, bonny lass, and both of you, follow us for the photos, quickly.'

They had reached the bottom of the steps when Evie heard her daughter call, 'It's not going to help the family photos, Mam, to have you and Aunt Ver in aprons, unless you're advertising the charms of our hotel, which I wouldn't put past the pair of you.'

Evie and Ver looked at one another, tore off their aprons and handed them to Bridie, who had run after them. Mrs Moore shouted as she reached for the handrail, mounting the first step, 'Bridie, remember to shut all the doors when you come. We don't want the dachshunds barking their barks, walking their walks, and deciding they'd like to be food tasters.'

Evie and Ver let Mrs Moore tackle the steps on her own, knowing that to offer help would go down badly. Instead they followed her up, keeping a close eye as she puffed and panted. Once she reached the yard safely, the three set off.

James had parked his father's Bentley in front of the second garage, white ribbons still attached. The first garage acted as a playroom for the children of staff and guests. There was an outdoor area with swings and a slide.

Together the women walked from the garage yard, into the stable yard, and then to the gravel driveway. Ahead was the marquee on the front lawn, and to the right, Easterleigh Hall. The three women were arm in arm, a monstrous regiment, so Jack and Auberon frequently called them. Ver's husband, Richard, wouldn't dare, he'd whispered to Evie.

As they crunched across the gravel, Mrs Moore sniffed. 'Did you see the vicar's bicycle clips on under his cassock when he conducted the blessing? Daft old thing, he is.' They marched on to take their place amongst the throng.

Chapter Two

Bridie adjusted the muslin. She adored cooking and baking, and would happily do it every day. Well, she did, daft lass. First, she, Mrs Moore and her mam had made the wedding cakes using a heavy fruit mixture. They had not only added brandy to the mix, but as the weeks went by Bridie had dribbled more onto the top until the fumes stung her eyes, watching it sink into the guts of the cakes.

Mr Harvey, the butler, thought they had used too much in these days of lingering economic depression, until Evie had pointed out it was an exceptional wedding, for Jack, and furthermore that the cake would be iced by Mrs Moore. At that, he had marked up the bottle in his account book with alacrity, and said nothing further. Mrs Moore was his wife and meant everything in the world to him, and besides, she'd tell him the error of his ways and not mince her words in the doing of it.

Bridie had also said that the remains of the cake would go to the pitmen at the retirement houses Gracie and her brother ran beneath Stunted Tree Hill.

Finally, it had been time to ice the cake. After her day's work in the kitchen, and before her riding therapy for the Neave Wing, Bridie had looked and learned, as Mrs Moore ordered. She had observed the spinning of cobwebs, the thicker piping, and breathed in the sweet smell. It had made her long to go to cookery school, to become the best pastry cook, and the best ever at icing.

'Come on, Bridie,' James nagged.

'Leave me be, man,' she snapped, as she tucked the muslin gently beneath the tiered cake stand, and made sure the knife was by its side and would not be forgotten.

Each day she had hoped that Mrs Moore would let her try her hand on something other than practice cakes, until finally she had been allowed to pipe much of the finery on the surface of the three tiers, and, last of all, the bow beneath the heart.

She stood back, tweaking a fold of the muslin which lay too heavily on the heart, saying to James, 'There's a great deal of looking and learning in life, isn't there?'

James hadn't been sure what degree to do, so had decided to work for a couple of years at Home Farm, where Bridie and her family lived, and her father, Auberon Brampton, farmed. It was as James had walked behind the plough, geeing on the Clydesdales, that he'd decided to read Classics at Oxford this October. He said it was something to do with looking at horses' bums for hours at a time. He also said that he understood why her father preferred the peace of farming to tiptoeing about like a spare part at the hotel, because in some ways it gave you time to think, but at others, no time at all. A good mix.

James came to her, wiping crumbs from his mouth. She snatched a look at the cool pantry. The door was open and she slapped his arm. He said, 'I only took one canapé, so hush yourself. I think they might be delicious, but perhaps I should taste another just to make sure?' His dark blonde hair flopped over his forehead, his blue eyes reflecting his grin.

She slapped him again, and hurried to close the pantry door. 'You dare and I'll have your guts for garters, you hear me? And answer me, please. Does Da make you look and learn when you work on the farm with him, or do you just "do"?'

When she returned he was peering under the muslin, and he whistled. 'She's a game old bird, isn't she? That really is good. No, your father says the best way to learn is to get stuck in. So there's your answer. Farm work is not a romantic notion, it's damnably hard, but, as he says, better than his generation had to put up with, given the war and all that.'

Bridie shut the door into the internal corridor, grinning through the glass at the kitchen staff in their sitting room across the corridor. Maudie, who was in charge of the scullery and laundry, was jabbing her finger at the clock on the wall. Bridie retaliated by miming that it was time for all of them to change for the reception.

Bridie noticed that the fourth generation of dachshunds, Raisin and Currant, were with them, ensconced on the sofa. James nipped into the pantry, leaving with yet another canapé in his mouth. 'All clear of dogs,' he said, spitting crumbs everywhere.

Bridie undid her apron and hung it on the hook. 'I bet you knew very well Maudie had them. You are a disgusting and greedy child, James Williams.'

She led the way from the kitchen, checking that James shut the door behind them. Out they went, up the stairs into the garage yard, while he grumbled, half laughing, 'I'm twenty, if you don't mind, so you can watch it, foul and unreasonable infant.'

It was no more than their usual mode of communication. As they started on their way they were diverted by Prancer's whinny and they went to his stall to stroke his neck. Then Bridie heard her mother's call, 'Troublemakers, where are you?'

'Coming,' they both replied in unison, and gave Prancer one last stroke. 'You're a grand old boy,' James crooned, then asked, 'How's young Tom finding it now? Is it helping him?'

Tom Welsh was the young miner who had lost a leg in a rare roof fall in Auld Maud, the Easton pit Uncle Jack managed.

Bridie smiled. 'Ah, we got him up the ramp in a wheelchair yesterday, then with Young Stan and Clive we hoisted him onto Prancer. We set up his balance just right and you should have been here, bonny lad. Within an hour he had made a circuit of the paddock, and his shoulders were straight, his eyes alight.'

James nodded. 'Well, clever girl, you. Sometimes, Bridie Brampton, you put two and two together and make four. Not often, mind, never could count, as I rem—'

They heard Evie call again. 'Better go.' They ran now, James in the lead, and he called over his shoulder, 'What about Prancer's daughter, Fanny, how's she training? And the mare, in foal to him? You have to remember, Bridie, he's an old boy who had a tough old war, so he can't go on forever.'

She shouted back as they ran along the gravel drive of Easterleigh Hall, past the wedding marquee set up on the lawn in front of the cedar tree, 'I'm sick to death of hearing about the war. We need to be thinking about today, James, because it's *like* a bloody war. Have you seen the latest newspapers? Have you forgotten the fascists are opening a British Union of Fascists' Meeting House in Hawton? A pit village, for pity's sake. So, we haven't time to witter on about the past, we need to see how we can stop these buggers right now.'

Colonel Potter was walking down the steps of the Hall and he looked up, startled, as Bridie ran past him, kicking up gravel. She called, 'Sorry, Uncle Potty, we're late.'

James called, 'Morning, Colonel Potter. Sorry about Bridie, appalling language and manners. Don't miss all the photos, and you too, Sir Anthony.'

Potty laughed and Bridie heard him say to Sir Anthony Travers, who walked at his side, 'Ah, the energy of youth. Makes one feel quite exhausted, what?'

Bridie was on the grass now, and her mother was gesticulating and frowning. 'Oh, heavens,' Bridie groaned. 'She heard me swear.' She reached Evie, who dragged her beneath the branches of the cedar. The shade was deep, and so was her mother's frown.

'I've told you several times, Bridie. You *will* mind your manners, you will not swear and you will address Colonel Potter properly, or I will want to know the reason why.'

Bridie longed to pull away, but knew better than to try. 'Oh, Mam. Yes, I know, and I try, but I've always known him as Uncle Potty, and I forget.'

'Well, don't. Not again. And don't rush about kicking up gravel, and I repeat, mind your language. It's disgraceful and won't do.'

Bridie swung round as Tim's voice carried to them, from the wedding party who were drifting about nearby. 'What's she done now, James? Isn't it time she grew up?'

Tim was standing near Sir Anthony Travers, who headed the consortium that sponsored the Neave Wing rehabilitation unit. The photographer was pointing at people here, there and everywhere for the group photograph. Bridie glared at Tim because his tone had been cold and harsh, not teasing like it used to be. She felt tired suddenly, and upset. She muttered, 'Families are damned confusing.'

Her mother warned, 'Language, Bridie.'

'Sorry, Mam.' She still looked at Tim, so tall and handsome, his hair with that red glint, his eyes almost black. He was ordering James about now, because it was what he had taken to doing. 'Surprised he's not wearing his Blackshirt uniform.'

'Sorry?' said Evie, starting to walk towards full sunlight. 'I didn't hear you.'

Bridie said, 'Never mind.'

Evie turned and beckoned to her. 'Come along now.' It was an order, given in *that* voice, which meant: you're on a knife-edge, young lady.

She followed. If he did have a uniform, would he take it to Germany tomorrow when he went out to see his mam again? Bridie felt the now familiar hurt at Tim's rejection of her and James, when they had always been so close. As she left the shade of the cedar, Tim called, 'Do hurry, and for God's sake, try and behave.'

Her mother turned and gave her a warning frown. 'Bridie, don't react. Not today.'

It was too late, and Bridie felt the words leaving her mouth, and she didn't damn well care. 'I am an adult, I'm working just as hard as you in your airless little office, if you don't mind, and why have you changed, Tim Forbes? Because you are a Forbes, you know. You're being corrupted, bonny lad, by your damned moth—'

'Bridie,' roared her father, who had been talking to the photographer. She stopped dead, horrified at herself. She saw that everyone had turned and the chatter had stopped. Jack had stiffened, Gracie had paled, and Tim had flushed. Above them birds flew across the blue sky; the clouds chased one another in the cool east wind. That was the only movement for what seemed like hours, and then her father took a step towards her, but Jack held him back, shaking his head, forcing a laugh. She heard him say, 'They always nitpick one another.'

James took a step towards her but Ver and Richard held *him* back. Bridie swallowed, her body so rigid it hurt. She shouldn't have said it, she knew that, but why did no-one say anything to Tim when he behaved like that? Were they scared he'd leave for good if they did? It was the first time she had asked herself that question and was frightened at the possible answer, because she couldn't bear never to see him again.

Evie almost ran back to her, saying in a voice low and fierce, 'How dare you, Bridie Brampton? Really, how damned dare you? We've all talked about this over the last few months. We will not make a judgement about Tim, do you understand, or are you too high and mighty to do as Uncle Jack has requested?' Her mother ended on a hiss.

Bridie rested her head in her hands for a moment, wanting to run from the whole lot of them. But then she looked up. 'You swore then, Mam, so it's not damn well fair.'

Her mam raised her finger, shaking it. 'Not one more word, Bridie, unless it is an apology, and keep your voice down. This is not your day, and I won't have you ruining it.'

'But Mam, he was so arrogant.'

Evie raised her finger higher.

Bridie wanted to bat it away, but instead felt her fury turn to an awful sort of silent sobbing in her chest. She swallowed, and again. Above her the cedar branches were moving in the breeze. She felt chilled, and alone. She whispered, 'I'm so sorry, but he used to like me. He was always there, the three of us. He made me feel safe, us feel safe. It's not the same now and it's as though . . . Oh, I don't know. It's all just empty, it's changed us all. Poor Uncle Jack, poor Aunt Gracie, and I've made it worse, and I hate it without him. Hate it. Hate him.'

The photographer was calling and beckoning to the family members, who came to life and began to move as directed. James looked over at her, and winked. She felt weak with relief. Good old James, at least they still had one another. He'd help her through the next few hours, even if everyone else was furious.

Her mother was saying quietly, 'Stand up straight, wipe your tears, put on a smile. Your uncle and aunt are married, and as Grandma used to say, far too often, "All will be well." But that, of course, will be after you've apologised to everyone.'

They straightened their shoulders, smiled at one another, and headed off to join the group. At that moment her mam squeezed her hand. 'It will be alright, Bridie, and you're right, he was horribly superior. If you hadn't said anything, I fear I would have done, so that makes me a hypocrite for snarling at you. What a pair we are. Now let's smile for the camera and remember that Tim is probably very muddled at the moment. Who wouldn't be, having a real mother coming back into your life? Let's keep thinking of that, and understand.'

Bridie wished that Grandma Susan and Grandpa Bob were still alive, because they wouldn't have put up with Tim's behaviour for one moment. Or would they? She didn't really know about much any more. She gripped her mam's hand, tightly. She couldn't bear it if Evie wasn't her real mother, and she hadn't thought of it like that before. Pity for Tim overwhelmed her, and as they reached the wedding party, she began her apologies. The first was to him, and heartfelt.

He smiled, and shrugged. 'Don't give it another thought. I won't.' Again there was that sneering harshness. She walked away.

Chapter Three

The wedding guests circulated within the marquee, or lingered outside where they smoked, talked, or just admired the herbaceous borders. Tim stood alone, and ground out his cigarette on the lawn, checking that Young Stan, the head gardener, wasn't looking. Instead he was talking to someone who had been introduced by Tim's da, Jack, as Herr Bauer.

Apparently Jack and he had met when Bauer was an officer at Da's German prisoner of war camp and had helped out Jack and his marras. They had kept in desultory contact since then, and as he was in the country he had accepted an invitation to today's wedding.

Young Stan was pointing out hyacinths, bluebells, peonies and a clump of something which had not yet bloomed. Young Stan looked around, saw Tim, and called across, 'Hope you put that stub into one of the sand buckets provided.'

Tim almost stood to attention, before picking up what was left of the stub. He waved it at Young Stan, who nodded before turning back to Herr Bauer. Tim half laughed at himself. Scared of a gardener, for heaven's sake, but then Young Stan had inherited his grandfather's way with words, and volume, or so Mam said. He couldn't really remember Old Stan. The laugh died in his throat because Gracie wasn't his mam. His mother was in Berlin.

He felt a rush of nervousness at the thought of seeing his mother, but this was mixed with excitement, and anticipation. Heine and Millie had been living in a little town near Hamburg last year, when she had first written to him, but since then Heine had been promoted, and was now an officer in the SS, the Schutzstaffel, a major paramilitary organization under Adolf Hitler and the Nazi Party, and they had just moved to a smart apartment in Berlin.

When he arrived tomorrow they would have a dinner party for him, his mother had said, and after that she'd take him to a coffee house. Perhaps they'd have a stroll round the lake, and later, the opera. He walked to a sand bucket and dropped the stub, where it lay amongst others. He sneaked a look at Young Stan, who nodded his approval, then walked on with Herr Bauer.

Tim moved to the shade of the cedar. Somehow it seemed to block out all noise, though that was impossible; it must just be psychological. He stared up through the branches. He realised he'd never asked who had blown up the original one and no-one ever talked about it. It was so long ago, he supposed, but what a foul thing to do.

He patted his inside pocket where he kept his mother's letters. He hadn't known what to think when he'd first heard from her. Of course he knew who she was, and that Roger, the valet, was his father, and had discarded her. But she'd left him with Da when he was really young, so the letter was from a stranger and had been a bolt from the blue.

He groped in his suit pocket for the gold cigarette case which had arrived from Heine and Millie just yesterday. It had a faint engraving on the top. He thought it was a candlestick or something, but it was so worn, he couldn't really make it out. It was antique, and their generosity overwhelmed him.

They'd welcomed him on the two occasions he'd visited as the long-lost son he was, and his mother had cried to have him back in her life. She had said she'd left him behind because of the uncertainty over her future with Heine, and that a little boy needed a steady, familiar home. She knew that one day he'd understand, but they had been years which had broken her heart.

He'd felt so sorry for her.

He closed the cigarette case, decided against risking Young Stan's beady eyes when it came to discarding another stub, and sauntered out into the sun again. The smell of hyacinths was carried on the breeze, along with cigar smoke. Ah, there was Colonel Potter, with Sir Anthony. They were both puffing on Havanas, no doubt. Bridie and James were passing, heads down, deep in conversation, and walking towards the back of the marquee. They, in their turn, saw him, and James called across. 'Tim,

Mr Harvey said we're all needed to take round the champagne and canapés now.'

Tim sighed, waved. For God's sake, there was no peace. There was always something needing to be done with this family. If it wasn't helping amputees to sit on horses, it was serving a load of guests. No doubt someone would hint before the end of the day that he should help Bridie muck out stables, or, because he was an engineer, ask him to design some piece of machinery that would help the wounded with their balance, or . . .

He thrust his cigarette case back into his pocket. Millie, his mother, was quite right when she said that when Evie, Ver or Gracie set their minds on an idea, everyone had to fall in. You could add Bridie, he thought, because using horses for the wounded had been her project. Why didn't they all get out of this backwater and really live?

He ambled along in the wake of the kids, as he'd come to think of them over the last year. Like puppies, they were, barking up the wrong tree, carrying on about the awful fascists. Couldn't they see what was being achieved on the continent? At the rear of the marquee, Ron Simmonds, who was a partner in the hotel, was waiting with Mr Harvey. Tim had always thought the butler was a great old bloke, but his mother had put him right on that. Interfering old tyrant, she'd called him, but not as bad as Mrs Moore.

She'd been amazed when she heard that Mr Harvey

27

had married Mrs Moore at the end of the war. How she'd laughed; it had made him uncomfortable. In fact, his mother's laugh was one of the things he didn't quite like about her. It didn't sound real, whereas Gracie and his aunts . . .

Ron called, grinning, 'In your own time, then, Tim old lad. Just you forget that we've a load of thirsty people in need of sustenance.' By his side, at the trestle table, Mr Harvey poured champagne carefully into fine crystal glasses, the bottle wrapped in a damask napkin, each glass tilted, his hand rock steady.

Tim picked up a tray of full glasses, and entered the marquee through the rear flap. Ron called, 'Take the left-hand section, if you would, Tim. Go as far as the cake table. Bridie and James are each taking the other two thirds, with others roaring about with the canapés.'

The marquee was huge and decorated with white hyacinths and myrtle, for constancy and love, or so Gracie had explained. The fragrance was heavy, contained as it was in the marquee, but as always he could smell the grass beneath the floor, though he could never understand why.

He gave a small bounce, and the floor didn't even creak. Grandpa Forbes and Tom Wilson, the old blacksmith, both of whom had devised false limbs for the wounded, had done a good job when they created the interlocking wooden sections ten years ago. The difficulty had been getting a tight enough fit. It had fascinated Tim, so Grandpa had let him help. That's when Jack had thought he'd make a really good design engineer. He was, and all.

Tim skirted the top table, holding the tray on his fingers, and entered the fray, smiling at the guests, who snatched the glasses as though they had been stranded in a desert. Within two minutes he was back outside, replenishing, then he turned on his heel, and re-entered. This time he reached as far as Edward Manton, Gracie's brother, who was also the vicar. Edward seemed awkward and nervous, but then, when wasn't he? A drink would do him good.

'Have a few bubbles, Uncle Edward.'

Edward muttered, 'Thank you, Tim. So kind.' He took the last glass and ran his finger down it, leaving a line through the condensation. He looked up thoughtfully. 'Thank you for escorting Gracie down the aisle. It made it such a lovely family occasion, one that warmed my heart.'

Tim smiled back, noticing that Edward still wore his cycle clips. What a silly old beggar; because it wasn't a family occasion, was it? If it had been, they would have invited his mother and Heine. Typical, his mother had said on his last trip, and he could see that it was. The family was so tightly bound together that they didn't live like individuals. He felt the sense of suffocation deepen; it was a feeling that increasingly threatened to overwhelm him.

Gracie was circulating on the right-hand side and chatting to Annie, who held a tray of canapés. Annie saw him, waved, and joined him. 'How's it going your side, bonny lad? Mine are being laudably abstemious with the caviar; all waiting for Bridie and Evie's little miracles, not to mention that amazing cake. Their food is something to behold, isn't it? I'm so glad it's a grand day for your da and mam.'

'They're really lucky,' he said, smiling. He liked Annie, who had worked in the kitchens throughout the war, though now she was married to Sir Anthony's son, Harry, and spent a fair bit of time organising the Neave Wing as well. Perhaps he should talk to her and try to find out exactly how it had been, back then, for his mother when she worked in the laundry?

Annie smiled and slipped away, back into her area, as a guest placed his empty glass on Tim's tray and took a full one. Soon others would do the same, if he didn't keep moving.

The marquee opened onto the lawn, and he saw Da manning the beer barrel, and heard his laughter, echoed by those all around. They were people Tim had grown up with, families who had lived here for years, and were still farming, still mining, still ... His smiled faded.

His mother had said that it must be dreadfully boring for him, and he hadn't realised until then how true that was. God, he was glad he had an escape route, one leading to Berlin where there were clubs, dancing, excitement, full employment, a country moving forward.

At the front, in the shade of the marquee, Kevin, the former bootboy, was taking over the beer barrel, which he could manage perfectly with his undamaged hand. Yet another war wound. Tim sighed. Everyone seemed to accept Sir Anthony's new idea of a Peace committee, even Bridie with her loud mouth, so why couldn't they see that becoming a fascist meant much the same? Who better to get on well with the Nazis?

Together the two countries could sort the unions, clear out the Reds looking to Russia for their orders, and anyone else causing trouble. They could then stride ahead, in full employment, and *never* have another war. What about that for a Peace committee? Tim smiled at Uncle Edward, who was still drifting about like a lost soul, and through the entrance he saw Uncle Aub coming across to his friends, duty done, taking a pint himself, deep in conversation with his da. It was all so predictable.

'Penny for them, Tim?' Young Stan stomped towards him, in his inimitable way.

Tim shrugged. 'Oh, just thinking of this and that.'

His mam came to him now, slipping her arm through his. 'I'll walk with you while we deliver this champagne, bonny lad.' She moved him around the room, talking all the time of her love for him, and for Jack, and how wonderful it had been that he had delayed his holiday with his mother so that he could be here.

'It would have been just awful without you. In

fact, I rather think Jack would have cancelled the thing and left me waiting at the altar for another twenty years.'

She wore her familiar Rose Garden perfume, and her hair was long enough to be coiled over her ears. Well, her one ear; the other had been dislodged by shrapnel in the war. Tim felt his shoulders relax, leaning into her, nudging her slightly as they passed Sister Newsome and Matron, who had arrived in 1914 and were still here. They were clearly squiffy and in need of food, as they giggled quietly at some naughtiness of old Dr Nicholls, who was widowed now, but still a lot of fun.

Then he sobered, because there they all were, happy, chatty, and where was his mother? Not here, not invited, though they knew he was close to her again. Suddenly he was enormously proud of Millie, for grabbing at a life for herself, and at last he understood why she had left him behind. If she hadn't gone, she would still be here, drowning in this awful little pool. It was as she had said: one day he would understand, and now the lingering hurt at her leaving him, and the time it had taken her to find him, disappeared, and he was light-hearted.

'Just look at your da.' His mam was pointing to Jack at the beer barrel, as Uncle Mart and several miners joined the group, including the union rep.

Tim had seldom seen his da looking so happy. How pathetic it all was. 'I'd better let you get on, dearest boy.' His mam moved off, doubling back to

Matron and linking arms with her, guiding the elderly woman to a chair in the 'let's take a break' area.

He worked his way through the melee of laughing, talking guests, until only one glass of champagne remained. Ahead of him was Sir Anthony with Lady Margaret – who liked to think she was Aunt Ver's friend, though the feeling was not mutual – and Herr Bauer. Sir Anthony insisted that Lady Margaret should have the champagne. Tim grinned. 'I'll return in a moment, if you can hang on, or I can call Bridie or James, they have a few on their trays.'

Sir Anthony shook his head, 'No, Tim. I'm happy to wait.' Tim smelt the brandy on his breath, presumably from a flask he carried on his person for such events. Not surprising when the photos took so damned long.

Tim looked at Herr Bauer, who nodded. 'Indeed, I too am more than happy to wait.' His English was immaculate.

Tim checked the German's lapel, but there was no badge that denoted he was a member of the Nazi Party, and he was disappointed.

He dodged his way back to Mr Harvey, who poured the champagne slowly, which was the only way to do it. Tim noticed the liver spots on his hands. God, he was old, his feet must kill him, but he only served on special occasions now.

Six glasses had been filled, six to go. It was

mesmerising. They'd had champagne in his mother and Heine's apartment near Hamburg to celebrate Tim's return to the fold, as his mother put it. He remembered how the champagne had fizzed and overflowed the glasses. He had laughed, taken the bottle from Heine, and shown him how to tip the glass. 'Slowly, slowly,' he had said.

His mother had told him later that it was rude to take over like that, and he must respect Heine. He had apologised in the morning, and Heine had just stared with those pale blue eyes and then laughed. 'It is nothing,' he had said. 'We must just get used to one another's ways, now we are a family.'

Tim watched Mr Harvey, who was the person who had shown him how to pour champagne, how to remove a cork from a wine bottle, how to taste and recognise the different wines: three more glasses to go. Ron Simmonds put his hand on Tim's shoulder. 'Mr Harvey, should we bring out another dozen bottles from the cellar, some more ice, and put them in the water bucket?'

The only thing that didn't move in Ron's mobile face was his nose, which was a replacement for the one that had been blown off in the war. It was the new plastic surgery procedure that had saved so many faces, Tim's mam had said – his mam, Gracie, not his mother, Millie. God, he told himself, it's so damn complicated.

Soon the time would come when he would have to make a firm decision about where he belonged.

He picked up the tray. Mr Harvey said, 'Yes, I think perhaps we should have those bottles, Ron.'

But Ron was pointing to the geese that were flying over, in perfect formation. The three of them watched it. Ron said, 'It's such an amazing sight.'

The Luftwaffe had flown like that, when Heine had taken him to a military exercise soon after Germany took back the Rhineland. The Versailles Treaty forbade re-armament, but Hitler knew what he wanted, and took it. Tim grinned. What strength the man had, and who had objected? No-one.

Mr Harvey continued to pour the champagne, engrossed, uncommunicative, which was what he said one should be: totally absorbed, or one made mistakes. When he'd finished filling the glasses he said, 'Perhaps you'd be kind enough, once everyone has a glass, Tim, to return for a bottle, and top them up.'

Tim entered the marquee again, snatching a look around. Bridie had gone, and it was just James handling the other side of the marquee. Aunt Evie and Ver were no longer here either, which meant they were beavering in the kitchen, and soon the guests would be called to the buffet set up along the right-hand wall.

He made his way back to Sir Anthony, his hand aching from the tray. Guests reached for champagne and he allowed the first few to do so before, dodging manfully, arriving with enough for Sir Anthony's group. Lady Margaret's daughter, Penny, had joined them. She looked alarmingly like her mother, with the same horsey face, and he smothered a grin. It was Bridie who had pointed that out long ago. Would Bridie kick over the traces and leave, or would she fester here?

He offered champagne to Colonel Potter, who had drifted up. 'I say, you counted well, dear heart,' he barked. 'Well done you. Just one glass left now.'

Tim eyed the remaining glass. 'I need to find a home for this tiddler.'

Sir Anthony said, 'For goodness' sake, young man. Put the tray down for a moment and join us.'

He didn't need asking twice. 'Only for a moment, though. Mr Harvey has a bottle I must bring out. By the way, it was so kind of you to give the caviar to Da, Sir Anthony.'

Sir Anthony said, 'My pleasure.'

Lady Margaret almost neighed. 'Dear old Harvey, still battling on, I take it. Such a tower of strength, that man.'

'Indeed,' Sir Anthony said, raising his glass to Tim. 'Cheers, and a happy and peaceful future to everyone everywhere, whatever boat they may crew.' His look was meaningful, and he held Tim's gaze.

'Indeed,' repeated Tim, and found he was flushing at the hint of friendly support.

It was Sir Anthony who had delivered his mother's first letter to him at his office in Newcastle. This wonderful old boy had met Heine at a cocktail party

36

in Berlin, apparently, and started talking of the Neave Wing, and hence the world at Easterleigh Hall. This was how his mother had found him, though he wasn't sure why she hadn't tried just writing. She had said it never occurred to her they would still all be here.

Lady Margaret was talking of the finishing school in Switzerland that Penny would be attending from September onwards, just for a year, after which she'd 'come out'.

Colonel Potter said, 'You'll learn to cook, I suppose, young lady, and converse in many languages, that sort of thing.'

Lady Margaret seemed to draw herself up another foot. 'She will become familiar with menus. She will not cook. One does not, Colonel Potter. One has staff.'

Tim studied his glass, twisting it round and round, and couldn't stop himself. 'Well, someone has to, Lady Margaret, as you well know. And some do it rather well. I think I can hear Mr Harvey's dulcet tones.' He half bowed, turned on his heel and weaved his way back through the crowd, surprised at his sudden wave of anger.

Lady Margaret was a snob, and what was wrong with Evie and Bridie earning a living? What's more, they made bloody good food too. It was then he felt his da's arm on his shoulders. 'Don't let Lady M bother you, lad. It wouldn't be the same if she wasn't upsetting someone. It's her life's work and

37

if I'm not much mistaken, Penny will also be that way inclined.'

Tim laughed, really laughed, for the first time today. 'You're not wrong there, but it's a shame, because Aunt Evie says Major Granville, Lady Margaret's husband, was the best sort. Died too young. Far too many went, far too many still need help, but it's not just us, you know. Germany suffered too, far more than us with that pig of a Treaty of Versailles round their neck.' He could hear the challenge in his own voice.

Jack walked with him to the back of the marquee, his arm still firmly around Tim's shoulder. 'Don't think we don't all know that they suffered, lad; after all, we fought them, remember. And don't you take any notice of our Bridie and her tantrums. She misses you, but you've a right to your opinions and decisions. That's what parliamentary democracy is all about. You just remember that, and if you need help, you come straight to your old da, because I'll drop everything and do what needs to be done.'

Jack's grip had become so strong his fingers hurt as they dug in. 'Never forget that your mam and I love you. I know I say it a lot, but I mean it. Don't forget either that we're coming to see you off from Gosforn tomorrow.' He hugged him, slapping his back, and it was then that the guests were called to the buffet, with the groom to lead the fray, 'With the missus,' someone bawled.

Tim watched his father go, loving him, loving Gracie. Or was it just habit?

Suddenly, he felt the breath catch in his chest, and it was as though he had been drenched in a shower of rain. For there it was, clear, in that question; was it just habit? Because none of these people were really his family. Not Bridie or James, not the Forbes, Bramptons or Williams.

He wiped the sweat from his forehead. For a moment he felt as though he was going to fall flat on his face.

Much later, as the guests departed or retired to the hotel sitting rooms or bedrooms, Sir Anthony came to the marquee. 'Might I have a word, Tim?' James and Tim were lifting a section of the flooring to store somewhere dry.

James grinned at Sir Anthony. 'Why not, sir? He's an old bloke now, and needs a break.'

Harry Travers took the other end of the section and tipped an imaginary forelock at Tim, who was led into the shade of the cedar tree. Sir Anthony dug into his inside jacket pocket and brought out a sealed package.

'I believe you are off to your mother tomorrow?'

'Yes, I am, sir, but I'm surprised you know.' Tim looked from Sir Anthony to the package, just making it out in the gloom.

'Well, Heine and I are in contact over this reha-bilitation idea he has for Altona in Germany, which supports my idea of "hands across the sea". I would be grateful if you would deliver these suggested plans for the unit. Seems a wasted opportunity, otherwise.'

Ron called, 'Come on, lazybones, we need you.'

Tim looked over his shoulder. Sir Anthony smiled. 'Off you go, lad, and mum's the word. Peace is a strange old game, and best to keep this between us. We don't want anyone putting a spanner in the works, and some in Germany are not disposed to "reaching out", or so Heine says.'

Tim tucked it into his pocket. 'It sounds a worthwhile project, Sir Anthony. Perhaps Bridie's riding therapy can be incorporated into the idea?'

Sir Anthony smiled. 'Ah, now that you've brought that up, I wanted to say how impressed I am with young Bridie's results. Many good things have happened here.' He seemed lost in thought for a moment, then he set off towards the Hall. He stopped, turned. 'Thank you, Tim. Remember, let's just keep it between us.'

Tim watched him reach the gravel, and then crunch across towards the steps. Ron called again, 'Enough skiving! We need you, lazybones.'

As Tim hurried back to the marquee he heard Prancer whinny. What would it be like never to see him again, or any of them? If he decided on Berlin, that could well be the result. He slowed, uncertain. A distant laugh intruded, and he saw Colonel Potter and Herr Bauer walking back from the direction of the ha-ha, looking like old friends.

It cheered him, because families weren't the only source of comfort, after all. Friendship was always at hand. He entered the marquee, and stopped. What was he talking about? He must remember that no-one here was family.

Harry called from the marquee. 'The sooner we finish, the sooner we can sup the barrel dry, Tim. I've sorted you a bed for the night. You can sleep off your hangover on the train tomorrow.'

That's what he needed: to get drunk, and stop all this rambling in his head.

Chapter Four

Jack and Grace waited on the platform of Gosforn station the next morning. They knew Tim would not arrive until nearer the time of departure, but neither could relax at home in Easton. Here, in the small commercial town, there was no sulphuric smell from the slag heap, no humming of winding gear, no clattering of boots as pitmen went on shift. As always, it seemed another world.

Jack made himself ease his shoulders and relax his jaw muscles. His son was off to Germany to stay with Millie and Heine, whose politics Jack abhorred. His son was a member of the British Union of Fascists, whose politics he loathed. His son was off to see his mother, whom he ... He stopped.

He refused to let his shoulders tighten and the muscles contract in his jaw again as Bridie's shouts of yesterday echoed round his head; her pain was also Gracie's and his, her fear theirs, for they couldn't bear to lose him either.

He could stand still no longer but paced the platform, Gracie keeping step with him, her arm in his. They passed a porter pushing a trolley of crates in which racing pigeons were grumbling. The porter would heave them onto the train, to be offloaded elsewhere. They would then be set free at a designated time, to race back.

His da used to wait by the pigeon loft in the garden of the family home in the lea of the Stunted Tree Hill near Easton, stopwatch in hand. It had been right bad when they'd had to distribute the pigeons after his da's funeral. He'd thought Tim, James and Bridie would never stop weeping, but they'd been the same when their grandma died. Jack was glad now that his parents were long gone, for what would they have thought of Tim? Perhaps they would have said that racing pigeons invariably return, so not to worry.

Grace said, 'We've had him for all these years, and it is only right and proper that his mam and her fiancé enjoy him now.'

Jack loved her at that moment, more than he had ever done in his life, and that was saying something. He stopped, turned, and held her close, resting his chin on the top of her head. Today she was not wearing a hat, a sign of her confused distress. 'By, Gracie, you and Mam were his mother, and you are being so brave, and so fair. I just want to go over and punch that bastard Nazi's lights out. He's welcome to Millie, but the boy is mine.'

She leaned against his chest, and they listened to the pigeons for a moment before she said, 'No, that's where you're wrong, Jack. Tim owns himself. He'll make mistakes, take a few wrong turns, like most of us do, but he'll find his way back, he's not daft.'

'But—'

She drove on, 'He's not of our blood, but he's had the families around him day and night for years and he won't forget that. Or if he does, something will make him remember. He's excited by the difference between us and them, but he isn't *her,* or Roger, so hoy that thought right out of your head, as your wedding present to me, bonny lad.' She pulled back now, and looked up. 'Trust him.'

Jack kissed her hard on her mouth before pulling her to him again. 'You're right, bloody Millie gave us a divorce, so we need to let it go.' He stroked her hair. She was pure gold through and through. 'D'you know, she asked Richard and Ver for better wages when she thought I'd gone missing on the front line, on the grounds that she was a widow?'

She hushed him, but he couldn't stop. 'Of course you did. It must have ruined her day when she found out I was a prisoner after all. Everything she did has been going round in my head, bonny lass, ever since Tim heard from her.' He tried again to make himself stop, but his thoughts kept going. 'She . . .'

A train puffed and steamed its way into the station on the other line, to pick up Gosforn passengers bound for Washington and beyond. Grace shouted over the screech of its brakes, 'Leave it. It's in the past. We can't change anything now.' Doors were banging on the other platform.

Meanwhile more passengers were arriving for the Newcastle train. Heedless, Grace kissed his mouth. 'We'll love him until we die,' she whispered. 'No matter what.'

Just then they heard a shout, one that was almost drowned as the Washington train finally huffed and squealed out of the station. 'Da, Mam, I'm here. The bus didn't come, so Richard brought me in the Bentley at about one hundred miles an hour. He's a crazy driver, even with a fake arm and leg, so lord knows what he'd be like if he had two of each. That's what engineers can do for you, Da – fix a car with controls that can make things possible.' He was standing in the entrance to the ticket office and a man pushed past him, ticket in hand.

Tim doffed his hat at him, apologising, then continued, 'Anyway, I'd not have made it, but for him. I stayed at the Hall, you see. Ron and Harry have hollow legs, James, too, and I have a bloody awful hangover. Richard's waiting in the car to take you back, but I thought I'd better check that you hadn't driven the Austin.'

Jack called back, 'Aye, I did, Tim. Can you wave him off? Quick now, lad, you've only got five minutes.' Tim ducked back through the doorway, but re-emerged a minute later, at the run, swinging his canvas holdall.

Jack loved every fibre of the lad's being, from the top of his head to his size ten clodhopping feet. Where did those come from? Roger's hadn't been big, and neither were Millie's. He'd never thought of it before, and he clamped his mind shut. No, things were complicated enough without doubting the fatherhood of the lad. But the under-gardener's feet had been huge, and Tim's colouring was the same. Again he clamped his mind shut, but stubbornly the thought came back. Thank God Bernie was long gone, deep beneath the ground at Tyne Cot cemetery, and it could be left there.

Tim had nearly reached them, and his excitement was obvious. It was almost as though his skin was alive. It was a skin free of miner's scars, for Jack had moved heaven and earth to keep Tim out of the pit. Apprenticeships had been scarce, so he'd finally pitched up on Sir Anthony's doorstep at Searton, asking if he could pull strings somewhere, anywhere, to get him a job. It turned out he had a contact at a marine engineering firm which was designing engines for yachts, until shipbuilding picked up. He was a grand bloke.

Tim let his holdall drop, and kissed Grace. 'Did I tell you how lovely you looked yesterday, Mam?'

Grace laughed. 'You did, many times. You didn't look so bad yourself in your suit, either. Now, are you ready, do you need anything? I packed you a few sandwiches, just in case.'

Tim laughed, and it was a real laugh. 'Thanks, Mam. I could be needing them, I reckon.'

Jack snatched a look at the station clock. The train

should be here by now. Tim followed his gaze. 'It'll be late, right enough. We're in England, but in Germany, Hitler's got the trains running to time.' There was defiance in his voice, and the set of his shoulders.

Jack smiled, making it reach his eyes. 'Aye, I expect he has. They certainly know how to work if the miners in the German pits were anything to go by. They were good to the prisoners too, in some ways. I remember once, when they shared some sausage . . .' He stopped. He could only go so far to meet his son, because too many prisoners had died of malnutrition, and brutality.

Gracie smiled her approval. Tim moved his weight from foot to foot. Jack found himself looking at them, and picturing Bernie again. Tim said, 'What're you looking at, Da?'

Tim lifted his gaze from Tim's feet. 'Oh, nothing, just thinking. I understand your grandpa now; he'd suddenly drift off somewhere else. Sign of old age, I expect.'

Gracie moved to his side, holding his arm, leaning her head on his shoulder. 'You're not old, bonny lad. You're wearing well. Must be down to the greens you grow and the good life you lead. What d'you think, Tim?'

Tim stiffened. 'A lot of people lead a good life.'

Jack felt Gracie squeeze his arm in warning. He looked again at the clock, his mind blank, knowing he needed to fill the silence that had fallen, but he

47

couldn't, because everything was such a minefield these days.

At last they heard the whistle of the approaching train, which was only five minutes late. The Station Master hurried from his office. 'Let's get them pigeons further to the rear, Thomas, for God's sake, man.'

Thomas shoved the trolley along the platform, dodging the waiting passengers. Jack said, 'You'll be on your way in a minute. Wonder where they're releasing the birds?' He was patting his pocket, checking that the envelope he'd prepared at dawn this morning was to hand.

They all stepped away from the edge as the sound of the train grew louder. Those on the platform picked up cases, or put away newspapers. A child darted forwards, only to be pulled back by her mam. The train drew in, screeching and puffing. Passengers hung out of windows, feeling for the door handles. The Station Master shouted, 'Stand away, please, let others disembark first.'

Some did, some didn't. Jack heard Tim mutter, 'Time people did as they were bloody well told, it's no wonder Britain's a mess. They won't work together, not like—'

Grace cut in, 'You take care, darling.' She kissed him.

The disembarking passengers rushed the guard who was checking tickets at the exit. Jack moved close to his son. 'Yes, take care of yourself, and have a good time. Please give my regards to your mother, and to Heine.' He hugged him, and eventually Tim dropped his bag and hugged him back. For a moment Jack wanted to say, 'Don't go, don't change, don't be wooed by her.' Instead, he said, 'I love you, lad. Whatever you do we're happy, all of us here will be. We just want what's best for you.'

Tim stepped back, embarrassed. 'I'm only going for a few days, Da.'

Jack felt all sorts of a fool. 'Of course, I just meant . . . Well, I have a bit of a hangover too, today. It's not just the prerogative of the young, and even though it was a special day, I should know better. It leaves me without much sense. On you get, then.'

Once the lad was on board, Jack slammed the door shut. Tim leaned out of the window. Jack dragged out the envelope and handed it to him. 'Some extra money for you, just in case. It's in sterling, but I'm sure you can change it. Buy your mother a cream cake and a coffee, too. Don't expect they drink tea in Berlin.'

Tim appeared to be about to give it back, then pushed it into his jacket pocket. He shook his father's hand. 'Thank you, Da, and for the sandwiches, Mam.' He sounded uncertain, suddenly, like the boy who had been asked if he'd like to go down the mine for a look, when he'd said he didn't want to bother with more education. He'd gone down in the cage, said little, but had accepted the marine engineering firm's offer of an apprenticeship.

The guard blew his whistle, the porter trundled his trolley down the platform, and the Station Master shouted, 'Stand clear, if you will.'

Gracie called, 'I hope it's a calm crossing. Stay in the fresh air, it will help.'

He nodded. It was what she said every time he went on the sea, because he always felt so ill.

The train started. Tim stayed at the window, as the steam billowed and the smuts flew. They waved until they could see him no more, and Jack felt utterly helpless.

The taxi drew up outside a Berlin apartment block in the late afternoon. Tim, exhausted and with a splitting headache, sat quite still. There had been a problem with a connection on the journey here, and he'd put up at a hotel overnight. It had been all too easy to change and use some of his da's money to drink himself stupid at the hotel bar. It had been a daft thing to do, but he'd had to stop the racing of his brain as it tussled with life's complications.

The taxi driver turned, sliding back the glass partition. Tim pulled out his wallet and tried to work out the money, including the tip, while a hammer played a tattoo inside his skull. The driver said, in accented English, 'You not hurry or make mistake.' In desperation Tim handed over a handful of Reichsmarks.

Through the open window, the traffic noise was intermittent, a few trams clanged their bells. A platoon of Hitler Youth marched round them, eyes front, in step. Nazi flags and banners flew from many buildings, fluttering in the breeze.

The taxi driver counted out his change, saying over his shoulder, 'Nice it is, this Charlottenburg area of Berlin. Before it bad, many fights, riots, strikers. Our SA boys and SS fought the communists. They crushed now. Germany better, every ways.'

He hesitated, searching for his English, 'The SA small now, the SS strong. There are many of SS in this block, now that it has been made – er – ah, yes, for use of Party members. Forgive me, it is some years since a war prisoner in your country. You treat me well and I remember your language. I work on it, ready for August, for Berlin Olympics. I am to drive some who come.'

Tim handed him a tip. The driver touched his cap. The Nazi Party badge on his lapel caught the light. 'All is better in Germany. I have passengers now.' He laughed as Tim opened the car door, dragging his holdall out after him.

'*Danke*,' Tim said.

The taxi turned into the desultory traffic stream, overtaking a horse and cart, and tucking in behind another car. Tim approached the impressive, heavy carved doors of the apartment building. There was a wrought-iron handle, but no bell. He opened the door and entered a cavernous foyer. The door slammed shut behind him, and he winced as the noise ricocheted inside his skull. Dear God, how could he cope with the planned dinner party?

In the dim light of a table lamp on a side table, on which lay neatly stacked unopened envelopes, he made out a lift at the far side. His heels clicked on the marble floor, and he was unsure suddenly. 'Thank you for the sandwiches, Mam,' he said aloud – it helped him to feel less alone – 'And for the money, Da.'

'Herr Forbes?' A woman came out of the shadows, her hair short and grey, her skirt long. 'I am Party Block leader. Herr Weber expect you.' She gestured him towards the lift. 'Please to press for floor two. *Danke.*'

She disappeared into the shadows, leaving him feeling a fool. Had she heard him?

Once on the second floor he checked the number on the letter his mother had sent. Fourteen. The passage was tiled, and smelt of antiseptic. His heels clicked again. He put his weight on his toes. He found fourteen and pressed the bell. Something small and rectangular had been removed from the door frame, splintering the dark wood. He was surprised it had not been made good. Grandpa Forbes would have sorted it in no time.

The door opened. It was his mother, and she rushed to hug him. 'Tim, dearest, darling Tim. I knew it would be you. So good to see you.'

He felt a great joy, dropped his holdall and held her tightly. 'It's so good to see *you*,' he murmured, and drew away. 'It's been so long. I've missed you every day.'

He stared at her hair. It was blonde when before it had been mousey. It was also plaited over her head and looked far too young, and not quite right. She saw him looking. 'Ah well, *Kinder-Küche-Kirche*, as they say, bonny lad, and the Party likes blonde traditional styles. So we do it for the Party, and for our men.'

Tim didn't understand. He'd been trying to learn the language from books, but hearing it was so different from reading it. 'I'm sorry, Mother, help me out here. *Kinder* is children, I think?'

She led him into the hallway. It was festooned with rugs, not just on the floor but also on the walls. They seemed to muffle all sound, and looked expensive. So Heine was successful. How wonderful for both of them, and how they deserved it. They must have saved for years for just this moment. He halted, swinging round, causing his mother to jerk to a halt. He said, 'I've forgotten my holdall.'

His mother smiled. 'Amala will take it to your room.' She shouted something in German. 'You see, we have servants now. Well, one. What would the Bramptons think of that, eh?'

An elderly woman came out of a room to the left of the hallway. He saw a bright kitchen and could smell a casserole, or something similar. Her grey hair was in a bun. She wore a black uniform, an apron, black stockings, and black shoes, which squeaked, even on the rugs. She picked up the holdall from the doorway.

Tim moved to help, but his mother caught him. 'Amala means "labour" and so she very much does.' She laughed her laugh, and hurried on ahead, almost running. He could sense her excitement. 'Quick now, Tim. Heine will be in soon. He's been at a meeting with a few of the other officers, something to do with his department. He's not inspecting the Labour Exchanges and camps any more, you know. He collects information and put it all into dossiers. It's really important. It's a step in his progress towards the intelligence arm, the SD.'

Tim hurried after her, and into a huge, dark-panelled sitting room with sofas, chairs and occasional tables. It took his breath away. There were oil paintings hung in heavy frames, and at the end of the room were two tall double windows with shutters folded back. Through the windows he could see the dark-ening skies.

His mother was stroking the back of one of the leather sofas, as though she could hardly believe it, any more than he could.

'It's beautiful, Mother. Honestly it is. May I?' he asked, gesturing towards the windows.

'By all means, lad.' She waited by the high marble fireplace, which sported a ceramic tiled stove. Tim walked towards the windows, past the sofas and a perfect glazed vitrine. He stopped, and returned to it. It was cherry, he thought, as he touched it. 'Mother, where on earth did you find this? It's so skilfully made.' It held a myriad of wines, liqueurs, flutes and glasses. He just stopped himself from saying how Grandpa Forbes would have loved it.

She told him, 'It's a Biedermeier vitrine.'

'Well spotted,' he said, but he had no idea what Biedermeier meant.

His mother was smiling, delighted at his pleasure, delighted at her new home. 'A sort of antique,' she explained.

'May I look inside?' he asked.

She nodded eagerly. He opened the glass cupboard, inspecting the hinges, looking at the glasses. He shut the door carefully, running his hand along the panel. 'You have so many beautiful things. I'm right pleased for you.'

Then he crouched to open the cupboard at the bottom. It was locked. He looked across at his mother. She flushed, and snapped, 'For God's sake, leave it, please. Things are locked for a reason, surely Grace taught you that.'

He stood again, dusting his hands, feeling lost in the face of her anger. 'I'm sorry, Mother.'

He crossed to the window and looked down onto the linden trees lining the street. It had begun to rain; the cobbles glinted, the tramlines too. There were lights inside the trams, and lights in the apartments across the street. His da would be coming home from the mine; his mam would be making sure there was a meal ready. James would be

55

finishing at the farm; Bridie would be busy in the kitchen, or grooming old Prancer.

He heard his mother walking towards him. She coughed. His head was getting worse. Why the hell had he had so much to drink? Bloody fool.

She said, 'I'm a bit tired, Tim. I shouldn't have snapped.' People were walking along the pavements, their heads down, looking as miserable as he felt. His mother was beside him now. '*Kinder-Küche-Kirche* means Children, Kitchen, Church, though change Church for the Party and you'll be nearer the mark. But Tim, I do so like being a hausfrau. After all, I was housekeeper at Easterleigh Hall so it's in my blood. I'm proud to run a good home for Heine, and it really is lovely, isn't it? I do hope you like it, because it is your home too. I love you so much.' She was holding his hand now.

Housekeeper? But she had run the laundry.

His mother said, 'Now, you look as though you need a lie-down, or would you like me to ask Amala to make us a cup of tea first?'

He could have kissed her, and did. 'Thank you, I just need a couple of hours' kip, I've such a headache.'

She hugged him. 'Remember, we have a dinner party for you this evening. Heine's friends will be here to meet you. Some have been in Berlin for quite a long time, but some have been in outer darkness like us, regulating the new ideas.' She laughed, and somehow it didn't grate quite as much. 'Let me show you your room, but before that, have you a package from Sir Anthony for me?'

She had moved to the card table. He shook his head.

She stared. 'You've come all this way without it?' She sounded angry again, or was it just this headache making it seem so?

He said, 'No, Mother, I've brought it, but it's for Heine. Sir Anthony has been in touch, has he, to alert you? He didn't have to do that; I'm reliable, you know.' Now *he* was being edgy. He pulled himself up short.

She hesitated. 'He telegraphed Heine to say he'd met you and passed it over for you to bring.'

He withdrew it from his breast pocket and handed it to her, looking down at the people walking in the rain, which was heavier now. Some were sheltering beneath the trees. He said quietly, again, 'But it *is* addressed to Heine.'

'Of course it is,' she snapped again. 'I am not official, not yet.' She was breaking the seal and ripping open the envelope, but then shook her head, and clutched the package to her. 'Forgive me, I feel rather worried, but thank you so much, dearest Tim, for bringing these. You are such a good son.'

'Worried?'

'Yes, you see there is a letter somewhere at Easterleigh Hall which is a confession written by me, saying that I stole some silver from that dreadful old Lord Brampton. Of course it is a forgery, but it must be found and brought here, so I have it safe. You see, dearest boy, while it's in existence Heine and I can't marry, and more, it will compromise his career. An SS officer must be without blemish. It's such a hateful thing for someone to do.'

Tim tried to keep up. 'A forgery?'

'Yes,' she almost shouted. 'Some awful person at the Hall, probably, to hurt me for leaving. I need it, Tim, or rather, Heine and I need it. Oh, life is so very difficult, and it would be so wonderful if only someone would look for it.'

She carried the package to a small card table. 'Put on the light, Tim, if you would.' He walked across and flicked on the standard lamp, designed to cast light on the green baize of the table. The shade was Tiffany, like the ones that were in the lounge at Easterleigh Hall. He felt pity for his mother, and confused. Who on earth would do something like that?

She withdrew what must be the Neave Wing plans, or similar, onto the table, and shook out another package, one that was also sealed, but with a note attached. She read it and smiled, with what looked like relief. He said, 'It sounds such a good idea, to try to set up something like the Neave Wing, and who better to help than Sir Anthony? He sponsored it, after all, with the consortium, and still does.'

He was rocking on his feet with tiredness and said, 'May I go to my room, Mother?'

She smiled and came to him, placing her hand on his cheek. 'Third door on the left, along the passage.'

'Well, you'll wake me, will you?'

She was walking back to the table. 'Set your alarm for eight, would you, bonny lad. I will have the dinner to supervise but will try to find time to make sure you're up.'

She blew him a kiss. 'Sleep well. Drink water from your bathroom tap, it helps with a hangover, I find.' Turning, she added, 'I will talk to you further, before you leave, giving you some ideas of where to look for the letter, because only you can help me with this. Forget about it now, though, and enjoy the dinner party.'

'Yes, Mother. I'll try.' He meant the letter, the dinner party, and he also meant he'd try to remember, but already he was just concentrating on staying awake long enough to get to his bed.

He found his way to his bedroom. Amala had hung up his clothes in the wardrobe. The bathroom was as palatial as the rest of the house. He felt shabby. Would his suit do for the dinner? Surely it wasn't black tie? Panic began to bubble up, but the headache overtook it. He stripped himself and left his clothes where they fell, grabbed a glass of water, gulped it down, and then sank onto the double bed. He was almost asleep before his head hit the pillow. His mam would have brought him a jug of water for his bedside, or a cup of tea. His da would have pulled his leg and sat with him for a while, to make sure he slept on his side.

But the Forbes did not have people to dine, or a wonderful apartment, or live in an exciting world that must be amazingly stimulating.

These were his final thoughts as, at last, he slept.

Chapter Five

Tim woke, startled by passing headlights illuminating a high, ornate bedroom ceiling. Where the hell was he? He remembered with a jolt, and checked the side table clock. Seven fifty-five.

He switched off the alarm and sat up, swinging his feet to the parquet floor. His head spun. He ran his hand over his chin. Stubble. He needed a shave. He clicked on the side table lamp and padded over yet more rugs to his bathroom. Amala had put his washing gear on the shelf above the sink. He switched on the light and stared at his reflection then groaned: he looked how he felt. He washed and shaved, pondering the size of the apartment, its position. He remembered the taxi driver's words, that it was for the use of Party members. Bloody hell, but surely they still needed to pay the rent? Or perhaps not. He grinned. If it came with Heine's job, then he'd like a job like it, too bloody right he would.

He changed into his only other suit, hung by Amala in the huge mahogany wardrobe. Should he leave the one he had just dropped on the floor for her, or pick it up? He wasn't used to staff. He hung it up. It just seemed so rude otherwise. The wardrobe was almost a walk-in. Heine had done so well to be able to afford all this.

There was a knock on his door. He called, 'Come in.'

His mother entered, wearing a smart green silk dress. 'Good, you're awake. Heine will be here any moment, with six of his colleagues. If you're up to it, dearest lad, come and eat. Oh, you've already changed? I thought you might wear your Blackshirt uniform?'

Tim turned up his collar and slung his tie around his neck. He shook his head. 'I never thought of it. It's only for meetings, Mother.' He saw the disappointment on her face. 'I'm sorry,' he murmured.

She smiled, though he thought it was strained. 'It's enough you brought the packet, Tim. He'll be pleased. Oh, and that you brought yourself too, of course.' She was already turning to leave the room. 'Be ready in ten minutes. Join us in the sitting room.'

He watched her as she reached for the door handle. His da had said his mother had named him for Timmie Forbes, his da's young brother, who lay in Easton churchyard, together with his marra, Tony, both boys dead before their time.

He said, 'Did you like Timmie?'

She stopped, half in and half out of the room. 'Yes, I did. He was always cheerful. He painted lead soldiers.' For a moment she looked relaxed, then almost shook herself. 'I'm too busy to think of that now.' She shut the door.

He stared after her, then hurried to the bathroom mirror. For the first time he studied his face for similarities. Their eyes were different, but there was definitely a likeness in his chin. Yes, and his hair was mousey, like hers before she went blonde. Tim grinned with relief. It was good to see them.

He moved to the window, looking out at the dark evening. It was still raining but the traffic was flowing, and the apartments opposite were lit by soft glows. Some had their shutters drawn. It made the room cosy, as his mam always said at Easton, as she drew the curtains shut. Yet again he felt strange; lost. He rested his head on the cool of the pane. He didn't really know who he was.

He closed his eyes. Immediately, to his surprise, he saw the cedar tree, calm and strong. He drew a deep breath, checked his watch and left the bedroom.

The sitting room was brightly lit, thanks to the chandelier. Over by the card table, Heine was examining the plans. He looked up, and smiled. 'Tim. How good it is to see you. I know your mother is delighted.'

His mother entered from the dining room, to the left. 'The table is perfect, Heine, and laid for nine as you wish. Is Bruno coming too?' She looked towards Tim. 'Bruno lives in the apartment on the next floor. He's a great favourite of ours, and tonight we celebrate because his sister has been chosen for the Berlin Olympics in August. She will be one of the eurhythmic dancers.'

Heine strolled to the vitrine and poured two beers. He looked smart in his black SS uniform, his black boots gleaming, his breeches pristine. His jacket was undone, as was the top button of his shirt. He brought the beers to the card table, handing one to Tim and putting his own down on the green baize, then he shrugged off his jacket – his braces were also black. For one moment Tim wondered if his underpants were too. He looked at the beer, unable to bear the thought of alcohol. 'That's grand.'

He didn't know what a eurhythmic dancer was and neither was he about to ask, because his mother had disappeared into the dining room, and Heine looked far too busy poring over the plans. On the table was the other, smaller package, opened, its seal broken.

Tim wasn't sure what he should be doing, but now Heine beckoned him over to the card table. 'It is good that you brought these. Sir Anthony has reached out to me, you see. I think that is what you say? He wishes us to work together on ... er ...' He groped for the words.

Tim said, 'Oh, you mean the Neave Wing. Yes, It works well. The covered walkways were a good idea and the ...'

Heine folded the paperwork up and returned it to the envelope. 'Yes, indeed. To be injured is not a good idea, as Sir Anthony's son, Harry, must know. To lose a leg is not a good thing. Co-operation and friendship can prevent all this, can it not, young Tim? We were put on this world to help one another.'

Tim nodded. 'I'm sure your injured will benefit from a place like Easterleigh Hall. Bridie is using horses now, to give the injured confidence.'

He realised he was speaking too fast, and Heine had lost track. There was a pause. Heine picked up the smaller package by the corner, as though it was a bad smell, and placed it back into the big envelope. 'And your BUF Meeting House in Hawton? Is that finished?'

'It's coming on.'

'Excellent,' Heine said, his eyes on the package. 'We just need everything to "come on", as you say, don't we?'

The doorbell rang.

The wine flowed swift and fast at the dinner, which consisted of a prawn mousse followed by coq au vin, though not up to his Aunt Evie's standard. Tim drank sparingly, knowing that what he really needed was copious glasses of water, and bed – again. But to admit that, in the company of these fit and powerful men, would be too humiliating to endure. He swallowed down his nausea and tried to think beyond his splitting head.

The talk was sometimes in German, sometimes in English. Heine's success was toasted before the remains of the coq au vin were removed by Amala. Millie stirred in her chair next to him and said she would take her coffee in the sitting room. 'As is proper,' she whispered to her son, since everyone declined dessert and cheese. She rose. Tim leapt to his feet and pulled out her chair.

The men also stood, their jackets off, their braces hanging down in loops, sitting only when the door clicked behind her. They attacked the brandy. The crystal goblets were poured fuller than at Easterleigh Hall, and not swirled, and the aroma not breathed in, which Uncle Richard and Uncle Aub thought was the best thing about brandy. Here, it was drunk in great gulps. Tim shook his head when the bottle reached him, the very smell making him even worse. He passed it to his neighbour, Walter, taking the opportunity to snatch a look at his watch. It was midnight. When could he leave for bed? He poured himself coffee.

Walter laughed, and waggled the bottle at him. 'You have no head for drink?'

Tim smiled, not daring to shake his head or it would fall off. 'I have done too well over the last few days. One hangover on top of another, and a rough sea crossing in between. Soon my head will explode, which will mess up my mother's decor.'

The men roared with laughter. 'You hear that, Heine?' Bruno shouted. 'An explosion, he says. What does this boy know of explosions?'

Walter nudged Tim. His coffee slopped onto the damask tablecloth, and he dabbed at it with his serviette. Heine said, 'Amala will launder it.'

Walter boomed, 'You should have been with us,

fighting those communists in the hellhole that *was* Berlin. Then you would have seen heads explode, and some were almost ours.' Again there was laughter, far too loud.

He was the one gulping now, but it was coffee, anything to neutralise the wine and try to kill the headache. Why had he had any this evening? Alright, he knew why, he was showing off, trying to keep up with these old soldiers. He refilled his cup. Damned small they were too, but such fine porcelain that it was almost featherweight. He called to Heine, 'You have a good eye, Heine. Lovely furniture, and this porcelain is right canny, as we say at home.'

Again there was laughter. Perhaps they hadn't understood. He said, 'I meant it is very nice.' The laughter continued and Heine grinned, waving his cigar and looking around at his friends. 'Ah, those who had the apartment before us were more than generous.' The laughter grew.

Bruno shouted down the table. 'Left us all their belongings. It is how things are done now, my boy, where some people are concerned.'

Walter slipped his arm across Tim's shoulders. Tim struggled to follow the thread of the conversation but it was hopeless. Instead he thought of the splintered wood in the front door frame. He called, 'I could mend that door frame for you, Heine, where someone has taken something down; I'll sand it, even stain it. It would be neater.'

The men looked from one to another, then at

Heine. Silence had fallen. Tim wondered what he had said. Heine pointed his cigar towards his plate, and the ash crumpled onto it. The end glowed red and grey. He said, 'Why not? The tenants were careless to damage SS property. It was not noticed in time and I had forgotten. Thank you for bringing it to my attention once more.'

Tim shook his head. 'It is only a small job, so I'll fix it tomorrow.'

Bruno and Hans, who sat next to one another, grimaced. Bruno said, 'Nothing should have been removed. Perhaps it should be mentioned to them, should it not, my comrades? After all, they are now living rent free.' They were grinning at one another.

Heine shook his head slightly, frowning at them. Tim sipped his coffee. Walter was laughing quietly beside him. Bruno pressed on, his face sweaty, his eyes those of someone who really should not have any more booze. 'It is a training camp, one might say.'

Heine called, 'Do not bore our guest, Bruno.'

Tim smiled at Heine. 'I'm not bored at all.'

Heine exhaled cigar smoke. Walter suddenly burst into song, squeezing Tim's shoulders. Hans called across the table, as he slammed his hand down in time with Walter's discordant notes. 'Do you know the Horst Wessel song, Tim? He died for us, did Wessel, fighting the Reds. You and your Blackshirts should learn it, because you are our friends, and Germany needs friends. We all need friends, and peaceful neighbours.'

Tim raised his coffee cup. 'Like Sir Anthony. To friendship and peace,' he said, knowing that Walter lived on one side of number fourteen, but wondering what the neighbours thought on the other side. Would they get any sleep tonight?

The men around the table were lifting their brandy goblets. Had the bottle gone round again already? 'To friendship,' they bellowed. He wished they wouldn't as the noise killed his head, and the poor buggers next door must want to punch a few noses.

Bruno said, 'France, our neighbour, wants peace, too. They proved it by letting Hitler take back the Rhineland with no protests. Our Führer leads us well. He knows his tomatoes, I think you would say in Britain.'

'I think it would be "knows his onions", though you all speak such good English.' A full brandy bottle replaced the empty one and began its way round the table.

Walter was watching the bottle's progress as he muttered, 'We aspire to the SD, the intelligence branch, just as does your step-father. He has the advantage of your mother, though. She teaches us well. It is good to know English. She is useful to us. Language, contacts . . .'

Heine shouted from the top of the table, 'Walter.' It was a warning. Walter flushed, slipped his arm from Tim's shoulders and reached for the brandy.

'Your mother teaches us English well, young Tim,' he said.

He poured more brandy into his goblet, then put a slug into Tim's coffee cup, which meant if he wanted more coffee he had to sup up. He passed the bottle on, drank his brandy, and knew immediately he shouldn't have. He reached for the coffee pot.

Walter hadn't finished, though, and Tim wished he had, because he was too close, shouting into his face, his spittle spraying like a shower head. 'You need to clear out your mediocre politicians and find your own Führer, then you too could have a grand apartment.' He gulped his brandy, then coughed. Spluttering, he held a handkerchief to his mouth and waved the conversation on.

The men laughed, and talked amongst themselves, and Tim understood not a word. He sipped his coffee, which was cold, but it didn't matter. He studied the chandelier; the crystal glittered and illuminated the fine frieze around the ceiling. Was Amala still working in the kitchen? Was Bridie too, at Easterleigh Hall? He shouldn't have been so damned rude to her, but she had annoyed him.

He sank back in his chair, letting the talk whirl around him, the laughter, the cigars; he loved it all, except for the smoke. His Uncle Aub liked cigars, but his da didn't, thank heavens, because they stank. Bruno was singing, and Hans rose, staggered, then found his balance, walking towards Tim as only the drunk can, and slumped down next to him, in Millie's empty seat. He put his arm round Tim's shoulders, and Walter, not to be outdone, slumped his arm around him again. The weight of the two of them almost crushed him but he felt proud to be accepted by these men, who had endured the same war as his da. It made him feel almost an equal.

Hans shouted in his ear, 'You are in the company of strong men tonight. You see our gold badges?' He pointed at Otto, who was directly opposite, his arms waving like windmills as he conducted the singing. Hanging on the back of his chair was his jacket. Tim saw a gold badge. He nodded.

Hans said, 'Yes, we are all holders of the Gold Honour Badge, because we are amongst the earliest to join the Nazi Party. It is we who carved a hard and bloody path through the rabble, making a future for our party. Darwin said it first, our Führer second: the fittest survive and the defeated deserve nothing. You think my English is good? I think so too.' He laughed so loud he coughed, and knocked Tim forwards.

The singing had stopped, and the others were listening. Hans banged the table with his fist. Coughed once more, then lowered his voice, wagging his finger at Tim. 'You, my boy, must listen to experts. We say, don't we, my comrades, put up your posters about your fascist meeting, taunt the Reds in your pubs in the days before. They will come to attack when you meet, so angry have you made them. You will be the defenders, then, to your community. Soon you will be seen as a force for law and order. You will become admired.'

It all seemed sensible but suddenly the room began to spin. He gripped the table and felt the bile rising in his throat. Oh, God. He stared at the silver salt cellar. They were all singing again. Oh, God. Walter and Hans belched brandy and sour cigar breath over him.

Hans and Walter looked surprised as he eased himself from beneath their arms. He nodded to Heine, who was watching him carefully. Tim didn't dare open his mouth. He nodded goodnight, and staggered to his own room. Somehow he removed his clothes and hung them, before crawling beneath the bed covers and praying that the room would stop spinning soon. Never again would a drop of alcohol pass his lips.

Chapter Six

Easterleigh Hall, June 1936

Bridie and James caught the bus to Hawton on Sunday at ten in the morning. They had wangled it as their day off after they heard about the trouble at the British Union of Fascists meeting the day before, and decided they needed to make a reconnaissance trip. Bridie had a basket on her lap containing sandwiches, which Mrs Moore had pressed on her, saying, 'You might need these, if you're hiking around and about.'

As the bus jolted into and out of a pothole, she saw that James was chewing his thumbnail. She tapped his hand away. 'You're too old for that.'

James frowned. 'You're as bad as Mrs Moore with your nagging, child that you are.'

In front of them an old man turned around, chuckling. 'Right canny lass, our Bridie is an' all, man.' He touched his cap to Bridie. 'Young Tom Welsh's picked up no end. He's walking good as new on that leg the Neave Wing made him, using just the one stick, he is. Up with you for an hour on Prancer later, isn't he?'

73

Bridie swallowed. She'd forgotten. She groped through her memory and finally said, 'Four o clock, isn't it, Mr Burton?'

'That's the one.' He turned to the front as the bus pulled into a stop and picked up Mr and Mrs Young, bound for chapel at Hawton. James pressed his arm against hers and whispered into her ear. 'We'll make sure we're back. It's only for a look, and to plan.'

'We must be or da'll kill me.' What she really thought was that she'd want to drop through the ground if she missed it, so her da wouldn't have to kill her. She leaned back, moving with the bus, the basket heavy on her lap. Tim had been back at work in Newcastle for two weeks and hadn't been to Easton to see anyone, not even Aunt Gracie or Uncle Jack. But had he been at the violent Hawton BUF meeting last night?

The bus trundled on, and she could imagine it almost panting as it revved itself up and over a bridge. It was one mile to Hawton now; its slag heaps smouldered in the distance, and the draught through the open windows was heavy with sulphur.

Had Uncle Mart, who managed Hawton Pit, heard the fighting? Had he seen Tim? Would he tell his marra, Uncle Jack, if he had? Would she?

James was chewing his thumbnail again. 'What do we do if we see him?' he whispered. 'Not sure we should have come, Bridie.'

'We need to know,' she whispered back.

'Then what?'

'Oh, I don't know, but it's what we decided, you daft bugger.'

She wasn't whispering now, and Mr Burton turned his head slightly and said, 'You'll be having your mouth washed out with soap, young Bridie, if Evie gets to hear that talk in public.'

James leaned forward. 'You make sure you tell Aunt Evie, Mr Burton. She could do with another clip round the ear.' They both laughed.

Bridie murmured, 'Enough of that, or I'll tip your cap out of the window, Mr Burton.'

'Fighting talk,' Mr Burton cackled.

When the bus pulled up at the market square, they followed the others off and slipped away, weaving through the back streets, as good people hustled to church, the women in their best, the men in suits. All the time the winding gear loomed; the sulphur was all-pervading.

On corners, groups of miners murmured, their heads close together. Some children swung from ropes attached to lamp posts. It was Sunday: no school, no washing or ironing, just church, or chapel. James kicked back a football to a group of lads, made of scrunched-up newspaper sewn inside a child's jumper. It was light and the breeze took it, but one lad was after it like lightning, calling, 'Thanks, mister.'

They took a turn left, but it was the wrong way. James tried a right, down between the backs of terraces. A wireless was playing church music in the scullery of one house. A dog barked in the yard of another, working itself into a frenzy as they passed. They came out onto Warton Street. 'It's up here,' Evie said. 'It should be on the corner, shouldn't it?'

James nodded. They both slowed, uncertain suddenly. Evie grabbed his elbow. 'Come on, we're only having a look, and he might not be there. Surely he wouldn't be violent? Surely?'

James didn't answer, just stepped out a little faster until they turned the corner. A group of miners milled on the pavement, peering towards the Meeting House across the road. Two of them eased away and propped themselves up against the side wall of the end of the terrace, rolling cigarettes.

The Meeting House was a hive of activity, with bangs and crashes coming from inside. Outside, there was a sound almost like chalk scratching on a blackboard as one man swept the glass from the broken windows into a heap. Another shovelled the piles into a wheelbarrow. Next to Bridie one man said to another, 'Aye, well, the Reds didn't half come with a wallop, so what d'you expect them Blackies to do? Gotta defend yerself, man. Stands to reason. Anyone came at me with an iron bar, he'd get a bloody fist 'n' all.'

Another man crossed the road from the left and walked along the pavement towards them, his boots crashing into the ground. He pushed past Bridie, his cap well down, a Woodbine hanging limp from his mouth. He shoved in between the men in the front, saying, 'Shut your noise, Sammy. Aye, I'd have stormed the buggers, an' all, for whipping up trouble like they did the days before. This is our town, our pit, and they come in here from God knows where, dropping them flyers, talking their talk in the pubs. Crazy buggers. They might as well have given invites to go along and smash 'em to smithereens, so think on, man.'

'Big Jim's got a point, Sammy,' one of the men leaning against the wall called.

The group laughed, without amusement. Sammy tipped his cap back. 'Now you put it like that ...'

'I bloody do, man,' Big Jim muttered, then raised his voice against the clatter and crash of glass, as the last bits clinging to the window frame were bashed out. 'There's a good few pitmen going over to this lot, forgetting their roots. Right fascist pigs, they are, clever 'n' all. Get your brains in gear, or this lot'll bash 'em out on the pavement, and it's that they'll be sweeping up next.'

He shouldered on past the group, who looked after him. One man said, 'He's right, yer know.'

Another ground out his stub on the pavement and toed it to the gutter with his hobnailed boots. 'Hush your noise, Bob. We need someone to take on t'owners, and this lot seem to have some ideas.'

James looked at Bridie. He was listening as hard as she was. Two women made their way past, one pushing a pram. The baby was crying. Perhaps, thought Bridie, he's full of common sense and doesn't

77

like the sound of banging, crashing and men putting the world to rights.

One of the men leaning back against the wall, the same one as before, shouted across, 'What are you talking about? We're right well looked after at Mart's pit and at Easton, and it's said that they're setting up some sort of co-op, like at the Hall hotel. Do I have to bloody spell it out, Sammy, and you too, Ted, that the workers'll get shares, or some'at like that, so they gets some of the profits? What do you bloody want, bells on it? We'll be the bloody owners then, without breaking windows, or heads.'

The conversation was interrupted again, this time by a load of bairns, running along, elbowing one another, shouting, 'First there gets the gobstopper.'

The men parted, then closed again, like the Red Sea, Evie thought. Sammy wasn't finished. 'Aye, and what if it's a load of hot air.'

James gripped her arm and nodded towards the shop. 'There he is, inside.'

Bridie saw Tim in his black uniform, talking to another man, also in uniform. The man was patting Tim on the back and they were shaking hands, laughing. Why, when their Meeting House was in such a state?

Bridie and James stood there, ignoring the buffeting of people pushing past them, just staring at their cousin. Bridie wanted to rush across and drag him away, back to Easton, back to them all.

James muttered, 'I didn't really believe it. Not

really, but to see him there, looking exactly like a fascist . . .' He turned to Bridie, his face pale and anguished. 'Which means he really is one, Bridie. I needed to see it to believe it, here, inside.'

For a moment they stood there, speechless. On the pavement the men still argued, the children still raced along. Together, hand in hand, they walked back down Warton Street. The lads were still playing football. One kicked it towards James. 'Give us a kick, mister.'

He kicked it back, barely looking. They walked to the bus stop, gripping hands all the way, neither able to speak, though Bridie's mind jolted with each step. He was a miner's son. He was part of a family that was socialist. How could he wear a uniform that stood for so much that none of them could bear?

'How could he?' she asked.

'Because he can,' James said quietly. She had never seen him so angry. Or was it anger? There was something else there as well.

He squeezed her hand. 'He's his own man, or perhaps his mother's man, and nothing to do with us any more.' His voice broke. She stared ahead.

Church must have finished, because there were women grouped around doorsteps; others walked towards them, in their smarts. Some were in a hurry. Her da said the vicar, priest or minister had to time it right: church doors shut, pub doors open.

She looked up at the sky. It was blue with a few

white clouds. It was all as it had been when they woke, but nothing was the same.

James sat next to her on the bus to Easton. 'We'll need to think, because we must protest, and it's nothing to do with him. We'd do it anyway.'

'Yes,' she said, but neither knew what they were really going to do. It was just noise.

They left the bus at Easton Co-op, when it parked up prior to its return journey to Hawton. They tramped the lanes, watching the larks, seeing that the wheat was ripening, and the lambs were fattening. They diverted to the beck, hurrying now, because it was 'home'. But when they arrived, it wasn't, because usually it was the three of them.

'I feel so useless because I can't change what's happening with him,' James said.

They returned to the road, walking along to the bridge. They gave their sandwiches to the boys leaning over, trying to catch minnows with jam jars.

'By, Bridie, that's grand, right nice cheese.' Jonny Earnshaw was lifting the corners of the sandwich and showing off the innards to his gang. 'Tell your mam, or Mrs Moore, that it's a sight better than bread and dripping, any day. ' His face was grubby, his father out of work. Bridie knew that Uncle Jack was trying to pump out an old seam to bring in the last few pitmen.

She hadn't known about the co-op idea, but just for once she would keep quiet. News like that had to be confirmed before it was given out as fact, even she knew that. Even she, she wanted to scream, so there, Tim Forbes, I'm not just a stupid child.

Jonny was staring at her. 'Your lug 'oles gone deaf, then, Bridie?'

She came back to the present and replied, 'I will tell 'em, bonny lad. Enjoy the sandwiches.' Mrs Moore would more than likely slap their wrists if they brought them back, convinced that they were on the point of starvation.

James leaned over the bridge, rubbing at the lichen. 'You've a good lot of minnows down there. Put 'em back before you leave, eh, lads.'

'Always do, James.' They pulled the jam jars out. The string dripped. They counted them up and scratched the various totals in the lichen, then tipped them out in a shower of water. They lowered the jars again, then hunkered down, their knees grubby. They were eating before Bridie and James continued on their way.

Bridie said, 'I wonder if Gracie knows times are hard for Jonny's family. There are the convalescent cottages she and Edward own, you know, the old Froggett houses, and they've turned the gardens into allotments and could help with food, and maybe some work.'

James said, 'Of course I know the houses. It wouldn't hurt to drop her a line, or telephone her at the manager's house. Will you, or shall I?'

Bridie said she would, but it would be a note. She didn't want to say anything about seeing Tim, and sometimes there was no filter between her brain and her tongue.

They both looked back at the bridge, then strode on, turning left towards Easterleigh Hall hotel. 'Easier when you're a child, isn't it?' James said.

Bridie nodded. They reached the gates and crunched up the drive. James said, 'It seems ages since we left.'

Bridie felt very tired. 'It is, bonny lad. It's bloody years, it really is. Everything is different.'

James put his arm around her. 'Don't worry, it can all change again.'

'Aye, lad,' she said, 'and I can see a pig flying from one cloud to another.'

Tables and chairs had been set out on the lawn, at which some guests were taking post-luncheon coffee. Others were strolling on the grass. For a moment Bridie forgot she was off duty and darted forward to help Sarah and Mary with serving the coffee. James caught her, and hauled her back. 'It's our day off, remember. All you've got to do is help Tom Welsh, and I'll be there, too.'

She relaxed. Harry Travers called from the top step of the Hall, 'Did you have a good hike, you two? Sandwiches devoured, legs walked off?' He was smart in his suit. Kevin stood by his side, his useless hand tucked inside his jacket.

James called back, 'We had a grand time, Harry. Have you and Kevin been busy?'

Kevin ran down the steps. 'You missed the excitement, both of you.'

They hurried over to him, Bridie calling, 'What's happened?'

Harry bawled from the top step, 'Prancer's a daddy again.'

Kevin swung round. 'You said I could tell them.'

'Ah well, you can go with them, how about that for a trade?'

Annie came through from the Great Hall, to stand next to Harry. 'Beautiful little foal, though she wasn't due until tomorrow. She's a grey, like Prancer. We left you to introduce him to his progeny, bonny lass.'

James was pulling at her. 'Come on, Bridie.' She ran with him, her empty basket swinging. Kevin joined them, streaking ahead. It was a race then. All three tore along, approaching the entrance to the stable yard, all in a line. She felt the others had slowed, and so they had, and they arrived beneath the arch together. It should have been with Tim, but it didn't matter, not this time.

There was supposed to be no running in the cobbled stable yard, except in emergencies, but they could hurry, so all three did, with Prancer whinnying as they passed his stall. Bridie called, 'In a moment, Daddy.' They entered through the stables' double doors, and saw the families lined up along the foaling stall, leaning on the horizontal wooden fence. They all turned, and Aunt Ver said, 'Ah, the hikers return.'

Her mother looked askance at Bridie, who sighed. Her mother was a witch, and clearly guessed that hiking had never been on the menu. She asked a question without speaking. Bridie nodded, her throat suddenly tight. Her mother came to her. 'Come on, you three, greet Primrose. She's bonny, and Marigold surprised the lot of us, including Bertram, the vet. She's an eager little mare and was determined to arrive early. He's just hoyed off.'

She walked her daughter to the stall, while James and Kevin followed. Uncle Richard and Uncle Jack, Aunt Grace and Aunt Ver and her da moved up to make room. She could see the foal now, nuzzling Marigold. Primrose was indeed bonny; new and fresh. It helped. She grinned at James. He said, 'It helps.'

The grown-ups looked puzzled, except for Evie, who told Bridie to bring Prancer. In his stall she put on his halter, and brought him along. He didn't seem impressed. He would be, though, because Bridie would train Primrose to handle the disabled, just as Marigold did.

'You'll be so proud, my lovely boy,' she murmured, pressing her face into his neck. He had helped her da and others, and he'd work with many more, whatever James said. She looked at Primrose. 'Yes, he's not that old, and there's the proof,' she said to James, and laughed, as he did.

Soon she must prepare him for Tom Welsh. This was her life. For James was right, Tim had his own. But she really wouldn't think about it, because she couldn't bear not to see him here with them today. She felt as James looked: lost, determined, angry.

Chapter Seven

The Jarrow March, 5 October 1936

Uncle Jack drove the Austin, while Uncle Mart sat in the passenger seat, telling him how to drive, and counting off the miles to Jarrow. He was seemingly unaware that Jack's knuckles were becoming ever whiter on the wheel. Bridie and James, with Charlie – the Easterleigh Hall gamekeeper who had been a POW with her da, Jack and Mart – sat between them, daren't look at one another, and instead stared out of the window at the scenery. Any minute now Charlie would chip in, and then Jack would yell, 'Who else wants to bloody take the wheel, or do you want to walk?'

At that point Mart and Charlie's game would finish, and the drinks would be on Uncle Jack.

Her da had been in Newcastle overnight with Uncle Richard on business, and they'd be making their own way. If there was too much of a crowd in Jarrow, they'd not even meet, but at least they'd each know the other was there. Perhaps Tim would come on his motorbike. If he did, would he be alone? If he wasn't, would the fascists make trouble: another

Cable Street, with its fascist marchers heading for the East End of London, until they clashed with protesters? It had better not be, or the Blackshirts would be on a hiding to nothing.

Bridie watched the raindrops course down the windows; some were faster, some were smeared by the wind and never reached the bottom.

Were the fascists surprised when the protesters barred their way? The newspapers said that bricks, chamber pots and heaven knew what had been thrown. 'You shall not pass,' a witness reported hearing one Jewish woman say. It had caused the police to require the fascists to disperse, for the sake of law and order. They'd finally ended up in Hyde Park, where she presumed they hadn't fed the ducks. She tried to laugh but couldn't, because of the question in all their heads, no doubt: had Tim been there?

They were passing through a small pit village now, the terraced houses blackened, the unemployed loitering on the corner, or in doorways, sheltering from the steady rain.

Charlie leaned forward, saying, 'Watch the corner, man. You're storming into it too fast, bonny lad. We're not charging across no-man's land into the jaws of death.'

Mart yelled over his shoulder, 'Not so sure about that. He thinks he's driving a canny tank.'

At that, Uncle Jack did the inevitable, drawing into the kerb and slamming on the brakes, so that they were all thrown forward. Bridie caught at the door handle as Charlie flung a protective arm across her and James, just as Tim had done when they were bairns. Everyone waited. Jack said, 'Any more ruddy nonsense and you're walking, the lot of you. Not another word, got it?'

'Aye,' Charlie said. 'Aye, think we got that, didn't we, troops? If we're good, the drinks are on you then, if I hear you right, Jack?'

The men were laughing as Jack drew away from the kerb, cursing under his breath. James leaned forward, looking past Charlie to Bridie, shaking his head. 'Same as always. Bairns, the lot of them.'

'Enough of your cheek, fellow me lad,' Jack called, changing gear and winding his way through the village. They were travelling in the wake of other cars now, and a few charabancs, all heading for Jarrow, it seemed.

Bridie grinned suddenly. She loved her da's marras, loved them so much it gave her a pain in her gut. They made her feel good. 'I spy with my little eye something beginning with "C",' she said.

Everyone groaned. 'Not that old chestnut,' Uncle Mart complained.

Bridie called, 'No, wrong, not a chestnut.'

The others groaned again. Charlie called, 'Church.' The spire she had seen in the distance was now on their left.

'Too clever by half.' Bridie could hardly speak for laughing.

'Your turn, Uncle Mart,' James shouted. He chose 'S'.

Bridie grinned at Uncle Jack as he snatched a look at her in the rear-view mirror, his eyes crinkling, his pit scars still visible. But scars like that stayed, because the coal became embedded. She thought it was like a sign saying, I'm a member of a gang, I have marras. We live together, and die together.

Perhaps it was a bit like that at Easterleigh in the kitchens. She smothered a grin. With her mam and Mrs Moore shouting the odds, sometimes it seemed as if death really was close.

Between James and Bridie, Charlie sat hunched with his big hands on his knees, trying to make himself smaller than he was, such was the tight fit. His hands had coal scars from the German mines where he'd worked with Jack and Mart until her da had got them out, and moved them to his officers' prison camp as orderlies and tunnellers. It was Jack and Mart who had developed the tunnel through which they led many to freedom.

'You started this, so join in,' James ordered. She listened then yelled, 'School. Too easy for the master of the game.'

'Ah ha, pride comes before a fall, pet,' Charlie said. 'So find us a corker then.'

Bridie snatched a look. He hadn't shaved too well this morning. 'I spy with my little eye, something beginning with "W".' That would keep them at it for a good while.

'No, no, no,' she kept replying, but her concentration was wavering. Seeing Charlie's scarred hands, and recalling the German mines, had made her think about what it was like for the miners. If she was Mine Manager, she knew that she'd do what Jack and Mart did, and go down the pit every few months, just to hear the grumbles, check the props, and listen to the creaking of the seams or whatever it was Uncle Jack said.

Perhaps all bosses should work with the men, so they could understand? Maybe, while they were waiting for the marchers to get going, she'd ask him and Mart what they thought about that idea, though what she really wanted to know was whether they were going to make the men shareholders. She wouldn't ask them that yet, though. Slowly, she was beginning to learn to wait for the moment. It could be something to do with her having turned sixteen a week ago.

At last James said, 'I haven't a clue, you horrid little worm.'

'Say you give in then, toad.'

They were drawing into Jarrow now, set on the River Tyne. Gulls were overhead, the rain was still pouring, the traffic was slow. Uncle Jack said, 'We'll park on the edge of town and walk in.'

'I give in,' James said, leaning forward. Charlie pressed himself back for her to answer.

She did so: 'Whiskers. To be exact, Uncle Charlie's; he missed some this morning when he shaved.'

James' howl of protest was drowned by the guffaws of the men, as Charlie ran his hand round his chin.

'Too tricky by half,' he murmured. 'We'll have to watch you, bonny lass. Mischief in the making, I reckon.'

They walked to Christ Church in the rain, and stood outside with hundreds of people who filled the workless town that day. Those inside were mainly the marchers, while most outside were well-wishers. Bridie wondered if this march would change things. Would Palmer's shipbuilders open up again, and if they did, who would buy their ships? If Hitler had the money in his pocket to buy a few, would Palmer's sell to the Nazis? The rain was dripping off her hair, and down her face. Gulls squawked.

Inside, an ecumenical dedication service was conducted, and prayers were said for a safe and successful conclusion to the march. When the marchers reached the House of Commons they aimed to present a petition, signed by more than eleven thousand people. Bridie said, 'It should weigh really heavy, with so many names, because they're more than names, aren't they, Uncle Jack? There's a lot of hope there, and pain.'

Uncle Jack nodded. He looked thoughtful. 'Aye, lass, you're right there.'

Uncle Charlie put his arm around her shoulder. 'Not just a mischief maker, then?'

James was putting up his umbrella, borrowed from his father. It was black and large, and more suited for a Durham club or the streets of Newcastle, or even London. He held it over Bridie, as well as himself. Jack, Mart and Charlie shook their heads at the offer to squeeze beneath.

'Caps will do the job, lad. Always have, always will,' said Uncle Mart, as the rain grew heavier and doused his cigarette. He threw it into the gutter. They all watched it shred.

Her hair probably looked like the tobacco, Bridie thought, because it was already soaked, and the water was running down her neck. She muttered to James, 'You could have put it up sooner, you daft beggar.'

He shook his head. 'No, I couldn't. I forgot about it, and besides, I like you looking like a drowned rat, it will keep you in your place.'

She dug him in the ribs. He seemed more himself today, though for the last few weeks he'd been scouring the newspapers, reading about the fighting in Spain as the Nationalists, who were fascists in all but name, staged a coup against the elected Republican, or socialist, government. She'd grown tired of hearing him mutter, day after day, 'How bloody dare they?'

The service finally ended, and the marchers began to sort themselves out, the front rank holding the banner 'Jarrow Crusade'. There was one more, further back. The crowd was talking quietly, and so too was James, who looked over his shoulder to check that Jack was not within hearing distance.

'Father says that the talk is that the BUF will be told they can't wear uniforms to strut about in any more, after the trouble at Cable Street. In fact, no civilians will be able to, so that's a shot in the foot for the silly beggars. Serve 'em damn well right.'

The march was beginning with Ellen Wilkinson, Jarrow's red-haired MP, leading the way. The cheering was ragged to begin with, but then it grew strong, and as determined as the marchers. Bridie could see very little because of the press of people, but she did see the top of the banner jogging past.

Mart called to Jack, 'Are we walking along for a bit?'

'Aye, lad, reckon we are.'

They set off, arranging to meet back at the car if they lost one another. The marchers were heading for Ripon, over sixty miles away, and destined to be there by the weekend. They would stay at village halls overnight. Their boots sounded like a company of soldiers marching. Still the gulls swooped. Bridie wondered how they would know if Tim had come. As they walked with the tide of men, women and children, she turned to James. 'Do you think Cable Street will have changed his mind and brought him back?' she asked.

It was Jack who answered. 'It won't be that easy.'

Jack and Mart had caught them up and were walking either side of the youngsters, with Charlie at the back. 'To stop you two getting up to mischief,' Charlie said.

Bridie knew it was to keep them safe. Rain still fell, the shops and houses looked dark and dreary, but after all, it was October in Britain. She said to Uncle Jack, 'We should do something. He could get hurt, he could—'

'Hush your noise, lass,' Jack said, peering over the heads of the crowd. They were keeping pace with the banner. 'Give it a rest. Let the lad find things out for himself.'

James almost shouted now, 'But what if he doesn't? What do we do then? He'll be one of us, but not one of us, and how can he not see what's happening out in Germany, to the Jews, to the communists, socialists, all those who fought his lot at Cable Street? When I met him for a drink, he said that I didn't understand how inefficient democracy was, that a leader was needed to drag the country out of depression, that it was the good of the whole that mattered, not the individual.'

Bridie turned on him. 'You met him, and didn't tell me?'

James shook his head, irritated. 'I can meet him, if I want to, but I bloody don't any more. Beggin' your pardon, Uncle Jack.'

They were out of the town now, and a gap opened in the crowds. James ploughed a way through, taking his umbrella with him, heedless of the rain falling on the others. They followed until they were walking alongside the marchers. Ahead of her Bridie saw James and a young marcher talking together. She heard James replying, 'A doctor, really? Looking after them on the march, are you? Oh, you're going over?'

She didn't hear what the man said, but she knew from the set of James' shoulders and the way he moved that it was something interesting. Other marchers were pressing forward, and James fell back, calling, 'Thanks for that. I'll have a good think, now I've a contact.'

Uncle Jack called from behind, 'What's he up to now, our Bridie?'

'I'm not a mind reader, Uncle Jack, but don't you worry, I'll get it out of him.'

His laugh was so like her mam's. 'I'm right glad you've got the lad to keep you company these days,' he said. 'It's hard when you lose a friend, even if it's only for a while.'

She looked at the marchers, already thin and tired. What on earth would they be like after a march of three hundred miles? She hoped they would be well fed in the towns they rested in overnight, but two hundred men was a lot to take on. When they got there, would it do any good? Would the government listen? How many of the MPs knew what unemployment and poverty meant? What the men needed was a safety net for when they were out of work. It would make things so much better.

She found herself saying to her uncle, 'Tim's not right, is he? We mustn't get rid of our parliament, our democracy, or our law. Would one Führer, like Mosley, make Britain fairer and more efficient?'

He put his arm around her shoulders. She was soaking. The rain was running down her face and squelching in her shoes. 'Aye, well, Bridie, they'd have your mam and your Aunt Ver to deal with if they tried that trick. Those women fought long and hard for their suffrage, and remember it took a war to give men of all classes the vote too. By, Bridie, I remember that call after the war – "If they are fit to fight they are fit to vote." Aye, it'll not be given up easily, you mark my words. As I say, give him time.'

He squeezed her to him. She said, 'You are so calm, so certain.'

'Maybe I'm certain, but calm? Not sure your Aunt Gracie would agree with that, but I know my boy has a good heart. One day he'll see past the blather, and know that though Britain is slow, no-one is locked up for what he is, or turfed out of the country.'

James was alongside them now, holding the umbrella over Bridie. 'But what if he doesn't see, Uncle Jack?'

'Then we'll have to show him, but until then, you two, let it lie. Promise me?'

His voice was so serious, so sad, that they both nodded. Uncle Jack dropped back then, as James and Bridie walked along together, and slowly the marchers drew ahead until finally, they were left looking after them, feeling gormless and useless. Uncle Mart suggested they head for home, and have their drink at the Miners' Club in Easton, with James too. They could drop Bridie back at the Hall. She had to be back for a patient who was going to try his hand at riding for the first time.

As they reached the car, James surprised Bridie by telling the marras that he'd like to be dropped at the Hall too.

James leaned back against the fencing around the exercise paddock and listened as Bridie read out details of David Weare's injury, weight and height. Poor beggar, James thought, hurt in a steeplechasing fall – how quickly life could change. The canny thing was that all David wanted was to get back on a horse.

James said, 'I wonder if it's just bravado, and once he's done it, he'll walk away. Well, roll away?'

Bridie shrugged. 'Not if Prancer's got anything to do with it. I reckon his daughter Fanny has the same gift. Wonder if Primrose will have it too?' She tucked the clipboard under her arm.

James watched as David Weare, who looked about thirty, appeared, pushing himself along in his wheelchair while Matron walked beside him on the concrete path from the Neave Wing. David's arms looked strong, but you never could tell. 'It'll be a total lift, I think, don't you, Bridie?'

She nodded. 'Can you?'

He smiled. 'These muscles can do anything, but just in case, I've asked Young Stan along. He's happy to leave sweeping the leaves for now.'

Matron waved, and now Sister Newsome appeared,

walking across from the Hall laundry where she'd left sheets to be laundered. She was never far away when needed, and James thought that the two women worked by some sort of telepathy. That would be a useful tool where he'd decided to go, especially after the talk with the doctor who was on the march. He just wished telepathy would work with Bridie, and then he wouldn't have to actually tell her of his decision to go to Spain with the International Brigade.

He stopped lounging, and walked with Bridie along the path to meet David. James called, 'Good to see you. We've Young Stan on his way to help with the lift; we might just need him. He's used to lifting sacks of spuds, and you'll be a damn sight easier than that, with those arms. Look like they could knock a few blocks flying.'

David laughed. Bridie had started this therapy by being polite and kind, but James had said if he'd lost the use of his legs, not to mention possibly his willy, he'd much rather be treated as an ordinary bloke. It seemed to work. They all chatted as they headed for the ramp and in between explained the procedure.

While they did so, Bridie and James studied him. People might say they were fine, but often, deep inside, they were petrified. It sometimes showed at the foot of the ramp, or when they saw Prancer, who was large; it was a long way to fall, after all. Clive, the groom, was standing with Prancer at the platform of the mounting ramp. He'd put on the double saddle. This time they'd decided James would get on board with David. It was Matron's suggestion, and she was always right.

'Two blokes together,' she'd said. 'We're one man down now Tim's busy, so you'll have to do a bit more, James. Bridie can't do it all. Well, she can, but it's good for you, young man.'

So that was that, James thought ruefully. She was right, of course, but fairly soon Bridie would have to do it on her own. Or he'd have to train someone up; perhaps Young Stan?

Bridie called, 'Are you going to stand there catching flies all day, James? Come on, don't know when the rain's going to start again, and we don't want David getting soaked.'

Matron said, 'We need an undercover paddock. I will talk to Sir Anthony.'

Oh dear, James thought, poor Sir Anthony. Bridie winked at him.

They were at the foot of the ramp, and now James shoved the chair up it, while David thrust at the wheels. Bridie slipped into the paddock and moved to Prancer's side, ready to guide David's leg. Young Stan was here now, but James said he would try to do it, if Stan would just wait in case he was needed.

James and David reached the platform, and again talked through what was to happen. Stan positioned the chair facing Prancer's head. James faced David, putting his arms securely around the rider, and knee-to-knee he lifted David forward, swivelled him around and lowered him onto the centre of the saddle in a side-sit position, never letting him go for a second. 'How are you, David?'

James' back ached; well, let it ache. At least he could feel it. This young man had broken his. Bridie helped James to ease David's right leg over the front of the saddle, while Young Stan supported David's back. All the time Bridie and Clive talked quietly to Prancer, who never moved a muscle, but waited, as though willing the rider to have faith and courage.

'Right, Clive,' Bridie panted. 'Let's slip this left leg just where it should go. David, Clive will ease Prancer forward and then help me put your feet into the stirrups. They're wooden, with a bigger platform, which seems to work better.'

James had left Young Stan on the mounting platform, where he was holding on to David's shoulders, and jumped down into the paddock. He took Prancer's head, moving him forward a bit, to make room for Clive to take up position by David's right leg. 'How are you feeling? Sick, dizzy, in a bit of a tizzy?'

David grinned. 'Bloody marvellous. I never thought I'd mount a horse again. Bit of a palaver, but worth it. Thank you.'

James let Prancer nuzzle his hand. 'Prancer is special. Bridie's da came home from the war minus a leg, and my dad left his arm and leg behind. Very careless. They both ride now. Prancer seems to know things we don't. Dad also drives a car and we wish he wouldn't. He seems to think if he drives it fast enough he can take off. A frustrated pilot, I reckon.' All the time he spoke, he kept his eye on David, monitoring him for sweating, paleness, panic. There was none. This man was bred for riding.

Bridie and Clive finished fixing David's feet in the broad stirrups, which Grandpa Forbes and Tom Wilson had designed. Bridie was at David's right knee. Clive at his left, and James at his front. Bridie asked, 'How's your balance? Should Young Stan release your shoulder?'

David nodded. Young Stan had followed David as James eased Prancer forward just a bit, but now he let him go, hovering a bare inch above his shoulders. Young Stan was a natural, James felt, with relief – for how could he leave Bridie without help? – and there was time to train him, on the quiet. They all watched, alert to rush to David's aid. Bridie was supporting his back from her side, and Clive was doing the same from his.

'Can I walk him?' David asked.

James laughed quietly. 'Thought you might say that. Clive will give me a leg up, and then I'll sit behind you; they'll walk either side. How does that sound?'

Clearly, rather good. Clive boosted James on board, and Prancer strolled around the paddock, once, twice. As they neared the ramp, Matron and Sister Newsome waved their hands. 'Enough,'

Matron called. 'We don't want to wear him out. When he's back in his chair he can go and have a look at Primrose and Marigold, and meet Fanny and Terry, and then that'll be his lot for today. There's always tomorrow, young man. Bridie combines kitchen duties with this, and James is intermittent, but it looks to me like Clive and Young Stan are coming along nicely – not that you knew you were in the picture, Young Stan. You are.'

The same procedure occurred, but in reverse. This time it was Young Stan who helped David roll down the ramp, pulling back so he didn't head down at a rush. As Clive slung Prancer's stirrups over his saddle, prior to walking him back to his stall, David said, 'He's a good horse; not that young, though.'

Bridie snapped, 'He's not that old, either.'

David and James exchanged a look. Something passed between them. David said, 'No, he'll never be *that* old. Horses like that aren't. They're always with us.'

Bridie wouldn't listen to this and strode ahead to check on Marigold and Primrose, and give carrots to Fanny, Prancer's other daughter, and Terry, who had come from a friend of her da and was absolutely trained up now, and ready to join Prancer in his work. As Clive took Prancer to his stall, to remove his saddle and bridle and replace it with his halter, she called back to Clive, 'Make sure he has a play in the pasture, won't you, Clive? He's been such a good boy.'

She leaned on the stall barrier looking at Primrose, who had been brought in with her mother because of the rain. 'She's a good mum, isn't she, Primrose?' she muttered to the foal, who was developing nicely. 'Bet your da's pleased with you, little Primmy.'

James and David were at her side now, with David peering through the horizontal slots. 'She's a belter,' he muttered.

'Prancer's foal,' Bridie said.

'She'll have his spirit, you can tell.' Primmy had come to David, who leaned forward and extended his hand through the gap. She nuzzled it.

Bridie smiled. 'His other daughter, Fanny, is the same, but she's out in the pasture right now. We're going to be able to help more people once we have them all trained. Fanny is five now, and almost ready. I do that in the evenings, or the odd hour off. Terry is just perfect, and we're already using him.'

They stayed for a while longer but then heard Matron calling, 'Time.'

David turned his wheelchair and trundled out of the stable, stopping at the doors. 'If you ever need someone like me to help, perhaps to give people confidence, I have my own money, but I have no life. I'd like to make mine here.'

Matron was waiting for him just outside and said, 'Good heavens, you're here five minutes and taking over, young man. Let's see how you do over the next few weeks, or months, and if Bridie and James can get you to the stage of a shining example, then it might be worth considering.' She pushed him out into the drizzle that had begun.

Bridie laughed. 'Well, no need to make a decision on that one then. Matron will tell us when the time is right, and will also say what it is we are to do, James. So we'll see you up on Prancer tomorrow, then, David.' They waved him goodbye, and Bridie said to James, 'I'm having a cup of tea before I get the dinner sorted. Come in and have some with me. You left your bike in the garage, didn't you?'

As she began to walk into the yard he pulled her back. 'I was talking to someone on the march.'

'Yes, I saw that. You looked interested. Come on.' She walked away, and he watched her go.

Perhaps he didn't have to tell her, not yet? But then he heard the words pouring from his mouth, 'Wait, Bridie, I have to tell you. Just wait, will you, and stop rushing everywhere.'

She stopped, and turned. He saw the consternation on her face and rushed on. 'We were talking about Spain. He's going out with the International Brigade to support the Republicans against Franco.'

'What?'

'Oh, don't look so dim, Bridie. You've read about it in the newspapers. You know the Nationalists are fighting the Republicans because Franco doesn't agree with the election results. The Nazis and Italian fascists are supporting Franco, and no-one but Russia is doing much to supply the Republicans. I'm tired of just complaining about Tim and the fascists here, so this is my chance to actually do something about the bastards. Arthur's given me a contact in London.'

'Arthur, who's Arthur?' Bridie said, right up close now, gripping his arms. 'Fight, you mean? You don't know anything about fighting, you idiot.'

She was shouting now, an inch from his face. He didn't move, but shouted back, 'Oh, don't be so bloody difficult, Bridie. Tim's up to his neck in something, and I'm just ploughing your da's fields, looking at horses' arses, and being useless.'

She was shaking him now. 'You're mad. Tim's not fighting; he's having the odd ruckus and being obnoxious. Don't. You mustn't. We'll heckle the fascists here.'

'I've been thinking about it, Bridie, since the Nazis started, and then there was the news about Franco, and someone has to do something. It's meant to *be*, can't you see? I wouldn't have met Arthur if it wasn't.'

'When?' she asked. 'When are you going?' She'd released his arms, and stalked towards the garage yard. It was only then he realised the drizzle had stopped and there were patches of blue in the murky grey.

He hurried after her. 'I'm not sure, Christmas or thereabouts. You mustn't say anything.' Now he was the one gripping her arms. 'Promise me, Bridie. Say nothing.'

She hesitated, checking his face. Could she see the

determination he felt? 'I won't, but only because you might change your mind.'

He knew he wouldn't. He was so angry at everything that had happened, and was happening. Democracy was everything, he knew that now; he'd known it when he saw Tim in his uniform, and when he'd heard Jack talking about his mother and Aunt Evie fighting for the vote. He knew Lady Margaret had been force-fed as a suffragette, though she had only done it for limited suffrage – votes for the well-bred – but nonetheless, she had done it. His da had fought for it in the war, and his uncles.

Bridie gripped his hand. 'I'm coming with you.'

He burst out laughing. 'Don't be so bloody silly, you're only sixteen. And a girl.'

'You're a pig, James.' She dropped his hand and ran towards the kitchen steps, James in pursuit. At the top of the steps leading to the kitchen, she said fiercely, 'Only a girl, eh? I expect that's what they said to my mother.'

She ran down the steps. At the bottom James caught up with her again, holding her back, whispering, 'Don't say anything. Promise me. Let me do it in my own way.'

She said, 'I promise I won't tell, but I haven't said I'm not coming. You're my best friend, James.'

He wished that was true, though he suspected Tim was the one who really mattered to her. Perhaps that was part of why he wanted to go – she might miss him.

Chapter Eight

Easterleigh Hall, November 1936

Bridie had prepared luncheon with her mother, while Sarah and Mary had served it. There had been several orders from hotel guests for the braised lemon cod, but more for the veal ragout, and only one for mutton cutlets and Soubise sauce. Sir Anthony had chosen a light lunch of cod with dressed cucumber, because he was holding a dinner in the old billiards room this evening, for that Peace Club of his. A few of these Peace Clubs had sprung up, Bridie had heard, after Hitler reoccupied the Rhineland in March, in contravention of the Versailles Treaty. The Peace Clubs were concerned that other countries might react – but they hadn't, had they? – and perhaps they should, Bridie thought.

She checked through her mother's cookery bible for her recipe for stewed pigeons. Why on earth he wanted those, she had no idea, but at least they were cheap. The first course would consist of Julienne Soup, to be removed by Baked Whitings aux Fines Herbes. This would be removed by pigeon casserole. Her mother felt, and Bridie agreed, that the flavour was quite strong enough in itself without marinating the breasts, but that a dash of red wine would perk up the casserole no end. Sirloin of beef and horseradish sauce would also be served, all to be removed by cheesecakes, and Charlotte à la Vanille. The leftovers of the beef would be used for something tomorrow, and no doubt they could use the pigeon too.

Bridie had prepared the desserts at the crack of dawn, after she'd ridden her bike across from Home Farm in the face of a cold and bitter wind. Had it carried the scent of snow? She wasn't sure, but no doubt they'd find out.

She was sitting on Mrs Moore's stool. Behind her the ranges gave out a gentle heat, and the furnace was gurgling happily. It would need more fuel in an hour or so. Her mother had been right; after a few months you could work out from the noises just how hungry it was for coal.

She found the recipe. *Hang for ten days.*

Well, the pigeons had hung for a week, and that would do. First thing this morning she'd removed the breasts and checked for pellets, while Susie, the kitchen assistant, had made the hotel breakfasts. She'd sauté the breasts later, and then capture the pigeon bones in muslin, add herbs, and sink it into the stock with the breasts. This way there'd be no need to double-check for tiny bones when decanting into the serving dish.

Young Stan and Uncle Charlie had been in seventh

heaven at the request last week, because it meant they could 'blast the thieving little beggars into kingdom come', as Young Stan had said, 'and someone would put them to good use'.

Bridie had shaken her head. 'I'll do the same to you if you blast anything, thank you very much. I want pigeons in good shape.'

Raisin and Currant were sharing an armchair today but were very definitely on their marks as they waited for her to straighten up, then wipe her hands down her hessian apron. At that point they knew it would be time to go. She looked into the servants' hall, beckoning to Susie, whose break was over while hers was about to begin. She grinned at the dogs, teasing them by returning to the bible, but only for a moment.

'This is it, you two,' she called, wiping her hands. They scampered across, just as Susie entered. 'Please can I sauté the breasts, Bridie? When is your mam coming back?'

Susie's da was the blacksmith at Auld Maud. They were having a hard time, although sales of coal seemed to be improving, but not by much. Jeb, the union rep, was being pressured to push for more money by Fred, the rep at Lea End, who was a member of the Communist Party and had just returned from Russia.

Uncle Jack said that the communists' intention was to knock down, not improve. Bridie tried not to listen to politics any more, because it was such a mess, with everyone shouting about something, and her two cousins making daft decisions, and if her uncle wanted to do something to shut up Fred, why didn't he push forward with the co-op idea?

'Bridie?' repeated Susie, and she brought the pigeon breasts out to the cool cupboard. 'Please can I do them?

Bridie hushed the dogs, who were jumping up and whining. 'Sorry, Susie. Yes, you can. You know how after all this time. Mam will be back from Home Farm in about half an hour, so if there's a problem, she'll help.' She checked the clock. 'Is that the time? Well, no, she'll be back in five minutes. I must run, I'm needed at the stables.'

Susie called after her, 'It's the blind lad today, is it? Daniel Forsyth. Weren't he at school with us? Grand lad, as I remember.'

'Aye, he was smacked on his head at the BUF meeting in Hawton last month.' The words stuck in her throat. She ran up the steps, refusing to think about it, but she had, ever since she'd seen that he was booked in for this afternoon. Was Tim the one who had brought a heavy great chair down on the lad's head? The police had not brought charges, because no-one was saying anything.

Perhaps Uncle Richard could find work for Daniel. It was what the Neave Wing did. She'd hoped that seeing the result of violence would make James think again about going to Spain. But why would it? Easterleigh had been looking after men who'd been hurt in that way for years, so he knew full well what he was walking into.

She hurried into the stables, calling out to Prancer, who whinnied from his stall. She could hear Clive crooning to him as he brushed the old boy. He stopped and called out, 'I'll be taking him across in a minute, lass.'

Clive had been here as long as Bridie could remember. He only had a thumb and forefinger on one hand, and one finger on the other. 'Damn great pigeon,' she'd heard him snap at James when he had asked how he'd lost them. But it was the war, of course.

She changed into boots, jodhpurs and a heavy sweater in the privacy of the tack room. Perhaps James had already changed his mind about Spain, because he'd not mentioned it since. Daft beggar – probably just a whim; he was prone to them. She said it aloud. 'Prone to them, aren't you, lad?' It seemed to set it in stone. She tried it for Tim. 'You'll come back to us, won't you, lad?' The words seemed to bounce about in the air and did no good at all.

Young Stan had promised to help her with Daniel, and Clive would be there, of course. Perhaps David would be at the paddock, watching from his wheel-chair, as he was most days. Matron thought he was serious about helping, but Bridie couldn't really see how that would work. Matron said that he would be invaluable as an emotional support.

This meant, in Matron's world, 'You will do this,

Bridie.' She shrugged. She was surrounded by women who never knew when to keep quiet, who thought they knew best. The problem was, they did.

Prancer was no longer in his stall, and she checked the stable clock. She was late again. She took the risk of running across the stable yard. 'Enough of that,' bawled Uncle Richard, his voice skidding her to a halt. She heard his laugh as he said, 'Oh, the power of command. Go on with you, gal. You may run this time.'

She took off again, shouting, 'Well, come and help us if you've a minute.'

She heard his limping gait following her. She slowed, late though she was, and they continued together, leaving the protection of the yards and heading towards the paddock to the right of Neave Wing. As the wind caught them she wished she'd put on a scarf as well. He asked, 'How are the preparations for Sir Anthony's dinner going? I gather your mother has left much of it in your capable hands.'

Bridie glanced at him. Was that a criticism? She said calmly, 'Well, let's put it this way, Uncle Richard. Yes and no. I've had step-by-step instructions and she's only left me for two hours. She'll be back any minute, breathing down my neck until it's cleared away this evening. I've let Susie sauté the pigeon breasts, it's about time.' Over his laugh she continued, 'I just don't understand why he doesn't entertain them at his Searton Estate?'

'Ah, in that case, you don't know our Sir Anthony very well. He is committed, not just to our rehabilitation work, but to the hotel. It is partly his son's business, after all, and he'd not miss an opportunity to introduce the delights of Easterleigh Hall hotel to yet more of his contacts.'

They were at the paddock now, and Young Stan was walking Prancer round the periphery. When Prancer came alongside Bridie and Richard, he stopped, whinnied, and nuzzled Bridie's hand. Bridie lifted her face and this time he nuzzled her hair. 'I love you, you're such a canny angel,' she murmured. She watched as Young Stan walked him on.

Uncle Richard said, 'I don't know who loves that horse more, you or your father.'

Bridie turned round and leaned back, spreading her arms along the top of the fence. 'About the same, I reckon. He's the grandest horse there's ever been. Uncle Richard, why are all these Peace Clubs sprouting up when no-one's taking a stand against the Nazis anyway, so they're not likely to be needed?'

Richard looked to the right. 'Here's Matron, with the lad. Look at that scar.'

Bridie said the words before she could stop them, 'It couldn't be Tim who did it, could it?'

There was a pause. Richard said, 'Dangerous ground, Bridie. Let's not even go there, for how are we to know? Now, why are the Peace Clubs sprouting up? Could be something to do with the alliance

Germany made with Italy in October. It's concentrating minds, making people anxious, and now that their rearmament programme is really under way, not to mention German conscription . . .'

'It's a mess, but we need to stand up to bullies,' Bridie ground out.

Richard said quietly, 'The world is frequently in turmoil, Bridie, and you're right. The problem is always when good men do nothing. That is why we must applaud Sir Anthony for doing what he thinks is right, and reaching out for peace. That at least is doing something, though it might not be what you and I would do.' He studied Prancer, murmuring, almost to himself, 'But then, we're doing nothing.'

Matron's voice reached them. 'There's young Bridie, Daniel, who is more trouble than you'd ever imagine, but you can trust her. A few of us do, but only a few. Others have more sense.'

Daniel laughed. Uncle Richard said, 'That laugh's not from the heart, young Bridie.'

'But it will be,' Bridie whispered to him. 'I promise you that.'

He shook his head. 'Like mother, like daughter. Heaven help the world.'

Chapter Nine

At seven p.m. Evie, Bridie and Annie wrenched off their aprons and removed their caps, then smoothed down their dresses before hurrying from the kitchen. They took the stairs up to the green baize door almost at a run, wishing they could just get on with the finishing touches to the meal. Evie said, 'Susie will do as instructed, she's a grand lass, but . . .'

Annie laughed quietly. 'Yes, indeed, but . . . Now is the time to smile and pretend we have nothing better to do, and thank him.'

They slipped into the grand hall, grinning at Ron, who was manning the reception desk with Kevin, then headed to the old billiard room, which was now the private dining room. There were only a few regular guests staying tonight, and they were already assembling in the sitting room for pre-dinner drinks. Bridie hesitated for a moment, but then relaxed. No, no, it was alright, Ron would take care of them, and they had simply put Sir Anthony's menu as à la carte for the guests. Her mam, as always, sensed her panic, and squeezed her arm. 'All under control, bonny lass.'

'Aye, mam. I just keep double-checking.'

Annie said, 'It's as well, that's how we keep the mistakes to a minimum. Well done, pet.'

They entered the private dining room, Bridie following behind her mam and Annie. Moira and Polly, the evening waitresses, were circulating with the canapés, while Harry, as a director of the hotel, did the same with dry sherry. Bridie scanned the room, but then Sir Anthony saw them.

He approached, kissing the hand of all three women. 'My dears, a triumph, as always.' He gestured around the room and at the flowers that Young Stan and his team of under-gardeners, Edward, Gerald and Gladys, had provided and arranged. 'And the canapés, Bridie . . .' He kissed his fingers. 'Another triumph. Now, come, meet my guests, some of whom you know.'

He led them forward and they followed, feeling like ducklings, ugly ones at that, Bridie thought, as some of the guests clearly wondered what on earth 'downstairs' was doing upstairs. Her mother winked at her and Annie grinned, so she put back her shoulders, holding her head high. Sir Anthony made for Lady Margaret, who was talking to Herr Bauer. Bridie was surprised to see Bauer here, but then, it made sense. This was a Peace Club, and Sir Anthony was reaching out.

Lady Margaret was in full flow, almost neighing as they approached, ' . . . Franco is such a good man. He'll sort out the Republicans, and not before time, and your dear Führer, Herr Bauer, will do all he can to help him squash the Reds, won't he? He's got the Luftwaffe, and my word, that Goering is such a charmer. A Great War ace, if memory serves me.' She looked so earnest, leaning forward, her face far too close to Herr Bauer's. Bridie thought someone should offer her a carrot.

So she'd met Goering then, and the dear Führer, or was she showing off? She was away a great deal, so it was possible.

Herr Bauer stepped back a pace and replied, 'Sadly, I'm not privy to such information, Lady Margaret. I do not move amongst those in power in Germany.'

'But dear Sir Anthony probably does, don't—' She stopped in mid-sentence when she caught sight of Sir Anthony with the staff. She flushed. Her hand went to the shoulder of her dress. Bridie saw a brooch, though it was more of a badge really, and one that was somehow familiar.

Evie said, 'How nice to see you again, Lady Margaret. Ver is sorry to miss you but they're visiting Richard's parents in Cumbria.'

Bridie and Annie looked solemn, because it was a trip that had been arranged the moment Ver had seen that Lady Margaret had booked in to stay. As she'd made bread she had said, 'She's become even more of a bore, such a snob. Do you remember the fuss when you and I fought for the vote for all classes, and she objected, feeling it should be kept for those of a certain social standing, on the basis that only a certain echelon were bred to rule? She'd absolutely love a dictatorship, if she was the dictator.' As she had spoken, she had pounded the dough to within an inch of its life, and the rest of the staff had roared with laughter.

Lady Margaret's smile was forced. 'Indeed. I shall miss catching up on her news. It would have been good for Penny to talk to James, too. Is he also away?'

Bridie replied, 'No, he's still at Home Farm, beavering away doing something dirty. It's only us cooks here this evening.'

Her mother reached around and poked Bridie's back in a warning. Harry had been passing, and now filled the silence that had fallen. 'Not just the cooks, if you don't mind, young Bridie. What about we men? Nothing wrong with a good day's work, eh?'

Sir Anthony forced a laugh, clearly feeling the conversation was out of control and also still a little uncomfortable with Harry's choice of wife. It was felt that he would, in his heart, have preferred someone from the same drawer as his family, but had never actually put this into words. He grabbed a glass of sherry off Moira's tray. Evie and Annie took one too. Bridie obeyed her mother's frown and did not, feeling a sulk coming on, until she saw the broad smile that Herr Bauer flashed her. 'Ah,' he said, 'never fear, young Bridie. The years pass soon enough. And your uncle, he is well?'

'Yes, thank you, Herr Bauer. Uncle Jack is very

well. I hadn't realised you were also Sir Anthony's friend as well as Colonel Potter's.'

Lady Margaret swung round. 'Colonel Potter, really?' Her tone was sharp.

Herr Bauer sipped his champagne, as though he was thinking. He said at last, 'Ah, I realise why you might think that. We passed a comment or two at your uncle and aunt's wedding, I believe, while we were looking at the flower bed with the estimable young gardener.'

Bridie thought back. It was later, when she walked across to see how the men were doing, that she had seen Colonel Potter and Herr Bauer deep in conversation as they strolled from the ha-ha towards the house. She started to shake her head, then saw the look in Herr Bauer's eyes. Was it a warning? Just then, Penny Granville bounded up like a colt, all arms and legs, jogging her mother's elbow. The sherry slopped. 'So sorry, Mother, but one of Sir Anthony's friends has a house in Germany. They would like us to visit. Please say we can. We could ski this time, rather than just shop and attend the theatre.'

Sir Anthony smiled. 'Ah, Penny, I believe you know Bridie Brampton and her mother, Lord Brampton's daughter-in-law, and here is my daughter-in-law, Annie Travers.'

Bridie was pleased and surprised that Sir Anthony actually sounded welcoming towards Annie. Could he be starting to value her, at long last? Penny bared her long teeth in a smile. Yes, very much like a colt.

'Yes, we've met.' That was that, and she was off.

Herr Bauer bowed. 'Ladies, so delightful to see you again.' He drifted off. Sir Anthony escorted them on to other groups who clearly had nothing to say to mere staff. Finally, Evie waved Sir Anthony to a halt. 'If you want to feed the multitude, Sir Anthony, we need to leave you to the canapés, and don our aprons again. Thank you so much for holding your dinner party with us. As always, you support us to the best of your ability, and your ability is very great.'

Sir Anthony smiled. 'You are a force for good, Evie. You always have been and always will be. I hope that I am able to help for a while yet.' He looked strange, almost sad. He turned to Annie and seemed about to add something, but the moment passed and he merely touched her arm. 'My grandsons are well?'

Annie's surprise was evident. 'Very, thank you, Sir Anthony.'

'Now, I must return to my guests.'

The three women left the private dining room. As they moved towards the green baize door, Annie muttered, 'Do you think he might be unwell? He asked about the boys, who in many ways don't exist for him.'

She was clearly torn between relief and confusion. Evie said, 'Perhaps he's coming round to the idea that you and Harry school them at Easton elementary, not Eton?' The two women laughed quietly.

Bridie clattered down the stairs behind them. 'Perhaps he looks at Penny and thinks how lucky he is to have you and not a pony.'

Bridie heard their laughter as they swung into the kitchen, where Susie was lifting the lid on the potatoes. Bridie scanned the table, checking that all the implements were laid out correctly. Evie shook her finger at Bridie. 'Penny's a perfectly pleasant young woman. Now, we've work to do, but I agree, Annie, Sir Anthony is not quite himself.'

The dinner party for Sir Anthony was much like any other, Moira and Polly reported, except that Tim had arrived. Worse, he had worn black tie when all the others wore lounge suits.

As one course was removed, to be replaced by another, they worked on, and in between they fulfilled orders off the à la carte menu for the other guests, served by Robert and Enid from Easton. At last, as the coffee and cognac were served, and the staff dismissed at Sir Anthony's request, they sat fanning themselves in the heat of the ovens. Moira and Polly headed for their beds in the staff quarters in the renovated attic, Robert and Enid cycled back to Easton, and Annie headed home with Harry to their house in the grounds, looking happy.

Evie eased herself from her stool. 'I'm heading to my bed too. Don't be long, Bridie, and don't forget the accounts for your da from Ron's study. Make sure you turn your bicycle lamp on the moment you set off, because some of our diners will be driving home, and I want you to be visible.'

Bridie raised her eyebrows as the list of precautions continued to flow from her mother. Maudie popped her head out of the scullery, grinning, 'Ah, Evie pet, she's as safe as houses using the back lanes, remember. You can't get a car down there, even if you wanted to. Mother Hen comes to mind, so it does.'

At that moment the bell rang in the passage. It was the private dining room. Bridie waved her mother home. 'I'll go.'

She ran up the stairs, feeling not in the least tired, because her meal had been a success, and she had been given more responsibility than ever before. She skidded across the hall and opened the door into the private dining room. Sir Anthony swung round; a gentleman was standing, speaking, down the far end. He stopped. Sir Anthony rose and came to her. 'I expect the staff to knock, Bridget.' His voice surprised her, it was so cold.

'I'm so sorry, I forgot,' she replied.

She saw Tim feeling embarrassed for her, but doing nothing to help as he would once have done, and she was glad he stuck out like a sore thumb sitting in his dinner suit. Sir Anthony asked for another bottle of cognac. 'Knock next time, this is a private meeting.'

'Yes, Sir Anthony, I'll send Kevin with it. He will knock.' She snatched a look at Tim. His dark eyes met hers, which she made sure were full of distaste. On his lapel was a brooch, or was it a badge? It was the same as the one Lady Margaret wore. Now she noticed that many of the diners wore such a one. It was only as she closed the door behind her that she realised what she had seen: it was the Fascist membership badge.

She asked Kevin to take in two bottles of cognac, then she walked from the kitchen to the stables. She hung over Prancer's stall, talking to him, her mind working. Perhaps these Blackshirts really were a movement for peace, or why else was Sir Anthony involved? But what about the fighting, what about Cable Street? What about the liking for the Nazis?

'Life's a tricky beast, isn't it, Prancer pet?' He nuzzled her cap, then her neck. 'You stay in your stall; it's simpler, lad.'

She was tired now, but still had to collect Ron's accounts which he wanted her father to check. She didn't know why Ron liked the upstairs study, but he said he could think more clearly there. The others used the one along from the kitchen, which Uncle Richard had organised.

She gave Prancer one last pat, and hurried down the steps into the kitchen, then up the stairs into the grand hall. The lights were on in the sitting room, and she could hear the murmur of voices. She checked to see if any of the regular guests needed anything. Mr and Mrs Stansfield and their daughter were chatting quietly. She waved as Mrs Stansfield grinned at her. 'Lovely meal again, Bridie. We so enjoy coming. Thomas sends his regards to you all, and a big kiss for Matron, though I will not be the one to deliver that.'

'If you want to live, please do not. Do you need anything?'

'Nothing more, but thank you.'

'Just ring if you do.'

She carried on up the stairs, smiling at Kevin, who sat behind the reception desk and would stay there until the last guest had gone to bed, or left the hotel. Thomas had been a wartime brain injury. Well, not quite brain, perhaps mind-injured would be better, or so Mam said. He had made a steady recovery, though it had taken time. He was now a surgeon. She made her way along the landing. A soft light spilled from the study, and she approached, puzzled, hearing movement. She stopped in the half-open doorway, then pushed it open quietly. Tim stood in front of the oil painting which hid the safe.

'What on earth are you doing here?'

He spun round at the sound of her voice, his shock clear. 'I thought you'd gone home.'

'Well, I haven't. What on earth are you doing?'

He moved to the desk. 'I was talking to Sir Anthony about Easterleigh Hall. He said the view from the study windows was wonderful.'

She pointed to the window. 'It's dark.'

He walked across. 'No, see, there's a hunter's moon. Then I saw the painting. It's lovely.'

She didn't move from the doorway. 'You've seen it before.'

'Oh, for heaven's sake, Bridie. Sometimes it's good to touch base with who you are.' He dragged a hand through his hair. In the light there was even more of a reddish tint. He looked tired, strained. Did he mean it? Was he really thinking about touching base? Her heart leapt and she smiled, moving towards him.

'You're right, it's a lovely painting, but not valuable. The safe's behind it, but it wouldn't fool a burglar, so nothing important is kept here. In fact, I think it's empty. But you know all this, so I won't bore you.'

He said, 'Why would I know it? I've never actually lived or worked here.'

That hadn't occurred to her, because as children, the three of them always seemed to be milling about all over Easterleigh. 'Come and have a look, lad.' She swung open the painting.

He laughed, almost with relief. 'Who're you calling lad?' It was almost as it used to be between them. He was next to her now. She opened the safe. It only had a handle these days, no combination. There were a couple of dusters in it. He said, 'Isn't there a back panel?'

'Ah, you have done your spying well.' She pressed the bottom of the back panel and it opened to reveal – nothing. 'There, that's your lot, bonny lad.' She closed the safe door, conscious of him standing so close that she could smell the cognac on his breath. She closed the painting, dusting off her hands. 'I must just pick up some accounts for Da. They'll be on the desk. Ron's the only one who uses this room now. I think Da keeps everything in his study at Home Farm. Ron wanted Da to double-check his accounts.'

She picked up what she needed and gestured Tim to the door. He in turn gestured for her to take precedence. 'Ladies first.'

'You are improving. It's usually "horrible child".'

He half laughed and said, 'I'm sorry, I should have asked before I poked about. It was rude.'

She walked ahead of him to the door and waited while he turned off the light. As they left together, Bridie said, 'You've as much right to be here as the rest of the family. You're one of us, Tim.'

She stopped herself adding 'aren't you?'

They walked towards the stairs, then he held her back for a moment, gripping her arm, almost whispering, 'I'm sorry I've upset you all, but Millie's my mother.'

'I know, Tim. I'm sorry too. I thought that all fascists were bad, but now? Oh, I don't know, because if Sir Anthony wants them round the table at a peace meeting, I suppose . . . Well, I suppose . . .' She stopped.

He let go of her arm. 'You don't want to believe everything you read in the newspapers, you know, horrible child. Some think we're a force for good.'

She nudged him as she used to and waited, barely breathing. What would he do?

He nudged her back. They walked down the stairs, nudging one another and laughing. As he turned right for the private dining room and she went left for the kitchen, and home, he said, 'I'll come and see you at Home Farm before I go to see my mother again. How about that, or will you and James run me off with pitchforks?'

'There'll not be a pitchfork in sight. Nice suit, by the way. Bit like a sore thumb.'

He shook a fist at her, and walked away. Bridie watched him, feeling strange, because it had been almost as though life was normal between them, but it hadn't sounded quite right. It was almost as though he had learned his lines.

Maudie was still there, having chased the scullery girls to bed. Harry was on duty upstairs, and it was Susie's turn for night call, so she would be coming down from her attic room to doze on the armchair in case any guest rang. Tomorrow night was Bridie's shift, and she sighed. She left the kitchen, wrapping her coat around her as she half ran up the back steps. Her bike was leaning up against the garage wall. She put the papers in the basket and rode away, too weary to think about anything more tonight.

Chapter Ten

Easterleigh Hall, March 1937

Bridie and the kitchen staff had worked all morning preparing the Sunday roasts. They had decided on a choice of rib of beef or chicken, but no goose. The usual apparent chaos had prevailed, but now that the five thousand were fed, and most of the clearing up was done, they could sit on the stools, sipping tea. Ver said, 'You're right, Evie, isn't she, Bridie?'

Bridie and Susie looked at one another, puzzled. Ver slipped her cap from her blonde hair, pushing back a few strands, and explained, 'You know, making goose a Christmas speciality only.'

Susie muttered, 'Horrid greasy birds, anyway, and I hate plucking the great beggars.'

Ver laughed. 'So, you have a supporter there, Evie.'

Evie pushed the biscuit plate towards Susie. 'Then you may have two, because today you are my favourite.'

Bridie poured herself more tea. The furnace was gurgling on a high note, which meant it was getting hungry. 'I think it's a grand idea to use fowl and fish that we use at no other time of year for our

Christmas menu. It's one more thing that Harry can use to interest the newspapers. He's found a reporter interested in food, and could tell him of our decision. I also think the reporter should be invited to sample new dishes and write it up in his column. I did tell him, and Ron, and Uncle Richard. Is that worth two biscuits too?'

Evie nodded, 'Help yourself, because you, too, are my favourite today. The girl has been thinking, not just checking on the workmen every minute. By the way, Ver, have you noticed that there's a rather handsome young carpenter helping to put up the all-weather exercise paddock?'

'Oh, Mam,' Bridie groaned, putting down her mug and heading for the coal bucket. His name was Derek. He was nineteen with a grand smile, and her mam had eyes like a hawk.

As she topped up the furnace, Ver called, 'How are Derek's lovely muscles getting on with the task, anyway?'

Bridie ignored her, and riddled the furnace loudly. Susie shouted over the noise, 'They're working hard. It's wood, so they can just shove on with it. Sir Anthony's right good, isn't he, Evie, to stump up?'

Now that the conversation was on safer ground, Bridie left the furnace to its own devices and hurried to the scullery to wash her hands. Pearl, one of the scullery staff who lived in Easton, stepped to one side, her spectacles fogged by the steam. 'Aye, Bridie pet,' she said. 'He's a bit of a saint, our Sir Anthony is an' all, and your da, because he's shared the cost, I hear. Them poor wee lambs in Neave Wing'll soon be able to ride through the worst of the weather. It's not right their riding has to stop when there's too much snow on the ground. It'll be better for Prancer an' all. His poor old bones must ache all winter. Look at it today – early March, and more snow. Only a bit, though.'

Bridie dried her hands on the towel hanging to the left of the sinks. 'His bones are *not* that old,' she snapped.

Her mother called from the kitchen. 'Didn't I see James down here when you were busy with the Yorkshire puddings?'

Bridie didn't reply immediately, but touched Pearl's shoulder. 'Sorry to snap, but he really isn't that old. You just have to look at him.'

'Aye, lass.' Pearl's voice was gentle. She was the wife of a pitman and mother of two bairns, the oldest aged twelve. Bridie wondered if her husband was listening to the strike talk that was coming to the boil around the villages. What her Uncle Jack didn't need right now was Fred, the communist rep at Lea End, putting pressure on the men of the area to come out. He was such a loud-mouthed idiot and always had been, even at school, her mam said.

Easton and Hawton were now in full employment with the most recent seam reopened, so Jonny Earnshaw's dad would be bringing home money.

But her Uncle Jack and Uncle Mart were looking more stressed as the days went by, and her da, as owner, was too. What were they doing about the co-op plan? Why didn't they say anything? Her da said they needed anything like that set in stone, and it would take time.

Her mam called out again: 'I see you changed into your jodhpurs when you checked on Prancer after lunch. I hope it's bikes you're riding with James, not Fanny and Prancer. I don't like them being out in this. He's an old boy, remember.'

Bridie sighed. Why was everyone obsessed with Prancer's age?

Helen Jones, the housekeeper, came in from the old butler's parlour, which had been renovated to provide a nice apartment for her after her husband's death. Bridie left the scullery and settled on her stool again.

'I have lists,' Helen announced, and waited, with a grin on her face. Ver and Evie groaned, and everyone joined in as James skidded down the corridor from the green baize door end, whistling tunelessly.

'Why on earth can't the dratted boy whistle in tune?' his mother shouted, so he could hear.

He entered. 'Pearls before swine,' he sighed, running his hand through his blonde hair, his blue eyes downcast. 'I lay my whistling at your feet, and it is, I repeat, pearls before swine, Mother dear; and why are you sitting there with a face like a wet weekend, Bridie Brampton? It's your afternoon off and we have bikes to ride, places to go, people to see.'

She laughed, happy now whenever she saw him, because he had shaken his head when she had asked him about his plans for Spain at Christmas, and said, 'For heaven's sake, don't believe everything I say, you silly beggar.'

Her mam waved them away. 'Off you go, don't skid, don't fall, don't get cold, don't . . .'

Bridie grabbed her coat, hat and scarf off the hooks in the boot hall and followed James up the steps to the garage yard. Her Aunt Ver called, 'Where are you cycling?' but neither of them answered.

They hurried along the yew hedge path, slipping in the inch or two of snow from time to time. They were able to run through the silver birches where, in the spring, primroses would create a carpet. The wind whistled through the branches; snow lay all around, crisp but not even, because it had drifted up against the trunks. Snow also lay on the north face of the thatch roof of the bothy, where their bikes were kept, but was sliding to the ground on the south side. Did that mean it was thawing? Well, Bridie thought, funny sort of thaw, as the wind cut her like a knife.

James heaved out his bike from amongst the others and called, 'The roads will have been cleared of snow by the traffic, and Young Stan's been along with sand and salt anyway, along the top end. Come on, we'll be too late to hear what's happening. We can heckle the communists and support the socialists. Surely the pitmen know they've got a fair deal?'

They cycled, head down, into the freezing wind, heading for the open air meeting at Old Bert's Field, the one which usually held the Miners' Gala and fête. Today, though, it was host to a miners' strike meeting. The pitmen would hear their union reps talking for and against strike action. Bridie supposed their reasoning for an outdoor meeting was that they might get too many men to fit in the back hall of the Miners' Club, but would many come out in this? James shouted back to her, as he powered ahead, 'We're late, they'll have been at it a while already.'

'Wonder if the Hawton fascists will be there?'

'If we've heard about it, so have they,' he panted.

What she meant was, will Tim be there? He had called in on Uncle Jack and Auntie Grace for a moment at Christmas, but had then rushed to Germany for a few days, and would be off there again at any minute, her mam had told her this morning.

All was calm as they arrived, but only just, to judge from the heckling. They left their bikes where they fell, just to the left of the field entrance, their wheels spinning, and ran, slipping and sliding towards the gathering of pitmen. Jeb, the well-respected moderate union rep at Auld Maud, was speaking on a temporary platform made up of wooden crates. They listened as he appealed for common sense, not agitation, which could only harm the Easton and Hawton mines and therefore the pitmen.

'Aye, Lea End still has its problems, but their seams are not as good as ours, though Jack and Mart are working with the manager there. They're trying to see if some of the flooded seams can be pumped out. Remember that our owner, Auberon Brampton, has listened to us; he is also talking to the Lea End owner. You fought alongside Auberon, Jack and Mart, or your fathers did. You trust them, so let's leave them to it. Aye, it takes time, but anything else will destroy what we've built.'

The cheers were louder than the booing as Jeb continued, his voice rising and falling. The pitmen stood with their mufflers up round their ears, their caps pulled down, their breath billowing like steam, only to be swept away by the bitter east wind. The sky was iron-grey. Two birds flew over, Bridie saw. By, she bet they were cold. In the background, as always, was the seething slag heap, the winding gear, the smell of sulphur.

Several men beside her stamped and clapped their hands together to keep warm; others were squinting above their Woodbines, murmuring to one another. James whispered, 'I bet they'd rather be back in the club, downing a pint.'

She grinned. James weaved his way towards the front, with Bridie in his wake, but increasingly the gap between them grew as the pitmen she passed caught her arm, asking her how she was, and what about her mam, and da? Telling her how much Tom Welsh had been helped by Prancer, how Jack and Gracie's Stunted Tree convalescent and retirement houses were essential, how the children's Christmas party at Easterleigh Hall had been appreciated, how cold it was, how she must keep her head down, there were some daft buggers expected today.

At last she caught up with James, who had stopped near the front, to the right. Some way in front of them, three men wearing red mufflers were shouting and baying at Jeb. One shook his head and spat.

'They're like a load of kids. Are they the commies?' Bridie asked.

James shrugged, but a pitman near them called, 'Why d'you think they're wearing red, man? Course they're bleedin' Reds.'

Jeb was leaving the stage. He tried to shake hands with Fred, the communist rep from Lea End, who took his place. Fred brushed him aside. The commies near them cheered. Fred stood there with his hands on his hips. He was also wearing a red scarf. 'Bosses,' he bawled. 'You 'eard him. Bosses, your old rep said. He needs to step down, 'e do. We still have bosses, when we should be the ones owning the bloody pits.'

There was a cheering from the three men, and from a few others dotted about the place. Now there was a press of men moving forward.

'Get him off,' a pitman near Bridie shouted, shaking his fist.

'Let him speak,' the pitman next to him bawled, throwing his stub to the ground. 'Bloody bosses.'

James muttered in her ear, 'I don't recognise those men over there, do you? With the mufflers?' He was pointing to a couple in the centre, and suddenly there were more men dragging red scarves from their pockets, strangers in the main. 'Have a look over there.' He nodded towards a couple of miners who yelled, 'You tell, 'em, Fred.'

Fred was shouting, gesticulating, just like the fascists. Why did people have to be so extreme? Did they just like the sound of their own voices? She said, 'Do they all wear scarves?'

A pitman in front turned round. 'Aye, or else they'd forget who they were, Bridie lass. How's your mam?'

A man behind them laughed, cupped his hands and bellowed, 'You're keeping us warm with your hot air, Freddy. Bet it's a mite warmer here than Moscow. Have a cosy chat with Stalin, did ye, on your last trip, man?'

Fred retaliated, 'There you are, then, lads. Listen to Andy over yonder, chatting to the owner's lass.' He was pointing now. 'He's a lapdog, a donkey led up garden path by a wee bairn.'

A pitman from way behind yelled, 'Or a donkey led by bigger bloody donkeys by the names of Jack Forbes and Martin Dore.'

Fred took up the thread, 'Not donkeys, but a pair

of bloody dachshunds sitting in the lap of bloody Auberon Brampton, and what a name that is to play with.'

Bridie found her voice now, 'That's not fair. You know that's not fair, Fred Benton. We've a grand safety record, good pay . . .' But she was only one voice amongst many, so she pushed forward, wanting to get close, and tell him to his face.

James pulled her back. 'Stay with me, don't you dare go off.'

All around her people were arguing, as Fred ploughed on. The crowd was shifting, lurching this way and that. Bridie was knocked to one side. James grabbed her, holding her to him, shouting against the furore, 'Stay with me. Damn it, Bridie. I shouldn't have brought you down this far.' He was shouting to be heard.

She shouted back, 'You didn't bring me, I came by myself, you daft beggar.'

The stewards were working their way through the crowd, calming it down. It grew quieter, and Fred continued, 'Oh, yes, shake your fists at us, but when the workers take over you'll be scampering along on our coat-tails, like pigs at a trough.'

'Who're you calling a pig?' a man beside her roared. It was Anthony Selwood from Hawton, one of Uncle Mart's pitmen, who had dressed as Father Christmas at the Easterleigh Hall party for the bairns. The yelling and shoving all around grew worse, and suddenly there was a push towards the stage. One steward fell, and was trampled. The others were swept along.

James' grip tightened. 'We're leaving.'

They tried to force their way back, but the press of people was too great. James yelled, 'We'll get to the side.' He took her hand, weaving his way through, but then there was another push, which became a surge, and on top of this the shouting grew louder, and then the yelling of men in pain, and men enraged. A group of men were carving their way across the front of the stage, heading for a group of Reds, while others, wearing red scarves, were barging the surge.

Someone yelled, 'It's the fascists.'

The pitmen near James and Bridie spun round. One grabbed James' arm. 'Follow us, there's going to be heads bloodied this afternoon, man. We need to get her out.'

'Leave the buggers to it, they can bash one another's heads in,' another yelled. 'Waste of bloody time, anyway, listening to Fred's rubbish.'

The pitmen were carving a path of their own, and James and Bridie tucked in behind, but then there was a surge from the left, and behind, and now more yelling, and the fascists were here, a mob of them, wielding their fists, knuckledusters and clubs, clashing with the communists and anyone else in their way. Bridie fell, James was knocked down. A pitman stepped on Bridie's hand, his boots gouging the skin; her blood seeped into the scuffed snow. He pushed on past, dragging his young son. Behind them she saw a Blackshirt punching a pitman, who was giving as good as he got.

She scrambled to her feet and heard James shouting, 'Bridie? Bridie, where the hell are you?'

She was buffeted on all sides. 'Here,' she almost screamed, her hand up high, though how would he see it in all of this? But he did, and now she saw him ducking and diving, and side-stepping his way back; he was charged then, by a fist-wielding pitman wearing a red muffler. James went down.

A fascist powered into the communist and they fought, stepping on James, kicking him out of the way. Bridie screamed as a boot just missed his skull, but caught his nose. It began to bleed. It was his blood on the snowy ground now. Another kick thudded into his legs.

Bridie forced her way through the heaving bodies. She powered into the back of the fascist before he could kick James again. He slipped and fell. The communist turned, barrelling into another brawl, leaving James on his knees, shaking his head; his blood sprayed through the air. She pulled at his arm. 'James, come on, get up.'

The fascist was rising, and then he grinned at someone. A punch caught her on the ribs. She felt a sickening crunch, and fell, as James at last got to his feet. Bridie lay, winded, the pain in her ribs like nothing she'd known. She looked up as the two Blackshirts nodded at one another, their faces alight with excitement. One was Tim. It was he who had punched her.

James flung himself at him. 'You hit her, Tim. You bastard, have you gone mad? And you shouldn't wear a uniform. It's outlawed. Outlawed, do you hear?' He was punching 'Outlawed. Outlawed.' The other fascist hauled him off, throwing him down next to Bridie.

Bridie saw the excitement disappear from Tim's face and confusion take its place, as she turned on her front and got to her knees, feeling as though she would vomit. Someone else ran past, knocking her flat again. She gasped at the pain of the jolt. She rose yet again, and now she was lifted to her feet and steadied by Tim, who gripped her face between his hands. 'I didn't know it was you, Bridie,' he said.

She whispered, 'But you knew it was someone. You shouldn't wear your uniform in a public place. It's been forbidden after your Cable Street march.' She knew she was repeating James, but it kept going round her head and it kept her from crying. 'You shouldn't wear it. Do you hear me? You shouldn't damn well wear it. And I don't know who you are, any more.'

She tore from him, and now James was on his feet, and together they pushed through the crowd. Behind them they heard Tim call, 'Damn you, James, you shouldn't have brought her. She's just a bairn, for God's sake.'

They cycled home. The wind was at their back. It

numbed the pain of her ribs, and seemed to have stopped James' nosebleed.

When they reached the crossroads where she would turn right for Home Farm, and he left for Easterleigh Hall, James said, 'I'm sorry. I'm so sorry.'

'For what, bonny lad? He was the one in the wrong, and I'd have gone on my own if you'd said no. He knows that, he's trying to squirm out of it.'

'I'll cycle you back.' He wouldn't listen when she said no.

He cycled her across the yard to the back door. She said, 'He's a stranger.'

James nodded, but said nothing.

He cycled away, knowing that he had to take a stand after all. Democracies had to be supported, and protected. There was time here for the country to come to its senses, but for poor bloody Spain it was running out. Franco and the fascists were gaining victories. But he couldn't go now and let Uncle Aub down. So he'd have to finish at Home Farm first, and then he'd be off. But he had to keep his mouth shut, or Bridie would come too, as she had said, and that couldn't happen. She must be safe.

Chapter Eleven

That same evening Tim arrived at Easton Miners' Club, though he no longer wore his uniform. He switched off his motorcycle engine and waited for a moment, feeling the pain of his knuckles, shocked at himself, remembering the thud as he punched Bridie. How could he not know it was her? How? Because he never expected them to be so stupid, and she'd been wearing those daft jodhpurs, so how was he supposed to know it was a girl?

He took off his leather gloves and stuffed them in the leather jacket Millie had given him at Christmas. He'd talk to Bridie, explain that it was a mistake, that she had to understand it was a battle bigger than them all. It was a fight against mayhem. He stared at the club. Tonight of all nights he didn't want to be here, talking to his da, for what if he'd heard about the fracas? But he needed that forged letter for Heine and his mother. His da would help. He always did.

He dismounted and walked inside, into the noise, the smoke, the smell of beer. He eased past groups of standing pitmen who huddled together, nursing beers and bruises. He pulled his cap further down.

His da was with Mart at a small table. Mart looked up, surprised. He said something to Jack, nodded to Tim, and rose. 'I'll get you in a beer, man.' There were beer rings on the scarred table.

His da nodded. 'You had a good afternoon, I hear, son.'

Tim's heart sank. He said, 'Can't have Fred having it all his own way, and being bloody rude about you.'

Jack nodded, watching his son closely. 'He won't get his own way, trust me. I've got it sorted, and all will be well.'

They both laughed at Grandma Susan's mantra. Did his da guess that it had nothing to do with Fred's insults and everything to do with implementing fascism? For a moment he was shocked, because he'd never actually put his mangled thoughts into order before. Mart reappeared, leaving a pint on the table for Tim, telling them he was going to see a man about a dog. Jack sipped his beer.

Tim looked at his. They sat, a heavy silence between them. Jack pushed his half-full glass away at last, leaned forward and said, 'You seem vexed, son. How can I help?'

Tim took a deep breath. It was what he'd been waiting for. 'It's Mother,' he said. 'She's glad you and Mam are married, but unhappy because she and Heine can't yet, because she needs . . .' He stopped, and then started again. 'Well, you see . . . I don't know why everyone seems to hate her so much, just for running off with a German. He's a good man, Da. Successful, patriotic, and he had the same war as you, even to the point of being a prisoner, so you should understand. You love Gracie, after all.'

Jack's gaze was steady on his son. 'The first thing is that no-one hates her, as far as I know. The past is the past, and we've all moved on. Your mam has a new life, and you're helping her to live it, which is grand. So . . . ?'

Tim felt irritation sweep through him. 'It's so easy for you; you have all this, and a family. She only has me.'

Jack looked puzzled. 'Well, you've just said she has Heine, and surely they'll have friends. I don't understand what you need, son?'

Tim took a gulp of his beer. It was warm. Heine drank his cold. 'That's just it, Da. She sort of has Heine, but there are rules now, she says. Rules on who can marry who, and . . .'

Jack looked stunned. 'But she's not a Jew, is she? I know her Aunt Nellie sent out her birth certificate. Now, if she is, that *is* a problem, and it damn well shouldn't be.'

Tim shouted, 'No, it's not that, just listen.'

People fell silent around them. Jack immediately laughed, and everyone relaxed. He was a clever man, thought Tim, in the way he knew just how to handle, or defuse, every situation. Tim said quietly, 'Of course she's not a Jew. Heine wouldn't touch her with a barge pole if she were. No, it's just . . .' He

143

groped for words. Around him talk and laughter flowed. 'Oh, forget it.'

He picked up his pint and downed almost half, gulp after gulp, while his da watched. 'Put your pint down, son, and listen. Your mam was always, how can I put this? She wanted things she didn't have – and why not, in a way? Her da was killed in the pit. She and her mam lived with Aunt Nellie in Hawton, and there wasn't room, not really. You've just said she has Heine, and will share his success. This will calm her. Most of all she has you.' His da's voice became harsh. 'What more could she want, for God's sake? Wherever she goes there's . . .'

Tim felt a shaft of fury take over: why the hell was everyone, his mother included, making his life so bloody difficult? He slammed his hand down on the table. His grazed knuckles were plain to see. 'There's what? Listen to you, Da. You married her, for heaven's sake, just to fill the gap left by Timmie, just as she said. Well, I'm not Timmie, I'm hers and Roger's. You lot took everything from her—'

'Jack, we need to talk.' It was Jeb, the union rep, rushing up, bringing the cold with him. 'I can't hold Fred back, he's stirring up a hornets' nest.'

Jack waved him away. 'Give me a minute, Jeb. We'll need Mart in on this, and I reckon he's in with the darts team. We've a plan to sort it once and for all.' Jeb nodded, and headed for the other room.

Jack swung round to Tim. 'You listen to me, lad.

You said "you lot". We're not a "lot", we're your family, just as much as Roger or Millie. You filled no gap, son. You're Tim, and your mam chose that name, to honour Timmie, and we were grateful.'

Tim stood up, shoving the table towards his da. For God's sake – parents, letters, bloody kids where they shouldn't be . . . He could feel his fist driving into Bridie's ribs. He'd enjoyed it, but he hadn't known it was Bridie. Or had he? That was the problem: had he?

He stared at his beer juddering inside the glass.

Jack said. 'Never fear, lad. You had our love.'

Had? Tim thought.

He lifted his head, and stared at his da. Around him he heard the murmur of the pitmen. Had? What did he care? This wasn't his world, it never had been; his da had seen to that, just like his mother had said. He was shuffled off to work in Newcastle as an engineer, when he could have sat his certificate and been in management here, as part of the family. But they weren't his family. Oh Christ.

His da still sat, looking up at him, shaking his head, as though to clear it.

Tim leaned over him. 'Had your love, eh? Just like it was for my mother, eh? As long as people do as you say, you'll love 'em. As long as the miners behave, you'll take care of them. If they step out of line, you'll get yourselves together and sort 'em out like you're about to do right now, together with Jeb and Mart?'

Jack stood up then, coming round the table, forcing his son to step back. 'What on earth . . . ?'

'Like my mother, I suppose. You lot fitted her up by forging that letter about the silver theft. It was you, wasn't it, just to spoil her new life? Well, be bloody glad, because you finally have. Without it she can't marry Heine, the SS have rules. You go on and sort the miners, because I'm going out to my mother and step-father tomorrow and I wish you well with the whole damn mess, and when I get back, if I ever come back, don't expect to see me. You and Mam are nothing to me, not any more.'

Around them, the men had fallen silent. This time Jack didn't laugh and make it alright. Instead he said quietly, 'Listen to me, son.'

Tim shook his head. 'I'm not listening any more, just as you're not. But hear this: I'm not your son, I'm not Mam's son either. You're so damned satisfied with yourselves and you'll do exactly what suits you, and to hell with anyone else. I know how my mother felt now and it must have been a great big loneliness.'

He turned away from his da, who had paled, his scars standing vivid and blue, and walked straight into Mart, who blocked his way. 'You're right out of order, you bloody little fascist. Apologise to your da, now.'

Jack moved then, pulling Mart to one side. 'Enough, man, he doesn't mean it. He might think he does, but he doesn't.'

The miners made a path for Tim to walk through. There was utter silence. He reached the door. Jeb was there. He too blocked his way for just a moment. 'You're bang out of order, son. You'll not come in here again until you've said, and meant, that you're right sorry. He's the best man out, your da is.'

Tim shouldered the elderly man aside, wanting to smash his fist in his face. 'Well, looking around, that's not saying a lot, is it? And they're not my parents, didn't you hear? Not any more.'

At his motorbike he dragged his gloves from his pocket. He swung his leg over the saddle and started the engine, looking towards the door. His da didn't come. He waited. Still he didn't come. He drove away and didn't know why he was weeping.

Bridie came in from feeding the chickens while it was still dark the following morning. Her mam had already left to supervise the breakfasts and lunch preparations at Easterleigh Hall. James had arrived at seven to head out with her father to ditch the top field and her father had cocked an eyebrow at James' black eye and swollen nose, but believed James when it was explained away as a slip in the snow. Bridie had exchanged a smile with her cousin and answered his own cocked eyebrow. *I'm fine*, she had mouthed. *Me too*, he had replied. Both were lying.

Her ribs hurt and were perhaps cracked, but she knew there was nothing to be done, except bear it. She put the empty feed bowls in the scullery cupboard, and passed through the kitchen to the hall. She heard her da in his study, and called, 'What did you forget, Da?' There was no answer. She entered. Tim was by the desk, his motorbike goggles on top of his head, his gloves stuffed into the pockets of his leather jacket.

'You, in someone's study, again?' She could barely look at him, feeling the crunch of his fist, seeing the light of enjoyment in his face.

He said, 'I didn't know it was you.'

'What are you doing here?' Her throat was thick, but it had been ever since she had walked away from him yesterday.

He was quite still, and so was she. He was pale, but so was she. He said, 'I need something which might be in the safe. My mother thinks your mother might have it. If you never speak to me again, do this one thing for me, open the safe. It might contain something that will enable her to marry Heine. It's too difficult to explain.'

She still stood motionless. 'Ask Mam.'

'My mother thinks she won't tell me, because she hates her.'

'I don't think my family hates anyone. You are the one with hate in your heart, which is something I don't understand.' She paused. 'I don't know the combination.'

'Please find it for me.' His face moved strangely, as though it was made of wood, and he looked anywhere but at her.

148

She made a show of checking in the two drawers, bending carefully, leafing through the papers, forcing herself to ignore the pain. She looked inside an address book. The combination was there, as her father had once shown her, the four numbers broken up, under A, C, F and G. She said, 'I can't find it. Look if you like.' She placed the address book on the table and stepped away from the drawer.

Tim searched through it. Bridie held her breath. He moved to the drawer and searched. He straightened, still unable to meet her eyes. He headed towards the door, his shoulders slumped, and said, 'Please, not a word, I beg you. I can't explain it, I hardly understand myself, but it will make my mother happy if I find it. It is something I can do for her, after all the years of her being without me.'

He walked on as Bridie stared after him. Why were his eyes so red? What must it be to have a mother in another land, one that had left you to go with a lover, who then asked you to get things, secretly? How would she feel if it happened to her? She snatched up the book. 'Wait, I have the combination here.'

She crossed to the safe and entered the combination, opening the door and standing aside. Now it was she who didn't look, as he hurried across. Instead she looked out of the window, and saw it was snowing again. Would her father give up the ditching? Would James return with him? Would they see Tim? Would he rush off on his motorbike, slide and crash? She felt nothing at the thought. She watched him now as he searched through the papers, opening envelopes.

He stared into the safe when he had finished and his shoulders were even more slumped, if that was possible. 'No, nothing. So perhaps it no longer exists.'

He carefully closed the safe door, spun the combination lock, sighed. She said to his back, 'If you'd asked Da, he would have let you look, you know.'

He nodded, and came to her. At last he lifted his head and met her eyes. She felt nothing. He kissed her cheek. 'I'm so sorry, Bridie. Sorry about it all.'

He left then, and she called after him, 'She's your mother. She'll love you whether you find it or not. Just as Grace would. All will be well.'

He let himself out through the front door. She moved to the window. He kicked the motorbike into action, dragged on his gloves, slipped his goggles down, and rode away without turning. The snow was still falling. She watched until he was out of sight, and then she leaned her head on the cold glass.

In the Easterleigh Hall kitchen Evie turned the bacon. She loved the smell but somehow, for her, the taste was a bit of a let-down and, anyway, she preferred it smoked, while the guests today had requested green. At the kitchen table Mrs Moore was beating the eggs ready for scrambling, the dogs were on the chairs, and Pearl was bashing pots in the scullery.

All was as it should be, cosy and rather less frantic than the rest of the day.

Once the bacon was frying gently she joined Mrs Moore and wiped the mushrooms, slicing off just the base of the stalks. She maintained that stalks were the tastiest part of a mushroom, and wouldn't toss them aside as some did. Now she scooped together the earthy bases and dropped them into the compost bin set to the left of the ranges. As she returned to the table, the side door opened. She looked up, and dropped her knife onto the cutting board. 'Gracie?'

Mrs Moore stopped beating the eggs and wiped her hands on her white starched apron. 'Oh my.'

Evie rushed across to Grace, who stood at the end of the table, bowed and weeping. 'Pet, bonny lass. Who? Jack? Who? What?' She held her friend close, feeling her shuddering sobs.

'It's such a mess, Evie. Tim went to the Miners' Club, he and Jack had words, the like of which they've never had before, and my lad stormed out. Jack didn't say any more than it was just Millie and her stupidity, and the boy's confusion over everything. But he cried, Evie, our Jack cried.'

Evie gripped her tighter and stared over Grace's shoulder at Mrs Moore, and Pearl who had come into the kitchen from the scullery. Gracie pulled away and stared at them all, disbelief in her eyes. 'Tim said, "*I'm not your son.*" Oh Evie, what are we to do?'

Evie tried to picture those words falling from Tim's mouth. Surely not? She said, 'Are you sure?'

Gracie shouted, 'Of course I'm damn sure, Evie ruddy Brampton.'

She stared wildly around, then fixed her attention on the table, wrenching off her leather gloves and thrusting them into her coat pocket. Evie put her hand out to her but Gracie rushed past and started tearing the mushroom stalks free of the cups, throwing them onto the floor. Pearl disappeared again into the scullery while Evie and Mrs Moore watched Gracie frenziedly chopping first one mushroom then another, and another, into little pieces. Her hair had fallen from beneath her felt hat, she thrust it back, then the chopping continued. After a moment, Evie moved across and gripped her hand, trying to make her stop, but Grace wouldn't release the knife. Mrs Moore tiptoed to the range and rescued the bacon, which had begun to burn.

Evie said, her hand still gripping Grace's, 'You can pretend these poor old mushrooms are Millie, Heine, or the devil himself, but it means no-one will have any for breakfast, unless you're prepared to run out to the fields and gather up a load more, bonny lass. Enough now.'

For a moment more Gracie resisted, but then she relaxed and let Evie take the knife, standing while Evie scooped the mushrooms, some chopped, some not, into a bowl, which she passed to Mrs Moore to sauté. Finally Gracie laughed. It was shaky, but it was a laugh. 'Oh Evie, thank heavens for you, and Mrs Moore, and Easterleigh. Of course breakfast is important. Everything must go on. You're quite right.' She sat on Mrs Moore's stool, quite suddenly, as though her legs had gone from under her.

Evie and Mrs Moore exchanged a look. 'Tea,' Mrs Moore insisted. She poured three mugs, and all three women sat around the table.

'How many times have we done this?' Evie pondered.

'Many,' Mrs Moore said. 'And there will be many more problems to solve in just the same way.'

Gracie muttered, 'But can this one ever be solved?'

The women sipped their tea, alone with their thoughts, but Evie knew that they would all arrive at the same conclusion. Only time would tell, and until then they just had to move forward, sticking together, and doing the best they could.

It was then that Jack appeared, pale and sad. He joined them, but said little. It was enough that he had come, knowing where he would find his wife, and needing the comfort of his family.

Chapter Twelve

Tim lay in bed, staring up at the ornate ceiling, feeling totally alone. Well, perhaps he was, and who was to blame for that? He closed his eyes, not wanting to think of his empty-handed arrival yesterday evening, and the fury it had provoked. He turned on his side, burying his face in the down pillow, wanting to shut out the sight of her face, the spittle spray as she had shouted, the slap.

It didn't work. He sat up and checked the alarm clock. He usually woke before it went off but this time he'd forgotten to set the damn thing. It was nearly nine o'clock. His mother would be even more furious with him, if that was possible. There was a knock at the door. Amala called, 'Good morning, Herr Forbes.'

He dragged his fingers through his hair. He didn't even know his name, not really. Was he Smith, like Roger? Or Thomas, like his mother's family?

'Good morning, Frau Dreher.'

'Amala is good,' she said. He had not known until now that the maid knew any English. He washed, shaved and dressed, noticing that he had the start of a bruise and a cut on his cheekbone from his mother's ring. He did not want to leave his bedroom.

154

Had his mother calmed down? Were the disappointment and anger of yesterday finished? Of course she was right, he deserved it because he had failed her, but as he said, there didn't seem to be any letter. He had obeyed her instructions, but to no avail.

He hurried to the dining room to get it over with, but there was only a plate with ham and cheese, some toast and coffee. And a letter propped on the coffee pot.

Dearest Tim

I have to attend a block meeting. Such a bore, but we need to get together to deal with one of the women whose behaviour is incorrect. I will be shopping today for Heine's birthday party tomorrow evening. It's a surprise, and because he's away until then, no need for him to know anything at all. He phoned late last night from Hamburg. I told him about the letter and he will give it some thought. Please amuse yourself and we will meet for dinner and I will tell you what Heine needs you to do. Forgive my bad behaviour, I was just so disappointed that the wedding cannot take place as I had hoped.

Your loving mother

He felt utter relief, because he'd thought he'd never be forgiven. He was suddenly hungry, which wasn't surprising, since he'd been sent to his room without any dinner, like a child.

*

It was hinting at spring in Berlin, to judge by the blue of the sky, and the tiny buds on the linden trees. As he walked he looked up but saw no birds, just banners and flags. They lifted his spirits and he was able to forget everything for a moment. He strode out into this vibrant city, so different from those at home, where everyone was struggling to survive. He realised it was the first time he had walked alone in Berlin, because his mother usually swept him off in a taxi to haunts she knew, telling him it was better to do it this way, and warning him that there were still some places it was best not to explore.

He sped past the slower walkers, saw a tram, and jumped on, not knowing where it was going, and not caring. The day was young, and his mother was his 'loving mother' again. He paid, and after ten minutes jumped off. Again he walked past shops, elegant apartments, a water fountain. He was about to cross the road, when his sleeve was gripped. He swung round. It was an old man, his coat shabby. He stank of poverty. 'English?' he rasped.

For a moment Tim hesitated. 'What?' he replied, pulling free.

His arm was gripped again. 'Help me. I am Jew. Please, beg take daughter. Take to England.'

'For God's sake.' Tim wrenched free but the man followed, limping. Again Tim's sleeve was grasped. The old man came close; the smell was appalling, he needed a shave. 'Please, take my daughter. I pay, diamonds. Take all. Nothing more I have. Home, work, gone. I get no visas. Please. She Jew, but she do anything. Take her, I beg.'

Tim tore free again, running across the road, stepping over the tramlines. 'What the hell are you people like?' he shouted over his shoulder. Reaching the pavement on the other side, he brushed his sleeve, feeling dirty. Selling his daughter, for heaven's sake. No wonder Germany had needed to be sorted out. Above, the sky was clouding over. He was shaking; how bloody stupid. 'Pull yourself together,' he said aloud.

He made himself continue walking and he no longer had to weave through people, as he was almost the only one on the street. At last the trembling stopped, and he could no longer smell the man, or see his desperation.

He wondered if he should buy Heine a birthday present. He answered himself – of course he should. He'd fouled up. He needed to make good or Heine would be in a mood. He stopped to look in the window of an antiques shop, interested in an inkwell, but he baulked at the price. He walked on, then turned right down a cobbled side street where there were far fewer shops, and people, thinking that it would probably be cheaper. He peered into a jeweller's, but all the goods looked second-hand, and there was nothing suitable.

He kept walking, and in a deserted street to the right he saw chairs propped up outside a building. He turned into the lane, which looked like the back street in any pit village, but the houses were tall tenements, and everywhere was the stench of poverty. The chairs were stacked against railings. Stairs wound down to a basement junk shop. He peered down, the door was open, and furniture was stacked in the entrance. There was nothing to interest a man like Heine who had everything.

He passed on. A child ran out of a tenement court-yard, in boots without laces. He ran to the right, then ducked into a doorway. Tim hurried now, anxious to find the main road. He came to the end and met a narrow cobbled alley, running north to south. He hesitated, and then turned north, hearing traffic, thank God, because this wasn't what he'd expected of Berlin. Almost immediately there was a shop window on his left. Again it was almost a junk shop, although he did notice a decent lamp in the window, but no, he had to find something personal. But what? He was feeling more confident now, and giving the lamp a final look, he walked on. Suddenly he heard something – what? A crash, shouts, behind him. He stopped and turned.

Two men ran out of the lane he'd just left, heading towards him, their caps pulled down; one perhaps in his thirties, the other just a boy it seemed. The older one turned and looked over his shoulder at two policemen who were gaining fast. Tim moved to stand flat against the wall, but too late, the man crashed into him, knocking him backwards, and then roaring on. Tim rebounded off the wall, clattering into the police, bringing them down like skittles, so that they sprawled at his feet, cursing. He tried to keep his balance, but more police came roaring past, and one clipped his shoulder, spinning him. He put out his arm, reaching for support, crashing back into the wall. He was winded, and couldn't think. Whistles blew, and somewhere a van revved.

A policeman ran up, his truncheon out, and caught him a blow on the side of his head. It knocked him down. He clambered to his knees, 'What are you doing?' he yelled. But the blows continued to fall. He covered his head with his arms. All the while the policeman yelled at him in German. A kick caught him on the thigh and he collapsed and curled up on the cobbles, but the men he had brought down were rising, and they joined in. He tasted the grit of the cobbled road.

All around were shouts, and the frantic sound of whistles, but at last the beating stopped; he hurt all over. He lifted his head; two policemen stood over him. He started to rise. One shouted at him, the other powered a kick into his ribs, panting. He vomited. He knew the men wouldn't stop, because the fire of excitement was in them, as it had been in him, for a split second, when he punched Bridie. At that moment he knew he *could* have stopped that one blow, but he didn't want to.

One had hold of his hair, and lifted his head. He spat out grit and blood, and saliva. 'English,' he said, but it was a croaking whisper.

A man in plain clothes was there now, and he said something in German, and there was no excitement in his eyes, just the same sort of coldness that was so often in Heine's. He was hauled to his feet, and pushed and shoved the length of the street to a green van, which blocked the far end. This was what had been revving. The doors were opened and he was flung inside, onto the legs of one of the two men in caps. The other was groaning alongside. The doors slammed. The engine revved, the van lurched and juddered over cobbles; they were thrown from side to side. He dragged himself off the prone figure and gagged, his body a mass of pain, his mind churning in a morass of panic and shock. 'What the hell did you do?' he murmured finally.

The two men were coughing and groaning. Their caps were bloodied and on the floor. Tim realised his own must still be in the alley. The younger man who had knocked into Tim lay prone, but the older one crawled over to their caps, snatched them up, and put them into the pocket of his torn and frayed jacket pocket. The van must have taken a corner fast because all three of them were thrown against the side, then back again. The older one heaved himself into a sitting position, and pulled out a broken tooth.

Tim's head was an agonising mass of pain; his face was raw and bleeding. The man tossed the tooth away and wiped his face with his handkerchief. In English he said, 'Why should we have done anything? It's enough that we exist. Freemasons they do not like. Mischlings they do not like. Jews, Reds . . . As I say, my friend, it is not something we have done, it is who we are.'

Tim dragged himself across to sit next to him. The man stuffed his handkerchief back in his pocket with trembling hands. 'Welcome to our brave new world, my friend.'

Tim asked, 'Mischling?'

The van took another bend. 'Half Jew, half Aryan. I had a good job in Hastings. I am a tailor. Not to mention a Freemason and a Mischling. My mother was ill and still in Berlin. I came last year to take her away from this.' He waved his hand.

His friend was stirring, and slowly raised himself to all fours. Tim saw that he was only a boy, perhaps James' age. The lad muttered something, then crawled across to sit next to his friend and said something else, in German. The older man said, 'In English, for our foreign guest. You see, my friend, Otto worked in London, in a restaurant. He came back some while ago, and though he has the misfortune to be a Freemason, he is not a Jew, so he will perhaps be alright.'

'I never saw them, Avraham. They must have been waiting for us. Did they get us all?' the young man said, groaning.

'You are hurt, Otto?'

'No, not really. I have a belly ache. They kick well, my friend.'

Avraham stroked Otto's hair. 'It will ease. I am

sorry, my English friend, to have knocked you. Tell them that I crashed into you. It won't help, but then again, it just might.'

Tim swallowed. He felt sick, and hurt so much. 'Your mother?' he said.

Avraham shrugged. 'I went to her apartment, but she was gone from it, to be replaced by Aryans. Her job was gone too, because an Aryan tailor took the Jewish business where she worked. It happens to some, but not to everyone yet. I found the tailor. He had just a diamond or two he had hidden but they had taken all else. He also had my mother, in his dark, tiny hole of an apartment. She was sad and dying. I went back to our home, to get the only thing I could save, for it was lodged, as is our way, outside the apartment.'

He drew out a small rectangular case. 'I saved our mezuzah case from the door frame. Within it is the parchment she inscribed with Hebrew verses from the Torah, as is also our way. It is what most of us make return for, in secret, to remove. Everything we have, otherwise, is for the new "owners". She died peacefully with it in her hand. I keep it with me. They will take it, and destroy it, but until they do, I will keep it.'

Tim was looking at the rectangular piece in Avraham's hand. He leaned back, his thoughts fragmented, but even so, he recognised the shape. He felt icy cold, and sleepy. Avraham nudged him. 'Don't sleep. Keep alert, it will help you recover.'

They moved with the van, the three of them together, and almost immediately it seemed they stopped, which was when Tim realised he had slept, and felt worse, much worse.

'*Raus, raus*,' a policeman shouted, leaping into the van and kicking them out.

Tim stood on the cobbles of a dark, forbidding square, surrounded by high tenements, or perhaps they were offices? He saw other policemen slamming shut huge gates. No, it must be a prison, because there were bars at some of the windows. Tim said, shivering, 'You should drop the mezuzah case or they will know you are a Jew.'

Avraham shook his head as they were pushed towards a single door. 'My friend, one gets so tired of hiding who one is, and look at me. They will know. We are in their hands now, and one of their delightful camps awaits us, but perhaps not for you. You must call a friend.'

'I'll ask for a solicitor.'

Otto and Avraham burst out laughing. The guards jabbed at them with their rifles, but as all three of them were racked with pain, what was a bit more?

They were herded towards a desk behind which a policeman sat. Tim insisted on a solicitor. Avraham repeated it in German. The policeman stared, took their names, then nodded to the guards. Manacles were slapped on their wrists. All three of them were shoved along the passage, then down slimy steps into a stinking basement. Somewhere someone screamed.

They were shoved into a cell, where manacles were also attached to their ankles. A chain linked their wrists to their ankles. The guard slammed the door shut. The men looked at one another. 'Best we sit,' Avraham said. There was only the cold floor. They all somehow slid down the wall to the stone floor. God, it was cold. Tim rested his head back. The walls seeped damp. He should ask them to contact Heine Weber. He would tell them he was an SS Untersturmführer.

But he couldn't, because now he knew the real Germany, and he was scared of discovering his real step-father, and his real mother, for he knew that a mezuzah case had been removed from their doorway too. He also remembered how clever Tim had sanded the wood until there was virtually no sign it had ever been there, and how Heine said he would find the owners and castigate them for damaging the property. Tim hadn't known what he meant. Now he did. Perhaps he always had, but had turned away from it. If Heine had indeed found and punished them, then that was his fault.

The manacles rubbed but he barely noticed it amidst all the other throbbing aches and pains, and the terror that had dried his mouth. His teeth chattered, and he thought he'd never stop shaking. All that was in his head were his da's words, from long ago, before he had found his mother, but after the

Nazis had started their march on democracy. 'A nation that dismantles its legal system is without restraint, and must be fought.'

Otto died in the night, quietly, without fuss. Avraham closed his friend's eyes as Tim looked on in shock and insisted, 'We must tell the guards.'

Avraham shook his head. 'My Christian half, and your whole Christian being, must say prayers for his soul, for they will not.'

They clanked themselves upright and said the Lord's Prayer and the twenty-third psalm. As they chanted it, Avraham's voice broke, and Tim found that tears were rolling down his own face. It was the shock, the fear and a sort of grief, but also the hell of it, and the outrage, because Otto was only a lad. When they were finished they called the guard, who flicked back the shutter over the spyhole.

'Later, it is two in the morning,' Avraham translated. 'The cart will come, later.' They sat until dawn with Otto.

Dawn passed. Hours passed. They talked a little, of their lives, their mistakes, their hopes, but these were scarce, so they preferred to remain in the past. It was this that Tim grieved for: the safety of the past, the goodness, and the folly of his erroneous beliefs and deeds.

Thirst was driving them mad. They grew quiet. The minutes and hours passed, and they heard men and the occasional woman being dragged along the passage, their chains rattling, their groans and pleading unceasing. They pressed their hands over their ears, but that did nothing to stop the rising panic and dread. When would it be their turn?

As the day drew to a close they were beaten up two flights of stairs, able only to take tiny steps in their chains. Avraham whispered, 'Tell them of Heine, your mother's friend. He will arrange for your release.'

Tim shook his head. He hadn't suffered enough for all that he had believed and done.

Avraham tensed as they hobbled along a corridor towards some double doors. 'I say goodbye, my friend. May your God go with you.' His eyes were fixed on the doors.

Tim looked from them, to Avraham. 'May yours go with you, though we both share the same one. If I get out of this, can I contact anyone for you?'

'Sadly, they are dispersed. I know not where. But my name is Avraham Walters. It is my father, now dead, who was Aryan. Should you by chance ever meet someone looking for a family member of that name, please tell them of me so that I may exist, if only in their memory.'

They were at the double doors now. The guards went ahead. Avraham leaned towards Tim, saying urgently, 'In thinking of my previous words, please, in my pocket is the mezuzah case. Quick, dig in your hands and take it and keep it safe, and put it in your house when you return, so something of my mother, father and I survive. That will keep me stronger and safer than it being stamped beneath their boots. Beware, it could endanger you. Say no, if that is your wish.'

Tim paused a fraction, then he took it.

Avraham said, as the guards clumped back, 'You are brave, you are good. Do not suffer for the past, for that is what I think you do, but change the future.'

Avraham was dragged ahead of Tim, through the doors. Tim called, 'Easterleigh Hall, if you survive.'

He was knocked sideways by the guard. He called again, 'You will exist in *my* memory, Avraham Walters.' The policeman hit him once more then shoved him down into a chair against the wall, while Avraham was pulled and pushed forward through another set of doors, which swung shut behind him.

Across from Tim sat a woman behind a desk, smoking a cigarette and writing. There were five such desks, each with a woman smoking, and writing. Across from them sat four men and one woman, shackled as he was. One of the men down at the end was slumped forward. The rest were talking in low voices as the women fired questions. A policeman stood behind each of those being inter-rogated, a truncheon in his hand.

The woman him stubbed out her cigarette and handed the man the paper she had been writing on, and a pen. She pointed at a particular spot on the paper. The man shook his head and proceeded to stoically read what she had written. She reached across and slapped him hard across the mouth. The sound resonated around the room. No-one even looked. The woman shouted, but the man continued to read. She hit him again. The man read to the bottom of the paper, and only then did he sign.

Tim knew he would remember this bravery for the rest of his life.

At that point the double doors to his left opened. The guard standing behind one of those being interrogated turned and pointed at Tim. He turned, his head heavy and sore, his mouth too, where he had cut the inside with his teeth at some stage of the beating. It was Heine, in his SS uniform. The shackles were unlocked. He stood, swayed. Heine did not reach out to help him. Tim clenched his fists, the nails biting into his palms. Heine said nothing but marched down the corridor, his voice cold and quiet, as Tim limped, trying to keep up. 'Your mother made me phone round when you did not return home, and I could not believe my ears. You have put me under an obligation – a common thug, they said, who stopped the police to allow criminals to evade capture.'

Tim said, 'That's a lie.'

Heine stopped. Tim collided with him. Heine stared ahead. 'I do not lie. The police do not lie. You will not speak again unless spoken to. You will help your mother prepare for my surprise party, and you will not tell her I know of her plan. You will then return to Britain to harvest the letter forged in your mother's name. The silver was someone else's theft.'

He marched on. Tim put his hand in his pocket and gripped the mezuzah case.

When he arrived at the apartment building, Heine stopped the car and opened the door. 'You wash, you shower, you help. You remain in your bedroom and do not attend the party, and I do not wish to see your face in the morning, even. You will do this to thank me for my actions. You will also, as I have ordered, find that letter.' Suddenly he smiled. 'Then we will all be friends.'

Tim limped into the foyer, up in the lift to the second floor. He approached the door and ran his hand over the sanded wood. His relief when he felt the very slight indent made his legs almost fail him. The spirit of the former owners remained. His mother answered his ring. She didn't hug him, but her moue of distaste said it all.

'I apologise, Mother. It was an accident. The police were chasing others, and I knocked into them, and down they went like skittles.'

'Stupid boy, you don't do that here, in Germany.' Her face was pale and frightened. 'Heine wants you to find . . .'

He lifted his hand. 'I know, I've had my orders.'

He walked away to his bedroom to wash. She shouted, 'Don't be so damned cheeky.'

He entered his bedroom and shut the door.

Later, he helped Amala set up the buffet table with mats, silver serving spoons, and forks. He carted in piles of porcelain plates, from the storage unit in the kitchen. For an hour he did her bidding, and with each item he wondered where the owners were now. He covered a side table in a white damask cloth. At last Amala gestured to the glasses and bottles in the vitrine. This was what he had been waiting for. He nodded. She disappeared to the kitchen.

He crouched down and examined the lock on the cupboard, which he had not been allowed to open. He removed from his pocket the slim penknife he had taken from his toilet bag. His da had shown him once how to pick a lock, when he was a child, and had lost the key to his metal money-box.

He listened, hardly breathing, turning the blade carefully. Click. He turned the handle and opened the door. Inside were many small silver items. He didn't need to check, but nonetheless he did. The initial stamped onto the bottom of some was exactly what he had expected. 'B' for Brampton. He didn't recognise the crest on the sugar bowls, or the exquisite brush and comb set, but knew it was some of Lady Brampton's family silver.

He thought he heard a noise, lifted his head, and listened. No, nothing. Carefully he shut the door and hauled himself upright, closing the penknife. So. So.

He reached for the side table. He was clammy with sweat. His body ached. His mam would have taken him straight to Dr Nicholls to be checked out; his da would have sat him down and talked him through it. Bridie and James would have supported and cheered him. Uncle Aub and Aunt Evie would have turned up to try and help, with Aunt Ver and Uncle Richard.

But he had chosen this woman who was his mother. In no way did he recognise her as such, now. He had chosen this world, which was black and evil, and he, in his turn, had become so too. He didn't know what he must do, except be careful, be clever, and get back home. No, he didn't deserve to say that any more, but he must return to England with no-one here knowing the truth of his feelings, or his discovery. It wasn't fear now, but terror, as it had been in the cell.

Chapter Thirteen

Easterleigh Hall, Late March 1937

Bridie, Ver and Evie had finished breakfasts and were drinking tea around the kitchen table, while Mrs Moore relaxed in one of the armchairs, her mug on the small side table. Currant and Raisin nestled down in the other. Edward VIII's abdication had been mulled over yet again, which led into a long discussion about how much one should give up for love. Each time they ended up as before, disagreeing. Bridie felt you should give up everything. The older women felt that duty was involved. As always, Mrs Moore, sick of the subject, introduced a diversionary thread.

'By, your da's done a good thing this week, bonny lass,' she called across to Bridie, who was reading the newspaper, studying the feature about the Italian fascist forces making advances in Spain. 'And your Uncle Jack's been leading the charge on it too, and that rascal Mart.' She looked immensely satisfied. The strike in Easton and Hawton was cancelled, and Fred and his gang of red mufflers seen off.

Bridie said, 'Aye, but they left it 'til the last minute, Mrs Moore.'

Her mother shook her head, relieved. 'It's taken time to set up the co-op project, just as it did here. Now the men have a stake in the mines, a profit share. Which makes them owners too. A good thing has happened this week, pet.'

Pearl and Maudie joined them at the table, and as Maudie reached for the teapot she stopped, her hand in mid-air. 'Bridie, before I forget, Clive was looking for you a while ago. He caught me as I nipped across for more washing soda.' She poured her tea, and a mug for Pearl. 'He was on his way back to the horses' pasture.'

Bridie asked her mam, 'We haven't anyone booked in for riding, have we?'

'Don't ask me, lass. My head's full of Mrs Simpson and the Duke of Windsor. I mean, how does she stay so thin?'

Bridie went to the diary on the side cupboard and checked, and as she'd thought, the day was clear. 'I'd better go and see what he needs.'

She left her tea, and still with her apron on, grabbed her scarf from the hook in the hall, and headed towards the back door. 'Wait,' her mam called after her. 'Finish your tea first.'

Bridie called back as she went towards the steps, 'No, I'll have it cold.'

She heard her mam say, 'She'll think it's something to do with Prancer. She and her da are soft as butter over that lovely old boy.'

Bridie shouted back, 'He's not old.' She heard

them laugh. She set off across the garage yard, towards the path. Clive would be with Prancer, Fanny and Terry. Though, of course, Marigold and Primrose had been turned out into the far pasture too, now that the weather was kinder. She ran down the side of the walled garden, head down into the wind. It was good to be out in the fresh air. She patted her pocket, knowing the horses would look for carrots. She had rushed out too quickly.

She pulled her scarf tighter.

Though it was still cold, the buds on the lilac, which grew close to the wall, were struggling through. She stopped running, the breath heaving in her chest, and strode along past the tool store on the corner, and the glass houses where the young plants and vegetables were being brought on.

As she walked she thought of the article she'd just read, and couldn't understand the brass nerve of these fascists. How dare the Italians go into someone else's country? But then again, Franco, who was leading the Spanish fascists against the elected government, probably sent them an embossed invitation to join him. Well, as long as James didn't feel he had an invitation to go across and take the beggars on.

She damped down her frustration, not helped by remembering how Tim had upset Auntie Gracie and Uncle Jack earlier in the month, and then shot off to Germany for a few days. It was all round Easton that he had been way over the mark with Uncle Jack in the Club, and what's more, he'd not been to apologise, or see any of the family, since he'd been home. Because he *was* home; Uncle Jack had checked he was back at work.

Young Stan stumped across her path with a hoe over his shoulder. 'Morning, Bridie.'

She grinned. Young Stan was always the same, a bit like the cedar tree.

'Morning to you, Young Stan.'

He passed through the gateway into the walled garden.

Young Stan would never hurt anyone as Tim had done . . . She felt the familiar thickening of her throat, the awful sense of loss. Her ribs were healing, but when she closed her eyes, she could still feel the blow, and see his enjoyment.

She cut through the bottom walled garden, between the asparagus beds, heaped higher each year, it seemed, and emerged into the deciduous arboretum that her da had started on his return from the war. 'We need one on the east side of Easterleigh Hall, as well as the west,' he'd said. 'I like trees, more so since the guns took so many. If you would be so kind, Young Stan.'

She was through the arboretum now, and heading up the lane to the field. As she approached she saw James leaning on the gate, straining forward. What on earth was he doing here? She ran, her mouth dry, but stumbled on a rut. Primrose? Terry? Fanny, Marigold. Not Prancer. Absolutely not Prancer. She straightened, her ankle hurting, but she tried to hurry on, calling, 'James?'

He turned, but switched to the field, then back to her. He looked . . . odd. 'For God's sake, where have you been, Bridie?' His voice was too high. 'Clive thought something wasn't quite right, and after mucking out the stalls, he left a message for you, then headed back to the field. Your dad and I were working in the lower field, and he hollered across, telling your da he was worried. I took the new tractor back to Home Farm and phoned the vet while your dad came here. Bertram came straight out. It's Prancer, he's down. He just sank, Bridie. I'd have come for you, but Clive had already sent you a message, though he wasn't too worried then.' His voice was getting higher and higher, and he was running to meet her. 'They've tried to get him up.'

She tore past him. Prancer down? No, he must get up. He'd die if he went down. He must, must, must get up. James was running alongside. As they clambered over the gate Marigold and Primrose whickered, but Terry and Fanny stood quite still, near the hedge on the right-hand side of the gate.

Bridie said, 'Just stay there, you two. We'll see how your dad is, Primrose. Look after her, Marigold.'

She ran towards her da, whose back was towards her. He was on his knees beside his beloved Prancer. Bertram squatted with Clive the other side. She threw herself down next to her da. 'Get him up, Da. We've got to get him up. Don't just kneel there, do something.' She was shrieking. She could hear herself on the wind.

Her da put his fingers to his lips. 'Hush, Bridie. Quiet now, let him hear you happy and calm, let him go out on that.' She stared at her lovely old boy, her dear friend, her love, who was so huge, so kind, so strong, just lying so still. She pressed her lips together and leaned forward, laying her face against his cheek. He was warm. He was lying on the stone-cold ground, but he was warm. 'Come on, my lovely lad. Come on, you can't. We've so much more to do. We've got David in his wheelchair, and what about Tom?'

Prancer lifted his head slightly, and then sank again. Bertram said, 'That's right, Bridie, he's been waiting for his dear little girl to come. You have to let him go. His work is done.'

Her da was stroking his friend, crooning to him. Bridie wept, hearing the sounds she was making. Her nose was running, tears dripped onto Prancer. 'Bridie,' her da ordered. 'He doesn't need that noise to be the last thing he hears from you.' She looked up. His voice was rock steady and firm, though running down his face was a steady stream of tears.

His hand was steadily stroking. She stopped, eased herself up, and stroked Prancer's soft muzzle. His lips fluttered against her hands. She said, 'I should have brought you a carrot, my love. I will if you stay with us, really I will, every day, or sugar. I will do anything if you stay with us.'

James had been to Bertram's van and was putting a blanket over Prancer. 'There,' she said, 'Good old James, he's keeping you warm.'

Prancer lifted his head an inch. Her da soothed, 'Easy, bonny lad. Easy with you.' Her da's hair flopped over his eye as it always did, his face pale, the tears dripping onto Prancer.

She saw Prancer's eyes glazing; a long breath eased into her hand.

James put his arm around her. 'It's alright, Bridie. Everything will be alright.'

She stared at the horse she loved, but knew that her love did not compare to that of her da. She stroked Prancer one last time. 'My dear old friend, my love,' she whispered. 'What shall we all do without you?'

James helped her to her feet, and they left her da kneeling beside his horse and moved over to the gate with Bertram and Clive. Marigold, Primrose, Fanny and Terry came to stand with them. 'It was his heart, the dear old soldier. A long war that he didn't deserve, and a long peace that he truly did,' Bertram said. 'I'll arrange the disposal.'

James shook his head. 'No, you won't. Absolutely you won't.' Now his voice was breaking, and his eyes were full. 'He stays here, at Easterleigh. I'll bury him, near the old oak up at the end of the pasture. He loved it there, but first we should get Aunt Evie and my mother. They need to take Uncle Aub somewhere else while I do it. I'll go, you stay here, Bridie.'

Clive was pale and distraught, soothing Fanny, while Marigold nuzzled his neck. 'Horses know,' he said. 'They need to grieve. I'll take them to him, just so they can say goodbye, otherwise they'll worry, thinking he's just abandoned them.'

He said to Bridie, 'I didn't know, Bridie. I just thought he wasn't quite right, or I'd have got you here sooner.' He walked to Prancer, and the horses followed. After a while, as the pigeons flew, and the clouds scudded, he led them out of the pasture, down the lane, to the stables.

Bridie waited, clinging to the top bar of the gate, feeling the ancient wood, deeply grained, watching her da and wondering what he was thinking. Perhaps it was about all those years, before the war, with Prancer? Perhaps it was about the war, when Prancer was taken by the army, or maybe about Aunt Ver finding Prancer again, and bringing him home? Perhaps it was the battle they had fought together to aid their mutual recovery?

She didn't feel the cold wind, but just watched over her father until she heard the others running up the lane. Her mam and Aunt Ver clambered over the gate. Why? When they could just have opened it. The two women flew to her da. They did nothing then; merely waited either side. James arrived with Uncle Richard. 'He'll want to bury Prancer himself, stubborn old beggar,' Uncle Richard said.

'He can't,' Bridie objected. 'The ground's too hard,

it's too much for a man with one leg. James said he would.'

'I phoned Jack. He'll bring Mart, and Young Stan's gone to find Charlie, who's out feeding the grouse. The marras will do it together. They have no need of any of the rest of us, but thank you, James, for offering. Stan'll bring along the spades and forks. Don't you worry, they'll see he's alright.'

Young Stan was stumping along the lane now, his wheelbarrow full of implements.

In half an hour Uncle Jack and Uncle Mart joined Charlie, who had arrived at the run. The three of them entered the field, while Aunt Gracie and Aunt Gertrude, Charlie's wife, joined Evie and Ver. James brought the tractor in after them, with tackle to move Prancer to the end of the field, when the time was right.

Bridie walked down the lane. If she didn't see it, it wouldn't hurt so much. She reached the road where Uncle Jack had left his Austin and waited. She would return in twenty minutes. She leaned against the signpost. Fordington and Easton to the left, Easterleigh Hall to the right. Her Uncle Richard had arranged for it to be erected to help to guide their guests. Two cars passed, one driven by a guest, who stopped and wound down the window. 'Bridie, are you quite well?'

She smiled. 'Perfectly, thank you, Sir Peter. Just waiting for someone.'

Well, she was, because Prancer was a person,

really. Sir Peter drove on, hooting his farewell. She watched, but she was drawn back by the sound of a motorbike. She stared as it roared along the road, then changed down through its gears and pulled in, the engine idling as the rider put one foot down to steady the bike. Tim pulled up his goggles. 'Bridie, I . . .' he started to say, then stopped, looking down.

She couldn't believe he was here, out of the blue, after he had done so much damage. She felt the blow, remembered the enjoyment he had felt, the tears her mother told her Gracie had shed in the kitchen, the paleness of her Uncle Jack when he arrived, the look of defeat and hurt she had seen on their faces too often since then.

Now he was here, on a day like this, when none of them needed any more conflict, any more grief. She went to him, so close, she could hear his breathing. 'Go away. You're like a bad penny, turning up, causing trouble. Well, not today, you don't. Leave us in peace, and never hurt my family again. It is *my* family, Tim, not yours, as you made quite clear to your da. How could you? You've broken their hearts.'

His mouth set, his lips clamped together. He started to speak, but she shook her head. 'Don't you dare come near us, especially not at a time like this. Prancer is dead, and I won't have your poison on top of it all. My father's heart is broken, his marras are needed, not you.'

She turned on her heel and ran up the lane.

James was waiting for her at the gate. 'Where have you been?'

'Just walking, and waiting.' They watched the activity at the end of the field.

James said, 'It will soon be over.'

'I can't believe it. It's all so strange. Everything is changing. I know I keep thinking this, but look at the world, look at today.'

James was staring up at the pigeons flying from the woods, just as she did, and as Tim once would have done. 'Something must have spooked them,' he said.

Over to the left, where wheat had been sown, green shoots were appearing. At the top of the field the marras were filling in the hole while the women looked on. James said, 'While we're talking of things changing, I'm definitely going to Spain, Bridie. Not yet. I can't let your dad down now this has happened. I'll wait until the end of summer, sometime in August. But I have to go. It won't just be the Italians helping Franco to knock at the Republicans' door, but Tim's friends will be there too. I need to do something to stop them. I decided a while ago.'

Two days later, Bridie finished a training session with Terry as David pushed his wheelchair over from the Neave Wing, with Daniel Forsyth tapping his white stick beside him. She led the roan back to the stables, her entourage in tow, David laughing and saying, 'It's the blind leading the legless, not the blind leading the blind.'

Daniel muttered, 'I'll let your tyres down if you go on.'

She called over her shoulder as she handed Terry to Clive. 'How *are* the pneumatic tyres?'

'Fine,' David said. 'As long as I don't go over anything sharp, which is something I wouldn't put past young fellow m'lad to organise, if he could only see where to put the tacks.'

She smiled, wiping her hands down her jodhpurs. Young Stan came into the yard. 'How did he do, Bridie?' he asked.

From the stables came Terry's whicker. Dave laughed. 'There you go, Bridie. Our Terry's heard his master's voice.'

Bridie laughed, but not inside. Yes, Terry did prefer Young Stan, just as Prancer had preferred her. She wasn't needed anywhere, not really, and soon James would be gone. She nodded to the two young men. 'So, are you staying here, Dave, to cheer on those who need help?'

Dave looked up at her. 'Of course I am. We're down to two trained horses, and we need a few young crocks to cheer on the beginners from the Wing.'

She walked away, striding out to the pasture, straight to the top end where the turfs were yellowing. Would they grow and green up? Young Stan said so. She stared down at them.

'What shall I do, Prancer?' She laughed slightly. 'Well, if you told me, it would be the shock of the century. So, it's up to me, bonny lad, I suppose. I want to go with James, but how? He would send me back, I know it.' She hunkered down, patting the ground. 'See you tomorrow, old lad.'

She headed towards the Hall, but at the last minute diverted to the cedar tree, where everything always seemed better. She stood beneath it, staring up, seeing glimpses of the sky through its branches, feeling her tension leaching from her. What was it about trees that did this for people? Her da had planted so many on his return that the new arboretum was larger than the one started a century ago on the west side.

Well, perhaps to say he had planted them was a step too far, her mam had said. Old Stan had got his weight behind the spade, but her da had helped manoeuvre the young trees into the holes, and sort out the supports.

Old Stan, eh? Now it was Young Stan. Forget Middle Stan, because he was dead, killed in the war, but there were still battles to fight. Would bullies never learn? Would others always have to stop them? Would none of it ever end? It wasn't twenty years since the end of the last war, for pity's sake.

There was a rushing in the branches above her, and a pigeon flew out to flap across the lawn towards the ha-ha. 'If Uncle Charlie sees you, it'll be pigeon pie again, my lad. There are too many of you by half, and you'll be after the grain and the shoots. We'll be sick of the taste of you,' she murmured.

She sat down, her back against the trunk, facing the Hall. Beneath her the roots would be reaching down and across. Was that the secret of the magic of trees? Did humans in some way think of those strong roots holding the tree steady in the face of whatever the elements threw? Unless it was blown up, as the earlier cedar was, by whom the children had never been told, but she thought she knew.

She felt the tension in her shoulders again. Surely it was Millie, and that POW, Heine, before they scarpered. Well, now the two of them had even destroyed the threesome she, James and Tim had always been. On top of that, James was off to fight, while she, Bridie Brampton, was just talking a good talk, and fiddling about stopping a sponge mix from curdling.

She heard her mam calling from the archway into the stable yard, 'Bridie, we need you.'

Some guests were walking their poodles along the drive: crunch, crunch, yap, yap. What on earth would Currant and Raisin think of these primped and precious little creatures with their pom-pom tails? Did they bark in French? Was Paris absolutely stuffed full of them? The idea of the dachshunds being faced with a flurry of them as they eyed up the legs of the Eiffel Tower, seeing if they were ripe for marking, made her laugh as she rose, brushed off her skirts and headed for the kitchen.

*

A week later, while Bridie prepared a large bowl of sponge mixture after luncheon for some fancies, she heard Mrs Moore tutting. The old lady sat in the armchair, knitting, with Currant on her lap.

Bridie called, 'Dropped a stitch?'

'More than one, pet. Sometimes my hands are canny and do what I want; sometimes they're a right pain.'

'Is it another scarf?'

'What else? I like to use bits and bobs of left-over wool, which the WI at Easton collect for me. I can't abide waste.' She laid down her needles, and Currant sniffed the knitting and then thought better of it, as Mrs Moore fixed her with a glare. 'Which brings me to you, lass.'

'What does?' Bridie had creamed the butter and sugar together and was now beating the eggs in a separate bowl.

Mrs Moore was untangling some wool. 'Waste. Now, my Bridie. There's change in the air, I can sense it. You're restless, James is like a cat on a hot tin roof while he waits for university, and Tim . . . Well, he's chasing around trying to find himself. You are making yet another sponge cake, and it will be delicious. But it is something you have done many, many times before. Sixteen and a half is almost old age, so what's to be done?'

Bridie folded some whisked egg into the cake mixture. It began to curdle, so she sieved, and then more egg, and then more . . . She could do it blindfold; and longed to have the time to try other things. She sieved, stirred, added eggs, sieved, stirred and sighed. She looked at Mrs Moore, and then around the kitchen, her beloved kitchen. It had been the same last year, the year before, the decade before. Would it be the same always? Good English cooking, fancies for tea?

She sieved the remains of the flour and slumped onto the stool. Raisin yelped in his sleep.

She stared at Mrs Moore, remembering the French poodles who had yelped for two hours one night in their owners' bedroom, and why not? A strange room, and a strange country. Their owners were from Paris, and had chatted to her about haute cuisine when they came to have a look at the stables. Mrs Moore had been there, listening too.

That was it. The confusion fell from her. 'You are a witch, you know, dear Mrs Moore. I think you have a cauldron in your apartment, one that you sit over while poor Mr Harvey wonders what spell you're about to cast. How can you sum up what's going on in my head, just like that, when I didn't even know what I was thinking, until this minute?'

'Aye, well, I've had your mother through my hands, and look what she and Ver got up to, attending suffrage meetings, organising the hospital, dealing with things you must hope you never see. Then there's Gracie, pacing her kitchen until she packed her bags and took herself off to war. So I know "restless" when I see it. The thing is, what are you going to do about it, apart from get on with that sponge before it spoils?'

Bridie poured the mixture into greased pans, and slid them into the oven. 'Cookery School,' she breathed. She'd go to Paris, learn haute cuisine. Then James could come to see her when he was on his way to Spain, and she would go with him, somehow, hanging unseen on his coat-tails, if that's what it took. Then Tim would see what a mistake he'd made: he was a Nazi; they were in opposition. That would teach him.

That evening, Bridie knocked at her father's study door at Home Farm.

'Come in, Bridie.'

She entered. 'Have you eyes that are not only in the back of your head, but that can see through doors?'

He grinned up at her. 'That's right, nothing to do with the fact that I've been hearing you knock on that door since you were able to walk. Come and sit with me. I'm just sorting out the stock ordering. You'll be fascinated, I don't think.'

She laughed, her heart lighter than it had been for what seemed years. She walked across the polished and spotless old oak flooring. Molly, the farmhouse housekeeper from Easton, ruled the house with a rod of iron, and the floor was her pride and joy.

She brought him a piece of the sandwich sponge she had baked that afternoon, while she and Mrs

Moore had worked on a plan to change the idea of a Paris cookery school into reality. He took the plate, as she settled herself in the 'swing around' chair he kept next to his.

He tried a forkful. 'Delicious. I love the gooseberry jam with the cream. Perhaps it would help if I put in an order to Home Farm dairy to feed the cows jam? Then you could just whack it in the sandwich. Is that why you're here – because I only have cake if I've been a *very* good father, or you want something *very* important? So I must eat it quickly in case I have to say no.'

He gobbled it up while Bridie laughed, but couldn't hide her nervousness. She gathered herself, then embarked on pretty much the same conversation she'd had with Mrs Moore, telling him that she was restless, that she needed to expand her experience, that she was sixteen and a half.

At that point her da put his plate on the desk, wiped his mouth on the napkin she'd brought, and sat back in his chair, looking not at her, but swinging round to look out of the window. She did the same. The trees, dimly lit by the moon, moved in the wind.

'Goodness,' he said, 'how very old. Sixteen and a half, eh, and needing a change of scene, and an expansion of skills.'

She rushed on, 'Easton lads were fighting in the war and working down in the mines at my age. Alright, the soldiers lied about their age, but . . .' She stopped.

He had swung back to his desk and was doodling on his blotting pad. She swung back too, used to the ritual. Her da said into the silence, 'Not sure that you can compare war with a cookery course, darling girl.' He looked up now, staring intently into her eyes. Had he guessed?

He continued, 'However, I think perhaps we could compare your mother's reaction to you leaving for Paris, to you asking to join up.'

'Paris? How did you know I was thinking of Paris?'

'Do you think Mrs Moore would let you go into battle on your own? She is more formidable than any sergeant major I have ever had the misfortune to come across, except perhaps for Matron. She has briefed me on every single aspect of your recent conversation.'

'Oh, Da, and you let me go on, and bring cake.' Relief and stress vied with one another.

'I need you to convince me, Bridie, that you will brush up on your French before you leave, though I know Gracie and your mam have taught you well; I need to know that you will work hard, and most of all behave. I want you to come back. I do not want you falling in love with a Frenchman and leaving us.'

Bridie busied herself, placing his napkin on the plate, because she wouldn't be back, not for a long while, anyway, and she had never lied to her father before. She swung round, looking out at the moon and the trees, and then turned back to him. She loved him so much, and her mam, but they had carved their own paths, so they would eventually under-stand that she needed this for herself, surely.

She pushed her guilt aside, taking his war-scarred hand. 'Of course I won't marry a Frenchman. He'd probably have a poodle, and Currant and Raisin would never come and see me. Will you talk to Mam for me, Da?'

He shook his head. 'Nope, that will have to come from you, but I will, what we used to call in the army, reconnoitre the land, and report on a way across.'

The next day her mother came into Home Farm kitchen, her arms folded, and no smile. Bridie turned back to the stove, stirring porridge, and wasn't about to stop, but instead would pre-empt her. She said, 'You see, I do feel that Easterleigh Hall needs to move forward, Mam. Haute cuisine is that way forward.'

'Yes, your da told me what he'd advised you to say. He can't pretend, and I know when he has something afoot, Bridie Brampton. You need to spread your wings, is, I gather, what Mrs Moore said.'

Bridie swung round, the wooden spoon in her hand. 'Oh dear.'

Evie stood there, a smile on her face. 'Put that spoon back and stop dripping porridge on Molly's floor, or you'll be down on your knees with a scrubbing brush until she's satisfied. I will decide at the end of the day.'

As the day continued over at the Easterleigh Hall kitchen, Bridie was so tense she was almost beyond talking, let alone breathing, because her mam seemed to have forgotten all about the decision she must come to. In fact, she was just as she always was, and Mrs Moore was as she always was. Since it was her day for taking it easy, her knitting needles were relentless, clickety-clacking as she sat in the armchair, with the dogs on the other one, curled up together most of the day.

Bridie slipped across to her while her mam was in the hanging pantry, examining the mutton and pheasant. 'How does Mam seem?' she asked. Mrs Moore was counting stitches and frowned, shaking her head.

Her mam returned, with the pheasant that she'd marinated overnight but without the mutton. 'Sole,' she said. 'That's what we'll have as an alternative, served plain, without sauce, as the guests we have staying at the moment prefer.'

Bridie flushed. 'Oh, Mam, but perhaps they'd like to try—'

Mrs Moore called across, 'Come and hold your arms out for me, Bridie. I need to wind some wool into balls. These scarves are using more than I thought.'

Evie concentrated on preparing the pheasant and

just said, 'Yes, that's fine, Bridie, but I want you to make sure the vegetables are ready within the hour.'

Bridie could have screamed, but she dragged up a stool and sat in front of Mrs Moore, and held the hank of wool until her arms ached, and all the time there was a question in her eyes, which Mrs Moore firmly ignored. At last they were finished, and as Mrs Moore nodded her thanks, the elderly woman whispered, 'Don't you be pushing it, young madam. Your mam will let you know her decision, and you might just like to show that you can await that decision like an adult.'

'She's goading me, though, Mrs Moore. The guests we have staying might well have liked my suggestion of a light lemon sauce. We did say last week that we might consider it today.' She was whispering in her turn.

'You need to give your mam her moment, pet, and behind the teasing she's really thinking everything through.'

After luncheon there was afternoon tea, and the usual sponge cakes and fancies to make. As she did so, Bridie actually kept her eyes shut. There, she thought to herself. I can do it without looking, which goes to show just how boring my world has become. She felt the tension rising again. What if the answer was no?

As she opened her eyes, she saw her mother looking up from her recipe bible, shaking her head as though she couldn't believe what she was seeing.

Was that a laugh behind her eyes? If so, what did it mean? She knew better than to ask, especially after she glanced past her mam to Mrs Moore, whose look confirmed it.

By the time dinner was cooked and cleared away, Bridie felt like a wrung-out dishcloth, and set off for home alone, unable to stand walking beside her mam while she ignored the subject as she had done all day. She was striding beside the yew hedge when she heard her mother call, 'Wait up, Bridie. We can walk together, because there won't be many more times we can, once you start your course in Paris.'

Bridie halted, turned and tore back to her mother, flinging her arms around her. 'I love you, Mam. I love you up to the sky and back down again, a million times. Thank you. Just thank you.'

Her mam's arms around her tightened. 'I'll miss you, bonny lass, don't you forget that, and I'll long for your return.'

Bridie pushed away her mother's words. She didn't know when she would return, but her mam would understand, if not at first, then eventually. Nothing could stop her now from going to Paris to start on something really worthwhile, a world away from cooking. But then, as her mother relaxed her grip, and they started to head for home, Bridie slipped her hand into her mam's, and didn't want to leave, not at all, because now it felt wrong, and the guilt and pain took away any pleasure. 'I love you so much, Mam, and I'll miss you all too.'

Chapter Fourteen

Paris, June 1937

She and her mam left from Gosforn station two months later. Mrs Moore and Mr Harvey came too, and James. Her da hugged them both, telling Bridie that he'd miss her and would expect culinary miracles on her return. He told his wife that he'd miss her every second she was away settling Bridie in Paris, and that she could buy as many hats as she liked, as long as she had a lovely time, but came back at the end of the week. 'I love you, dearest Evie, you too, darling Bridie. Just make the most of it the next four months, that's all I ask.'

Aunt Grace arrived with Uncle Jack. They still looked sad and drawn and as they hugged Bridie, she wondered, for the first time, if she had done the right thing to send Tim away, but if he'd come to compound the hurt, at that particular time, it would have been just too dreadful, especially if she'd been the one to allow him through. The guard whistled, and the porter, Gerry Wilkins, shouted, 'Bridie Brampton, if you don't get on the train, I will throw you on myself.'

She leapt aboard, and waved until the train rounded a bend.

Bridie gazed at the Eiffel Tower. 'By, Mam, the boys . . . well, James, would love this.'

'Tim would too. Just because he has had a few tantrums and has different ideas to you two doesn't mean he's changed completely.' Bridie caught the uncertainty in her mother's voice, 'But I did expect him to come to help the marras support your da when Prancer was dying. I phoned Jeb, you know, and asked him to get a message through to his office, in the hope . . .' She trailed off.

For Bridie, the sun seemed to have gone behind a cloud at these words, and she realised she had stopped breathing. Oh, God, she didn't know he'd been responding to a message. She drew in a sharp breath, almost a gasp.

'Oh, Bridie pet, we need to forget about all that, and concentrate on today.' Her mother was holding her arm. 'Come on, time to buy a few hats, and then we'll return to Madame Beauchesne, I promise. Just a few.' Evie laughed.

Bridie stared at the tower, dragging her thoughts back to Old Bert's Field, to Tim's face, to the savage enjoyment, to his uniform, to just about everything he had become, and knew that she'd been right to send him away, whether Jeb had given him the message or not. Nothing would have changed him from the person who told Uncle Jack he wasn't their son. Nothing. He'd come to gloat, to laugh at her wonderful Prancer, to hurt them all again.

She felt again the soft muzzle, the last exhale, and for a sharp, slicing moment, wanted to be home. To be under the cedar tree, looking at Easterleigh Hall, both of which were the only things that never changed, in essence.

Shrugging, she allowed her mother to pull her along and was soon laughing with her.

Five hats later they were still sauntering along, following the map her da had tucked in her mam's handbag, saying that he knew if there was a chance of Evie getting lost, it would happen. They stopped for a coffee, strong and black. She almost felt the caffeine knock the top off her head as they sat at a pavement café. 'I wonder what I'll learn at the Haute Cuisine Institute?'

Her mam was looking in one of her hat boxes, 'It's so gorgeous, and as for the Institute, you'll learn far more than I've been teaching you, as well as more than the mastery of Mrs Moore, and let's just draw a veil over what Aunt Ver might have taught you.' They both roared with laughter, because Aunt Ver's strength was helping Harry at front of house and doing a few basic cookery chores. 'You will learn so much, and then you'll return at the end of September and introduce all you have learned, just in time for the start of the winter. But, pet, we'll miss you until then.'

Bridie sipped the dregs of her coffee. She wouldn't

be home; she'd be fighting for a cause in Spain, with James. Yet again she felt the wave of discomfort and guilt that had been sweeping through her on and off since they had arrived. 'I'll miss you too, Mam. All of you, but it's something I have to do. You must remember that, and tell Da.'

Her mother called for the waiter and paid. 'Come along. You sound as though it's forever, but the time will fly. What's more, your French is so good that you will adore Paris, and love the course, but you'll ignore the debs who will be there, finishing their "finishing". Instead, you will make sensible friends, and come back showing off, until Mrs Moore slaps your wrist.'

An elegant woman walked by, with a white poodle on a lead, which made her think of Raisin and Currant.

Bridie said, 'You'll look after the horses, and the foal? Primrose is coming along so beautifully. Dave, Clive and Young Stan know what to do. Young Daniel is doing very well, but there will be others that Matron will want to send to riding therapy. Tell Young Stan that Fanny's trained sufficiently, but to keep an eye on her.'

'Everything is set up for the few months you're away, so stop fretting. Now come along, you carry three of the hat boxes and I'll take two, and I promise not to buy any more on the way to the train tomorrow. Madame Beauchesne will wonder where we've got to, or worry, because she knows too well.'

Her mother handed her the hat boxes. What would her father think and when would she actually wear the frothy concoctions? Bridie smiled. Well, whatever her mam did was wonderful in her da's eyes.

That night, in bed, trying to sleep, it wasn't Spain that kept Bridie awake, but the thought of the Haute Cuisine Institute, and trying to imagine what it would be like. Her mother had told her that one of the tutors was a cousin of the Allards, who had looked after her da following the explosion which took his leg. It wasn't during the war, but afterwards, when he had been helping them to clear shells along the old front line.

She lay on the bed, not in it, such was the heat of Paris in June, and remembered the Allards coming to Easterleigh Hall six or so years ago. The chef had spent more time in the kitchen, applauding all her mam was doing, than strolling the grounds. He had shown Bridie how to make shortcrust pastry, unaware that her mother had shown her when she was eight. She checked her clock at three a.m., and then the next thing she knew it was dawn.

Bridie arrived at the Institute alone, at her own insistence, and with her mother's map. Her mother would leave for home today, and had no need of it. 'It's best I go alone, Mam. It's not school, it's more like a university, and I need to seem independent and strong,' she'd said.

She climbed the wide steps to the impressive old

building, which had ancient gas lights on either side of the doors. She halted, peering back to the corner. Her mam was still there, hiding under an umbrella though it wasn't raining. She grinned, loving her to the depth of her being. She called, 'I love you, Mam. Remember that, and thank you for guarding me, all my life.'

Her mother lowered the umbrella. People were sidestepping her, probably thinking, *'Folle Anglaise.'*

Evie waved. 'Caught in the act. I love you, Bridie Brampton, we all love you. Make sure you write to tell me how your day went. Are you sure you won't let me stay just for another night?'

'Go home, Mam. I'm a big girl now.' She waved and blew a kiss as other girls arrived, some climbing the steps uncertainly, some boldly. Her mam returned her kiss, and walked away.

Bridie felt utter relief, because as long as her mother remained, the lie loomed too large, and the need to stay with her family grew stronger.

When she entered the foyer the girls were standing still and silent, staring up at the high ceiling with its chandelier, then, as one it seemed, they turned to look at the gracious staircase. Bridie said in English to the girl next to her, 'By, it's grand, isn't it? I wonder if the kitchens will be as posh. Ours at the Hall is old-fashioned and we still use the stoves, not electric or gas, but we produce good food for the guests. I want to get better, though.'

The girl, red-haired, tall and obviously older than

Bridie, spread her hands and replied in French, 'I cannot understand.'

Effortlessly Bridie switched to French. 'It's beautiful.'

'Your French is perfect.' The girl was smiling. Her eyes were almost the same green as Aunt Grace. Bridie felt her heart twist. She wanted to go home, and be content to let the world do what it had to do.

'No, it is not but I hope it will be. I was taught by my mother and my aunt, because I am a cook and need French. It's a beautiful language, and my Uncle Jack and Auntie Gracie speak it too.' She was speaking in French, her words running one into the other out of sheer nervousness. She said, again in French, 'I am a cook. I need to improve. Let me say that again in English, slowly, if you would like me to?' The girl nodded, and so she did.

A small group of girls near them were whispering together, and now Bridie heard, 'Oh, my God, did you hear, she's actually a cook. I thought they'd all be like us, finishing.' The girls tittered and agreed.

A man's voice boomed from the top of the stairs, speaking in French. 'Welcome, ladies. If you will follow me, we will start immediately. There is much to learn.'

The French girl with the red hair walked alongside Bridie, as the British group pushed past them, their Chanel perfume lingering like a choking cloud. She repeated in English, 'I am a cook, I ...' Then in French, 'Now I've forgotten.'

Bridie told her again, quietly, adding, 'Don't worry, we have three months.'

The French girl said, 'Four. We have four months.'

Bridie just nodded because she only had about three, perhaps less, because then it would be August and James would be here. They were at the entrance to a huge salon. A smart woman dressed in black stood in the doorway, indicating places on the small, close-packed circular tables where the girls were to sit. On the stage was a long table covered in a white damask cloth, set up with what seemed like hundreds of wine bottles. The woman pointed Bridie to a place at the table with the English girls, and the French girl to a neighbouring table.

Once seated, the French girl turned, and told Bridie that her name was Marthe Deschamps. Bridie introduced herself as Bridget Brampton, but commonly called Bridie by her friends, 'So Bridie to you.' She repeated it in English, slowly.

She turned back to the girls on her table. One had just whispered, 'Can you see her hands? I expect they're really rough.'

'You girls, however, may call me Bridget.'

They flushed, and then rallied and introduced themselves as the Honourable this, that and the other. She grinned, because in her home no-one used titles if they could help it.

A man in a dark suit made an entrance, sweeping between the tables, heading for the front. His black hair looked dyed, and was cut short. His neat moustache was similarly dark. He sprang up the three steps onto the stage, and introduced himself as Monsieur Favre. He talked in heavily accented English about wine, to the thirty or so girls who sat around the room. There were five girls to each table. Bridie saw that Marthe was struggling to understand, as were several others around the room. Still sitting, she shoved her chair across to the neighbouring table. It scraped on the wooden floor.

Monsieur Favre stopped, looked and called, 'Ah, Miss Brampton, I believe. Are you on the move for any reason, or merely because you felt like it? Are you bored, perhaps?'

The girls at her table tittered. She stood, and said in French, 'Certainly not, Monsieur Favre, but you risk boring those French students in the class who understand little English. I was taught, as a cook, that I should learn French. I suspect that here, in France, it is not suggested that French cooks absorb English. Why would they, when recipes are invariably in the French language?'

She did not sit down, but waited for his reply. First he repeated in English a precis of all she had said, then fingered the white wine bottle he had been using to explain the bottling process. He pursed his lips. Bridie felt the eyes of the room switching from him, to her, and back again, and wondered if this was to be the shortest course for any student in the history of the Institute. She almost turned, to walk out, rather than be humiliated, but saw the

Honourable Edith Hardcastle tittering at the table, and whispering to her friends. No, she'd wait it out.

Monsieur Favre now held the bottle up to the long windows along the length of the room. In his fractured English he said, finally, 'Indeed, Miss Brampton, you are quite correct. Usually we have an interpreter, as our students from across the Channel perhaps do not have our language. Out of courtesy we thought we would speak your language; however, I promote you. For today you are our interpreter, and let us see how well you manage.' He gestured to the stage. 'Join me, Miss Brampton, and remedy the shortcomings of the Institute.'

The girls tittered again. Bridie made her way between the tables and mounted the stage, her heart beating so hard it seemed to be about to burst up and out through her throat. Without pause he commenced in French, explaining how to taste and examine wines by developing an evaluating technique he described as *'sensorielle'*, and suggested that those who were not writing notes should do so. She hesitated for a moment over *sensorielle*, but took a stab at 'sensory', and from his single raised eyebrow and slight nod she knew she had guessed correctly.

The woman had by now joined them on stage, and as he drew to a close, he explained to the room that he would be bringing spittoons to each table. They would activate the skills he had just outlined, and instead of drinking, they would use the spittoons. The next step would be to take a drink to cleanse the palate, and spit again, and taste the next wine. At that stage they would write down their thoughts. He then bowed to Bridie, and gestured that she should resume her place at the table, to applause from the audience.

Bridie picked up her chair, which remained next to Marthe, and tried to fit it back into her place. The 'Hons', though, had closed the gap. Bridie kept ramming until the girls were jolted enough to move, just enough. The atmosphere was frosty. The Honourable Beatrice Gordon said, sotto voce, but designed to be heard, 'One does not exhibit oneself, if one knows how to behave.'

On the table to their left, a girl with a blonde bob turned in her chair and articulated impressively, 'Or, of course, if one cannot speak the language.'

She reached across and held out her hand to Bridie. 'Lucinda Fortnum, at your service – though my friends call me Lucy – and I know that you are Bridget. Well met, indeed.'

Monsieur Favre was at Bridie's table now, with two spittoons. The woman followed, carrying a tray with six bottles of chilled white wine. 'You, ladies, will smell, swirl, sip, spit. Miss Brampton, I have managed to translate as I have travelled the room. However, when Monsieur Allard takes over this afternoon to conduct an exotic gastronomic tour, you will be needed. While I am here, he asked that I send his best wishes to your grandparents, Lord and Lady Brampton.' He winked and moved on, stopping by Lucinda, 'Enjoy your tasting, Lady Lucinda.'

There was a silence around the table. Lucinda leaned over from the other table, grinned, and held up her empty glass to Bridie's table companions. 'Touché, I feel we can safely say, don't you?'

That evening, as Bridie strolled down the steps at the end of the day, Monsieur Allard followed her, catching her up as she reached the pavement. 'You will find, Mademoiselle Bridie, that your mother will have taught you all that you need to know. Here, in your case, the best we can do is to refine and broaden. For many of the others, pouf, they merely want to be able to instruct a cook. You, my dear, *are* the cook, the magician.' He swept on, neat and small, but without a moustache, and his brown hair was longer than Monsieur Favre's.

Bridie set off in the direction of Madame Beauchesne's apartment, but paused as Marthe ran down the steps after her, her jacket swinging in the breeze. They strode along talking about their aims, and the kitchens they'd worked in, for Marthe was a cook in her father's restaurant in Lyon. They talked of the joy they felt creating dishes, the need to learn. Before they reached the first corner, they heard, 'Wait up, you two.'

It was Lady Lucinda Fortnum, a good egg, as James would have said, with a wink. Together, still in French, they talked cooking and wine, for Lucinda Fortnum was determined to drag her family's estate into the modern age. She felt the need to improve the gardens and perhaps charge people to have a look around. If this succeeded, then a restaurant would be essential. 'There's such a ghastly great roof on the whole pile, needing to be repaired. All I have to do is convince the old dears that it's an excellent scheme,' she drawled. They reached the Café Adrienne, and by tacit agreement took a pavement table, ordering a coffee.

After coffee, they moved on to wine, and this time there was no spitting, just a lot of swallowing. It was unusual for Bridie, and within minutes she felt her mind slip into some easy place. After an hour they went their separate ways.

A letter from James awaited her at Madame Beauchesne's, and a cup of coffee, thick and black, which she needed. Madame Beauchesne, grey-haired, elegant and charming, had been a friend of the first wife of Lord Brampton, and was now a friend of Aunt Ver. She spoke perfect English but insisted that Bridie use her French, gently correcting flaws of accent and grammar, and applauding her tale of being a temporary interpreter. She listened intently to the descriptions of the girls she had met, the nice and the nasty.

After a dinner prepared by Cécile, the cook, who had trained at a similar institute, they listened to the wireless, though Madame Beauchesne leafed through her book on English gardens that Evie had brought as a gift while she did so. All the time Bridie was aware of James' letter in her pocket and longed to retire to her room. As though reading her mind, Madame Beauchesne stirred as the gold clock on the mantelpiece chimed nine o'clock, placing the book on the side table, removing her glasses. 'Bridie, my dear. I retire early, as you know, and this evening I feel it advisable for you to do the same.'

Almost before her hostess had finished Bridie was on her feet. Madame Beauchesne smiled. 'Yes, there, in the privacy of your room, you can read your letter. Perhaps it is one from an admirer? Soon you will be seventeen, such a lovely age, a time of joy, fun and hope before the serious business of marriage, perhaps at eighteen?'

She switched off the lamps on both tables, and led the way towards the door. She stopped for a moment at the photograph of her husband, in a French officer's uniform. As she had told Bridie and Evie on the night of their arrival, he had been killed at Verdun.

'Please God, Bridie, that Germany does not see fit to rise again, though the signs are not good. You will know that the Germans' Condor Legion bombed Guernica, the Basque capital in Northern Spain, in April. Should they even have an air force after the great war, one asks oneself? Should we not have objected to that unpleasant little man, Hitler, being allowed to issue his edicts and carry out his adventures?'

She picked up the photograph. 'Some say the

bombing was a rehearsal, but if so, I ask, for what? Or am I wrong? Perhaps they are prancing buffoons and harmless?'

She replaced the photograph and turned to Bridie. 'I do so wish someone would reply, for I need to have answers to these questions, but all seem asleep. Hitler signs a friendship with that fascist, Mussolini. He signs a pact with Japan. Why? As I say, all seem asleep.' She touched her fingers to her lips, then laid them on the face of her husband. 'Goodnight, my love. Come, Bridie, take no notice of a lonely old widow living in France, which does not have a Channel between it and the Nazis. I have seen my country destroyed once, and fear for it again.'

Bridie closed the door of her room, and leaned back against it. Yes, she had known that Guernica had been bombed; it was after Prancer died. She and James had talked of little else when it happened. She sank onto her bed. Her room smelt of lavender, and had windows that opened onto a square around which tall buildings clustered. Some of the windows opposite were shuttered, some were open with lamps burning. Each building consisted of apartments, probably similar to this. She ripped open James' letter.

Dear Bridie
I do wonder how the Institute is managing with
you there. Are you causing mayhem, or is it too

early for you to get going? I hope that you enjoy every minute. I know it is something you want to do, and it will help Easterleigh Hall.

Sir Anthony has had another of his meetings at the Hall, and missed you, though Annie and Aunt Evie were called in to circulate for a moment. Lady Margaret and Penny were there, and when they left I saw that Lady M was wearing a fascist badge as you said, but it seems it's all in the cause of peace. After all, as you say, Sir Anthony is at the head of their little club. Annie and Aunt Evie were helped by two Basque refugees who arrived at Easterleigh Hall recently, Maria and Estrella. A friend of mine knew of them, and asked if I could help find employment. Of course, my mother and your mam were only too happy to help. I have tried to talk a little to them in my pathetic Spanish, but it's laughable. I nip in for tea from time to time, and listen hard to their Basque to try and pick some up. Without much success, I have to say, but I will keep at it, as it will be valuable.

Young Stan is managing Terry and Fanny very well, and David is good with advice. I help most days. I will leave at the end of July, not August, as your father has a new boy starting in time for the harvest. I still have Arthur's information, you know, the medic I met on the Jarrow march, and will find the enrolment office in London. Who knows, I might see him in Spain. I will come to Madame Beauchesne's to say farewell, probably early August, then leave for Spain, straight away.

Mother is writing to her to ask if I may stay for two nights, as I have explained that I wish to travel the continent before university. I will return by the start of university if I am more useless than I hope to be. But I hope that I get the hang of things quickly, and can make a difference. If I do stay, then tell them where I have gone, will you? But insist that you knew nothing, and that I wrote to you from Arles with the news.

If they think you were in on it, you'll be put in the corner, for not stopping me. The horses will be glad to see you when you finish the course. So will Young Stan, because for a short while he'll be without both of us helping.

I will write again soon, Bridie. I do hope that you are regaining your old enthusiasm, and that the wine tasting listed on the prospectus is interesting. In France you should learn how to actually drink the stuff. Perhaps I will help a bit more with that when I come.

Your loving cousin,
James

Bridie ripped the letter into shreds, gathered the pieces up, and dropped them in the bin near the window. No-one must know his plans, because they were her plans too. She had brought her stable boots, which had annoyed her mother when she had helped her unpack. 'Why on earth have you brought these?'

'In case I find a riding stables.'

Her mother had shaken her head, and put them in the bottom of the wardrobe, with the jodhpurs she also discovered. 'I don't know, I'm surprised you could drag yourself away for even a few months, as it's the toss of a coin whether the horses will miss you more, or you them.'

For a moment, during this first day at the Institute, she had faltered in her aim, loving the pleasure of learning, thrilling at the thought of helping Easterleigh Hall hotel. But James was going to do something, so she must also.

Chapter Fifteen

Paris, August 1937

Today, the Terrible Trio, as Bridie, Marthe and Lucy had been named by Monsieur Allard, met at the food market at seven thirty in the morning. They were to prepare their own version of mushroom soup as part of their certification. He had insisted that he wanted a flavour that he had never experienced before. Together they hunted for the mushrooms of their choice, selecting the best, before taking time for a coffee at the market café. They sat outside, chatting about the two Basque refugees that Easterleigh Hall was employing in the kitchens.

Marthe almost spat as she cursed the Nazi Condor Legion, which had bombed the port. 'We know the Hun too well, from the war. We are without a ditch, like you, my dear Bridie. How lucky that you have the Channel.'

They sat for a moment with their thoughts. Lucy said, 'They won't come again.'

Again the silence.

Bridie checked her watch and leaned back in her chair. Though it was still only eight o'clock the early

August sun was already warm. She loved the feel of it, and knew that soon, when James arrived and they reached Spain, it would be even hotter. She hoped he was progressing with his Spanish, as she was trying to, and also picking up some Basque, and could teach her. 'I forgot I need dill sprigs,' she murmured.

The others laughed. Lucy picked up her basket, and stood. 'Trust Bridie: food first, and politics a long way behind.'

Marthe just shook her head, gulping her coffee. 'Crazy English.'

'Mushroom soup takes first place in any situation,' Bridie said, leading the way back to the market. It was best that her friends thought of her in this way, because then, when James came, they wouldn't suspect her plans and try to stop her, or worse, tell Madame Beauchesne.

In the kitchen at the Institute, there were many workbenches and many electric stoves, and half as many cooks as there had been. The debs who had shared Bridie's table had lasted a mere two weeks. It seemed that getting their hands dirty was not part of their 'finishing'. Others had followed in their wake, and now the Institute class contained debs who had, to their surprise, found themselves interested, and a few cooks who, from the beginning, had known why they were there.

Bridie liked the chatter all around; it reminded her of home. She liked the friendship of Marthe and

Lucy, but always she kept a slight distance because she would have to leave them. Monsieur Allard was at her shoulder now, looking at the coarsely chopped mushrooms, which still retained their stalks.

'Perhaps it would be best to discard the stems,' he suggested.

She replied, 'Mam says that most of the flavour resides there.' She found she was using his terminology more and more.

'Ah,' he said. 'Well, if Mam says, then who am I to disagree?' He patted her shoulder and moved on, as the class laughed, with her, not at her. He called, 'Remember, girls, we must make these last few weeks count. For as autumn falls, you return home, and put into practice what you have learned, or not, Michelle.' Again laughter, but friendly and kind, for Michelle was a girl who liked to pick and choose the days she attended.

Bridie sliced two cloves of garlic, which she had not used at Easterleigh Hall, but which she felt she had 'discovered' under Monsieur Allard's tutelage. She chopped the dill, not sure if that was indeed the right herb, but she was going with her gut, as her Uncle Jack would have said.

Though Lucy and Marthe had decided to use vegetable stock, she had hesitated, then chosen chicken, which she had prepared yesterday. Which was right? She didn't know, but her mam used chicken. Was she teaching Maria to cook? And what about Estrella? Would they be able to take her place for as long as she was away? And what about the horses, Terry and Fanny? Was Young Stan good enough? Would he stick at it? Well, he'd just have to, and that was that.

She looked at the chopped mushrooms and removed the black gills from beneath the caps, keeping them for garnish. She should have done that first, but she hadn't thought about it soon enough. She fought to concentrate. She needed to learn as much as possible, so that when she did return to Easterleigh she would be of use, because she must make up for what she was about to do.

'Concentrate,' she said aloud.

Lucy looked up. 'Are you alright, Bridie? You've been a bit distracted these last few days.'

'I had a letter from my cousin; he's coming to Paris for a day or two any day now with a few friends.'

She moved to the stove and melted butter in a pan, as Marthe was doing on her hotplate. Marthe said, 'How exciting. We must all have wine together.'

Lucy was melting butter too, and all along the row of stoves, others were beavering away. Bridie said, 'Yes, he'd like that.' But would he? Or might he be worried that questions would be asked?

She added the mushrooms, garlic, salt and pepper, then covered and simmered for five minutes, until all were softened but not discoloured. She lifted the lid and breathed in the steam, and the smell. Wonderful. Gently she added the broth, slowly,

slowly, and then, almost drip by drip, added half a cup of cream and half the dill. She replaced the lid and simmered again, for ten minutes.

Monsieur Allard was behind her again. 'I would suggest, Bridie, that you do not add the dill so early. Perhaps leave it as a garnish. It might stain the soup. On the other hand, it might not. Interesting. Yes, interesting.' He moved on.

She would miss him. She would miss them all.

After ten minutes she sieved the ingredients through a fine hair-sieve. She hated doing this at Easterleigh, because everything was always such a rush. When she had complained about this to Monsieur Allard last month, he had shrugged, throwing his arms wide. 'You think you will find a kitchen that is not rushed. Ah, Mademoiselle Bridie, think again. Such innocence.'

Well, today she did have time. Her arm ached when she was finished, and he was right, her soup had a slight green stain. Damn. She added salt and pepper to taste, and whisked in more cream. It frothed and did seem to lighten.

'One more minute only, and by then it must be served, ladies,' Monsieur Allard called, standing in front of the workbenches, his arms crossed, his chef's hat as pristine as ever.

'Crikey,' breathed Lucy next to her. 'One minute?'

'*Merde*,' muttered Marthe, the other side of her.

'Damn,' murmured Bridie, and removed the pan from the heat. She whisked some cold cream, ladled the soup into the waiting bowls, then swirled the cream onto the surface of the soup. It shone cream against the hint of green as though it was an intended difference. She scattered the gills and remaining dill. Then stood back as Monsieur clapped his hands.

The girls all looked at one another and stepped back as he tasted along the line, talking to each cook as he did so. It was important, because it would count towards the certificate. She stopped. A certificate she would not receive. Suddenly her throat was full. She loved this place, these people.

Monsieur Allard tasted hers. He replaced the spoon on the workbench. 'This, Miss Bridie, is a happy accident, or perhaps, like your mother, you have the gift. More than perfect, and I have never said that before. Inspired. The cream is a successful trick, but one that you must use again. Come, gather round, all you young ladies. Bridie used the dill in the cooking. I felt it would stain the soup and ruin the presentation. She rescued it with cream, changing the "mistake" to a statement. Bravo. You will take your certificate home, if you produce more work like this.'

He continued along the line, praising Marthe and Lucy too, but not as effusively. Later, as they washed up their utensils, he said quietly to Bridie. 'You have a gift. Remember that. Your mother was right to send you to us. You bring credit to her, and to us.'

She felt the pleasure, and then the pain. But as her mam had said for as long as she could remember,

218

'Smile. It's what those at Easterleigh Hall do, however dire the situation.'

At the day's end, she walked with Lucy and Marthe, and they stopped as usual at the café for a coffee, sitting at a table outside, and then ordering a glass of red wine. They sat under the shade of the awning as the sun beat down. Bridie leaned back, soaking up every second, because soon it would be only a memory – but one that would sustain her, just as much as Easterleigh Hall. Lucy brought out her gold cigarette case and offered it round, as she always did. As always, Bridie and Marthe shook their heads. Lucy lit up with her gold lighter.

She had said, on the first day, that her father had given it to her before she left, saying that gold always held its value, and she was to keep it with her always. Just in case.

'In case of what?' Marthe had asked.

'Just in case,' Lucy had said. 'We're Jews, and it pays to have a "just in case".' She looked serious, for the first time since they'd known her, as she replaced the case and lighter in her handbag.

Bridie remembered Tim's cigarette case then, which Heine had given him. It was gold, or was it silver? She couldn't remember. Was he still giving him such presents – in other words, buying him? She shut off the thought, as a familiar voice roared out, over the sound of running feet, 'Bridie, I'm here. We got an earlier boat.'

The girls spun round, and there was James, blonde hair tousled, running towards her, his rucksack bouncing on his back. There were two others with him who stood around grinning as he hugged her, and shook hands with the two girls. James said, 'Bridie's told me all about you,'

'All?' queried Lucy, arching her eyebrows. 'I do hope not.'

The boys laughed. James introduced them, and explained that Archie and Ian were staying at a hostel tonight, and were meeting up with other friends there. They drew up chairs and crowded round the small table as the waiter brought wine, not asking whether they'd prefer coffee. He was right, because they fell on it, but only after they'd chinked glasses, and said in unison, 'Happy days.'

Bridie sagged with relief, thinking Ian and Archie might have mentioned Spain, but met James' eyes, and saw the slight nod. They knew better.

Archie was a student at Cambridge University, and said that it had been the most wonderful journey, from the moment the gangplank was withdrawn. 'It was a perfect night, and the stars were magnificent. We watched the lights of England fade, and stayed on deck until we reached Dieppe. Had to wait for the train to Paris, and here we are.'

Marthe said in her fractured but improving English, 'Bridie say you are travel in France, then, 'ow you say, back to studies. Is right?'

Archie nodded. 'More or less.'

Ian said, 'Not me.'

Bridie froze, and so did James, the glass halfway to his lips. Ian continued, 'I'm a plumber, so I ain't got no studies, just leaks.'

There was a pause, then a burst of laughter, led by James. Lucy said, 'Now if you mended roofs I'd be picking your brains.' The pair of them launched into a discussion about a mate of Ian's who might be able to help her, and how big was the roof? His face was a picture when he was told. He gathered himself, and said he'd drop a line to his mate, who might be able to gather up an army of roofers if the price was right.

At eight o'clock, the waiter brought coffee and cognac for them all. Bridie gave hers to Ian, who threw it back in one gulp, before heaving his rucksack onto his back. He headed off with Archie, promising to have some more thoughts on roofers, which he would tell Lucy tomorrow evening. Archie bowed over Bridie's hand.

Bridie and James headed towards Madame Beauchesne's apartment. Once they were out of earshot, she said, 'It's grand to have you here, bonny lad. Do you want to go out after dinner, to see something of Paris?'

'Another time, Bridie. I'm absolutely whacked. I know I have to have dinner with our hostess, but perhaps you can carry the conversation. My French isn't enormously good, as you know.'

Madame Beauchesne, as perceptive as always,

merely smiled when James explained that his French was limited, and he hoped he'd be better company tomorrow, after a good sleep. 'Of course,' she said, in English. 'I too am, as you say, under the weather. Rather a headache, so I will be eating little, and sleeping much. Now, dinner is ready, so tell me news from Easterleigh Hall as we eat.'

During the meal James mentioned the Basque refugees, Estrella and Maria, and described their perilous voyage to England, where people had greeted the dispossessed, mainly children, and taken them under their wing.

'They will stay when Bridie returns?' asked their hostess. She looked pale, and had left her dessert of chocolate macarons and cream half finished.

'I'm sure, or if they prefer to move on, then my mother will help them with whatever they wish to do.'

Madame Beauchesne patted her mouth with her serviette. 'It is a good thing that your family does, but forgive me, I have a most dreadful migraine, they are the bane of my life. I will need to stay in bed for some of tomorrow if it takes its usual course, so I bid you farewell, dear James, until tomorrow evening.'

She looked at Bridie. 'You are quiet tonight? You too are tired, I feel. So, my dears, Bridie, you and your James sit over a cognac, and catch up on his news.'

She rose, and James helped her to the door, asking

if she needed his help mounting the stairs. She declined, 'I know the procedure for my headaches, my dear. A darkened room and peace and quiet is all that is needed.'

When James came back to the table, Bridie asked, 'Are you alright? You seem more than tired.'

'Lying to so many people, including Mother and Father, doesn't sit well with me. I'm glad you don't have to do the same. I will leave a letter with you to post to them. Just say that I called in to say fare-well before heading off on my travels and that you knew nothing of my plans. Now, dearest Bridie, please do not pour me a cognac. All I want is my bed. So come and show me my room, and we can talk more in the morning.'

The next day passed far too quickly. James had things to do, and Bridie had an exam to take, on wine. They all met at the café, and the air of excite-ment and apprehension around the boys was tangible. They laughed too loudly, and drank too much. Marthe and Lucy grinned at Bridie. Lucy said, 'The excitement of holiday time. Soon it will be our turn, girls.'

Within moments, it seemed, James and Bridie were walking back to Madame Beauchesne's apartment. James talked of his meeting with the group who were setting off by train for Arles in the morning at eight thirty, of the need to disembark there, rather than Nîmes, to confuse anyone who might want to stop them. 'The authorities are determined to prevent their nationals enlisting in the foreign army of the International Brigade, so they are watching those who disembark at Nîmes carefully.'

He told her the time of the train and gave her his letter for his parents, to be posted in a week, when he would be safely in the Pyrenees, and beyond their reach. She, in her turn, had secretly placed a letter in Marthe's bag, tucked into her sauces notepad, which she would need for the session on Friday. It was in an envelope on which she had written, 'Please post this letter to my mother at the address on the envelope, but not before a week has passed.'

Madame Beauchesne was still unwell and had left a note of apology, which Cécile gave them. Bridie's relief was immense, because it made her exit so much easier. She packed that night, stuffing her jodhpurs and boots in her carpet bag, together with underwear, books, a notepad and some money she had saved from the allowance her parents had sent her with. She added her jacket, umbrella, and woollen jumper, as the winters could be hard, she thought.

She rose at six in the morning, and slipped a note under James' door, saying she had forgotten in the excitement that she had an Institute visit to Poitiers, and would see him at Easterleigh Hall on his return. She wished him bon voyage.

She left a note for Madame Beauchesne with the cook, who had prepared croissant and coffee. In the note she explained that she had forgotten to tell her that Monsieur Allard had arranged a trip to Poitiers for the Institute students, to sample the food in a restaurant. While they were there, they were taking the opportunity to stay with the parents of one of their fellow students south of Poitiers. She would contact her with her approximate time of return.

She also thanked her, from the bottom of her heart, for all her kindness, and hoped that she would recover soon.

She arrived early at the railway station and went straight to the ticket office, where she asked for a one-way ticket to Arles. At the ticket seller's raised eyebrows, she changed it to a return, blaming her faulty French. He nodded. She hurried out, her straw hat pulled down, and waited alongside some trolleys piled high with trunks, watching for James, Archie and Ian. People were milling about – women with smart hats, and others with headscarves, some with smart handbags, some with baskets. The men wore hats or berets. The engine, five carriages down, was shooting out steam, smuts were falling, sulphur hung in the air. It smelt like Easton, with its glowing slag heap.

At last she saw the three of them, and nearby was another small group of young men, and behind them, two more groups of three, and so it went, all piling into the same carriage, but not the same compartment. She hurried into the carriage behind them, feeling sick with nervousness, with shame, because she had lied to so many people, and she could hardly bear the guilt. But she must. Someone had to do this.

The train jerked, spat sparks, wheels ground on the tracks, slipped and then caught, and slowly they pulled free of the station. She had packed three of the croissants, loaded with butter and jam to sustain her. Her water bottle, bought in a walking shop, was full, and as the heat of the day built, she knew she would need every drop.

She listened to the desultory conversation of the passengers, breathed in the garlic oozing from the pores of the man sitting next to her. He was reading a newspaper. She looked out of the window. France was so flat. Had her father marched along here, and Uncle Jack, and all the others? How strange and awful to have war played out on your own land. How much noise there must have been with the artillery firing on and on, so that the ground shuddered miles from the front line, as her da had said.

He'd be bringing in the cows for milking, just as Fred Froggett would, at his farm under the Stunted Tree Hill. Did James miss Home Farm? Did he miss the chats he would have had with her da and Fred Froggett on market day? She watched from the window as the French farmers harvested ripe wheat, bleached by the sun. They passed through towns, and the train stopped in the stations. Then more countryside, and slowly she relaxed, and slept, waking with a start at a station when the man next to her rose, left, and slammed the door.

She searched for a sign to tell her where they were. The woman across from her, with a headscarf and basket on her knee, said in French, 'You sleep and I will tell you when we arrive at your station?' There was a question there.

Bridie hesitated a moment, 'Arles,' she said.

The woman frowned and stared, but then nodded. 'Very well, but . . .' She shook her head. 'Sleep. I will wake you. We have hours yet. I go to Nîmes.'

'Thank you, Madame.' It seemed safer to sleep than talk, for then the questions in the Frenchwoman's eyes might progress to words.

She dozed, waking to see drier land. The train stopped or slowed frequently. She dozed again, this time waking to vineyards on sloping hills, and olive groves. The heat was harsh as it beat in through the windows, and the shadows sharp and dark. The train was slow. She sipped from her water bottle. It was warm. The woman opposite was knitting what looked like a child's cardigan. They were passing Roman-tiled farmhouses, stone built. A small herd of goats grazed on sparse shrubs halfway up a hill-side. An old man with a stick guarded them.

Eventually, night fell. The train continued, then stopped for a long time, it seemed, and finally drew into Arles at dawn. She hauled her rucksack from the seat beside her, then leaned out of the window, watching the carriage in front of her. There they were, alighting onto the platform. She opened the door, called, 'Thank you, Madame.'

She jumped down and hurried after them, staying out of sight. They were heading for the bus station, and she saw they were splitting up, much as they had when embarking, but this time into pairs. She and James could sit together. She ran now, catching up with him, pulling him round. 'I'm coming with you. I need to do this too. We must make a stand, together, all of us.'

Archie was walking beside James. 'What the hell?'

James was staring at her. 'For heaven's sake.' He gripped her arms. 'Bridie, what are you doing here? You've got to go home.'

Archie glanced across as a man shouldered himself towards them, barging through the flow of boys and men heading towards the bus station. 'Here comes Stephen Sadler. Now you're in trouble, James.'

'Williams, what the hell is this?' the man seethed.

James lowered his voice, and explained to Sadler, 'She's my cousin, and has followed me here, with some ridiculous notion of joining us. Oh God, Bridie, how the hell could you?'

Archie was looking from one to another. The stream of boys and men had stopped to stare.

Bridie said, 'Ridiculous? And what do you mean, how could I? You lot are going, so what's ridiculous about me—'

'Oh shut up, Bridie,' James said.

Sadler waved the others on, and Archie and Ian. He glared at her, hissing, 'You damned little fool.

It's hard enough without this sort of rubbish. You're not coming, and we'll be bloody lucky if you don't blow the whole thing sky-high. What the hell are we going to do with you? We're trying to be inconspicuous here, and it's ended up a bloody circus.'

Bridie couldn't believe this was happening. She reached forward, clutching at James' arm. 'James, don't be like this.'

'Bridie, you've done enough damage. Just be quiet.' As he spoke he was shrugging free of her and turning away, shaking his head.

Damn them, she'd head for the border, clamber the Pyrenees on her own. She swung round, then stared about her. How? She hadn't an idea which way. Suddenly her head spun, and frustration and disappointment drained her of all strength.

Ian had returned. He patted Bridie on the arm. 'Keep your pecker up.' He turned to Sadler. 'Tell you what, sir, why don't we settle 'er in a pension. I bet she's left a letter with someone, telling 'em to post it to her parents in a week or so, like we all 'ave. She will have said she's away for a few days, just so no-one gets alarmed, so how about we make her swear to stay here for a couple of days. Then she can go back, just as she's said, and it's all tickety-boo, everyone's calm. She can stop the letter being sent, and send yours.'

Stephen Sadler dragged his hands through his hair. 'Bloody women. You, James Williams, had better bloody sort her out, because I'm not having this idiot jeopardising our plans. Half an hour to settle her, and then we leave.'

Bridie saw the fury in James' face as he looked from Stephen to her, and couldn't believe he could be like this. She'd walked away from everything to be here, because it was so important. She only realised she had spoken aloud when James said, 'For the last time, Bridie, shut up and bloody well grow up. This isn't a game. Easterleigh needs one of us. How could you bloody do it to them? Come on.' He grabbed her arm and yanked her forward. It hurt. His face was white with rage.

Ian took James' rucksack. 'You've lost two minutes with that little tantrum, Jamie, my lad. Get a bloody move on, then get back 'ere, or the boss'll go without you.'

Bridie pulled free, shouting, 'Why do I have to go back? Why can you go off and fight, and not me? Well, I'll take myself over the mountains. Get on your damned bus.'

James grabbed her again, pulling her to him, whispering. 'People are looking. I'm taking you, and making sure you actually book in, and if you don't do as Ian said, I will never, ever forgive you. I need to do this. You don't, and mustn't. You *have* to wait two days, then go back.'

She let him lead her down street after street, her mouth dry, her legs shaking, until finally they found a pension, where the owner, Madame Colbert, said she had a room free. He booked her in, took her to her room, and made her promise to stay quiet. She looked into his face, which was closed and cold. She had done so many wrong things, and she said this to James, sobbing, and at this his fury faded, and he put his arms around her. 'Dearest Bridie. What a mess. Why didn't you talk to me, as I talk to you? Then I could have explained why it's no place for you.'

She leaned on his chest. 'That's why I didn't say anything. You would have said no.'

He hugged her tightly. 'Bridie. You have to listen to people sometimes. Stop rushing into things, making irresponsible decisions. You're not a child, not any more.' He checked his watch. 'I've got to go.' She felt him kiss her hair, and then he pulled free. 'If I'm not back for university, I will get in touch by October, somehow.'

'Be lucky, be safe,' she said, still sobbing. 'The pitman's prayer. Come back to me, James.'

He checked his watch, and ran from the room.

Chapter Sixteen

The next day, the early morning sun sliced through the gaps in the old, weathered shutters as Bridie forced herself to leave her bed. She had not undressed or washed since James had left. She had just cried. Now, as she pushed open her shutters and opened the windows, she wondered how it was that the man with the cart containing something in large baskets, covered by a cloth, was trundling along, that the woman setting up her market stall near the boulangerie could smile, and talk to that other woman. Surely the world should have stopped?

The windowsill was split. She ran her finger along it. Was it age, or the heat of the sun? Would it be cold on the pass through the Pyrenees? Would James be laughing with Archie and Ian about the fool of a girl who had followed him? Would his blue eyes still be as angry? She'd never seen him like that, not even with Tim.

The man with the cart stopped, and was lifting off the cloth. He folded it carefully and put it beside the cart. The baskets contained tomatoes, and the square was becoming busy with customers. As she looked, more stalls were set up, and the noise level grew. She heard laughter and thought that she would never even smile again. The heat rose over the square. She wept again. He had gone, and she had left the Institute and lied to everyone, and it was all for nothing. She was a fool.

Madame Colbert tapped on the door. Bridie called in French, 'No thank you, Madame Colbert. I'm not hungry.' It was what she had said all day yesterday, and so it would be again today, because although she had money to pay for the room, she wasn't sure that it would be enough. Was it tomorrow she could go back? And what about Madame Beauchesne? Would she guess she had lied? What about the letter? How would she retrieve it from Marthe?

She walked about the room, thinking, thinking, but then heard a slight tap at the door, and a man's voice saying quietly, as though his mouth was pressed to the door, 'I think we should leave, Miss Brampton. We have a journey ahead of us. We could eat on our journey.'

Bridie turned slowly, dragging her hand across her face, wiping her mouth. 'Who? What?'

'Ah, we have met, but a while ago, first at your uncle's wedding, and then at Sir Anthony's dinner. Perhaps you remember me. It is Herr Bauer.'

'But . . .'

'First, before any more "buts", may I suggest that you pack, and we embark upon our train. I took the liberty of obtaining a ticket, as I think you might

233

have expected to only need a single journey. It is usual, if heading for Spain.'

Herr Bauer? He knew about Spain? The heat bombarded her through the window; the noise of the street was growing louder. Herr Bauer, who had been with the fascists at Sir Anthony's dinner. Herr Bauer knew she was here? Herr Bauer, who probably knew the Nazis who bombed Guernica and Bilbao, and killed Maria and Estrella's families. Had he followed her? Was he after James and the others? She peered down into the square, but it was too far to jump.

He said again, quietly, 'I would prefer not to spend too long convincing you that I am not a villain as we have a train to catch, Miss Brampton. May I just say that Madame Beauchesne phoned your family, as Lady Lucinda Fortnum was concerned at your absence and so "exposed your cover" is what I believe you would say.'

Bridie stood stock-still.

He tapped again. 'After this complicated journey of words, Miss Brampton, Colonel Potter suggested, as I was in the area, that I try and locate you in Arles, a common disembarkation point for those off to do Spain. If located, Colonel Potter requested that I accompany you to Calais, where I have further business. Your mother awaits you there. Colonel Potter asked me to convey the fact that your mother said that if you do not come, she will come to Arles and drag you back by the hair.'

These last few words convinced Bridie that Herr Bauer was indeed acting on behalf of Colonel Potter and she wept again, with relief, because she needed her mam, needed to go home. She opened the door. 'I have a return ticket,' she said.

Herr Bauer took her rucksack as she left the room, having washed, and tried to straighten her skirt and blouse. She snatched it back. 'I'm not helpless,' she muttered.

His smile said, Oh really? But he said nothing.

They hurried down the stairs to the lobby. Madame Colbert was behind her desk and merely smiled, waving them past. Bridie halted. 'I need to pay.'

'Monsieur Williams has already done so.' Herr Bauer moved her out into the heat of the morning. It was still only eight thirty. James had paid. Perhaps he wasn't as furious as he had seemed. Herr Bauer was striding ahead of her, carrying an attaché case, requesting that she keep up, or they would miss the train, which might further annoy her mother. She hurried alongside.

Once they were near the station, Herr Bauer checked his watch, bought a newspaper, and indicated a pavement café. He bought croissant and coffee for them both, then buried his head in the newspaper. Bridie hadn't realised just how hungry she was, and thirsty. There was a carafe of water and glasses on the table. She gulped down the water, then the coffee, then the croissant, while he merely

sipped his coffee, his eyes never leaving the newspaper. The moment she had finished, though, he
was up, tucking the newspaper into his attaché
case, and hurrying into the station, then on to
the platform, and then the train. He insisted they
use the ticket he had purchased for her, as they
could then sit together as their seats were reserved.
At that point no-one sat near them. She said, as they
settled next to one another, 'You knew James wasn't
with me.'

He nodded. 'You had booked a single room.'

She persisted, 'But you *knew* where he had gone.'

Herr Bauer hesitated for a moment, before smiling.
It was then she realised that his smile seldom reached
his silver-grey eyes, which were almost transparent,
and never seemed to be still. They reminded her of
someone, but who? She couldn't think.

He said, 'I deduced. For where else do the romantic
go to jeopardise their lives today, not realising that
it is a cause that is surely already lost?'

She barely listened, so intent was she on remembering, and then it came to her. It wasn't someone,
it was Uncle Charlie's springer spaniels, looking,
scenting, alert, seeking, always seeking.

'Why did you say you were you in Arles, Herr
Bauer?'

He shrugged. 'I wasn't *in* Arles. I diverted to Arles
at the request of Colonel Potter, who wondered
perhaps if I would be in time to collect a package
of two young people. I only managed one, you.' He

nodded to his attaché case. 'I have business to attend to, as grown-up people do, Miss Brampton.'

His tone was ironic.

Stung, she retorted, 'He wouldn't let me go with him, when I've given up everything to *do* something, to stop the fascists. Franco is lucky, you Germans are helping him, and what are Britain and France doing? A big fat nothing to protect democracy. What else are you fascists and Nazis going to do, or should I say, to take, and that's not just me, but what Madame Beauchesne says, and a lot of people too?' She crossed her arms and slumped back as the train started.

He said nothing, merely began to read his newspaper again. She said, quietly, because another two people had found their way to seats near them, 'Anyway, what is Uncle Potty going to do to get James back?' She was scared now. 'He might get hurt.'

Herr Bauer continued to read the newspaper, or so she thought, but he said, still scanning the French news, 'I presume he thought about that before he went. You clearly didn't, which is why he showed a glimmer of sense when he refused to let you join him. Your friend, Uncle Potty, can only do so much to protect foolish young people from playing dangerous games. He hoped I would find you both. I haven't.'

'He's not a child, and neither am I. I'm nearly seventeen.'

He turned the page, the paper crackling. 'Then, Miss Bridget Brampton, may I beg you to start behaving like an adult, and cease to cause others to break from important tasks. You would do well to sit quietly and think about that, and how you are to rescue your life, and repair the trust you have damaged.'

Evie paced the deck of the ferry she had taken to Calais. The last time she had done this alone there had been hospital tents visible along the coast, the pounding of audible guns, and a heart that was clasped by an iron hand of fear. She had come to collect Gracie, who had been hurt by shrapnel, and amongst other things, had lost her ear. Now another hand clasped her heart, one that seared; full of disappointment, rage and worry.

As they drew into harbour she waited at the site of the gangplank, barely able to hold herself still in the face of so many conflicting emotions. It seemed an eternity for the ship to edge towards the quay, by which time the passengers were gathering either side, and behind her. She thought of all those who had embarked on the return journey along with Gracie so many years ago, the mutilated, the distraught, the exhausted. Here she was, fetching home an idiotic daughter, who had lied so convincingly about how she longed to take Easterleigh Hall forward, who had let James go off on some escapade during which he would, in all likelihood, be killed.

Bridie had not only facilitated him, but had conspired to go with him. How could she?

Evie dug her clenched hands into her jacket pockets and made herself count the wheeling gulls, and listen to the specifics of the chatter around her, or she'd . . . Well, she didn't know what she'd do, but she had to somehow find some control before she put one step onto the quay. But even as she thought that, Ver's devastation, Richard's misery and Aub's shock and pain added to her own, and swept over her like a crashing wave.

There was a jolt as the ferry closed on the quay. Hawsers secured it, the gangplank was set up. She clenched her fists tighter still as the excitement of the passengers surrounding her grew. She breathed deeply, telling herself that she must calm down, but instead she remembered Mrs Moore's heartbreak, her disbelief that the young woman she adored could make such plans and lie to their faces. It was then she spied her daughter standing against the press of people streaming away from the ferry. She stood alongside Herr Bauer near several bales of rope.

Evie stared at the bales, not at Bridie. Were they for transportation or a permanent fixture on the quayside? Above, the gulls still called and whirled, and passengers still streamed past her and down the gangplank. At last, when she was in control of herself, she joined them, still fixing her gaze on the bales. Once on the quay she stopped, standing to one side of the passenger stream, unable to move towards her daughter because love had caught and held her. Bridie looked so pale and exhausted, but still with her shoulders braced in defiance. She felt such pride, but such fury and disappointment, such enormous love, and pity. Dear God, where could they go from here when trust had been so badly damaged?

Herr Bauer strode towards her, a newspaper folded beneath his arm. She walked towards him. Bridie remained by the bales, as well she might. Herr Bauer lifted his hat, and stopped a mere two feet from Evie. He bowed slightly. 'The package is contrite, angry and feeling inordinately foolish and guilty, or so I think, Evie, if I may call you that?'

'Of course, Herr Bauer. I am so grateful to you, and to Colonel Potter, who has used his extraordinary contacts to pull the irons from the fire for us. And it is not the first time. He helped us in the war.'

'Ah, indeed. Yes, he asked me to make a slight diversion. It is of no consequence, but I must now resume my journey, just as you, my dear Evie, will probably re-embark on this ferry for the return trip? I wish you well with everything. The young are impetuous but seldom mean harm.' He bowed and left her, clipping along the quay, merely nodding at Bridie as he passed.

Evie saw Bridie lift her hand, as though it was very heavy, and call, 'Thank you, Herr Bauer. You have been very helpful and kind.' Evie's love soared again.

The passengers had all disembarked, and the last, an elderly man, limped in Herr Bauer's wake. Evie gestured to Bridie to join her, and as Bridie approached, the anger returned, and Evie spun on her heel and hurried back up the gangplank. She heard Bridie call, 'Mam, please wait for me.'

Evie couldn't wait. 'You've managed this far without any of us, Bridget, so just follow me, because I can't find the words to speak to you at this precise moment and until I do, I suggest you try to make good the hurt you've caused to those who love you.'

Two days later Bridie was leaning back on the wall of the indoor exercise arena in her jodhpurs, having mucked out the stables because she couldn't bear the ongoing silence in the kitchen any more. She watched Dave to the left of the mounting platform. He was in his wheelchair and talking to his blind friend, Daniel Forsyth. On the mounting platform Young Stan was guiding an older man with only one arm, and two legs, but one foot, onto the double saddle, with one of the under-gardeners standing at Terry's head.

Clive was standing on Terry's right-hand side, guiding the man's leg over the double saddle. She heard Clive saying, 'That's the way, Norman, you know the ropes. Matron said you're up to this, so that's that, you ruddy well are.'

Norman said something as Clive put his hand on his back, and Young Stan showed him how to hold the reins with just one hand. Clive laughed and said, 'You shouldn't use language like that or she'll deal with you in her own special way.'

Since her return, Aunt Ver and Uncle Richard had not spoken to her, beyond saying, almost in unison, 'What were you thinking? Why didn't you tell us his plans?'

Her mother had said nothing more on the ferry until they had set sail, and then, though the wind had been fierce, Bridie had heard the fury and hurt in her words, the accusations of betrayal towards Monsieur Allard, Madame Beauchesne, Bridie's friends, her family, herself. In reply, Bridie had screeched, 'Someone had to do something, the Republicans need me and James. And you did something too, when a cause needed you: you fought for votes; Da went to war.'

Her mother had held up her hand. 'You talked us into sending you to a prestigious institute, and then you used it to follow James. You left your horses and your patients, and *they* need you just as much, if not more, than the bloody International Brigade. Tim has never lied. He's just done what he needs to do, and not hidden who he is. That's what's wrong with you, madam.'

On her arrival home, Mrs Moore had whacked her with a wooden spoon across her knuckles, then wept. She had whispered, 'Bridget, what have you done?'

Since then, the kitchen had been virtually silent.

She had suggested macarons. Her mother had ignored her. She had suggested her version of mushroom soup. Again her mother ignored her, and Annie too had avoided her since her return. Maria and Estrella had been embarrassed, as though it was their fault. They had offered to leave. Evie would not hear of it. Bridie had written letters of apology to Madame Beauchesne, Monsieur Allard, Colonel Potter, and through him, Herr Bauer. Lastly she had telegraphed Lucy and Marthe and they had replied, missing her but enjoying the remainder of the course. It had hurt but she deserved it. Today, in her break, she had plucked up courage, at last, to visit the paddock.

No-one had looked up when she slipped through the entrance, but Terry had whinnied.

She heard the panic in Norman's voice, as Clive carefully removed his hand. Someone should be up behind him. Who would it be? Clive replaced his hand. Perhaps it would be no-one, but that wasn't wise. Clive must at least walk beside Norman. She stood upright, but said nothing. She had no right. Just as she had said nothing when her mother had held up Tim as a shining example. She had wanted to say that she had found him in Da's office, but she had promised she would not. That he had punched her, that . . .

She shook her head now. She had not because she had done worse: she had sent him away when Prancer died, and she had told no-one. Perhaps she should have done, because it wasn't her decision to have made.

'Well, are you helping or not? Don't just stand there miles away. I've said it twice and I won't again, young madam.' It was Dave, bawling across his wheelchair. 'I need someone up on the saddle, you runaway. You've had your adventure, stop feeling sorry for yourself and do something.'

Young Stan was grinning at her as he crouched down, next to Norman. 'She's been a bad, bad girl, has our Bridie. But we're all allowed to be, once in our life. Isn't that a fact, Norman?'

Norman said, as Bridie hurried across the paddock, kicking up the sand, 'I don't give a monkey's arse who does it, as long as someone does, before I fall off the bloody thing.'

She skirted round Dave's wheelchair, whispering, 'What's this I hear about you and Estrella? Fast worker, eh?'

Before he could pinch her, she was up the ramp, face to face with Young Stan, who looked her straight in the eyes, waiting. She murmured, 'I'm sorry—'

He shook his head. 'Louder, and face the front, so we can all hear, including Terry. He's missed you. None of *us* have, but *he* missed you.'

She breathed in, and pushed back her shoulders. 'I'm sorry,' she shouted, her voice reaching the back of the building. 'I'm right sorry. I should have thought of you more, all of you, and this.' She waved her hand around the exercise building. 'All of this,' she repeated. This time she gestured to Easterleigh Hall.

'And?' Dave called up. 'You haven't finished, Bridie.'

'I acted like a child. I thought I must do something, because no-one is doing anything, not really, to stop them: the Nazis in Germany, the fascists in Italy and Spain. But I ignored the fact that to do that I had to lie; I ignored the things and people who need me here.'

'And?' Dave called again.

'I'm sorry, alright? I've said I'm sorry. What more do you want?'

Dave was still looking up at her. 'I'm getting a crick in my neck waiting, Bridie. And?'

Terry shifted his weight; the under-gardener, who she remembered was called Ron, held his bridle; Norman gripped the saddle; while Clive held him. Young Stan squatted to reassure him, twisting round, saying, 'Get on with it, bonny lass. It's getting boring here, and me back's killing me.'

She didn't know what they wanted, and anger surged. 'Alright, I'm really sorry, but I still think James is doing what he thinks is right, just as everyone else has always done. Look at Mam with her votes, and Da with his war, and Aunt Gracie, and everyone. But I was wrong in the way I did it – I bloody know that – but I was still right. So bloody there.'

Young Stan looked down at Dave. They both nodded. Clive grinned; the under-gardener, Ron, laughed and rubbed Terry's nose. Norman said, 'Now she's said it, can we get on?'

'On you get, Bridie pet,' Young Stan ordered. She slid into the saddle behind Norman, in spite of being in her skirt. She clenched Terry with her knees, put her arms around Norman. 'You'll be fine, bonny lad,' she breathed.

He said, 'Aye, I'm getting better.'

Ron eased him forward, and she said quietly, 'Getting better?'

'Oh aye, it's a set-up, bonny lass. They wanted to get you back on track. Apologies are alright, but they wanted the real Bridie back.'

'Mam thinks that, too?'

Norman shrugged. 'That's another kettle of fish, lass. Have to wait and see on that, but I expect Estrella will be whispering any updates into Dave's ear.'

Bridie turned to look back at Dave, who was chatting earnestly to Young Stan and Clive, gesturing and pointing to the far corner of the building. She knew that he'd always thought a tack room should be set up here. 'I heard. It's really grand.'

'Aye, but shall we get a bit of a move on? Matron will be here to pick me up, and if we're dawdling about she'll be thinking her plan didn't work.'

Bridie laughed, knowing she was lucky to have these people, hoping that one day her family would forgive her, all of them. She thought of James, clambering over the Pyrenees, and she prayed he would be lucky too. Safe and lucky.

James, Ian and Archie waited at a farmhouse for a couple of weeks, while others arrived. It seemed forever since he had left Bridie. Finally, several of them went to Nîmes, where they took another bus. It was an old, beaten-up vehicle, which bumped along the lanes, its lights dimmed, until it turned onto a dry, hard-packed field. 'Alright, lads, let's be having you,' Stephen called. They filed from the bus. Stephen, who had only grunted at James since he had returned without Bridie, led the way in the dark. They walked for an hour, and finally saw another dark farmhouse, which looked deserted. Inside were two guides, and tables with pâté and bread and wine. There were more men sitting at the table. Stephen said to them, 'We have a few more for the International Brigade.'

They moved along the benches to make room. In all, there were about forty. Stephen said, 'Eat. Later we go over the mountains and into training.'

The murmur of voices gained momentum, as the various different nationalities chewed the cud. Some were communists, some socialists, some who just felt fascism should be stopped, and if their governments wouldn't, they would. They all talked, sitting in their language groups. All the time, James wondered about Bridie. Was she alright? Was she still crying? Did she phone home as she had promised? Would she forgive him?

He remembered the smell of her hair, the feel of her in his arms. He was in love with her, of course, which was crazy, because she was his cousin, his playmate, his best friend. But she was in love with Tim, and he wondered when she'd realise that.

Archie nudged him. 'Eat up, we have important things to do.'

'I know. That's why I'm here.' James nodded, as Ian held up the carafe of wine, and poured.

Chapter Seventeen

Spain, August 1937

At the farmhouse, at dawn on the third day, they were handed *alpargatas* – rope-soled sandals – that were useful for climbing, and what's more, as Ian said, no-one would 'ear a bleedin' thing. They were to wear their boots to start with, and change into the sandals in due course. With two guides in the lead, and Stephen walking at the head of their group, they began a long trek through lanes, past farmhouses, or hamlets. Sometimes dogs barked. No-one spoke because frontier guards were alert for groups such as theirs.

They cut alongside a field now, keeping their eyes on the man in front as the darkness deepened. James could hear running water, a mule brayed. He shrugged his pack straps into a more comfortable position and as he did so, he remembered the rope Uncle Aub had fixed to a branch across a dry, wide ditch for the three of them.

Out by themselves that afternoon, Bridie had swung through the air and fallen with a crash at the bottom of the ditch. For a moment he and Tim had thought she was dead, so quiet did she lie. When they rushed down to her, she was sobbing silently as blood spurted from her nose, her forehead and her shoulder, which had been pierced by a sapling that had snapped under the force of the fall. They'd had to lift her from it, and the blood had poured. Tim had ripped off his shirt and shoved it hard against the wound. 'Hold it,' he'd said to Bridie.

His thoughts were interrupted briefly by Stephen walking back along the length of the trail of men, repeating in a whisper, 'No clanging of water bottles. Keep them separate.'

Tim had carried Bridie at a run, to Home Farm barn. Uncle Aub had said nothing, though they had feared he'd tan their hides. Instead he'd bundled them all into his old jalopy of a car and driven like a lunatic to the Neave Wing. Dr Nicholls was in attendance, with Matron. Matron had sent them from the room. Aunt Evie had arrived, sent for by Sister Newsome. She had started to shout at the boys, 'How could you?'

Was that what she'd say to Bridie now? A stone clinked. A man cursed. Everyone froze. Then started again, bent over now, to make themselves smaller, though whether it would make the slightest bloody difference was a matter of opinion. Archie poked him from behind, and he grinned, then the smile faded at the thought of Uncle Aub, that day, holding Aunt Evie to him as she repeated, to the boys, not him, 'How could you?'

He had pressed her head to his chest, hushing her. 'I put it up. Bridie chose to swing on it. They didn't drag her to it. It happened and she'll learn to be more careful. It's no-one's fault, and therefore, my darling, neither is it yours. So, enough, and before you start on me it isn't my fault either. It just is.' They had all laughed.

Tim had stood there, his chest bloodied. Bridie had been stitched and bandaged and did not mention her fall again. She had just powered on.

They were now skirting a derelict shepherd's hut and the ground was inclining. They must be at the foot of the mountains. They were instructed to stop, and change from their boots into their *alpargatas*. They were then to tie the boots by their laces to their rucksacks, one to each side, so there was no chance of them clashing together. They set off again, with Stephen clapping them on the shoulder, whispering as they passed. 'I'll be off to pick up more of you hooligans but will come and see you while you're training. You are a grand bunch, keep your heads down.'

They kept going, and for a while James felt lost without their leader. A sliver of a moon lit their way and he thought again of his uncle that day, the way he had taken over. He and his marras had a wisdom, almost a weariness, as though they had seen the worst the world had to offer but had survived, and achieved a sort of calm. But was it calm? Because everyone was really still struggling, Uncle Jack and

Mart at the mine, the pitmen, young Jonny Earnshaw who they'd seen catching minnows on the bridge, with his da out of work, women too. Was that what peace was? If so, was anything worth fighting for, or against?

He walked on. The answer was yes. Sometimes you could not stand aside, but in the end life would be just as it always was: imperfect, some of it good, some of it loving. If they survived this, they would be lucky enough to know that it could have been worse, perhaps, if they had not stood against the bullies.

He shook his head. What a load of guff, surely he wasn't becoming like Uncle Edward? He'd need a pulpit next. He clambered on, following Ian, trying to keep to the path. He stumbled, caught his balance, righted himself, and as he did so, he saw Tim again, and his bloodied chest from carrying Bridie. He stopped, and Archie banged into him. 'You alright, James?' he hissed.

He moved on, but the image remained. What if Tim was here? What if they fought?

Ian half fell. James caught him.

'Jamie, you're a pal,' Ian whispered. 'My bloody feet've got blisters like I don't know what.' They laughed quietly together. James dropped in behind him again.

They only travelled little used trails, in order to avoid the non-intervention patrols. After two hours they halted for a brief rest. Ian touched the ground.

'This is France, soon it'll be Spain. Never thought I'd get this far. Don't seem real, some'ow.' James knew what he meant.

They set off again, and somehow he felt an inner peace, because he knew, now, that his Uncle Aub would calm his parents, as he had his wife after Bridie's fall, and that, when Bridie returned, she would be safe and Aub would not allow her to be blamed. It was as though a load had been taken from his shoulders and he could press on with all he had to do.

As the sky lightened towards dawn, it somehow teased scent from the trees. Dawn actually broke as they neared the summit. Mists drifted in and around rocky crags. He wished Bridie was here to see the colours, but he would tell her. They moved onwards, and the whisper went along the line, 'Almost there.'

Archie and he were helping Ian, who had almost collapsed in the thin air. Three others were similarly helped, but no-one had turned back. At the summit they lowered Ian. They would not be stopped now, because they had reached Spain and would carry the fight to the enemy. What would he do if he saw Tim? Could he fire? He knew he could not. Would Tim fire? He didn't know, that was what was so awful. He just didn't know.

Ian ate some of the biscuits that they all carried, and managed the descent into Spain. It was afternoon when they reached the foothills and started to pass elderly Catalonian farm workers who clenched their fists and shouted, *'Salud, camaradas.'* The sun beat down, the light was harsh, as they approached a mountain outpost. The pace quickened, and their guides were greeted like old friends and so too the group of volunteers. One of their guides shouted, 'Fall out. Trucks come soon, *camaradas.'*

Archie eased off his rucksack and pointed to the stream. 'Last one in's a cissy.'

The race was on. The clothes came off, the bodies went in, and the feel of the rushing water as it powered down to the plain washed away the exhaustion, and the aches, and the life before. The trucks arrived after they had dressed, and they bumped along the track for an hour or so, to a sign off to the right, *Las Brigadas Internacionales* – The International Brigade. They pulled up eventually at a large stone building. The guide in their truck called, 'These your barracks. Climb staircase at end, iron one, outside.'

Ian murmured, 'Not more bloody climbing.'

James laughed. 'No help this time, my lad. The air's thick enough to get into even your weak muscles.' They jumped down onto the dusty ground.

'Speak for yourself.' Ian threw his *alpargatas* at him. Archie, in turn, threw one of his at Ian.

They all ran towards the barracks, dodging *alpargatas* and returning fire, up the staircase and into the dormitory, and soon the whole room was awash with flying sandals, until an Australian bawled from the open doorway, 'Wonderful, damn it, we leave you ankle biters for a ruddy minute, and you're playing games.' He cast a long shadow in the afternoon sun.

'Ankle biters?' queried the communist, Otto, who had been chased out of Munich in '34.

Archie replied, 'I rather think he means two-year-olds or younger.'

'Ah,' the Australian replied, entering and looking around at them. 'We have an adult amongst us, I see. Well, you're boss for the moment. Get this lot across to the mess room in the building opposite so we can get some tucker down you before training begins.'

Ian called, 'But we ain't slept for more'n twenty-four hours.'

'Well, a few more hours won't hurt, then, will it?'

The Australian marched out, his boots crashing on the rough wooden floor, his wide-brimmed hat pulled down against the light. They put their boots on and followed Archie down the steps. He stood at the edge of the square, pointing doubtfully across to the building. They strolled towards it, until the Australian appeared in the doorway of the building and roared, 'At a bloody run, if you don't bloody mind.'

James did mind, actually, but he said nothing, just ran with the others, clattering into the mess room in their boots, then doubled back out again at a scramble as the call came, *'avion'* – aircraft.

The Australian called from behind, 'Run, to the

slit trenches to the left at the edge of the square. Left, you bleeding idiot, I said.' Archie had run right.

They dived into the trenches, scanning the skies, Guernica and Bilbao in their minds, but the planes passed and no bombs dropped, this time. James stared at the ants running along a narrow ledge in the trench wall. They were unaware. He closed his eyes for a moment and heard his grandma's voice: 'All is well.' *I bloody well hope so, Grandma*, he said silently as he followed the others back to the mess room, his legs trembling, not with tiredness, but from fear.

The next day they signed on as soldiers of the Spanish Republican Army, and the days took on a uniform pattern of being 'bugled' awake in order to rush to the water trough, wash, then to the mess room to gulp down coffee and bread, probably to be interrupted by another air alarm. Then, to form into squads for firearms instruction and drill.

In the evenings they had to learn enough Spanish to follow orders in the field. Also in the evenings, they played football, though chess was Ian's passion: he had lugged a set along in his rucksack, and found several opponents to thrash. 'Crazy bloody English,' snarled the Australian, Sergeant Neil Coffey, then proceeded to sit down and beat the lot of them.

On the seventh day a load of uniforms and boots arrived, which in no way, shape, or form, fitted. Sergeant Coffey handed out needle and thread. 'You sat at your mother's knees, so get sewing.'

The *avion* warnings continued, and each time James watched the ants rushing along their ledge in the trench, just as they had done at home. On one particularly hot day, he had crouched with Bridie in the height of the summer, when the ground by the beck had cracked. The ants emerged, one after the other. These were not the ants they knew, but ones that had wings, and which took off, in a sort of swarm, at which he and Bridie had run screaming. So they must have been really young. How young?

He searched the skies now, and the ground shuddered, but the bombs were falling some distance away. How long would their luck hold? He watched the sand in the walls of the trench trickle down. Were they Nazis or Italian bombs? Were the Republican Russian airplanes bombing Franco's men? He concentrated on the ants, remembering he must have been about ten, and Bridie only five. Where had Tim been?

He remembered now. Tim'd been swimming in the beck, and had clambered out, rushing after them, grabbing them with his wet hands, pulling them to him. He must have been about twelve or a bit older. 'What?' he said, his face scared. 'What? Are you hurt?'

They had told him, and he had held them both to him for a moment, and it hadn't mattered that Tim was cold and wet, and they became so too. It was enough that he was there. Tim said, 'They're the males, the drones, and there'll be a female, a queen, too. They're looking to start a new home, a new place, that's all. They're not looking for you.'

They had all traipsed back, but they couldn't find a single ant. 'They've gone,' said Tim. 'So, into the beck, all of us, and Bridie, you must swim to the other side by the time I've counted ten.' She had done so, and James had felt quite safe.

These must be the workers, he thought as he watched the ants, as another wave of planes flew over. The drones might come out any minute and fly, and if they did, so what? He wasn't about to start running about screeching. There were far more ugly buggers flying about these days.

The all-clear whistle sounded.

Tim was in the corner pub, the one near his bedsit in Newcastle. Why the hell was August so bloody hot? It was the twenty-seventh, so surely it should be cooling down by now? He'd had four pints, but he needed more: to sleep, to get through the days, to live, really. Work was busy, thank the lord, as more orders were reaching them from around the world, for the rich were always demanding, and yachts were still being built. Now much bigger ships were being built, but not here – in Germany.

His boss, Mr Andrews, had wondered today what he'd do if he got an order from the Nazis. Tim hoped he'd turn it down, as the very thought of Germany brought back the nightmares of the beatings, and the cell, the death, and the final sight of Avraham as he was taken through the double doors, of Heine, and his mother, and her silver, and her use of him, her supposed love, which he very much doubted had ever existed.

He moved his glass around, feeling it skate in the spilled beer. It was summer bank holiday on Monday, and he wanted to be lolling over the rails of the exercise paddock with Bridie and James, working out how they could get more horses, what they could do now that Prancer was gone. It had been the lovely old grey who had trained Fanny and Terry, really. Yes, Bridie had done a lot, but it was Prancer who would nip them, and keep them on the straight and narrow.

He felt the cold of the cell, saw again the light fading from Otto's eyes. He reached into his pocket and fingered Avraham's mezuzah case. Maybe he should ditch it. It might help him to leave it behind, but in a way, he didn't want to forget. As long as he had it Avraham existed.

The ashtray was full of his stubs, and the air in the pub was its usual smog. A bloke was playing 'Begin the Beguine' on the piano, and he bloody well hoped no-one was going to get up and sing. He rose, staggered and grabbed the back of the chair, then gathered himself and fought his way through the crowd towards the bar. Sunny the barman, tea towel slung over his shoulder and cigarette wedged in the corner of his mouth, eyed him. 'Haven't you had enough, Tim?'

Tim shook his head, digging in his pocket for money, blinking as he counted it out and tipped it onto the bar. Sunny handed him his pint. 'Make it your last, there's a good lad.'

He sipped it, standing there. Someone jogged him. 'Watch your bloody self,' he growled.

'Sorry, man.' The customer was reaching forward to pay.

Sunny warned, 'Go and sit down, Tim. Now.'

He did so, dragging out his packet of cigarettes – not the case Heine had given him, because he'd realised on his return that the faded insignia was a menorah, a Jewish candlestick. One day he'd go back and find the Jews to whom the apartment had belonged, and all the goods within it, like this.

He lit up and chucked the match in the ashtray, inhaled deeply, exhaled, then coughed. He should eat, of course. His boss had said his clothes were hanging off him.

His mother had written from Berlin, nagging him about finding the letter again. He said he was hunting for it as they had insisted. He was really busy with work, which meant he couldn't go to Hawton meetings, but he was keeping his fingers on the pulse. It seemed easier, and something – he didn't know what – stopped him from cutting the ties completely.

He had also told Sir Anthony that he was too busy to go to the Peace Club meetings at the moment. Sir Anthony had said, 'I understand. We'll be pleased to see you, Tim, when you can manage. Peace and co-operation are more important than ever.'

Tim had wanted to bang the table, and say, 'Open your eyes, you silly old fool. Do you think the fascists sitting round your table are reasonable people? Listen to them.' But perhaps they were. Perhaps they were on the trail of peace – but at what price?

He drank the tankard dry. He wanted his dad to be here, so much, so he could tell him what had happened, and apologise. He wanted his mam to clutch his hands in hers, and say fiercely, 'We love you. We knew you'd come back. You have just made a mistake, like we all do.'

Well, he'd tried after Prancer died, but perhaps it was too early. Bridie must have been there to send him away. One day, he'd try again.

He staggered to the bar, and Sunny relented. 'Just the one more, and go and see someone about those nightmares you told me about, or talk to your da. He'll have had 'em after the war, like me. He'll understand.'

Sunny said this every night. Tim counted out his money, the coins tipping into the spilled beer. He took the pint, sipped it, and was jogged again as a bloke muscled alongside. Tim said nothing, just staggered back to his seat.

At Easterleigh Hall kitchen, Bridie waited by the scullery door. It was Friday evening, and they'd been busy preparing for the summer bank holiday weekend, but her da had sent a note to everyone insisting that they be here at ten o'clock. Her mam, Auntie Ver and Mrs Moore sat on their stools. Uncle Richard, Harry, Annie and Ron stood around, all busy with their own thoughts, from the look of it. The kitchen and scullery staff, including Maria and Estrelle, sat in the staff hall across the passage.

Bridie heard his car enter the yard, then the slam of the door. She clasped her hands in front of her, as though she didn't care. Was he going to shout at her again as he had done when she'd arrived home, chastising her for lying, and for causing them such worry about her well-being? Well, that at least would be a change from the continuing frostiness here. Just how many times did she have to apologise? Well, she couldn't do it any more. She felt her throat contract, but she wouldn't cry.

Her da entered, pulling off his gloves. 'Lovely evening,' he said. 'The harvest is finally in, and the drive over from Home Farm was delightful.'

The others turned to look at him. Mam and Auntie Ver had poured cognac into goblets, and his waited for him at the head of the table. Bridie's tea was cooling on the corner of the dresser, where she'd left it. Mrs Moore was sipping hers. Her da pulled out the stool and sat. He picked up the goblet, breathed in the scent of cognac.

He snatched a look at Bridie, and she watched his face twist with sadness, and then anger. He raised his glass, looked at each in turn, including Bridie. 'Cheers.'

They raised their glasses, and Mrs Moore her tea. Bridie didn't reach for her mug. What was the point? 'This has to stop,' her da said, keeping his voice friendly and calm. 'I will not have Bridie penalised for James' decision, or, any more, her own actions.'

Bridie stood ramrod straight. Her mam also straightened, slamming her glass down onto the pine table, opening her mouth. 'No,' her da insisted. 'Evie and Ver, you went in to bat for votes, without a by your leave to anyone. You didn't come out into the open, if I remember rightly? Remember, Ver, you didn't share your suffrage activities with our step-mother. And Evie, you changed your surname in order to work here because my father didn't like the Forbes family.'

Auntie Ver shouted, 'Fighting for votes wouldn't get us killed – well, only in some rare instances.'

Richard moved round the table and put his arm around her. 'But joining the army, as we did, could. Listen to your brother, for pity's sake.'

'Exactly,' Aub said. 'Our daughter was loyal; she didn't give away her cousin's intentions at any stage. She lied, I agree, so that she could follow her beliefs. So?'

He held the balloon glass to his lips, breathing in the scent, then sipped from it. 'I've been thinking hard about this ever since Bridie returned, and I want you to ask yourselves how what she's done is different from what anyone around the table has done, really? Yes, you're worried about James, and were worried about her. Yes, you're embarrassed that she attended the Institute and used them. Yes, you're embarrassed that she used Madame Beauchesne, but have you spoken to either of them, other than to write blathering apologies on top of Bridie's?'

The two women looked down at the table. The others shuffled, embarrassed at the family palaver. Her da shook his head, and she was amazed, because even when he'd shouted at her, he had not been this annoyed.

'Well, I have. Lucien Allard applauds her endeavour, both as a student and as a person who wanted to do what our assembled governments won't: to defend democracy. Even dear old Sir Anthony is involving himself in the international situation, in the wrong way, with the wrong people, in my opinion, but he is addressing it.'

'But . . .' Auntie Ver spluttered.

'I have also spoken to Madame Beauchesne. She feels that Bridie's heart was completely in the right place. If Captain Beauchesne had been alive, she feels he would have driven her to the Pyrenees himself. What's more, he'd have carried on with the pair of them to do his bit. As for the lies, she says, "pouf".

'So, I repeat, this stops now. Evie, my darling, Bridie is our daughter, she is so like you and I doubt you would have done anything different. Ver, your son is his own person, just as you were, and Richard.'

He held his glass towards Bridie. 'Bridie, another time, you must trust us enough to tell us the truth. We might try to talk you out of it, and indeed, we would have forbidden you until you were older, but you can see that on this occasion we would have been right. James turned you away at the behest of his leader, for your safety, and theirs. I suspect that this has made you an adult. If not, then see that it does, by the morning. Do we have an understanding, everyone.'

His voice was such that they knew it wasn't a question.

He looked at Mrs Moore and they shared a smile. At that moment Bridie knew that they had decided on this plan of action together, and she wouldn't be surprised if Matron hadn't also been in on the act. Now she reached for her tea, and sipped it. It didn't matter that it was almost stone-cold. She listened as everyone chatted, and it was as though a safety valve had been released as the men talked about how the Japanese were occupying Peking, and the women contributed, and then moved on to tomorrow's menu.

No-one had spoken to her yet, or even met her eyes. Her father, however, was smiling at her, and she loved him to the sky and back down again, just as she always had. Her mother called out, 'Let's try that mushroom soup soon, shall we Bridie pet?'

Bridie smiled, 'Aye, Mam. Let's.' She was forgiven. Her mam was gesturing to her.

'Come and tell us how to do it again. Your da is quite right. We were wrong. Ver and I would have done the same. I'm sorry, dearest girl.'

Ver smiled at her, pale from worry about her son. 'Of course, Bridie. I don't know about *you* needing to grow up, but certainly there are a few of us here who do. I should be the first, methinks.'

Bridie smiled. It seemed over, but it wasn't, because she hadn't told the truth about Tim. He had come but she had sent him away. She put her tea down and opened her mouth, but she could say nothing. Not now, or it would all start again, and she was too tired, too upset, too worried.

Chapter Eighteen

Spain, Mid-September 1937

James sat in the back of the truck, clinging on to the rifle propped up between his legs. Archie was looking at the mountains, which seemed just a stone's throw but were much further.

'So,' drawled Frank, the American. 'What d'ya reckon advanced training means? More running, more press-ups, more God-awful pasta. It's alright for you, Jamie boy, with all your ploughing and hedging, and whatever the hell else you did for your uncle, but us lot, from offices . . .' The grimace said it all.

James rested his chin on his hands, which formed a cushion on top of the rifle butt. The barrel was well oiled, the stock shiny. Ian nudged him. 'Studying yer navel again, are yer? Shouldn't bother. It's the same as it was yesterday.'

James grinned. Ian had struggled with basic training because the most exercise he said he usually got was putting his Woodbine to his gob. He'd kept at it, and swallowed Sergeant Coffey's orders for extra press-ups and joked his way through. He was the best shot in the platoon, a fact that had surprised them all, especially Ian. He'd said, 'I just imagine it's your bum, Sergeant Coffey, and it all happens.'

He was given extra press-ups, yet again, but he maintained it was worth it.

Today, when they'd left the compound, the others saluted Sergeant Coffey, then waved as the truck revved away. Ian, however, bowed and bellowed, 'You're a right bastard, but you're our bastard and I have muscles to prove it. I s'pose I'm to be grateful.'

The others had dragged him down, and for the first time, Sergeant Coffey had laughed.

On their arrival at a barracks in the lea of a hill, they were greeted by Sergeant Miller and Corporal Badia, a Catalan. They led them through ever more rigorous terrain, while a platoon of Badia's Catalans ambushed or sniped at them with blanks. James began to realise even more clearly why his uncles and father were different from those who had not been at war.

The following week they were trained in light machine guns, which they fired until the barrels grew hot, and each evening some of the platoon was allowed into the nearby village. Finally it was the turn of their group. Together with Frank and Boyo, they headed down the track towards the lamplight, hearing the accordion playing, and discordant voices, long before they arrived. They drank wine and cognac at the café, as moths batted at the lamps.

Men were entering a house opposite the café, then leaving half an hour later. 'A brothel,' Ian declared. 'Who's up for it?' None were. Instead they drank steadily, quietly, and again James took himself back to Easterleigh Hall: its formal gardens, the herbaceous beds on the front lawn, the arboretums. To watch things grow was precious.

He wondered if David was helping Bridie with the injured. How did you go through life in a wheelchair? Would that happen to him? Then his thoughts moved on to the horses, and he wondered how Terry was working out, and if he had Prancer's sense of care.

They staggered back, drunk as skunks, and it felt good. Sergeant Miller met them at the gate and insisted, 'Water, lads, lots of it, or you'll want me to chop your heads off in the morning. Why? We've had the signal. Up at sparrow fart, if you please, ready and willing to join the British Battalion.'

They set off in a convoy of trucks at dawn, taking a last sip of decent coffee in the mess room, and grabbing the half loaf they were to take with them. They stuffed it in their packs with their water bottles, their heads throbbing in spite of the water. Sergeant Miller travelled in the back of the truck with them, Corporal Badia in another.

They ignored their aching heads and constantly searched the terrain, as they'd been taught. They scanned the sky, and listened as they roared through canyons, up hills and along valleys, dotted with trees and bushes, and the occasional small wood. Who knew what was hiding in there? They were on alert as never before. Finally, as evening fell, they pulled into a camouflaged lay-by in a long valley.

They jumped from the truck and followed Miller at a run, up a gentle incline that was hidden by trees and shrubs until they reached Battalion HQ, which was a ramshackle stone farmhouse. The exhausted adjutant, in a uniform as shabby and ad hoc as their own, allocated them to different companies. Archie, Ian and James were designated to No. 4 Company, along with Frank and Boyo.

The HQ was set up amongst trees and bushes, and all around were *chabolas*, or lean-tos. They were directed to B Company lines. Their section leader, Alan Douglas from Sussex, pointed towards the spot where they could erect their own shelter. He told them to lay their blankets out on the pine needles, and sleep. 'You'll eat in the morning, so no complaints; you've had some bread, Miller tells me.'

He stomped on, pretending not to hear the groans, and Ian's voice, 'Ray of bleedin' sunshine, that bloke.'

James slept immediately, and it seemed only seconds later they were woken by a bugle and heard their section leader, Douglas, calling, 'You lot, jump to it. Get to the ablutions early and you'll stay clean. At the bloody run, lads.'

They diverted on their return to pick up axes, because today they were to build their *chabolas*, having grabbed bread and cheese from the mess hall. They ate as they headed into the pine trees and James knew he would not be heading home to university because, he told himself, he had done nothing to earn such a luxury.

Later that afternoon he talked to Sergeant Miller, who said he'd try and get a letter out of Spain, via the guides back at base training. They'd take it back to France to send from there.

'They'll do their best, they always do.'

He slept soundly again, the letter written, and his mind at rest.

Two days later they marched at night and rested under cover by day. As they marched they kept to the sides of the tracks when the occasional truck passed. In the light from the moon they could see the red crosses on the canvas. The next night, with the valley starting to box in, they headed, footsore, into the dawn, hearing sounds of firing probably just a half kilometre distant, if that. They hunkered down by a dried-out river bed, looking for, and eventually finding, water in potholes, then clambered up towards the shade of a small outcrop. The mountains blurred in the far distance.

They chewed at their dry crusts and sipped their water, always alert, examining the landscape, and James couldn't believe they were actually going into action, heading for the front line. He slumped into his little bit of shelter, a dip he had found, and stared up at the early morning sky – and then rifle fire cracked, machine guns chattered, mortars exploded all around. They smelt the explosives, heard Miller roaring, 'Take cover, take cover.'

Men were shouting; rifles were firing at the enemy flashes on the opposite slope. The *avion* whistle blew, and the planes with German crosses came over, strafing and bombing, but their aim was off, and by mistake they pounded the opposite hill. James felt the ground shudder, the percussion hitting his eardrums, and saw the dust and debris fill the sky. He heard the screams too and for a moment he froze.

Archie yelled, 'Bloody German planes, couldn't hit a bloody barn, they couldn't.'

'Shut your noise,' roared Miller. 'Keep your head down, they'll be back.'

The *avion* whistle blew again after they had been returning fire for a few hours, pinned down by the enemy. James hugged his dip, feeling sand in his mouth. He saw Ian doing the same, behind a bush. James put his arms over his head as this time the road caught some of the fire, but now it was catching the lower slopes on their side.

The screams rose, the ground shuddered, the smell of burning was overlaid by cordite, and above it all, the roar of the engines, the shadows of the wings. The planes roared on, and they heard Miller yelling, 'Follow me, up and over the hill, while we've a smokescreen. We'll work our way down the slope to the front line. At the double, before they return.'

They scrambled up and over the top, through the dust, smoke and debris, and James' legs were weak from fear. He slipped and slid down, hanging on to his rifle, keeping it clean and functioning.

Almost at the bottom, a Lieutenant Mieras gestured them forwards, towards the front line. Bloody hell, they were really doing it. The fear deepened as James followed the others, bent over, still slipping on the slope, between the clumps of olive trees and scrubs. Ian was panting at his elbow. James swung round, almost knocking Ian off his feet. 'Where's Archie?'

Ian looked confused. 'What? Can't hear. The blast caught me lug 'oles.'

Miller was shrieking, much as he did when someone turned left instead of right on the parade ground. 'What the hell are you two doing? This is no time for a cosy bloody chat. We're needed at the front. We need to hold it or the fascists will outflank all our forces.'

'It's Archie, Sarge,' James called as he ran on, his pack banging on his back, the sun burning his head. Damn it, he'd lost his hat without realising.

Sergeant Miller waved them forward, looking calm, as though daring any bugger to shoot him. 'Sorry, lads, he bought it. Saw it myself.'

They reached the forward battle zone by late afternoon. The fascists had been repulsed but were ensconsed on the hills either side and ahead. Immediately B Company received orders to follow Miller to the foot of Hill 300, eastern sector. They were to be an advance party, and must dig in, and warn of any incursion.

It was cloudy, and the darkness gave them cover to crawl forward on their bellies, up the lower slopes. With each yard James saw Archie's face. He felt grief and rage, and he didn't care if Tim was at the top of the hill, because if he came upon him he'd crack his rifle butt across his bastard fascist face. His leather ammunition pouch caught on the rough ground and made a scraping noise. He froze. Just then the clouds moved and the moon lit the terrain like a spotlight. Machine gun fire chattered. There was a shout, a grunt.

The cloud came over, the firing continued, but so did they, crawling forward, fury in their bellies. There were shouts, groans, and orders to keep going. There was another shout, a muffled scream. The man nearest James was hit. Christ, not Ian? He hissed, 'Who is it?'

'Tommy,' came the reply.

James slid across to the lad. 'Where are you hit?'

'Leg.' Tommy was panting.

Ian joined them as James drew out his handkerchief, dyed black so it wouldn't be visible, and tied off the leg. 'The medics'll be along,' he whispered. He and Ian shared Tommy's ammunition pouches and grenades, and crawled on. The mortars had fixed on the main force coming up behind them, and in the light of the explosions they lay low as the shells roared over them, then crawled on when the light had dimmed.

Miller was everywhere, directing, organising and encouraging the small advance party, and they all found some sort of cover as mortars, machine guns and rifles fired down on them from the hills either side. There was a pillbox just under the summit over to the left; the machine gun was in there. Miller nudged Ian. 'Prove yourself, man. Shoot the bugger.'

Ian steadied himself, and when the next round flashed from the slit he fired. The firing stopped, but now there was movement at the base of the pillbox, and they both fired round after round until their rifle bolts were too hot to handle. The advance guard were pinned down as firing from the right grew steadily stronger and they dug in deep, as ordered. As dawn arrived the barrage continued over them, and there was desultory return fire from the Republicans, but so far no infantry attack.

To their left was the now silent pillbox; in front were neglected terraces that sloped away, their vines ruined. To the right were some olive and pine trees, and it was from there the firing still came. The hair prickled on the back of James' neck. Ian, who made it his business to stay beside him at all times, whispered, ''Ere we are, sitting like bloody ducks, so what do we bloody do if they come? Say 'ello and ask 'em for a bleedin' cuppa?'

Sergeant Miller crawled to them on his way who knew where, and grunted, 'What you do is stop your bellyaching and use your eyes and ears to catch the first sight or sound of feet on the ground heading our way. Then we set off the flares.' He handed one to Ian. 'It'll give the main force time to sort themselves out while we hold 'em off. Crucial, you are, young Ian. Could be the high point of your miserable and possibly short life.'

'Always a comedian,' Ian grunted, as Miller crawled on his way. Their group, including Frank and Boyo, scraped out the ground beneath them over the course of the long day, until they had an excuse for a trench. All the while the enemy artillery roared over them, aiming for the main force. The ground shuddered, the noise deluged them, and shrapnel flew.

The setting of the sun brought hope of some respite, but another night passed with more of the same. The next day, the enemy infantry came in a rush, and Miller set off his flare, shouting for Ian and another man to do likewise. The pillbox and the firing from the right kept their heads down, so they didn't know if the enemy was charging from the front. They clutched their rifles to them, while the pillbox machine gun chattered, and bullets spattered and hissed around them.

Suddenly the gunfire stopped, and the enemy charged past them in a rush. The men aimed their rifles, but from nowhere another squad came from the rear, shouting in English, 'It's over. Hold your fire.'

James and the others spun round, then half

lifted their rifles, but it was suicide. Just then Miller shouted and raged at the fascists from his trench, diverting their attention for a moment. James and Ian tried to heel their army papers into the bottom of the trench to avoid giving any information to the enemy, but the ground was too damned hard.

The soldiers left Miller to others, and booted and jabbed with their rifle butts until James' squad were out of the trench, while one of the fascists collected up the papers. They were threatened with death if they didn't run to the olive trees. They all ran, Miller too, then on down the slope until they were in the valley, their guards in close order around them. All the while the main Republican force engaged the enemy.

Miller said quietly, 'Well done, lads. We let them know in time.'

In the valley they were robbed of everything worth a farthing. Their boots were taken and tried on for size by the enemy troops before being tied by the laces and slung round their new owners' necks. In return the Republicans were given stinking ancient *alpargatas*, their hands were tied behind their backs, and they were herded like goats further along the valley, rifle butts jabbing at them and punches landing. There was no food, and no water. Their tongues swelled.

Every minute James wondered how he could walk because his legs were shaking so much, and Ian said, far too often, 'Makes me realise me old dad wasn't so bad after all.'

Miller tried to keep their spirits up. 'It'll be better when we're in a proper camp, lads,' he told them, then, his voice low, 'but keep yourselves alert. If the opportunity presents itself, be ready to make a break for it.'

Chapter Nineteen

Easterleigh Hall, November 1937

It was early November and nothing had been heard from James. 'So, he's staying in Spain, fighting, not exploring the Classics,' Bridie murmured as she waited for her turn to stir the Christmas cake mixture.

Her mam looked up from grating orange peel for today's menu, wild duck à l'orange. 'Keep making the cakes, it's all you can do.'

'He said he'd be in touch,' Bridie complained. 'If they can get into Spain, letters can get out. I should have made him come back.'

'Hush, we're not going through all that again. Anyway, Ver and I have come round to his way of thinking, and yours, that we should all do something, so we've written to the letter pages of the newspapers, all of them. Needless to say, they haven't been published.'

Ver stopped stirring the cake, having made her wish, her knuckles white on the spoon. Mrs Moore took it. She in her turn stirred then handed the spoon to Bridie. 'Make it a good wish, lass.'

Bridie made her wish, which was twofold: one for James' safety, and one for Tim's safe return to them. She lifted out the spoon, and some mixture dropped back into the bowl. She said quietly, 'I made two. Is that going to weaken the wishes?' Panic gripped her.

Gracie took the spoon and stirred. 'Don't worry, Bridie, I've done the same.' She handed the spoon to Maisie, Mart's wife, who was pregnant for the first time, and feeling exhausted, as she wasn't a young thing any more, as Matron had pointed out.

Her mother laughed, but it was strained. 'It wouldn't dare weaken, not with this monstrous regiment stirring like mad. Potty is telephoning with what news he can glean of James' whereabouts from his extraordinary contacts. We will wait. Our wish could have been answered.'

In Richard's study, along the internal corridor, he, Jack, Mart, Charlie and Aub sat around his desk, waiting for the phone to ring. Potty had said he'd get back to them by three with what news he could find out about James. The phone rang, on the dot of three. Richard picked it up, pale, with sweat beading his forehead. 'Hello, Potty.'

As always, Potty's voice was so loud that Richard held the phone away from his ear, wincing. 'Dear boy, I've burrowed like the little hamster I am, if indeed they burrow, and good news, though somewhat of a déjà vu, if you get my drift?'

Richard shook his head, as though to clear it, an

action mirrored by the others, and he wondered how his old friend had bumbled along in the military for so long, though he seemed to spend most of his time swanning around his clubs as far as Richard could tell. Well, maybe that was where his contacts also swanned. 'I don't altogether follow your drift, Potty. Perhaps you could elucidate?' Why the hell did he get all long-winded when he was talking to Potty?

'Elucidate?' Potty boomed. Richard winced and held the phone even further away. 'Indeed I will. The old dear is a prisoner, held by the delicious and delightful cream of Franco's mob.'

The others stared at one another. Somehow they had all been hoping he was on his way home.

Richard looked up at Aub. 'What can we do?' he murmured.

Aub shook his head. 'I don't know.'

Potty bawled, 'Can do nothing this end, old son.'

Richard shook his head, trying to think, desperation clouding his mind, a mind too full of Estrella's tales, some of which she'd witnessed, of captured prisoners being starved, beaten and shot.

Just then, the women came in. 'We heard the telephone,' Ver said, coming to Richard's side.

'Just a moment, would you, Potty?' Richard put his hand across the mouthpiece. 'He's a prisoner, but Potty can do nothing, only give us information, which is good of him, of course.'

Bridie was staring at him, and suddenly reached

over and snatched the receiver. 'Uncle Potty, you have Bauer. Can't he do something?'

Potty's voice was very quiet now. He said, 'Bridie, I believe. Well, young lady, I don't *have* Herr Bauer, as you say. He was good enough to help you, when I understood him to be visiting a mutual business acquaintance. I am actually merely on nodding terms. I repeat, I barely know the man. Do you understand? Now pass me back to your uncle, if you please.'

His voice was at full volume as he spoke to Richard, so they all heard him say, 'I repeat, I can do nothing, but it's best for the laddie if someone can; we've heard tricky stuff's being done – by both sides, it has to be said. You have someone who perhaps *can* help, of course. A someone who has a contact in Berlin who might be able to hoick him to safety. Perhaps you should ask that someone. I refer of course to young Tim. Now, must away, lots to do, people to see, and a nice Pudding Club meeting to attend later.' There was a click. Richard replaced the receiver.

After a moment, he looked up at his wife, then his gaze went slowly from Gracie to Jack.

Mart, Charlie and Aub ranged themselves alongside Jack. Mart protested, 'You know how difficult that is, Richard. I was there, in the club. He didn't even come when Jeb phoned him to tell him Prancer had died, and we'd be at the field and needed him. He did nothing.'

Jack held out his hand to Gracie, who came to stand with him. 'Perhaps we could try again,' she said, her voice shaking. 'It's James we're talking about. Maria and Estrella tell such stories.'

Bridie slipped to the door, feeling so hot, she thought she'd melt. She wanted to leave. She felt for the door, but her mother saw her, and reached out. 'Bridie, pet. Don't worry, we'll find a way.'

Bridie didn't look at her, but at Gracie, who was still standing with Jack, gripping his arm. It had gone on too long. Bridie said, 'I didn't know then that Tim was responding to a message. He came, you see, on his motorbike, to the lane when Prancer died. I thought he'd come to be unkind again. I said he wasn't wanted, and he was to go and stop dripping his poison, because things were bad enough without that.'

There was utter silence, and she waited. Please, please don't make me say it again, she begged silently, and please don't hate me. I hate myself enough for the whole room. Gracie turned. Jack put his hand out, but she tore free and ran, pushing Evie to one side, and slapped Bridie right across the face, before Jack could reach her. Then he was dragging Gracie off while Aub stood between Gracie and Bridie, looking at Gracie, his hand out, but speaking to Bridie. 'Bridie, are you sorry?'

Bridie's nose was bleeding. 'Yes, I'm sorry. Of course I'm sorry.'

Her father said, 'Did you ever tell Uncle Jack and Aunt Grace that Tim punched you at Old Bert's Field and cracked your ribs? Did you tell anyone, ever?'

She shook her head. 'No. James was there, and we said nothing.'

Jack looked shocked. Gracie had begun to cry, wailing, 'Oh, Bridie, why didn't you say?'

'Because it wasn't him, not really, or I didn't think it was, to begin with, but then I saw he enjoyed it, so how could I tell anyone that? But his face was different when Prancer died. I should have seen it. I didn't. I just kept seeing him when he hit me, and I knew how mean he'd been to you. It was enough that Prancer was dead, without more. I'm sorry. I wanted to tell you, but I was a coward.'

Her father said, 'No, you were not a coward. I failed you. I could tell there was something from the way you moved, and I made it my business to ask general questions about the melee at Old Bert's Field, but nothing more.'

Evie was with her now, leading her from the room, but Gracie came after her with the other women. Gracie slipped her arm around her. 'Poor Bridie. Let's clean you up. I'm so very sorry, about it all. How could he? How could I? What's happening, that's what I keep thinking: to the world, to him, and now, to me? Where on earth is it all going to end?'

Though her nose throbbed, Bridie felt as though a darkness was lifting. James was a prisoner, and not dead, and Jack would talk to Tim, and they might all be friends again. It wouldn't matter if he couldn't help, because she knew that if he was the old Tim, he would at least try.

She said, 'I'm sure he felt sorry when he came, because now I see him, I see myself when I came back from Arles. I'm so sorry, everyone, and so sorry for Tim. I need to tell *him* that, too.'

Mart, Charlie and Aub walked with Jack to the indoor exercise yard, drawing up their collars in the whipping easterly wind. Aub thought that the waves at Fordington would be a sight and sound to glory in. 'What can we do, Jacko?' Aub asked quietly as they entered the exercise barn. Immediately the sound of the wind faded, and they watched Clive take Marigold through her paces.

'Nothing, bonny lad,' Jack said. 'It's what I have to do, and should have done a long time ago, but after Prancer and his no show, Gracie and I felt it was up to him. Bloody hard for us it's been an' all. So now I'll go and try to sort it all out, and not before time. My lad came for Prancer, and was sent away. No-one's fault, not really, and nowhere near as bad as punching Bridie. D'you know, lads, he doesn't go to Hawton BUF any more, I've been checking.'

Mart said, 'But that means nought, for he could be a member in Newcastle. Do we know if he's still hand in glove with Millie and Heine? I hope he isn't, but right now, I bloody well hope he is.'

'No matter what I said, Bridie still shouldn't have turned him away; she's not the world's policeman.' Aub's tone was weary.

Jack toed the sand as they all leaned back now against the wooden wall of the building. 'She was protecting us and hitting out at the same time, like most Forbes or Bramptons are prone to do.'

Charlie stuck his hands in his pockets and whistled slightly in the pause that followed, then said, 'Aye, I can see that, quite clear, I can. It's just like the bleedin' Forbes and Bramptons, so I think you should all get birch twigs and give yourselves a good whipping.'

Aub laughed quietly, watching Clive use his knees to back Marigold slowly and calmly. She'd come on well, especially since Bridie had been back. He sighed and muttered, 'I do think that Bridie is less impulsive and probably wouldn't send your lad off with a flea in his ear now. She's seventeen, and seems to have changed, and who wouldn't after her rather frequent falls from grace. The thing is, Jacko, I admire her, damn it, just as, in a strange way, I admire Tim's courage in being open in support of his politics.' Well, Aub pondered, someone had to say something good about Tim.

Marigold was trotting forward now with a steady stride, one that moved her body very little. 'She'll be perfect for the injured,' Aub said.

Jack nodded, preoccupied, and for a while there was total silence between the four men.

Mart repeated, 'So, Jacko, what can we do to help?'

Clive had dismounted and was walking towards them. Aub searched in his pockets for the carrots he always carried. 'She's looking right canny,' Charlie said, as Marigold whickered and took the carrot, huffing her warm breath into his hand.

'Aye,' Clive said. 'Your Bridie's done a right good job on her. Best lass out, she is, and always has been, and I reckon we're right proud of her, all of *us* lot, anyway, and that's all I want to say.'

There was a challenge in his voice as he stared at each of them in turn. They levered themselves off the wall, and almost saluted as he passed on by, and then they grinned at one another. 'Well, that's it then,' Mart laughed.

'It is indeed,' agreed Jack. 'Now I've a son to see about a number of things.'

Chapter Twenty

Jack drove the Austin into Newcastle that evening. Gracie had said that she would not come, because someone had to stay outside the centre of the conflagration. 'The boy needs a harbour unconnected with this particular discussion.'

When she had said that, he knew how badly hurt she'd been by the thought of her son striking a girl, even if it was in a melee. He parked in the next street and walked to Tim's building, looking up at his window. It was dark, but it was only nine, so of course a youngster would be out.

But did he live here still? He hadn't even tried to find out; he hadn't reached out his hand after he thought Tim had not come when Prancer died. What sort of a father did that make him? He noticed that the building next to Tim's block had been changed into flats. It had been a warehouse before, surely. He knew he was prevaricating, and opened the door into the main entrance of Tim's building.

He checked the mail in the hallway. There was an envelope addressed to Tim, with a German stamp. He held it up, peering at the date. Ten days ago. It was Millie's handwriting, and he dropped it, wanting to wash his hands. Ten days? Was Tim away? A young woman in a headscarf came through the front door, pressed the light switch, and headed up the stairs. He called after her, 'Does Tim Forbes still live here?'

She called back without stopping, 'Tim Forbes changed his name to Tim Smith, and now he's Tim Forbes again. Daft, I call it. Yes, he's still here, but he'll be in late, he always is.'

The light went out. She called down, 'Press the light switch, would you, man? It's on a timer; we've got a mean old devil of a landlord.'

He did, and followed her. His son had changed his name to that of his father, Roger, but then back again. He felt a surge of hope. The light went out on the second floor. Tim's bedsit was at the top. He clambered on up to the fourth floor. He sat outside, on the floor, twisting his cap, waiting in the dark. At eleven thirty the light came on, and he heard steps on the stairs. They sounded like his son's. The light cut out after thirty seconds.

Jack stood, reached out and flicked the switch. The light came on, as Tim almost reached the landing. He blinked, rubbed a hand across his face, his cap on the back of his head. Jack could smell the booze and stale sweat on him even from here. Tim was looking at the next step, and then the next, and hadn't seen him. Jack stayed silent, not wanting him to run, wanting him within arms' length so he could grab him if need be.

At the head of the stairs, Tim fumbled in his pocket. He staggered towards his door, bringing out a clutch of keys. He looked up. Jack reached out, and Tim flinched away. The lights went out, and Tim stumbled against the wall. Jack grabbed him, and his son fought him off. 'No, get away.' It was more a sob of terror than a shout.

Jack lunged for the switch. In the light he said, 'It's me, it's your da.' It was too late, Tim was stumbling towards the stairs. 'Wait, son.' Jack went after him, snatching the keys from his hand, holding him close, in a bear hug. Still Tim fought. Jack almost dragged him to the door, then looked for a key that would fit. He opened it, and hauled in his son, kicking the door shut, the stale stench making him cough. They were plunged into darkness. Tim tore himself away. There was the sound of a chair or something crashing over. Jack found the light switch by the door, and flicked it on.

The bed was unmade, the linen was filthy, the small sink full of dirty dishes. On the draining board were half-eaten meals, with cigarettes stubbed out in the remains. Tim slumped onto his bed. Jack dragged across the wicker chair he and Grace had brought the day they had helped him move in.

He placed it in front of his son, but after a moment, he moved to sit next to him, taking him into his arms again. 'It's your da, bonny lad. It's only me. What's happened to you?'

There was no answer. They sat in silence and

gradually Jack felt Tim's body begin to shudder, and as it grew worse he held Tim tighter, and tighter. 'It's your da. I'm here. I was always here, I always will be.'

Tim began sobbing, great hoarse cries, and Jack rocked him. 'Oh, my boy, what's happened to you?'

At last the crying stopped, and Tim straightened, digging in his pocket. 'Let me go, Da. I need a handkerchief, and I can't breathe, man.' He was trying to laugh, but it was a creaky sound, as though it was strange to him. Jack dragged out his own handkerchief, pristine white, and handed it to him. 'I didn't know you'd come to help with Prancer. Bridie's only just told us. She didn't want us hurt. I should—'

Tim smiled, stuffing the handkerchief in his pocket. 'Bridie, God bless her, she's an army all on her own. She was right to look after you, it's what I would have done, should have done. I'll wash the handkerchief and send it to you, as I expect I'm not welcome.'

'You're always welcome.' Jack said nothing about the punch Tim had dealt Bridie, but waited. His son was exhausted, thin, unshaven; how had he held down his job? Or had he? What the hell had happened? Was it Millie? God, he would swing for her.

Then it all came out: his belief in fascism as a way to get the country on its feet, the increasing anti-Semitism in Germany and at the Hawton meetings which he had totally ignored, feeling perhaps that all collateral damage would be rectified when things were sorted. 'But that's a bloody excuse, Da. I just didn't give it a moment's thought, man. What the hell's wrong with me?'

He drove on, telling of his last time in Berlin, the beatings, the cell, Otto's death, his fear, no, his terror. At last his realisation of the nature of a state with no democracy, the absence of a legal presence, the evil of it all, which was why he no longer considered himself a fascist. Finally he said, 'It's the nightmares. So damned silly. If I go to sleep I dream, so I don't want to sleep. I stay awake, and instead I hear and smell it. I'm so bloody tired, and all the time I need a drink. It's the only thing that blunts it. I'm on a warning at work, and I don't blame them.'

Jack waited a moment, and then said, 'I had those, after the war. Lots of us did; they ease and then end, in the main, if you talk to someone and are patient. I was beaten, as a prisoner, and locked up in a cell in a salt mine. That is what I remember most about being a prisoner: the terror of being alone, the worry about my men, because if I still fought against the enemy then me marras suffered penalties too. That's something I never discovered the answer to . . .' He drifted off into his memories, which was a place he preferred not to be, and knew that tonight he would dream about it again. 'And there was no law, not really, in a bloody enemy salt mine, or any other of their mines. So I know exactly what you mean.'

Tim looked at him now. 'I thought you would.'

Jack said, 'You have a letter downstairs from your mother?' It was a question. Somewhere a clock was ticking, or was it a tap dripping? He looked around. It was the clock on the mantelpiece, next to a photograph taken when Tim was ten, with Bridie and James. There was another, of Tim with Gracie and Jack, another of Tim with Mart, Jack, Charlie and Aub after a day at the races. There was not one of Millie, or Heine.

'Mam is my mother.' Tim was picking at the skin around his thumbnail, a nail that was dirty. Well, they all were. Jack placed his hand on his son's, and held it, as he had done when he was a child. He placed his other around it. 'You're right, son, and she always will be.'

Jack felt a growing relief. Then his son explained about the earlier need to find the letter which Millie had said was forged, and the stolen silver. He added that, of course, the family probably knew that Bridie had found him searching, and had tried to help.

Jack shook his head. 'No, she said nothing. You asked her not to, I reckon?'

He saw his son's eyes fill with tears, which he brushed away. For a moment, neither said anything and Jack pictured his niece, so like her mam, so rock solid, so formidable, but vulnerable.

A memory came to him from that terrible day when his son had hurled abuse at him in the club then stormed out: amongst all the ranting, there had

293

been something about the theft of the silver and a forged letter. Now it all made sense. He said, 'I certainly remember about the stolen silver. Lord Brampton reported it to the police, and then set his private detectives on it. They harassed your grandparents until your Uncle Aub put a stop to it.'

'I know she lied to me, because the silver is there, in her vitrine. They need the letter so she can marry Heine, or so she says. But it's probably something to do with his job. I'm never going back, Da. I don't trust them, either of them. They were so angry last time, and there's just something about people who take apartments from others, who wade through lives . . .' He trailed off and shuddered. 'There's an evil . . .' He gave up.

'Come with me now and see your mam. She knows I'm here, and just loves you, so much. We all do, especially me.' Jack's mind was racing. Heine needed the letter, and they needed Heine to help James, but not this way, not using his son. There was no way Jack was going to let him back into that cesspool, so how else could they use that lever? He'd have to be the one to go, that's all.

'Da?' Tim was looking at him, his head cocked to one side, as he did when he knew there was something happening.

Jack repeated again, 'Come back with me, lad, let your mam look after you for a while.'

'What's up, Da? Why have you come now? It's not one of the youngsters, is it? What have they been up to?' He laughed again, and this time it sounded amused. He was patting his pockets, and drew out a packet of cigarettes. His fingers were nicotine stained. He offered one to Jack.

Jack shook his head. 'I'm just here to check on you. I know you haven't been to the Hawton meeting rooms, and I just wondered what your beliefs were, and how *you* were, but I know that now.'

Tim threw the packet of cigarettes on the bedside table next to an overflowing ashtray. He pushed himself up and walked to the sink, running the tap onto the dirty dishes, the old water heater on the wall flaring. 'I live in a pigsty. Help me?'

Jack tipped the unfinished meals into the bin, found a tea towel, and dried as his son washed.

Together they stripped the bed and remade it with clean sheets. Tim bundled up the dirty ones into his linen bag for the laundry as Jack tipped the ashtray into the bin, washed it, and returned it to the table. He ran a cloth over the surface of the small table at which Tim ate, and Tim put the linen bag by the front door. 'So I don't forget it in the morning.'

He stood watching as Jack washed out the cloth, and muttered, 'It can only be Spain. Bridie's back here, so it's not her. James was so dead set on doing something, and that's where the young men are going. It is, isn't it, and it's gone wrong? Just tell me he's not dead.'

Jack sat down at the table, exhausted suddenly.

It was all such a bloody mess, and Tim would think that he'd only come to put him in the lion's den.

Tim stood at his side, and now as he put his hand on Jack's shoulder, it was he who comforted his da. 'You have to tell me, Da. I need to do something for you all, really I do. And I know you would have come anyway, sometime.'

Finally, Jack told him that James was a prisoner. 'Potty has strongly advised we do all we can to get him home, and I thought that you might still be in with the Nazis through Heine, but you're not, and I'm having no part in sending you back into that situation. So I'll take the letter over there, if it still exists, and maybe he'll do an exchange.'

Tim shook his head, squatting before his father and clasping his hands in a strong grip. 'Da, I need to do this. You must all look for the letter, and if you find it, I'll come at the weekend to collect it. It might work – they were in a right lather about getting it, and probably still are. I'll know when I read the letter. Don't worry, it will all be alright. Now you must go home, Da. I'm tired and I need to think, and I need to sleep – and tonight, maybe I will.'

Jack eased himself up. Tim said quietly, 'Don't tell the others about my change of heart. You don't know who is around the place, reporting back to the Nazis. It's safer, Da. If I've learned nothing else from them, it's that. You have no idea how long their tentacles are. So let the family continue to be wary of me, even to hate me. Until this is over.'

After leaving his son, Jack hadn't gone home to Easton, but driven straight to Home Farm to speak to Aub and Evie. He'd explained that his son was still in touch with his mother and would act on James' behalf, but had said nothing of the lad's feelings and beliefs, and they had not asked. Since then the families had all spent every spare moment up until the weekend looking for the letter, which Evie had forgotten all about. Finally, it was Bridie who found it, on Saturday morning, in the Hall kitchen, tucked in one of Evie's cookery bibles, which was where she had also pressed the first flowers that Bridie had picked as a toddler. She had telephoned her mother at Home Farm immediately, and pedalled like fury down the lanes to deliver it.

Bridie arrived just after the postman, who had delivered a tattered and stained note from James, saying that he could not return, not yet. In it, he explained that the note was to be carried across the Pyrenees by one of the guides.

Ver was there, and handed the note to her niece, kissing her. 'Look at the date. It was early on and before term started, but enough of that. You've found it, the lever we've all been hunting for, so thank you, dearest Bridie. I had almost given up hope.' Her face was pale with worry. She had lost weight, as had they all.

Bridie said, 'You need to thank Tim, it's he who has to do it.' She left for the stables, where things were simpler and she didn't have to see Tim, who was still a fascist, still happy to pop across to his Nazi mother.

Evie read Millie's letter aloud to Richard, Aub and Ver as the clock moved towards eleven o'clock. Ver sipped a sherry with hands that trembled, as they did all the time now, and would until her son returned. God knew what would happen if he didn't.

Well, Evie,

The tree is my goodbye present for you. I said I'd get you, but you probably still don't know why. It's because you're just so smug, so bloody perfect with your hotel plans, with your do-gooding. You and your family is always at it, and so I got to do it as well, and will have to go on doing it, if I stay, because you'll get your hotel, you see if you don't, and I'll have to do the laundry, or something.

It's been hell, working in a freak show. And it's not over, because Jack will come home, and we'll have his bleeding shouting all night and who knows what he'll look like, and if you're daft enough to think them Bramptons will still be friendly and nice when they don't need us, you got another think coming. They'll be back to the masters and we'll be the servants.

I have a right to a whole man, with nice skin, no blue scars, and I'm going to have him. Heine likes me, and I will make him love me. I will. And we've got our start in life, thanks to the bloody Bramptons. We're going on a boat, but you won't know where, and now things will work for me. Just look after Tim, because Heine doesn't want him. I had to choose. You Forbes took him away from me anyway. He loved his gran more than me, so now you lot can do the donkey work, and anyway, Jack loved the bairn, not me. Don't think I didn't know that. Just like you he is, the big person helping the little people. Well, get on with it, and thank you for the silver. I hid it in the garage attic, so you got that wrong. But I was right, it will make a good train play area. Put up a plaque with my name.

Millie Forbes

Evie said, 'We can't let the lad see this, we really can't.' The others were looking beyond her, aghast.

Tim said from the doorway, 'I don't need to, I've just listened to it.'

Evie folded the letter and stood quietly. Her nephew was pale and thin, but clean-shaven.

He said, 'So the tree was their goodbye present? They're the ones who blew it up. Well, well . . .' His voice was expressionless. Was he proud of his mother? Or appalled? She couldn't tell.

She said, 'People change, Tim.'

299

Behind him stood Jack, his hand on his lad's shoulder. Grace had her arm around her son's waist. Evie didn't know what to think, looking at him, for she saw Millie in the set of his chin. Would he really help them?

'Are you sure, Tim?' She smiled, but knew it didn't reach her eyes.

'Yes, Aunt Evie, I'm sure.' He looked at the letter, not at her. 'It's more than time I paid another visit. She is my mother, after all.'

She handed him the letter. 'I will do what I can,' he said simply, then turned and left, his parents by his side.

Ver ran after him. 'Thank you, Tim.'

'It's my pleasure,' Evie heard him call, his voice still expressionless. Would he, Millie and Heine sit around the dinner table in Berlin, mocking them? Were Jack and Gracie to be hurt all over again? Questions, questions, when all they could do was to wait.

Before Tim left, his father took him into Aub's study and they telephoned Potty. A few days earlier, Jack had told the Colonel about Tim's change of heart and willingness to co-operate, and Potty had agreed with Tim that it was best to pretend to everyone else that he was still a fascist, because Nazi agents were almost certainly active, especially within the BUF circle. Now Jack read out the letter to see if Potty felt it was enough of a lever.

Tim listened too, his head pressed hard against the earpiece.

Once Jack had reached the end of the letter, Potty said, 'It might be enough, because it does mention Heine by name, but if they think Tim could be useful to them in other ways – intelligence, for instance – they might be prepared to put themselves out a bit more. Put Tim on, would you, Jack?'

Tim took the receiver, and now it was Jack who pressed his ear against the receiver. Potty said, 'Strange bit of business, dear old pumpkin. I did a trace for the police records on your mother's case. All gone. At about the same time a constable with fascist affiliations left the force and bought a fish and chip shop in Hartlepool – in 1936, about the time of your father's wedding, actually. I'm wondering if a package was delivered to your mama and Heine at about that time. Not via you, was it, Tim?' His voice was quiet now.

Tim shook his head. 'Absolutely not.' Then he paused. 'The only package I delivered was from Sir Anthony to do with the rehabilitation project.'

'Ah, of course. Good idea, that, what?' There was a long pause. 'Telephone me from Newcastle, a public telephone if you will. I do so enjoy novels such as *The Thirty-Nine Steps*. One learns so much. I will beaver through it, and others, to see if there are more things writ large that might keep you safer.' The line went dead.

*

Tim watched Bridie as she leaned on the fence observing David and Estrella with Terry. He'd been glad she hadn't been at Home Farm, because he couldn't meet anyone's eyes, after all he'd done to them. Now he had an apology to make to this girl. Estrella was riding, wearing a pair of Bridie's jodhpurs, and David was near the mounting ramp, giving instructions. Tim heard Bridie laughing quietly, heard her call, 'Leave her be, bossy boots. Let the girl feel her way.'

Tim said, 'Who's the bossy boots?'

She swung round. 'I heard you were coming. I thought it would be best I wasn't there. You'd think I told, and besides, I sent you away—'

He cut across her, 'You didn't tell them I hit you, you didn't tell them I was poking around in your house and Easterleigh Hall's study for the letter, so what is the ticking off you gave me in comparison? Walk back with me?'

She shook her head. 'I'm needed here. But thank you for agreeing to take the letter, or rather, the copy of the letter. Da and Uncle Jack said Uncle Potty had given some odd advice, something to do with *Thirty-Nine Steps* and other books? Dear old soul, I think he's going a bit batty.'

Tim shrugged. 'Yes, perhaps Potty is a bit cracked, but he's a good old buffer. It's little enough for me to do. Don't fret, Bridie, I'll do all I can to get him home, but it might take some time.'

She turned back to Terry. 'Thank you,' she said. 'I'm really grateful.'

He walked slowly towards the garage yard where he'd parked his motorbike, wanting to say more, but unable to do so. She was so grown up, so beautiful, so cold. Well, he was still a fascist in her eyes, and in those of the rest of the family, and must remain so, but not forever. He strode on, feeling happier at the thought.

As he walked he was sure he was being watched, and swung round. He was, by Bridie. She waved. His heart lurched. Confused, he felt the breath struggling in his chest, and he couldn't believe how much he wanted to stand and look at Bridie, with whom he had swum in the beck when they were young, Bridie who had told no-one that he was searching their homes, who had tried to help, though he had punched her. She was so extraordinary. What had happened to the child she once was? He realised: she had become a woman.

From this minute it was as though his world had been turned upside down, because he had always loved her, but this was different. He knew, without a doubt, he would not only kill for her, but die for her. He started to walk back towards her, but she turned away to watch Terry, leaving him bereft.

He roared off to Newcastle, permitting himself the space of the journey to think of her eyes, her soft, blonde hair, the tilt of her head, her defiance. He allowed himself to smile, to remember their days as children, but once he arrived at his bedsit, it was time to think of what needed to be done, and nothing else.

He telephoned Potty again from a public telephone box. The old boy told him he'd asked some questions, and a club member knew someone in Newcastle who would copy the letter quickly. 'So helpful, dear boy, to have membership to so many clubs. One hears the most useless information that suddenly comes in handy.'

Tim photographed the letter, and took the film to the man Potty had recommended. He took the original letter to a safe deposit box, also as Potty had advised, because Heine might baulk at helping once he had the original of the 'lever'.

He then re-read all his mother's earlier letters to him. He absorbed the gushing, the need for the forged letter, the words of love, which now rang sickeningly hollow. There were later ones, asking if he had received her letters. *Why aren't you replying?*

He had been mulling this over and decided that he would tell Millie that he had only received this last one, that she must have put the wrong number on the envelope. But no, saying she had written the wrong number wouldn't work. Millie wasn't stupid. He would think about that, and come up with something better, something that could be checked by their snoopers. He realised then that he was learning to think like them.

Chapter Twenty-One

Mid-November 1937

Tim checked his watch as the wind whistled through his overcoat and almost took his cap. He rammed it on more firmly and tightened his scarf. He was in Dover, and it was an hour before he needed to board the early morning ferry for Calais, so there was just time for a cup of tea.

He found a café outside the docks, relieved to be away from his da's anxious eyes, and his mam's determined cheerfulness. He had chosen, as always, to take the train from Newcastle, in order to catch the quickest ferry. For someone with his tendency to seasickness, anything longer was a disaster.

It was steamy but warm inside the café. He undid his coat and took his tea from the woman serving, her hair tied up in a headscarf. He used the spoon, attached by a chain to the counter, to stir in some sugar. He stared at the chain, feeling the manacles, the chains that had bound him in the police station, or was it Gestapo headquarters? He didn't really know, nor did he want to, because he was breaking out in a sweat, and the spoon was clattering against the inside of his cup as his hand shook. A man standing next to him at the counter boomed, 'Are you going to stir that all day, dear boy, or can someone else use it?'

Tim jerked back to the present. He saw it was Potty. For heaven's sake, what . . . 'Well met, dear heart,' Potty said quietly. How odd. He was so seldom quiet. How odd he was here at all.

'I'm just having a cuppa, Colonel.'

The Colonel actually whispered, 'Potty, dear heart. Potty is perfectly fine. Let's sit.'

Although it was a whisper, it was also an order, and one that Tim found himself obeying. He followed the man into a corner seat away from the window.

'What are you doing here?' Tim asked as they sat down.

'Got the copy letter, have you? All tucked up safe and sound in your breast pocket, and another in your suitcase, as a fallback? You put the original in a safe deposit box and you've let your mother know you're on your way?'

Tim shook his head, amused. Dear old Potty, he was almost more involved than his da, but perhaps he had nothing better to do. He realised then that he knew nothing about this man who had waddled about on the periphery of their lives for as long as he could remember. Hadn't he been connected with James' father in the war – adjutant or something?

He sipped his tea as Potty settled himself more comfortably, beaming at him. Tim said, 'The family's

306

been in touch again, has it, and given you instructions to see me off? You all need to stop worrying. I'm doing as they want, and it will be fine. I've done all that you advised.' Even as he said it, the sweat beaded his forehead.

He checked his watch. In ten minutes he must go. Across from him, Potty was digging into his overcoat pocket, but then appeared to think better of it. He leaned over the table.

'Your father said you've been brushing up on your German, but best not to let on about that, to anyone. That way people will talk freely, so keep listening, because you are unsafe with Herr Heine Weber. Above all, try to keep him sweet, and your mother too. Never lose control. If you need help, use a telephone number I will give you, which you must memorise and destroy. Use a café telephone, as who knows who is listening to whom, with what bugs, in an SS block. Trust no-one. I do believe that offering Heine a deal is dangerous. He won't like it.'

This was not the usual Potty; this one had gimlet eyes, with a brisk, quiet delivery. Tim tried to think of something to say, but he was reeling from the information.

Potty was standing now, his avuncular self back in place. 'Come along, laddie, mustn't miss the boat.' Tim gulped his tea, rose, and shook Potty's hand. He felt the piece of paper in Potty's. Tim nodded and put the paper in his coat pocket, then picked up his case and followed Potty.

Outside the café, Tim turned towards the docks, and Potty turned the other way, then stopped. 'Just one thing. You might bump into someone unexpectedly, the way one does. Remember, be circumspect, don't trust anyone. Keep up your fascism.'

He waddled away, but Tim realised, watching him as he reached the corner, that the man had covered a lot of ground in a short space of time. In fact, he did in all ways. He thought he heard him call, 'We'll meet on your return.'

Tim checked his watch again and set off, almost at a run, reaching the ferry just in time, and taking a place on a bench on deck, knowing from experience that the last thing he must do, for everyone's sake, was to leave the fresh air and the horizon or there would be consequences. He walked and sat, walked and sat, until Calais came into view, and as they drew alongside he heard yet another familiar voice.

'Is that you, Tim? Your mother said we might meet.' It was Sir Anthony Travers, his hand out.

Tim shook it. 'Are you well, sir?' Tim asked.

'Indeed, but busy, as is everyone. I am bound for Paris, but have papers for your mother and Heine. The last of the co-operative plans, which is all rather exciting, I must say, and productive, one hopes. We have to talk through our differences, don't we, man and country? Yes, indeed we do.' He had answered his own question, so Tim just smiled. He liked this man, well, almost loved him. He did so much good, and if anyone could moderate Heine and his pals, it would be him.

'Look, Tim. Would you deliver them, as I have to meet up with Lady Margaret and her daughter, for some birthday shenanigans? All rather irritating, but don't tell them I said that.'

Tim took the package.

'Take care of it, dear boy,' Sir Anthony said. 'I'd do anything to save young men like you from another war. Anything.' He walked away, his shoulders hunched, looking like an old man, which of course, he was. It was just that Tim had never noticed it before. Tim watched until Sir Anthony Travers merged into the streams of other passengers. The ferry was manoeuvring into the quay. There was a bump, the hawsers were thrown and secured, then the passengers began to disembark. Tim joined them, hearing Potty's warning. Yes, he had met Sir Anthony unexpectedly, but to think ill of the man was rubbish, just as it was rubbish to think his plans were stolen police papers. Sir Anthony was their benchmark for goodness.

As he walked down the gangplank, the gulls soared and called above him, and his mind disobeyed him, and insisted on playing with the meeting. Sir Anthony was on his way to Paris; he had intended to dispatch the package from the city. Tim had only telegraphed his mother two days ago, saying that he had what she wanted and would be with her on 18 November. Tension threatened to take over, and he forced himself to relax. He was getting sucked into one of Potty's spy novels.

In Berlin, he took a taxi from the station, past the flags and banners fluttering in the icy blast of the late afternoon. There was a light smattering of snow. He passed a few accordion players. Passers-by threw a few pfennigs into the caps, also dusted with snow. The taxi reached the SS block. He paid, got out, and stood on the pavement, bracing himself for what was to come. As he looked up at the blank windows, he suddenly realised that he hadn't told Potty where Millie and Heine lived, so how could he know that the building had been appropriated for the SS?

A passer-by slipped on the snow and knocked into him, but regained his balance and hurried on. The taxi drew away and he mounted the steps, opened the heavy door and entered, heading straight for the lift at the rear of the foyer. The block leader came out from her cubby-hole. He forced himself to smile, hating her, hating the foyer, hating every damn square inch of this bloody country, and its politics. More, he hated himself for having aligned himself with them, but then again, perhaps that would turn out to be a good thing after all, if he could get James home.

He took the lift to the second floor, walked towards Heine and Millie's door. In his pocket, as always, was Avraham's mezuzah case. He touched the place on the door frame that he had sanded, and then rang the bell. Heine opened the door, with his braces hanging in loops either side of his trousers, his shirt unbuttoned. Tim held out his hand. Heine just looked at it, then waved him through, saying, 'After all I did to release you from your interrogation and we hear nothing. Our letters are not answered. But here you are, a bad penny, you say in England, I think.'

Tim had prepared himself, and now his mother was beside Heine, her hair still dyed blonde and in that ridiculous Nazi plait around her head. 'Mother,' he said. 'I thought you were angry, because it was only a few weeks ago that I received a letter. I have had no others.' He sounded hurt and confused. But there was no confusion in his heart. 'Did you address it to fifty-nine A? That A is important.'

It was their turn to look confused. 'A? But that didn't matter before.'

Tim put his case down. They were all still standing in the hallway, as though they were about to throw him out. Well, that wouldn't happen when they saw the letter – or would it? Was it enough? He'd have to wait until Heine had read it. He forced himself to smile, keeping them sweet, as Potty had said. 'I wrote to tell you, but had no reply. You see, the building next door has converted to bedsits, and now *they* are fifty-nine.' Thank God he had thought of this, and best of all, it was true, and mail did get muddled.

Heine reached for Tim's case. Was he going to

throw it out of the door? Tim beat him to it, lifting it. Heine said, 'So why did our last one reach you?'

Tim shrugged. 'Because I spoke to the postman, asked him if he had delivered any letters from Germany and he said yes, but to the new fifty-nine. The people in the other building threw them away, I suppose. People in bedsits don't care. So he delivered the last letter from you.' It sounded thin, even to him, but as the two of them looked at one another, he saw they accepted it.

Tim grimaced. 'I've also been in a bit of a state, my last visit shook me a bit. I was drinking.' Somehow he felt they could find out about this too, if they hadn't already.

Heine stepped back, his eyes narrowing. 'And you say you have the letter?'

'I found it, would you believe, Mother, in one of Evie's old recipe bibles. She was using it as a bookmark.' He saw the joy in her face and the relief in Heine's, and hated them even more.

Heine said, 'Come along and sit down. You must be cold and tired. Millie, instruct Amala to brew coffee.'

He led the way into the sitting room. Was the silver still there? That didn't seem so important now. Tim had heard poor Aunt Evie's distress as she read the letter, and Aunt Ver's too, distress on his behalf. Aunt Evie had said, when they saw him listening, in that warm kitchen at Home Farm, 'People change.' *That* family was his, not this.

Heine was waiting by the card table, but Tim sat on the sofa. He was at least going to have a cup of coffee before the bastard slung him out. Amala brought the coffee. He sprang to his feet and insisted on taking the tray. His mother said, 'For goodness' sake, Tim. She's staff.'

He said, 'Well, *you* wouldn't have liked it.' Millie flushed, anger flashing across her face. He held himself in check and continued, 'If you had ever been in her position.' Millie sat down as he put the coffee on the table, sat next to her, and said, 'Will you be mother?'

She looked confused and checked his face, as though for irony. He kept his smile steady.

Heine barked a laugh. 'That is a good joke, Tim. Yes, I like it.' He joined them, taking a cup of coffee.

Tim drank eagerly, as though it would be snatched from him. Once he had reached the dregs, he replaced his cup in the saucer and drew from his pocket, first, Sir Anthony's packet, and handed it across to Heine. 'I met him on the boat.'

'Oh, so he found you,' his mother said, before Heine slated her with a look. She flushed again. 'I mentioned that you would be coming once I got your telegram. I didn't know which ferry, of course, so that was lucky.'

Tim smiled. 'Of course it was – lucky, that is.'

Heine was hurrying to the card table. Tim strolled across, feeling the mezuzah case in his trouser pocket. It gave him courage, as Heine folded what looked like more plans, and faced him, his hands on his hips. 'The letter?'

Tim kept his smile, feeling the sweat trickling down his back and praying it wasn't breaking out on his forehead. He brought out the creased, grease-stained envelope from his pocket, and now Millie was with him. 'Did you read it?' she asked.

Heine was taking the photographic copy from the envelope. 'Of course he did. This is a copy, so he photographed it, and has given us this.' He threw it onto the table.

His mother said, 'You must understand, Tim, it is a forgery.'

She couldn't meet his eyes. Tim said, 'I took it to a forensic analyst at the university, with a copy of your laundry lists. He verified the writing as yours.' His voice was totally pleasant, but firm. In fact, it was a contact of Richard's who had taken it. 'I thought I would keep the original. One never knows when one might need things like' – he paused – 'originals.' Could they hear the hammering of his heart?

His mother flushed even more, and Heine almost spat at her, 'Like mother, like son, I see.'

Tim didn't understand, but he didn't have time to think about that now. His cousin was in a fascist prisoner of war camp and he needed to get him home. He explained that the original was quite safe, that one other person knew where it was, and if he didn't return, then that person would publicise it, that he admired them enormously and wouldn't hurt them for the world. 'But I have learned from my fellow fascist members, and the Nazis who arrested me, that weakness is a fault. Now, like Hitler, I believe in Darwin and only the fittest should survive.' He didn't tell them that the person was Potty.

He waited, while his mother and Heine looked at one another. Finally, Heine said, with a look of reluctant admiration, 'Indeed, like mother, like son. So, Tim, what do you want?'

'You will remember Lady Veronica, Mother?'

'Of course, Tim, don't be silly.'

His mother had crossed her arms, and was staring at him. He continued, 'Well, James, her son, is in a Spanish prisoner of war camp, and they want him home. He, of course, was on the side of the Republicans, so they're welcome to him, daft beggar. But for the sake of peace, I thought Heine could pull some strings. I won't release the original, which proves you took the silver, Mother, and in which Heine is implicated, but I will keep it tucked away nice and safe.'

He saw even more admiration in Heine's face. Nazi bastard, he thought, and strolled to the sofa and sat down before his legs gave way. He waited as Heine scanned the letter. He spoke to Millie in German, 'He's right, I am implicated.'

Heine said to Tim, 'I am expected at a club this evening. We will go, you and me. I am meeting a friend, and others will come. You will meet them, and then I will see what I can do.' He almost marched from the room.

Millie came to join him, and Tim forced himself to unclench his hands and look relaxed. 'Do you really want to marry him, Mother?'

Millie nodded. 'Oh yes, Tim, he is my passport to security. Germany is soon going to be much more important than it is now.'

'But does he want to marry *you*?'

She smiled. 'He needs me. I bring him contacts to enhance his stature with his department.'

Contacts like me, Tim thought. He poured them each another coffee. It was cold. She ignored hers but he drank his, unable to leave the thought of her here, with Heine, alone. 'But he is ruthless, so are you safe?'

She laughed, and relaxed back against the cushions stacked behind her on the leather sofa. 'Like you, I've learned. Shall we just say that I have proof, locked away, that his father is not his father, but,' she leaned towards him, 'someone, shall we say, not of the Aryan race, and you, as a fascist, will understand the importance of that.'

The cup shook in Tim's hand. God in heaven, what a pair. Linked to one another by a perverted admiration, and hate. Or was it love? Who the hell knew, or cared? He just wanted to be home, away from this. But he forced himself to smile.

She said, 'Tim, I'm proud of you, you are strong

and clever, but it would be better to produce the original letter, because he might change from admiration to dislike.'

'Well, I'm getting used to that. They don't like me at home, either, especially Jack. And I am one of two who knows where the original is, so why should I care what Heine thinks of me?'

This was what he and his da had decided he should say. It would be what she wanted to hear. She smiled, and pointed to the door. 'Off you go and change, and promise me, Tim, you'll let your poor old mother have the original of the letter, on the quiet, as soon as you can.'

He pretended he hadn't heard.

Later, at the end of the evening, Heine put Tim in a taxi and thrust money at the driver. 'Get him back, and don't leave until you've made sure that he's gone through the doors.'

Tim forced himself to stay awake as the taxi drove off, thinking of Bauer, who had been there in the club, sitting with Otto, Hans, Bruno, Walter and the other SS friends. So, it was Bauer, not Sir Anthony, who Potty thought he might meet. The relief was enormous, and he had listened, like a good boy, to all that was flying around the table, in English, out of courtesy towards Heine's guest. It was boastful rubbish, on the whole, until Bauer replied to a question in German, from Hans.

Bauer had smiled, and began to talk of the

bombing of Guernica, though Otto jerked his head towards Tim, frowning.

Heine said, in German, 'He knows no German, for all his fascist talk.'

Bauer continued, telling them of his days observing the bombing of Guernica from nearby hills. Tim had been able to follow most of it, learning of the relentless waves of bombers, the devastation of the Basque town, the deaths. The SS friends smoked cigars and banged the table. They toasted a Luftwaffe pilot who sat at the next table. Quietly Bauer had added, 'After all that, the bridge they had wanted to be destroyed was still intact.' He had said it in German, almost to himself, but Tim had understood.

He stared at Bauer, who met his eyes, as though coming back to the present, and said, immediately, 'Such a waste of armaments, don't you all think? It shows we must improve upon the rehearsal.'

Walter, the SS officer sitting next to Tim, had nodded, and said, 'Indeed, Herr Bauer.'

Tim had said nothing, because, of course, as far as they all knew he had not understood a word.

Tim stayed for just two days, pleading that a return to work was necessary. He was, after all, on a warning from his employer, he explained, though somehow Mr Andrews had seemed more flexible this time. Heine walked him to his taxi. He said, 'Your cousin will be located. He will then be returned.

You are aware that you are now under an obligation to me.'

Tim said, 'I still have the original letter.'

'Ah, but I have your mother.'

Tim nodded, paused, and then said, 'Yes, I understand that.'

On his way to the station he knew he needed the name of Heine's father, and the proof his mother spoke of. Then, the obligation would be Heine's again. Where did that put his mother? He didn't really care. He smiled slightly. He was getting as bad as Potty, and his spy novels.

Chapter Twenty-Two

At Dover Potty was waiting at the bottom of the gangplank, his hat pulled down, but his portly body would be identifiable miles away. Tim had half expected him, because, while the ferry lurched and keeled as it drove through the buffeting swell, he'd fixed on the conversations he'd had with Potty as a way of remaining vaguely in control of his seasickness. When they came into harbour, not only did his stomach calm, but his thoughts clarified, much like puzzle pieces slotting into place. Potty, a silly old buffer who spent his time reading spy novels? What nonsense. He was very much more than that, and Tim couldn't understand why he hadn't seen it earlier.

Potty said, 'Walk with me.' It was eleven in the morning, his train wasn't until one o'clock, into London, and then he'd get another to Newcastle. So Tim walked. Potty ordered, 'Talk me through the people you met, and all that happened.'

Tim did, but left out Sir Anthony, because that was nothing to do with anything. He also held back the mystery of Heine's parentage, though he wasn't sure why. He mentioned Bauer, though, and that he had stated that they hadn't destroyed the bridge, and something about it being a rehearsal.

'Did he indeed?' Potty murmured, as though he was making a note of it.

Again Tim smiled, because that was exactly what the man was doing. He said, 'I should tell someone what he said. It could be important. What do your books say about who to go to? Have you any ideas?'

They were clear of the dock now. The gulls were screaming, the wind was howling, somewhere a ship's hooter boomed. 'You're going to the station?' Potty asked, ignoring Tim's question.

'Well, I'm not walking to Newcastle,' Tim said. 'I have to tell Da that Heine's bringing James out, in return for the letter.'

'Let's phone him. The sooner he gets the news the better. Come with me.' Potty led the way along streets which became progressively narrower, reminding Tim of the one in which he'd been caught in Germany. He fingered the mezuzah case. They stopped at a laundry situated on a corner. Steam belched out of vents along the side of the building. Potty opened the door, a bell jangled. They walked into a cloud of damp heat, and the smell of clean washing. Somewhere washing machines were sloshing. There was a woman behind the counter, in an overall, checking off some neatly folded sheets.

Tim said, 'I thought we were finding a telephone?'

'Indeed, dear boy.'

Potty tipped his hat at the woman, lifted the

hinged counter, and walked bold as brass into a corridor, and then through to a back room in which were a desk with a telephone, chairs and filing cabinets. Tim followed, playing the game. He made himself sound embarrassed as he asked, 'Shouldn't we ask?'

'Take a seat,' Potty said, pointing to a cushioned chair in front of the desk. Potty took the chair behind the desk. Tim sat, as Potty pushed the telephone across. 'Please, make free.'

Tim did so, assuring Da that he was well, that Heine had rolled over in the face of the presentation of the letter, that he would be home when the train arrived. He'd contact him then, unless it was the early hours. He ended, 'I love you, Da.'

He heard his da say, 'You know how much I love you, lad. I'll let Aunt Ver and Uncle Richard know, and that now we wait.'

He replaced the receiver and sat back in his chair, looking around the room, waiting. He felt quite calm. Potty smiled, tamping a pipe he had produced from a rack on the desk. Tim looked around. 'Good to be home, is it?' Potty said, reaching for his matches.

'You have no idea.'

'Ah, perhaps I have.'

Tim thought. Yes, Colonel Potter, you no doubt have, and damned glad I am of it, or who knows what mess I would have got myself into. But he said nothing. He checked his watch. He wanted to catch his train, but there was still an hour, and he guessed

Potty had more to say. He would, however, kill for a coffee, now that the ground had stopped moving, which always took about an hour after disembarking. Perhaps Potty was a mind reader as well as everything else, because he pressed a button on his intercom. 'Gladys, we have a laddie here who's probably parched.'

A crackly voice replied, 'Alcohol or coffee?'

Potty raised an eyebrow at Tim. 'Good God, coffee, please. I'm not good on the sea,' he explained. 'Takes a while for things to settle.'

'You heard that, Gladys. Coffee for us both.' Potty clicked off the intercom. He lit his pipe, puffing madly. Finally it took, and Tim did wish it hadn't, as clouds of smoke smelling of cabbage leaves billowed out.

The coffee arrived. Gladys, the woman from behind the counter in the laundry, scowled, and opened the window at the rear. 'You're disgusting, sir, isn't he, young man?'

'Enough, Gladys,' Potty said, puffing madly. 'Now go and tend to your sheets.'

Potty leaned back in his chair, pointing to the coffee. 'Pour for us, if you would.' Tim obeyed, and pushed a decent-sized cup and saucer across to Potty, then sipped one himself. Potty had his hands behind his head now, and he was staring at the ceiling. Tim looked too, noticing a water stain. Potty said, 'Have you heard of the night of the long knives, when Röhm, the leader of the SA – the *Sturmabteilung* – and his cohorts were killed on Hitler's orders, after they become too powerful, and a possible threat?'

Tim had, because Heine and his cronies had laughed about it, and how it had elevated the SS into the position they now held. He nodded.

'Well, laddie, if Röhm had had intelligence – in other words, agents or spies – he might have been one step ahead and dodged the bullet. That's the way wars are prevented, or if push comes to shove, wars are won. Intelligence, laddie, is the magic word. Intelligence which is gathered by people who have contacts, brave people who put themselves in harm's way, people with a cover, and a belief in a cause. People who might have an "in" with others who feel they are owed a favour in return. People who appear to be what they are not.'

Tim drained his coffee. Potty was looking at him through the fug of his foul tobacco. Ah, now they were getting to it. Yes, Potty's knowledge had kept him safe, but not just for his own sake, it appeared. He, Tim Forbes, had an 'in', and someone who felt they were owed a favour, but to be one of the 'brave' was a step too bloody far.

'If you think I'm one of these people, you must be joking,' he said, pouring himself another coffee.

Potty continued to stare at the ceiling. 'Is there something you really want? Something that you think I could do for you, to make you at least consider it?'

Tim repeated, 'You must be bloody joking, man.

I've done what needs to be done, and now I'm going home, with a big thank you for all your help.'

'Forget the thank you, but do reconsider, old son, at your leisure. You operate well, you keep calm, you carry out the task. We need all the help we can get, Tim. You told me Bauer said the pilots needed more practice, but for what? Why do they need the bombers? They talk of *Lebensraum*. For you, I'll translate.'

Tim interrupted, 'Living space. I have some German, as you know.'

'So, they have the Rhineland back – so what, or where, will be next, one wonders, to provide this living space? We need more people capable of listening, of travelling to and fro. We need you.'

Tim said, 'Goodbye, Potty.' He rose. He had no intention of ever setting foot in Germany again.

Potty stood, smiling slightly. 'Let's say au revoir, dear boy. Goodbye is so dreadfully final. Now, dear heart, I trust I have your discretion, and don't feel bad. I must just soldier on and perhaps I will find somebody else. Travel home safely, and congratulations on your courage these last few days.'

As Tim left the room, he was aware of Potty slumping back in his chair. He nodded towards Gladys, who smiled, and handed him a card printed with a telephone number. 'Just in case you change your mind,' she said.

He left the laundry and walked towards the station. Had Gladys had her ear stuck to the door?

Or had she listened on the intercom? Or was he one of many, and she knew the script? He passed people choosing vegetables from a greengrocer's outside shelves, then a flower seller. Were there still shop-keepers in Guernica, and Bilbao? What must it be like to be bombed, to have planes overhead, dropping something you could not escape? He looked up at the sky. The gulls were wheeling. Well, Estrella and Maria knew. James too, no doubt. His gut twisted. Stupid little sod, but at least he should come home.

Bombs killed. A rehearsal – for bloody what? He felt he knew.

Tim tumbled into bed just before midnight. He was exhausted, but struggled with Heine in his dreams, as the bastard tried to strangle him with his black braces, again and again. After work the next day, his da was waiting in his Austin outside the engineering firm and drove him back to Easterleigh Hall, where Aunt Ver and Uncle Richard waited in their apartment. He repeated that Heine had agreed to do what was necessary to prevent the original of the letter surfacing. He said nothing of his mother's more damning hold over Heine.

By this time Evie and Aub had arrived with Bridie. He tried not to look at her, but how could he not? She waited by the door while the others sat talking nineteen to the dozen of how wonderful it was, how grateful they were, how James could continue his life, go to university. Tim stood up. 'You must remember that it will take time, and until then he is in jeopardy. There's a civil war raging.'

The talking stopped. Bridie stared at him. He said, 'The leverage should be strong enough, but it's chaos in Spain, so you must keep on hoping until he's here.'

His da smiled at him, and nodded. Tim moved to Bridie, wanting to explain that he was no longer who she perhaps thought he was, just as he wanted to tell the others. She whispered, 'I'm grateful to you, but I'm not sure James will be able to bear the thought that a fascist secured his release by using the Nazis, any more than I can.'

This time it was he who felt he had been punched. She left and he longed to chase her, tell her how sorry he was, that he had moved on, but something stopped him. Damn Potty. He fingered the mezuzah case.

Two hours later he used Richard's office telephone to call Potty on the number that Gladys had given him. He said, his voice low, 'I need to know who the Jews are who occupied the apartment my mother now lives in. I need them out of wherever they are, with permission to settle in Britain, and a way of getting them here. Once this is arranged, although it is still a bloody joke, I'll do it, and I'll do it well.'

There was a silence. Tim waited, because he knew quite well that it was something that would not be easy to arrange. However, those were his terms, and he was amazed at his strength, his coldness and determination.

Eventually Potty said slowly, 'I think it can be done, but we need to maintain your cover at all times, to everyone but your parents, who already know. Forgive me, dear boy, but you know that you must resume and maintain your attendance at the Hawton BUF Meeting House, you must resume your Peace Club attendance, you must *be* a fascist, and no-one else may know you are not. No-one.'

The person he most wanted to tell was Bridie, but he knew that he couldn't. She must continue to hate him, in her uncompromising way, because that would maintain the illusion more than anything else.

Potty repeated, 'Your dear parents, but no-one else.'

'Yes, I agree, but first, I need that Jewish family safe. So I will wait. Incidentally, just to keep you happy, Millie has some proof about something that would give us an additional and powerful lever over Heine. It is her security. I will tell you when you find that family and have arranged their escape from whatever hellhole they are in – I suspect it is a camp.'

Potty said, 'You're suitably tricky to be made for the role, laddie.' There was a click as the receiver was replaced.

He now understood why he hadn't told Potty the details of Millie's security earlier. He was learning about the politics of power, the need to keep something in reserve.

Chapter Twenty-Three

Spain, January 1938

James, Ian, Frank, Boyo and Sergeant Miller were amongst a small band of about twenty who had been marched from temporary hellhole to temporary hellhole since their capture. They were exhausted, hungry and footsore, and trying not to lose track of time. Their idea of heaven was escape or a proper camp. All the time they marched they noted landmarks – the distant mountains, villages, hamlets, churches, farms – so that they could work their way back, should a chance to escape occur. There had only been one break-out possible, and two men had taken it. Both had been shot. The guards were too alert, too determined.

Christmas had been and gone, and they were into the New Year and were on the move again. Marching was too strong a word; they were straggling along a trail through the usual small olive groves, the occasional pine, and acres of scrub, stones and dust. James remembered his Uncle Jack saying that the relief he felt when he arrived at a camp with structure, routine, safety and order was immense.

Well, he could bloody well do with that – they all could.

Ian stumbled beside him, regained his balance, swore quietly, but James was looking at a clutch of derelict farm buildings in the distance, a wire fence strung around the perimeter. Sergeant Miller rasped, 'Who knows, this could be a late Christmas present, our very own home from home, lads.'

His voice sounded as dry and cracked as James' throat felt. The guard at Miller's side gestured with his rifle. Miller grinned at him. 'José, just passing the time of day.' José smiled slightly, and shrugged. He'd been with them from the start and must have been as sick of it as they were, but at least it kept him out of the firing line.

They shambled on and reached a fork in the track. Would they go left, which led away from the buildings, or right? They went right, and relief gave them some energy, and even the guards stepped out. Sergeant Miller ordered, 'Straighten up, then. March, if you please. Remember who you are. Left, left, left.'

They marched the last three hundred yards, and in through the entrance, shoulders back. Now they could see that it was small enough to be a transit camp, yet again. Disappointment clutched at James; Ian swore; Boyo and Frank kicked at stones as they marched. They all scanned the wire for breaks, just in case. There didn't seem to be any, though there was another entrance at the far end of the camp, with the gate hanging open, as though half derelict. It seemed devoid of other prisoners, and just a few soldiers loitered around. Yes, a transit camp. James knew the others would be feeling the same disappointment.

Sergeant Miller ordered a halt. They stood. Their own guards mingled with the other soldiers, back-slapping, chatting, smoking. Ian said, 'I'd kill for a drag.'

Miller kept his men at ease. They waited. A small man strolled out from the roofless farmhouse, shouting orders in Spanish. James named him Garcia in his head. It was what he did on these occasions. He didn't know why, but somehow it helped. The guards who had accompanied them on the march looked at one another, and spoke to those already there, who shrugged and threw away their half-smoked cigarettes. One pointed to a barn set further back. José led their own guards over to its shade, and they helped themselves to water from a well before grouping together, lounging on the ground.

Garcia's men selected ten of 'Miller's Men', as the twenty now called themselves, handed them picks and shovels, and pointed to the ground a short distance away, which looked as though it had once been a pit but was now half full of rubbish, sand and rocks. What it must have been used for James had no idea. Perhaps they protected some sort of crop in it during the height of the summer.

Ian was amongst the ten who were ordered to dig it out. James and the others had their hands tied behind their backs, and were forced to kneel a short way from the working party. They sighed, wondering what the game was this time. James felt the rope dig deep into his wrists and scanned the skies. Who knew, perhaps Garcia was expecting Russian planes? Was this his idea of a safety trench? Would there be a chance of escape? He shook his head. No, if he had to bet on it, it would be a game.

They'd given up protesting at the indignities they had suffered. The only thing to do was to put up and shut up, because it would end, the bastards would become bored. They'd be released, to find shade and sleep. Perhaps even water and food. To do anything else meant a bloody good hiding.

His tongue swelled in the heat. Their knees hurt beyond endurance. Sergeant Miller demanded water from Garcia for his men. He was ignored. He tried again. James saw Garcia mutter to a guard, who stalked across, lifted the rifle butt and calmly and clinically clubbed Sergeant Miller to death, in front of them, his hands still tied behind his back.

The shock rippled down the line. The diggers didn't see, working with their backs to them as they were, their shovels clinking, the rocks crashing as they threw them onto the edge. Boyo stared from Sergeant Miller's body, to James. His lips were cracked, his eyes blank with horror, and an inability to absorb what had just happened. It was the same with them all. Their own guards were sprawled in the shade of the barn. James saw José start to rise. Another, Miguel, pulled him back down.

Was this a game? What sort of bloody game? James tried to speak but no words came. Garcia walked in front of him and the others, the smell of garlic oozing from him, mixing with, but not overlaying, the smell of Sergeant Miller's blood, which pooled and then seeped into the sandy ground. Ian and the working party continued to dig; James and the others continued to kneel, past the point of processing anything. The sun beat down, although it was winter.

Garcia fired questions at them in poor English. They refused to answer anything beyond their names, shock killing the pain of their knees. The smell of Sergeant Miller's blood was suffocating, and James thought he'd never be rid of it. They were invited to beg for their hands to be released so they could perform a fascist salute. They refused, and instead followed Boyo, who said, 'We are fighting for a return to democracy.' Garcia smiled, gestured, and each one kneeling received a jab to the head with a rifle butt.

Finally Garcia seemed satisfied with the hole. The diggers were instructed to throw their shovels onto the far edge. It was only then that they turned. For a moment it was clear that they couldn't work out what they were seeing. James saw that some of their own guards had emerged from the shade and were talking amongst themselves, shaking their heads.

José hurried off, keeping to the shade of the buildings, and was hard to see. Then he was through the far gates, running down the track which skirted the hill.

Now Garcia was shouting and James, along with the others, was grabbed by the soldiers and dragged along the ground. He fought, twisting and turning, because they were heading to the pit, and now he dared to think what the game was that was to be played.

Boyo said, 'No, they bloody don't.'

They were all fighting, leaving streaks of blood on the earth as jagged stones gouged flesh from their legs, but it was no good. They stopped on the edge of the pit. The guards wrestled them back into a kneeling position.

Frank said, 'They could be just shoving us in?'

Boyo said, 'Another bloody game?'

But no, there was Sergeant Miller. James' mind had frozen.

Several soldiers were aiming their rifles at the diggers, gesturing them out. They scrambled up onto the surface. They were corralled and forced away, held at gunpoint to one side. Their own guards were hesitating. Some stepped forwards, calling and gesticulating, then turning to look at the far entrance. José had not returned. Had he gone for help?

Garcia approached the kneeling line-up. They all watched as he stood at the end, by James, for a moment. He drew out his revolver from his holster belt. Everything seemed so slow. The man didn't fire it. James breathed again, but instead he walked to them, and behind them. James could smell the garlic. He heard a shot, smelt cordite. Boyo fell to the ground next to him, dead from a bullet to the head. The officer kicked him into the pit as James peed himself.

Garcia shot every other one of them in the back of the head, and kicked them into the pit. Sergeant Miller's body was then dragged and tossed in too. James and Frank were amongst the survivors, all of them kneeling in their own urine. Ian and the other nine stood like stone, pale as alabaster.

Ian's group was gestured towards their shovels. They began to refill the pit, covering their friends. Two soldiers cut those left kneeling free of their binding. One laughed, the other didn't. His hands were shaking, and he too had paled. James and the others were given shovels. The handles of the shovels were hot. Above a raptor glided on the thermals. Everything seemed quiet. There seemed to be no clink of shovel on stone. Nothing. They worked like automatons, just seeing the earth, sand, stones. Their friends must be buried.

Could any of this be real? How could it be? As they finished, and rested on their shovels, and stared at the blood-soaked ground, their minds began to work. Slowly they felt the horror really take hold. James looked at the shovel in his hand. He turned towards Garcia, who was smoking a cigarillo at a table that had been set up in the shade of the ruined farmhouse. On the table stood a carafe of wine. James lifted the shovel. He put one foot in front of the other, raising the shovel higher, heading for Garcia, the garlic-stinking officer who had killed his friends and his sergeant, his bastard bloody wonderful sergeant. Others were walking too.

Rifles were lifted, Garcia laughed. He gave the order. James took another step and then there was shouting. Miguel and the rest of their own guards were running towards them, their weapons out, but pointing at the soldiers, not at the prisoners. He didn't care. Another step, but then a rider galloped between them and Garcia, hauling his horse to a stop in a swirl of dust, sand, and the clink of a bridle. It was an officer, large, incensed, screaming his orders to his men, who ran behind him, panting, sweating, and there was José. He'd brought help, but too late. The air was full of outrage. James took another step. Garcia's men lowered their rifles but James and the others kept walking, shovels lifting higher, higher.

The officer set his men to face the prisoners then turned to fist the stinking Garcia to the ground, kicking aside the table. The wine spilled, red as blood. It seeped into the ground. It was then that James stopped, and laid down his shovel, along with the others, able, quite suddenly, to hear and see properly.

He heard Ian calling, 'You bastards.' He heard the recently arrived soldiers shouting and herding those other Spaniards away from the pit, at gunpoint.

'*Gracias por tus esfuerzos*,' he called to José, not sure if he had found the right words to thank him for his efforts.

José bowed slightly. '*No es de todos nosotros.*'

The recently arrived officer, unshaven and exhausted, kicked at the murderer on the ground, and turned to the survivors. 'Indeed, it is not all of us. My apologies.'

Ian muttered, 'But though the others didn't do it, they let it 'appen.' His voice was cold and shocked.

'*We* let it happen,' James said quietly.

They were herded into trucks and taken to an established camp, an old farmhouse. There was the sound of distant firing. They were thirsty, their tongues were swollen, their stomachs hollow. They sat in the cool of their room, and no-one really spoke, not for hours, or was it days, or weeks? Those already there had greeted them, and wondered at their silence. At last, Ian said, 'We dug a pit, they shot every other one. They killed our sergeant. We refilled the pit, clink clunk. Now bugger off, and don't ask again.'

They had not asked again, but a German socialist of the International Brigade had brought a handful of twigs and shown them how to play 'Pick up a Twig'. He told them it was February.

There was snow on the distant mountains. There

was one meal a day, sometimes. Gruel. There was structure, a sort of safety. Uncle Jack had been right. They ducked when *avion* was called. The firing in the distance was continuous. The days were long and filled with Pick up a Twig. They were getting rather good. Ian or Frank kept the score.

They lost three men in the camp from malnutrition that week. Two the next, one from malnutrition, one from a beating, or was it illness? James' knees were healing. They didn't complain, because the International Brigade was lucky in comparison with the Republican nationals. But then, it was said to be no picnic for fascists who were caught by the Republicans.

Ian thought they might be saving the foreigners for use as hostages. One man was released in return for a delivery of a mortar. They laughed. Rumour or fact? Who knew?

Who knew anything?

Chapter Twenty-Four

Easterleigh Hall, March 1938

James was unable to sleep, so he rose and walked down the side of the yew hedge, unable to believe that he was home. He reached the silver birches. The primroses carpeted the ground; birds sang, protecting their territory; the birch leaves were in early bud; the wind was cold. He reached the bothy and stared at his bike. The handlebars were rusty. He pulled it forward. The chain needed oiling. Perhaps he would do that. Perhaps.

He walked across the drive; the gravel crunched. He reached the arboretum and stared up at the sky. No bombers. He shut off his mind. The others would still be there, where he had left them. He shut off his mind again. He. Had. Left. Them.

He hadn't known then what it meant when the Italian officer arrived at the camp in his sleek black car, and strode up the steps to the commandant's office. All the prisoners had stopped what they were doing, because sometimes this happened, and people were dragged away. The fear was so tangible you could almost smell it. After a while three guards had left the commandant's office, while the Italian strolled to his car, slapping his swagger stick against his shiny boots, nodding to his driver. James had watched as they headed straight towards his Pick up a Twig group. Each of them, as though of a single mind, had stood, braced together.

'You,' the squat, brutal guard had said. He had pointed at James, who felt his legs almost go from under him. Ian grabbed one of his arms, and Frank, the other. He had swallowed the bile that had risen to his throat, forcing himself to stand upright.

'Why?' he had croaked.

'You,' the guard had shouted again. The other two had bashed Ian and Frank away and grabbed him.

'Why?' he had repeated, wanting to struggle, but refusing to show these bastards such fear.

Instead he had called back, as he was hustled away, 'I'll be fine.' Ian was nursing a broken nose; Frank was dabbing at a split lip. He'd walked to the car. 'Why?' he'd asked the officer standing by the car. He opened the back door. James said, 'I know nothing that can help you, except the rules of Pick up a Twig.'

'Get in,' the officer had ordered.

Inside was a German officer. He patted the seat beside him. 'Ah, Herr Williams. You have powerful friends, or someone somewhere is offering something of value in exchange for your return.'

James sat. The Italian slammed the door and eased into the front passenger seat. As the German's words sank in, James grabbed for the handle. It did not exist. 'I don't want to leave. They are my friends. How can I leave?'

The driver spun the wheels and took James away.

He reached out now, and touched the branch of a sycamore. It was smooth. The wind was chilly. Here there was food to eat, wine to drink, but even after two weeks at home, his stomach couldn't cope. He sighed, feeling as though he was looking at everything through thick glass. Primrose was beyond the leggy stage; Terry and Fanny were old professionals, ably taking over from Prancer. David was doing a grand job. Estrella and Maria were more settled, but had said little to him, beyond that they were happy he had survived.

It was as though Easterleigh Hall had flowed on undisturbed. There was a peace in that, he supposed, but the only thing he felt was a burning rage. It made him too hot all the time, it made him want to run, it made sleeping impossible, and when he did there was the sound of ragged shots, the voices of his friends calling, as he was shoved into the back of the Italian's car.

He ran headlong between the trees now, enjoying the pain of his ribs as they jolted and jarred, still not healed from one or other of his beatings in the prison camp. He arrived, panting, at the cedar tree. He checked his new wristwatch, given to him by his parents who had not been able to tell him quite how much they loved him, how relieved they were, and how much they wanted to box his ears for not telling them he was going, but knowing why he had not.

Tim was there as he had promised, because James had said he must thank him. He didn't want to, but he must.

He put out his hand, Tim shook it. James said, 'Thank you, but . . .'

There was a pause. Tim said, 'But . . . You left people behind. You feel guilty. You have nightmares. You wish in many ways you were dead. You want to try and get them out.'

James let his hand drop. How did his cousin know all this? Tim said, 'I will try to secure their safety. But . . .' Now it was his turn to stop.

Both men, for that was what they were now, James thought, turned and looked at the big house. Tim said, 'It's so solid, isn't it, James? It never seems to change, just runs on, no matter what bloody mess we get ourselves into.'

Just then, the dachshunds, Currant and Raisin, rushed round from the stables, barking, jumping up on Tim, licking, squealing their joy, snapping at one another so they could be first to be petted. Tim reached down and pulled their ears gently, 'Well, you two. You're pleased to see me, at least. How're you doing, you dear old things?'

Bridie's voice cut through the yaps, 'Come here, you two. Just come away.' The anger in her voice made the dogs cringe, and they slunk back along the lawn, and then the gravel, skirting round her and scuttling through the stable yard into the garage yard, and then the kitchen. She stared at Tim for a moment longer, her expression unreadable. She turned on her heel, and followed the dogs.

James dug his hands into his pockets. He wished they wouldn't shake as they did. He said, 'Do you remember the beck, Tim, when Bridie and I saw the flying ants?'

Tim nodded. 'Aye, bonny lad. We ended up in the water, as I remember.'

James said, 'When we were being bombed by your Luftwaffe mates, there was a line of ants busy on a ledge in the trench. Each time they were there, and I remembered the three of us together. I remember you coming when we screamed and ran. I remember you holding us to you. You were all wet. You made us wet too. What's happened to us, Tim? How did we get to the place we are now?'

He saw that Tim's hands were shaking too. Or had they already been when they shook hands? He looked closely at his cousin. 'Look at me, Tim.'

Tim turned. His eyes were full of tears, his hands *were* trembling and in his face was the memory of nightmares that James saw in his own, whenever he looked in a mirror. 'What happened to you, man?'

Tim turned away, dragging a hand across his eyes. He muttered, 'Just glad you're back, James. That's all.'

It wasn't all. James wasn't a fool, and neither did he want to stand here feeling his whole body racing, as well as his mind. He needed to move, to run. He said, 'For old times' sake?'

Tim turned. 'What do you mean?'

'The beck, now. Race you?'

It was something they used to do, but always slowed for Bridie so they could arrive at the finishing line together. The finishing line being the beck. Tim laughed, 'You're on.'

James counted them down, and they were off, running down the drive, the gravel kicking up behind them, James' ribs jolting, his legs weak from the prison camp. Tim powered ahead, stronger, fitter. They ran along the road to the crossroads, Tim well in the lead. James was panting, but he'd win over the bugger. Tim might have put James under an obligation, but . . . Now he placed the fury. That was it. He owed Tim, fascist Tim, the one who'd betrayed the family, the one . . .

He found energy from somewhere, and he began to gain on his cousin as they pounded along the road. A car passed and hooted. They took no notice. He was catching Tim now, though the breath was jagged in his chest. Tim was passing the church on the right, but James was only twenty seconds behind. There were sheep in the pasture beyond. Uncle Aub had put them out now the snow had cleared. There were crows pecking at the ploughed field on his left. They'd have to get the bird scarers out.

He was tiring, his legs were about done, he had to think of one step, and then another. One. Another. He had no shovel this time, no garlic-stinking officer . . . He reached the turn to the beck. Tim was still ahead but he was slowing. James powered on. Tiring, was he, the beggar? Well, *he* damned well wasn't, because the fury was back, driving him on. There were just over a hundred yards to the beck, and now he was pounding along the lane. The cobwebs in the hedge shuddered. He was drawing close. He was passing.

He snatched a look at Tim's face, but saw only a burgeoning sadness and disappointment, while in himself there was searing triumph. The beck was ahead. He could see it, and he was going to beat the bastard. The sun was glinting on the still surface, just as it used to. For a moment he heard their laughter, and Bridie's call, 'Wait for me.' He remembered their pace slowing, heard her panting as she reached them and they ran on, together.

In that second, the fury that had fuelled him since his return dissipated.

Now, he was the one slowing, and steadily Tim drew alongside, matching him pace for pace, until they reached the bank, together. As one, they bent over, gasping for breath.

'I'm getting too old for this,' Tim said, straightening, and dragging out his cigarettes, offering them to James.

He heaved himself upright and took one. Tim lit them with his lighter. 'What happened to you, bonny lad?' James asked again.

'Life,' Tim said flatly. 'Life is what happened, but what keeps me going is Easterleigh Hall, and the people in it. That's all you need to know, James. Just be happy you're home. You owe me nothing. It's been a good result and led me to what should be done.' He seemed tired.

James didn't understand. 'You're still going to the Hawton meeting hall, I hear?'

Tim paused, inhaled, exhaled. 'Yes.' That was all. They walked back together, side by side. 'The nightmares will fade,' Tim said.

'Yours have, then?'

'Listen.' Tim stopped, turned James around, gently. 'You don't want to know about my nightmares. You don't want to know about my life, not for now. It is enough that you *see* that I am still a fascist, but perhaps we can still be cousins. I love you, James. Remember that. I'll use my contacts to do what I can for your friends.'

They walked on together. James said, 'I don't und—'

Tim put up his hand, it still trembled. 'We're who we are. Get better, James, go to university, make a good life. Look after our family, if ever I can't.'

Neither spoke again until they reached Tim's

motorbike. James waited while Tim put on his gloves, his leather helmet, his goggles. They shook hands, but it wasn't enough for James. He pulled Tim to him. 'I don't know what the hell is going on, but something is. No matter who or what you are, I love you, and you need to take care.'

Tim pushed James away, mounted his motorbike, and thrust down on the kickstart. The engine fired. 'Thank you, but it's better if you hate me. Do you understand?'

For a long moment they looked at one another. 'I hate you,' James said. 'Don't worry, I hate you, very much.'

He watched Tim power down the drive. He didn't understand what was happening in Tim's life but he was left with a sense of the complexity of the world, and a feeling that a game was being played, one that was reserved exclusively for the lonely and the brave.

Bridie listened to the chatter as Evie and Ver prepared breakfasts for those who had risen late. Annie, her work at the Neave Wing done for the moment, hugged a mug of tea and said, 'Honestly, Matron and Sister Newsome are driving me scatty, fretting that David's burning the candle at both ends, what with the horses, *and* Estrella. Silly old dears don't seem to understand that the best thing in the world is for him to have a pretty girl sitting on his knee, as long as the brake's on, of course.'

347

Evie laughed, jerking her head at Bridie. 'Steady, less talk of s-e-x in front of the young ones.'

'Mum,' Bridie protested as the women burst out laughing.

Annie spluttered, 'Oh, Bridie, calm down, girl.'

Bridie shook her head. They were totally impossible, but she loved the lot of them, daft beggars.

She heard James then, rushing down the steps, whistling. They all looked at one another. He hadn't whistled since his return, so it had done him good to thank Tim. Well, good for him, because Bridie still found it difficult to be grateful to a bloody Nazi, because that's how she thought of him, and she was furious with James for getting in a situation where the family had to kowtow to someone like that for help. He should damn well have put up with prison.

He bowled in as though nothing had happened, calling, 'Any coffee on the go?'

Bridie slammed the kettle on the hotplate.

Her mother looked at her. 'Bridie?'

'Your bacon's burning,' Bridie snapped.

James looked from one to the other. 'Did you get out of bed the wrong side, Bridie?' he laughed.

'Well, that's better than getting into bed with the *wrong* side.' She barged past him. 'I saw you, all over him. I hope you're pleased with yourself.'

James was after her like lightning, and caught up with her in the doorway. 'Oh, shut up, Bridie. Look further than your—' He stopped. 'Just shut up, and grow up. He helped, when he didn't have to.'

'He's showing off, being the big hero, can't you see that? Look at Uncle Jack and Aunt Gracie, they're all over him like a rash.'

She ran off now, wanting him to follow her, wanting to wail, 'I love him, and I hate him, and you shouldn't be friends with someone like that.'

Chapter Twenty-Five

Potty had contacted Tim at his office a few days before James had arrived home, asking him to return his call at his convenience, as there was a problem with his laundry. Tim telephoned him back from a public telephone, feeling ridiculous. Potty told him that they had located Dr and Mrs Gerber, the previous occupants of Heine and Millie's apartment. Plans were being drawn up for their exit from Germany. 'Is that sufficient?' Potty asked. 'Or would you prefer them to be safely ensconced on our shores?'

Tim had thought of Sir Anthony's invitation on the mantelpiece in his bedsit. 'I trust you.'

'Thank you,' Potty replied.

Tim explained that he had received yet another black tie invitation from Sir Anthony, which he would accept. It was a bit late in the day, but he was such a nice bloke, he wouldn't mind. Tim still had his fascist badge and was attending not only Hawton BUF Meeting House but the one in Newcastle. They were pleased to have him because membership was down, apparently. The violence of the marches in the East End had put people off.

'Indeed, though we know without a shadow of a doubt that their friends, the Nazis, are still donating funds. Is this to support them if – well, if it comes to fisticuffs between Germany and us, one wonders, dear heart?'

Tim's grip tightened on the receiver. One did indeed wonder.

Potty was still talking. 'So we must continue to keep them under very close surveillance. Remember, you are re-injected with enthusiasm by your time in Berlin, and the excellent people you've been meeting, the help they've given you with James. Remember also that you speak no German, if any should slip into that language. Just listen, and report.'

Someone tapped on the window of the telephone booth. 'Just a moment,' Tim said into the receiver.

He opened the door to an irate elderly woman. 'So sorry, it's my mam. She's worried about my da so I'm having to talk her through the process. She's rather a grumpy old soul, but I must do this. Would you mind waiting, just a moment.'

The woman standing there in her headscarf smiled. 'Aye, lad, you help her. I'll wait.'

'Hello,' he said into the receiver, feeding coins in for more time.

'This is your grumpy old mam talking.'

They laughed. 'So, off you go to Sir Anthony's little soiree, and though I cast no aspersions on his good intentions, knowing him of old – at school together, we were – I have severe doubts about the paths some others might be treading. Eyes and ears, dear boy. Incidentally, we have an account at Norton's in Newcastle. Nip along for a *decent* dinner suit.'

'We?'

'Don't be obtuse, dear heart. The SIS, of course. Secret Intelligence Service. Report, please, soon.'

The dinner was at Sir Anthony's club in London on 13 March, and Tim enjoyed the food, but not the company. He sat next to Lady Margaret and opposite Herr Bauer, who was a guest – again. Somehow he wasn't surprised and felt sorry for his da, who must have no idea of his friend's connections. Or was this indeed still a Peace Club? He looked at Sir Anthony, so good and kind. Yes, surely it was, or at least from this philanthropist's point of view, and perhaps from Bauer's? Perhaps.

Lady Margaret was in full neigh, and Tim brought himself back to the point, fixed admiration on his face and dripped it over her, as she toasted the latest donation from 'our friends'. At the end of the table Sir Anthony smiled at her, but it didn't really reach his eyes. He looked as though he'd lost more weight. Tim toyed with his food, as Lady Margaret asked about Berlin.

'Wonderful,' Tim said. 'So exciting. The flags and banners, the night clubs. Though I haven't been for a few months.'

Lady Margaret patted her hair, which was going grey at the temples, and perhaps it was thinning a little? She had put it up in some sort of bun. Tim couldn't get the picture of Fanny's mane out of his head. Bridie would laugh if he told her. James too. He found the thought grounding.

Lady Margaret was talking, 'Such a fine body of men, so blonde and tall. It must be so much purer in Berlin now that *all* – for surely it is all – the Israelites have left. One does so wish,' she stopped, lifted her glass of German hock at Tim, and then Herr Bauer, 'that we find the will to similarly cleanse our country.'

Tim lifted his glass and touched it to his lips, but he couldn't drink to it. Across from him Herr Bauer toasted Lady Margaret. 'Perhaps you will be able to visit Berlin soon, Lady Margaret.' He replaced his glass. Sitting next to Herr Bauer was a faded older woman, and next to her was a man Tim thought he recognised, but he didn't think they'd been introduced. Perhaps he just hadn't heard in the hubbub of chat.

Sir Anthony said, 'I suppose Germany has had to sort out its internal affairs; it was in such a parlous state, economically and politically. I do know that many communists are Jews, and that they owe their allegiance to Russia. As such, I can see that they can be considered a threat. I believe your father, Tim, has experienced some extreme action by communist union representatives, and they have been voted out.' He sighed. 'One must hope it truly is all for the good.'

There was a silence, which Herr Bauer broke. 'Your cousin is home, I believe, safe and well.'

Tim smiled, and it was he who lifted his glass now. 'Yes, my step-father arranged his release. It helps to have people who know people.' He sipped the hock. He supposed it was good, but a beer would be better. He could take a bloody great gulp of that to wash the distaste from his gob.

Lady Margaret sipped her wine, replaced her glass carefully and said, 'I so admire you, Tim. You seem to have escaped the Easterleigh Hall curse of celebrating the common man, and I do mean common. I had this argument so many times with your Aunt Evie and Aunt Veronica when we fought for votes. They wanted universal suffrage, whereas I agreed with Emmeline and Christabel, who felt that it should be restricted to women of a certain education. Herr Hitler sees that most clearly. Only those with breeding and education can understand what needs to be done, and have the courage to do it.'

Sir Anthony said, 'I won't hear a word against all that Easterleigh Hall does, any more than young Tim, I suspect.'

A silence fell. Lady Margaret flushed and looked confused. She gestured for her glass to be refilled. Tim smiled, though he actually wanted to shove Lady Margaret's face into her veal in white wine. It wouldn't spoil it because it wasn't a patch on Bridie or Evie's, but instead he said, 'I can just imagine the battles you had, Lady Margaret, and what's more, perhaps because times were different, you were able to overstep the mark, and live to tell the tale.'

Sir Anthony nodded. Across from him, Herr Bauer raised his glass. 'Very adroit.'

Lady Margaret didn't understand the irony and tittered. The conversation resumed along familiar lines, until the faded woman asked Tim if he had attended the theatre in Berlin the last time he was there? He shook his head. She was on her fourth glass of wine, though had not eaten very much. 'We attended on our last trip, didn't we, George?'

George said, 'Mr Forbes doesn't want to hear about that, my dear. All far too boring.'

But Mr Forbes did. Tim said, 'Sounds interesting, so perhaps I should go again soon. Yes, I think I will. What did you see?'

George laid his hand on his wife's. She shrugged him off. 'Don't be a bore, George.'

No, please don't, George, thought Tim. I'd love to know when you were there and who you met, because it had come to him at last that this was Sir George Edgers, a high-up in the Foreign Office, which was where Sir Anthony also worked. 'Do go on, Lady Edgers,' he urged.

Lady Edgers did indeed go on. 'Oh, what is the theatre called? Well, never mind. You go onto the Lutherstrasse, in the Schöneberg district, you know, not far from the Kaufhaus des Westens department store, which you and Herr Bauer will know as KaDeWe. My dears, on stage were girls in perfect unison doing the cancan, wearing costume after costume. Their marching matched the SS for perfection, honestly it did. Our hosts were tapping in time. So smart in their uniforms.'

Tim let her talk, but they left soon after. Lady Edgers, Sir George decided, was unwell. Tim thought, not so, dear heart. She's absolutely drunk out of her mind. Oh God, he thought, I'm becoming Uncle Potty.

Lady Margaret's friend, Freda Wilson, sat the other side of Herr Bauer and she was wittering about Spain, and the marvellous progress of Franco. He'd like to put her in a room with James. At the thought of James he smiled slightly. He was safe, they had shaken hands, James had told him he hated him very much, just as he had asked. But it wasn't hate. Not any more.

On his way home from the railway station in the small hours, he asked the taxi to drop him off at the telephone box. He phoned through his report to Potty, and slept well, feeling he was fighting back, and knew where he was going.

The following evening, the wireless carried the news that the Nazis had annexed Austria. Potty wrote him a note: '*And so it begins. Suggest a trip to Berlin, very soon. Mr Andrews will not object.*'

Chapter Twenty-Six

A few days after Sir Anthony's dinner party, Tim's telephone buzzed in his office. He left his design board and crossed to his desk, his mind on the dynamo that the Royal Navy required updating, as soon as possible. Since the Anschluss there was a sense of urgency, where before there was none. It had seemed to be reiterated in the frenetic screaming of the gulls as he had hurried to work early this morning.

'Good morning, Anthea,' he said into the receiver.

The telephonist they now employed said, 'Nothing good about it, young Tim. I have a private call for you, from someone who calls himself Sir Anthony Travers, and you should tell your friends to stop using silly names. Also, you need to get yourself a home line. I'm not your private secretary. Or, on the other hand, you can take me out for a drink.'

He laughed. 'A drink would be cheaper.'

'Don't bank on that, bonny lad. I'll put him through then, shall I?

'Yes, and he *is* a Sir, for your information.'

'You still need to get your own home line.' There

was a click. He heard Anthea say, 'Putting you through, sir.'

Sir Anthony came on the line. 'Forgive the intrusion, Tim. I'm in a bit of a rush and I know this is a working day for you. I gather from your kind note of thanks that you are to visit your mother soon. I did wonder, yet another little task. A packet. I will send it with my driver, if that is alright. He will wait in your reception to deliver it into your hand, as I feel these things can become lost. Would this be a possibility?'

Tim kept his voice level, 'Of course. Yes, I am on my way soon as I have some holiday owing. I thought I must try that theatre that Lady Edgers was telling me about. I will ask Anthea to buzz me, and I will come down and collect it. Will it be this morning?'

'Tomorrow, at eleven thirty. I'm in London, so he'll drive up with it. Things are looking more, shall we say, uncomfortable, but one must keep the hand of friendship extended, the way open to peace, though . . .' He trailed off.

Tim said, 'Are you still there, Sir Anthony?'

'Yes, indeed.' He sounded brisk again. 'I have business in Carlisle tomorrow, and as I say, my driver will take me, and then deliver it to you. My thanks, Tim. My regards to your mother and that . . . and your step-father.' The line went dead.

Tim replaced the receiver slowly. He had written to his mother just after Sir Anthony's dinner party, as Potty had requested, with the news that he would be visiting them, to thank them so much for returning James. Potty had also told Tim to spread it around at the dinner party, to see what transpired. And now Sir Anthony wanted him to deliver a package.

He pictured the lovely Sir Anthony, his trust in people, the packages he had carried for him, Heine's hunger for them. All thoughts of the dynamo he had been working on completely receded as he rose and stood by the window. The sky was grey, but clearing. Soon it would be blue.

He had thought to walk at lunchtime, but longed to be out in the air now, smoke drenched though it was, and busy with trams, cars, lorries, buses, hawkers, shoppers, the employed, the unemployed, because they were his people, his traffic, his smoggy air. Instead he opened the dirty window and leaned out, just a fraction. He didn't want to go to Berlin. But Dr and Mrs Gerber were out of the camp – soon they'd be here – so he had a bargain to which to hold firm.

The telephone buzzed again. It was Anthea. 'It is your own private secretary here, and now that's two sherries you owe me. It is a Mr S-m-y-t-h-e wanting to talk to you now. I know that it's with a "y" because I repeated Mr Smith, and he spelt it. Cheeky beggar, as though I care how he spells his name. So, shall I put the idiot through?'

Tim was laughing as Potty came on the line. It was the name they'd decided upon. 'Are you there, dear boy?' he bellowed. 'Give me a tinkle in an hour or so to discuss that little job on the side.' Click. Tim looked at his design and sighed. He had proper work to do, but that seemed irrelevant to Potty.

He put in almost an hour, then sprinted down the stairs. 'Taking an early lunch,' he said as he hurried out.

'Huh,' sniffed Anthea. Her hair was red this week, burnt auburn, she'd called it. She was married to a sailor and loved him to the heavens, she had told Tim last week, after his ship had set sail for six months and her eyes were swollen with crying.

He had thought that described his feelings for Bridie. Or did it? Sometimes he didn't know what was real, what was imagined, because the change in his feelings had been so sudden. All he knew was that when he saw her, or thought about her, everything else faded to nothing. She was so beautiful, such a bloody handful, so different from everyone, but then she always had been. Today, just as every day, he ended up pushing Bridie away, because it was one muddle too many.

He telephoned Potty from a different telephone booth. He had discovered last week that Potty's telephone number connected to a central switchboard, from where it was transferred to whatever office he was working in at that moment.

Potty answered. 'You've had a telephone call.'

'Is my telephone bugged, or is his?'

'Now, now.'

'Yes, Sir Anthony has been in touch, Potty. He would like me to take a package to Germany, but this is Sir Anthony we're talking about, for goodness' sake, the best man in the world.'

A lorry revved as it passed, the fumes noxious. He coughed. Potty was saying quietly, 'We've been watching Sir Anthony for some while, fearing he is accessing files within his sphere of information, and passing them through you, or whoever else, to Heine. He started by just sending his own plans of the Neave Wing, when he met Millie and Heine "by accident". As you say, he is the best, a good-hearted, peace-loving plum, ripe for the picking. Like Topsy, though it's growed. Oldest espionage trick in the book.'

'What do you mean, growed?'

'The dear old lad thought it was hands across the sea – "none of us want another war". He must have thought it so wonderful to meet like-minded Germans. Then, wonder of wonders, after the Neave Wing plans, perhaps some photographs of suitable sites in Britain, so they can find comparable sites in Germany. They will now have this in a file, for use in an invasion. Then it was plans for a dam of an existing British reservoir, to service a drought-stricken area.'

'A dam?' Tim queried.

'Ah, Tim, my innocent boy. Once you know how it's built, you know its weakness – a short cut to destruction. A great gush of water is a powerful weapon. This, too, will have been popped into a file. Then perhaps the minutes of meetings, because there is no way out now for Sir Anthony, except ruination, and how will that damage his son? Who knows how many others are doing the same thing, because they've been hooked in the same way, or are doing it out of conviction, or for money?

The pips were going. Tim fed in more coins. Above the sky was clearing as he had thought it would, and blue was showing. Was it enough to make a pair of sailor's trousers? So many questions, so few of the answers he wanted to hear.

'So, what happens to the Sir Anthonys of this world?'

'Finally, as it goes on, one has to lay a few traps, unpleasant though it is. A further piece of misinformation has been left, in plain sight, just to prove to ourselves . . .'

'A further piece?'

'We don't rip people's hearts out unless we absolutely have to, so it's best to test them with information that is of no use. I've tried to chat around the subject, when we have met in the club. But ever the gentleman, he sticks to banalities. He is not looking well, and that could be because he is being squeezed by your esteemed step-father. It must be doing Heine's career no end of good.'

'What about Herr Bauer? I hope you're keeping an eye on him. He knows too many people and is always there, like a black spider.'

'Leave me to deal with Herr Bauer.'

'I don't want to stay too long over there.'

'Don't, just tell him you're busy at work. He'll be interested in that. Provide some innocuous information, if you will.' Click. He was gone.

Tim arrived in Berlin just a few days later, to an atmosphere that was euphoric. The Hitler Youth were, as ever, marching in the street, but probably a new intake, another load of youngsters for the Hitler-mill. His taxi gave a squad a wide berth. Tim forced a smile. Once there, he almost ran across the foyer to the lift, waving to the block leader, pressing the button. Come on, come on. It came. He pulled the gate shut. It rose, stopped. He walked along the passage, touched where the mezuzah case had once been. Potty had said the plans to bring the Gerbers home was complete, and soon to be put into operation. He braced himself, and rang the bell.

His mother opened the door, hugging him, drawing him in. He dropped his bag, held her, breathing in her perfume. It smelt expensive. He explained that it was a flying visit, as work was so busy. 'So sad, so usual. You are a busy boy, and you must tell Heine all about it, darling Tim.'

She pulled him through to the sitting room. She was holding out her hands, showing off her wedding ring. 'I am officially Mrs Weber.'

He feigned delight. 'How wonderful! If I'd known I'd have brought a present.'

'We can go and buy one. Let's try KaDeWe, on Lutherstrasse. I went not long ago with a lovely couple, the Edgers. He's a Sir, you know. So, don't take off your coat. I'd like a jacket for the summer, so much to celebrate. What fun, darling Tim.'

He followed her back into the hall. 'Wouldn't you prefer something for the apartment that you could enjoy together?'

She laughed, almost running to the lift. 'Good heavens, why? We have everything we could possibly need.'

As Tim shut the lift gate he muttered, 'Of course, how could I forget?' Then caught himself. 'After all, you deserve it.' His mother's frown changed to a smile. She really was the most stupid of women, he thought, but knew that he needed to keep a close watch on himself, in case he found traces of her in his character.

They took a taxi to Lutherstrasse, and swept into the Kaufhaus des Westens department store, and for the next hour he experienced hell, as she went from one overheated floor to another. In the end she chose a pale blue lightweight jacket, and a more expensive necklace to go with it. The necklace she paid for, thank God. Her wallet was stuffed with notes. Everywhere there were excited shoppers; the talk was all of their success, or the wonderful Führer. He pretended he could understand none of it and in the taxi home she chided him for his lack of progress with the German language.

He said again, 'We have so much work on.'

Again she said, 'You must tell Heine.'

Again they passed a Hitler Youth Brigade. He watched them but said, 'So, the wedding. Did his family come? Where did you say he was born?'

'Somewhere near Marburg. You wouldn't know the village. Such a department store, isn't it, Tim? Nothing like that in sad old England, just pits and slag heaps and a few nobs on the hill.' Tim gripped her parcels too tightly, but it was better than slapping her.

They arrived, and waiting for them in the sitting room, by the card table, was Heine. Tim strode across, his hand out. 'I hear congratulations are in order, Father.' He laughed. After a moment, Heine laughed too. There were bags under his eyes, and a frown deep between his eyes, but walking into other people's countries was tiring, Tim supposed. Though there were those who said that the Austrians had welcomed them with open arms.

Heine was tapping his foot. 'Is there anyone in? Or are you asleep?'

Tim realised he had been deep in his thoughts. 'So sorry, did you say something?'

'The package. Please, so sorry, but it's very busy in Berlin at the moment, as you can well imagine.'

'Ah yes, I can indeed imagine. Our own work is extremely busy too, which is why I'm really just on a turnaround trip, though I had to come, to catch up. It seems too long since the last time. So pleased

365

I came, especially as you have just married Mother, and I needed to thank you for James' release too. Perhaps we should go for a meal, or to a club?' He was diving into his inside pocket. Potty had met him at Dover, at the laundry, where he had photographed the contents, then resealed it. Heine examined the seal, noticed nothing and opened it. They were carbon copies of minutes of a meeting, Potty had told him. Real minutes? Who knew? The trap around Sir Anthony had closed. But they would do nothing, yet.

Watching Heine, Tim felt sick. Poor, stupid Sir Anthony. Out of his goodness, his panic to avoid death and injury to others, he had misjudged. There were some people you could only stand up to, or stand against, but he must know that now that he was in their web.

The doorbell rang. Amala answered it, and called, 'Frau Weber.'

Millie left. It was the telegraph boy, with a message for Tim. Millie brought it into the sitting room. 'Not bad news, I hope?'

He ripped it open. Who? Not his da, or Mam? Only they knew he was here, apart from Potty and Sir Anthony. 'We require you to return immediately stop work is pressing stop apologies to your mother stop be at the station at eighteen hundred hours. Smythe'

Potty. What the hell? He checked his watch, handing the telegram to his mother, who read it aloud. Tim said, 'I must leave, it's five already. But first, may I use the conveniences?'

He went into the room which was his bedroom. He did not use the bathroom, but instead snatched a photograph frame from the dressing table, and a small porcelain pot. But the loss might be noticed, and if it was, Amala would be blamed. He put them back. He hunted for something else to give the Gerbers when they arrived in England, whenever that was. He checked the drawers. There were hatpins, several. He took two, stuffed them in his pocket. There were also some hair ribbons. He took two of those too.

He returned to the sitting room. 'That's better. But I must rush.'

Heine smiled. 'I would like to hear your work problems, so I will come too. We will use my car or you will not be there in time. When you are safely embarked, I will then proceed to the office. We workers, what lives we lead.'

In a rush they used the stairs, as there were already three queuing for the lift. Tim's brain ached as it searched for some sense in the telegram.

The traffic seemed to part for Heine's black car. Did the other drivers know it was SS? Perhaps from the number plate? The driver knew the back ways, which helped. Heine pumped him for information, and Tim talked of a mythical problem, and the difficulties the warships were experiencing because of it. Potty would call it misinformation, dear heart.

They drew up at the station. Heine said, 'I will come.'

He left the driver, and as they hurried to the concourse, Tim's mind was racing. What had happened, why that train?

He heard someone shouting, 'Heine, how delightful, and Mr Forbes. How extraordinary.' Herr Bauer was hailing them, hurrying from a booth which sold refreshments. Tim checked his watch. Herr Bauer flashed a Heil Hitler towards Heine, and pumped Tim's hand. A note was passed. Tim's hand closed over it, and he tried not to stare at Herr Bauer, who had moved between Heine and Tim, taking the SS officer's arm.

'Well, this is a delight, Heine. I need to talk to you on an urgent matter, how fortuitous.' He turned to Tim. 'And you look as though you are on your way to a train, Mr Forbes, please, don't let me stop you. Now, Heine.'

Firmly he led Heine, pristine in his uniform, over to the booth. The crowds parted before the SS officer, as though they were the Red Sea. It was fear, Tim saw that now, but there was admiration in the eyes of some. Tim called after them, 'Goodbye. I must rush.' They were too far away to hear.

He headed for the train, checking over his shoulder. No-one followed. He read the tiny note, cupping it in the palm of his hand:

Expected package (Dieter) in seat 12 and (Bernat)

17 Carriage 9. Your seat 14. Make contact carefully. Paperwork with them.

Agent unexpectedly unavailable. Be alert.

Tim coughed, with his hand to his mouth. He ate it, thinking that the spy novels he was reading were surprisingly helpful, and realising that the package must be the Gerbers.

He clambered onto the train, the whistle blowing as he did so. Sweat was pouring down his face. He checked Seat 12. A middle-aged man was there, his hat pulled down, reading a newspaper. His hand was skeletal and trembled. There was as yet no-one next to him. Tim sat, then made a show of checking his ticket. He said, in bad German, 'Wrong seat, my apologies, Herr Dieter.' The man looked closely at him. Tim nodded, and smiled gently.

He moved along, to Seat number 17. He took the spare seat there, and said something similar to the painfully thin woman, who also read a book, upside down. As he left, he turned it up the right way, and smiled. She looked petrified. He patted her hand. He found his own seat, saying to the woman sitting next to him, in English, 'I find foreign travel very trying. I get confused.' He showed her his ticket, in the face of her incomprehension. She nodded, and turned to the window.

His heart was beating out of his chest. What the hell had gone wrong? Was an agent even now in some stinking cellar spilling his guts to the Gestapo? Would the Gerbers be picked up as they travelled across borders on their way to Calais? Would he fight for them? He felt sick with fear.

And Herr Bauer? God, the man must have nerves of steel to live such a lie, because it was now clear that he was Potty's man.

By the time they reached the ferry, at fifteen hundred hours the next afternoon, Tim's clothes were damp with sweat and he felt he'd aged fifty years. There were only the embarkation papers to come, but so far, the Gerbers had floated through all controls. They did so again, with Tim a pace behind, steadying them with his presence, it seemed, though not a word was spoken between them. The gulls were soaring and screaming as they, along with many others, made their way up the gangplank, and at last, onto the deck. Within moments, the ferry set out for Dover.

It was then that Frau Gerber sank to her knees, weeping. Her husband and Tim helped her up, and to a bench along the side of the boat. Frau Gerber said, 'We leave our daughter beneath the earth, but she is with us, in our hearts, always. She was twelve, ill, and we had no hospital that would take a Jew. Yes, she is in our hearts.'

The Gerbers sat together; Tim sat a space away. Tim said, looking at the surging sea, 'Would you like to go inside? I can't, it makes me sick. I'm not a good traveller.'

Herr Gerber smiled. 'If you had extra hands, you

370

could press an energy point on your wrists. It would help. But no, we will sit here, if it is safe for you to be seen with us.'

'I think it is safe, but just in case, let us look at the horizon, not at one another. I will also "read" my book.' He dug out his book, *The Thirty-Nine Steps*, which he had brought to give him courage, looking around for over-curious passengers. The weather had changed to a light drizzle, however, and no-one was daft enough to remain on deck. He withdrew the cigarette case from his pocket. He took it with him when he visited Heine, to reinforce his assimilation into the fold. He had hoped that one day he could return it to its rightful owners. 'My step-father gave me this. I believe it is yours.'

He placed it on the bench between them, while looking at the horizon. Herr Gerber took it, tracing the worn menorah. 'It is my father's. You have no idea how important it is to us. My brother lives in America. He will be so pleased too.'

The couple who must be in their late thirties, if that, looked much older as they fingered all they had left of their life in Germany. Their tears fell when he also placed the hatpins and the ribbons on the bench. They had used the ribbons for their daughter's hair, Frau Gerber murmured.

Tim said, 'I wanted to bring more, but it would have been noticed, perhaps, and the maid would have been suspected.'

'So much for you to think about. So much,' Herr Gerber replied. 'We can never thank you.'

Tim shook his head. 'You don't understand. It is *my* mother who lives in your apartment.'

Herr Gerber shook his head. 'Your mother is not you. A man whose face we never saw came to our camp, at night. We didn't believe him. We thought, if we went with him, he would lead us to our deaths. He explained. He is a brave man. We don't know who he is. If you do, please thank him. And we thank you, all of you. I am a doctor, I heal the sick, but could not heal my own child, though I helped a former patient, a Gentile. For this, we were sent to camp.'

Frau Gerber leaned forward, as though to see the waves more clearly. Behind her hand she said, 'Remember, you are not your mother. Now, should we move to sit elsewhere? For your safety, as there are people now?'

The drizzle had stopped. Passengers had emerged. Tim turned a page of his book, his eyes scanning the deck. Who was that man over there, with the cap, watching the people milling? Who was that woman to their left, who seemed to be reading a book, just as he was?

'Perhaps if you took a walk up and down, and found a seat near, but not too near?' They did, walking arm in arm. The wind was high, and soon Tim felt too ill to care who anyone was, and seriously considered throwing himself over the side.

At last they arrived at Dover. At the bottom of the gangplank, a man in a mackintosh stood waiting. He shook hands with the Gerbers, looking at them, but saying to Tim, who was a pace behind them, 'Fall back a pace or two, I have them now.' He steered the Gerbers ahead. Tim followed behind.

The man had a fit of coughing, and had to stop. Tim almost knocked into him. The man gripped his arm as though in apology. He said, 'Check your pocket.'

The man turned back to the Gerbers. 'Come along, let's get things sorted. You are quite safe now.' They hurried away. Tim made a great show of checking his watch, patting his pockets and drawing out his book, nodding with relief, as though worried he had lost it. With the book he also withdrew the expected note, and placed it in the book, as though a bookmark, noting as he did so, *'Agent lost. Need to reconsider your position. Cover possibly blown. Telephone Smythe.'*

Tim went on his way to the station, thinking of the lost agent, and Herr Bauer.

Chapter Twenty-Seven

Easterleigh Hall, April 1938

Annie, Evie, Bridie, Mrs Moore and Ver spent two days making plans for Sir Anthony's surprise seventieth birthday in May. To finalise everything they called a meeting at ten thirty in the morning. They sat around the kitchen table with Maudie, Harry, Richard, James and Mr Harvey, while Kevin and Ron guarded the reception desk.

Mrs Moore muttered, 'And what, exactly, will you be doing for my ninetieth birthday?'

Evie groaned, 'Surely you're not still going to be going strong by then?'

Bridie put her arm around Mrs Moore. 'Sticks and stones may break our bones, but words they cannot hurt us, eh, Mrs Moore?'

'Ah, rebellion in the ranks,' Aunt Ver said, brandishing pen and paper. 'For that you can write the invitations, and remember, we do not make comments about the guests, as this is for Sir Anthony's sake, not ours. So write them with good grace, please, young lady.'

She tossed the list on the table, and pointed to the invitations on the dresser.

Bridie did as she was told.

On 5 May, in the ballroom, the assembled guests consumed virtually the whole of the buffet, which had included many of Bridie's haute cuisine classics. At the end of the meal the tables looked like a train crash, she thought, with their scrunched-up napkins, and some knocked-over glasses. She looked around for the temporary staff and gave them the nod, because all the regular staff members were guests, at the behest of Sir Anthony.

The guests assembled around Sir Anthony, and his birthday cake. Bridie had iced it. It was not as good as Mrs Moore's would have been, but it was passable. Well, more than that, she thought to herself, trying not to look at Tim, who stood with Lady Margaret and Penny, near to Sir Anthony.

Her mam thought Lady Margaret might marry Sir Anthony. Bridie did hope not; she was such a horrid woman, and he was so nice, and the whole thing was so odd.

James stood beside her and whispered, 'I do so hope the speeches don't go on forever, as I really want a slice of your masterpiece.'

She folded her arms. She was cross with him, still. Tim stood across from them. 'Look at him,' she hissed. 'With that stupid girl fluttering all over him. Why can't he see them for what they are?'

'Perhaps he can, and . . .' He stopped.

She said, 'I'll finish it for you. Perhaps he can, because that's who he is, too. We all know that, so why are you always defending him?'

James flushed. 'You can be so – hard. I think there's something else going on, he's . . .'

She put up her hand. 'Yes, let me finish it for you. He likes her, so I've said it for you.'

Her da was beside Sir Anthony now, tapping his wine glass for silence. 'I hope you've all topped up your glasses for the toast, to Easterleigh Hall hotel, and the Neave Wing's generous benefactor. It's been our great pleasure, Sir Anthony, to know you for many years, and to celebrate such an important birthday. We admire your goodness and kindness more than you can ever know. We admire your drive for peace, we applaud you for all your good works, and toast the honourable example you have set us all. Ladies and gentlemen, I give you, Sir Anthony Travers.'

All assembled raised their glasses and repeated, 'Sir Anthony Travers.'

Bridie brought the glass to her lips. Across from her, Tim looked so sad, and his shoulders were slumped. The glass was in his hand, at his lips. He didn't drink, but brought the glass down and just held it. What was the matter with him?

Now Sir Anthony spoke, 'I thank you all, and you,

Auberon. I feel I am not an example.' He stopped. Tim was looking at him, his shoulders rigid now. Behind him she could see Potty. Did he touch Tim's shoulder? No, there was no hand there now. Sir Anthony continued, 'I feel that I have been remiss. I have been busy supporting this, that and the other, and somehow I have found little time for my family.' He held out his hand now. 'Annie, would you come and help me cut the cake?'

Bridie looked for her mother, and they lifted their eyebrows at one another. Annie? At last. 'You see,' Sir Anthony admitted, 'I have been blind to many things, so focused have I become on my need to change the world.' He laughed, and so did others, who knew of his urge for peace. Did they also know how many of the Club were fascists? Probably not, because today they weren't wearing their badges.

Sir Anthony said, 'I asked Annie and Harry to bring the boys this evening, though I fear they have been bored beyond tears.' He raised his glass to the boys, who shook their heads, like the little gentlemen they were. 'I want to say, though I have said it before, that they are the most wonderful family. I am proud of Harry and the way he has created a valuable role for himself; I am proud of Annie, for running the Neave Wing as she does, and my wonderful grandsons.'

Harry was standing next to Annie now. They both looked pleased but confused. Well, Bridie thought, they're not alone. James whispered, 'I do wish they'd cut the ruddy cake.'

She grinned suddenly. Trust James to break the moment. He had changed since his return, but not that much. He was just more grown up. Sir Anthony said, 'Now to cut this magnificent cake, made and iced by the clever Bridie Brampton.'

He cut the cake now, with Annie's hand on his. The temporary staff moved in, to cut the rest, and circulate to the tables, as people headed back to their chairs. Harry set the band playing, and suddenly, as Bridie moved across and tried some crumbs, everything was wonderful, because the cake tasted just as it should. As good as any her mother had made, and Sir Anthony had called it a magnificent cake, and what's more, he had praised Annie.

As the coffee arrived dancers took to the floor, including Tim, who led out Penny. They danced and Penny floated as though on gossamer wings. Bridie wanted to kick her feet from under her. She hadn't realised Tim was a good dancer, but why would she? He usually said he couldn't. He had yet another new skill, then.

She turned on her heel, fury and jealousy raging. She bumped into James. 'Shall we?' he grinned, bowing.

'No, we shall not.' She swept through the glass doors which opened to the terrace. Two couples were dancing out here. She stormed past, and out onto the lawn, breaking into a run and only stopping beneath the branches of the cedar tree. She heard James panting behind her. 'Crikey, we used to slow down so we could reach the beck together, but you'd outrun us both now.'

She stared back at the Hall, loving it, waiting for it to work its magic and soothe her. She said, 'We're not those children any more. That won't ever happen again.'

'No, Bridie, you're wrong, it did. Tim waited for me, that day when you shouted for the dogs. He waited and we reached it together. Bridie, you have to let it go. We're not a police state yet, people have a right to be what they want to be.'

'I can't. I won't, and how can you say that?'

'Because I love you. Because you're just so stubborn. Because you prattle about democracy but you won't live it.'

She shook her head. 'I won't live it, not for this. He goes to Berlin. He supports cruelty and evil. He pitches up at that damned meeting house where they spout their prejudice, their hate. He has dinner with that horse-faced woman. He dances with her daughter.'

James waved his finger at her. 'That's it, though. He dances with her daughter. Have a good look at yourself, Bridie. Perhaps he's made his choice and it's not you. But I'm here.'

She stalked off, calling back, 'Oh James, don't be daft. You're my friend, my cousin, and so is he. We all belong together, which is why he should be here too.'

Tim led Penny back to her mother, and obeyed Potty's minute gesture. They had not been in contact for a while, as Tim had been instructed to lie low after helping the Gerbers to escape, and he was curious to know what Potty had to say now. He followed him out onto the terrace, but it was too crowded. Potty strolled out towards the cedar tree, passing Bridie on the way. 'Evening, Bridie,' Potty called.

'Oh shut up,' she shouted at Potty, stalking past him and Tim.

Potty stopped, and stared after her. 'Goodness,' he said to Tim. 'Lovers' tiff – look at young James, striding towards the ha-ha at a rate of knots.'

Tim looked from James to Bridie's retreating figure. Oh God, he hoped not, because he wanted to be the man she chose to love. Potty called him, 'Come along. We have things to talk about. And isn't she rather young for you?'

Tim shook his head. 'There's something about Bridie that was born strong, bold and old. She might say a lot, but it usually needs saying, and it's always the truth, unlike us, Potty, and I'd die for her. Now, what did you want to say?'

Potty blew on the ash of his cigar. 'Walk with me to the tree. It seems to have the wisdom of years, which it has inherited from the one before, I suspect.'

He waited until they were there, safe beneath its branches, looking at the soft light streaming from the windows of the Hall, and listening to the music. Potty said, 'Please God the lights do not again have to go out over Europe. I did think, for one moment, that Sir Anthony was going to confess all to the assembled company, and I'm pleased he didn't. There would then be no way back, and he's a good old cove. I am working to find a way that he can honourably face what is left of his life.'

'Does he know he's blown?'

'Not yet. We are using him to our advantage and I hope that in due course, when it is time to haul him in, that will serve to expiate him in his own eyes. He is clearly aware of the murky waters in which he's paddling, but we can't throw him a life-belt yet, or we will be unable to save his name. We have to work carefully and patiently and hope to God he doesn't blow the gaff before we are ready.'

'Using him to our advantage, you say?'

Potty laughed slightly. 'Yes, but, dear heart, the world is short of good men.'

It was a relief to be able to talk freely with Potty. Besides, he liked the man. 'What about me? Am I blown?' He wanted Potty to say, Yes, never go again, it's too dangerous, because he'd received a letter from his mother, wanting the original of the letter or Heine would be forced to take steps. What those were, he had no wish to know.

Potty said, 'We're fairly sure you are safe. We did

381

lose our man on the ground in Berlin, but no-one seems to have made a connection with you, or registered that Dieter and Bernat were the Gerbers. We feel that it is thought they are roaming free, somewhere on the continent.'

'So, at some stage you will be sending me to Germany again?' He barely breathed, waiting for the answer.

'Possibly, old tosh, though I feel that the time will come when you are of more use working within Britain. There will be agents here to be turned, or exposed, such as the Lady Margarets of this world, who could take their infatuation with the master race into the realms of treason, if she has not done so already. Penny has potential also, one feels. An asset, though not in the way she would wish.'

'She is just a young woman,' Tim protested.

'One who is a rabid anti-Semite, who, in her own words, insists that Germany is not a dictatorship but a system that is merely simplifying democracy, to enable them to march into the East, the West and wipe the place clean of sub-humans. I quote verbatim.'

Tim objected, 'She's a stupid young woman who hasn't seen all that we have, and is parroting her mother. You can't manipulate her in that way, it's too damned cynical.'

'Bless you, dear boy. She has been to Berlin several times with her mother, and rather enjoys the incidents of persecution. Oh, did you not know? I have several rather interesting photographs of her, one of which portrays her clapping when an elderly Jew is made to sweep the pavement with his hands after his shop window was heaved in by a few of Hitler's finest. I gather the cuts were rather severe. That photographic evidence is by no means the worst. What say you to that?'

Tim leaned back against the tree, his hands in his pockets. He fingered the mezuzah case. 'Bridie would rather clean the pavements like that herself, than allow it to happen to anyone else. What's more, she'd tell them all the time what bastards they are, and get herself killed.'

Potty laughed, loud and long. 'Oh yes, I do believe you are right. She'd be a fat lot of good in our game.' He looked up through the branches. 'She loves you.'

Tim jerked upright. 'What on earth makes you say that? She hates me.'

'Of course she does. She wants you as you were, because your supposed politics make her love impossible. You are right, she's a stubborn little baggage, too honest for her own good, too strong, and in too much pain to ever be nice to you as things are. I've always had a soft spot for our Bridie, and for the whole family, come to that.' He looked at the Hall. 'It's a special place, with special people. I hope against hope that it doesn't end up being a hospital again. Though if it does, they'll be lucky buggers, the ones that make it this far. So, for the moment, life is back to normal for you, young man.'

Tim said, 'Almost. I have the long weekend training session north of London soon, in spycraft, or somesuch.'

'Indeed, dear heart, but that is your normal, from now on. Be aware, it could save your life.'

'Now, that's a thought to conjure with,' Tim murmured. They both laughed.

Chapter Twenty-Eight

Easterleigh Hall, August 1938

Life had proceeded with great calm at Easterleigh Hall over the summer, with David Weare taking much more of a role with the riding therapy and Estrella drawing closer to him. As June had turned to July, Matron and Sister Newsome seemed to finally understand that the young man was not about to have his heart broken by this young woman, who was not the flighty Jezebel they first surmised.

Bridie liked to think that it was because of her own heavy comments dropped kerplunk when the occasion allowed, but Matron had flapped her hands and told her it was because they had eyes in their heads, and had assessed the situation for themselves. It was no surprise to any of them when David Weare and Estrella Aiza announced their engagement as the sun beat down on the wheat, and the Stunted Tree shimmered in the heat.

Evie and Ver insisted that Easterleigh Hall would host the wedding reception as their gift. Aub, Richard and Harry put their heads together and offered David the position of second in command to Bridie at the riding end of the Neave Wing. It was Bridie's suggestion, as she was finding it increasingly difficult to share both her cooking and riding duties.

'Accommodation for the pair of them?' Bridie queried, as she walked with her parents towards Easterleigh Hall early one morning after the engagement announcement.

Her father raised his eyebrows, and sighed. 'And you have decided – what?'

'I've decided nothing, Da,' she laughed. 'I just asked Matron and Sister Newsome to put their heads together to work out where the two of them can live. It's alright for our couples who come for a holiday to share a hotel room, but David and Estrella can't squash into one permanently, can they?'

'Perhaps they're perfectly happy to squash,' her da objected.

'Oh Da,' she sighed. 'That's not nice.'

Her mam started to say, 'I think it probably is n—'

Bridie held up her hand. 'Please, don't say another word, either of you, and actually, I asked a friend of Harry's to draw up some plans to convert the far end of the third block into an apartment. That gives them some privacy but still easy access for David, as it has all the ramps and walkways. If that's alright with you, of course?'

She saw her da and mam exchange a look. Her mam said, 'That wasn't a question, was it?'

Her da laughed. 'Oh lordy, where have I heard all this before?' He stroked his wife's hair, as they came to the end of the track demarcating the end of Home Farm land. Bridie looked away. He was going to kiss her mam, his love shining out like a beacon, and she felt inexplicably sad, because she was almost eighteen and most girls of her age had a beau. But the man she loved had put himself somewhere she wouldn't go.

She reached down and swept her hand through the long, dry, yellowing grass of the verge, hearing the quiet conversation her parents were having, envying the deep waters of their lives. They left behind the wheat fields, and now sheep grazed on one side, and cows on the other. Easterleigh Hall had its own pasture, its own wheat, a legacy from Uncle Richard's management of the land during the Great War. He and Harry still managed it. Overhead larks sang. She felt momentarily peaceful, as the pain of love settled, as it sometimes did.

The wedding was on 1 October 1938, just after Chamberlain had flown into Croydon Airport waving the Munich Agreement. The newspapers had quoted his words: *Peace for our time*. It seemed to Bridie that the agreement was a bribe, which gave Germany the right to reclaim the Sudetenland region of Czechoslovakia in return for peace in Europe. At six in the morning, she listened to her mam and Aunt Ver as they praised the Prime Minister, while she wanted to slap him. She hurried up the stairs to the ballroom, lifting the muslin covering the wedding cake. It was all her own work, and her mam was pleased, and so too was Mrs Moore. The glasses were ranged on a table along one wall, the buffet implements on another. The tables and chairs had yet to be arranged.

She slipped to the stables, because Fanny should have foaled yesterday but had not. Clive was in the stall. He shook his head at Bridie. 'She always was a lazy girl.' He stroked her neck, as the bay mare guzzled her oats.

'She looks about to pop,' James said from behind Bridie.

Clive grinned at Bridie. 'You look pretty done in, lass.'

'That's what comes of sleeping on a camp bed in the tack room, and waking every hour to check on the old bag. Her teats are waxed up, so she's thinking about labour.' Bridie leaned on the open stable door, listening to the chomping, the swish of the tail, the neigh from another stall. She called, 'Alright Terry, we love you too, but you're not about to heave out a foal, so stop fussing.'

James came alongside. 'How are we going to do the stable shifts during the wedding?'

Bridie snatched a look at Clive, and said, 'Clive's here during the service. You'll be here for the first two hours, then David's taking the next shift.'

James gripped her arm. 'You can't, not the groom, not even you can do that.'

Clive burst out laughing, and Bridie shook her

head at him. 'Ah, he's so easy, Clive. Just so very easy. No, then it's me, then it's you, and then – oh, have a look at the schedule. I have the canapés to check, the vol-au-vent cases to bake, the . . .'

James backed away, his hands up. 'Fine, I've got it. I'll come with you, because I'm on furniture moving duty in the ballroom.'

They headed across the yard, James muttering, 'Not sure about Chamberlain's damned bit of paper. We should be standing up to Hitler, not creeping around, playing nice. Everyone's forgotten what's happened in Spain, if they ever think about it at all. All that practising. I gather the International Brigade is leaving, now that Franco's won.'

The easterly wind was its usual cold self and Bridie pulled her cardigan around her. James continued, 'At least I found Archie Leadbetter's address before the recruitment office closed, so I was able to write to his parents. They were pleased to know he didn't suffer. But I bet he bloody did.'

They headed down the steps. He said, 'You're quiet?'

'What can I say, when it's all a damned great bloody mess?'

They entered the kitchen and the dogs came for their stroke. She picked up Currant, while James lifted Raisin. Mrs Moore was making puff pastry. 'Not sure about not knowing what to say, bonny lass. You're right, it's a mess, right enough, and I don't believe a word that nasty little man Hitler says, and

Chamberlain is a pushover. But the buffet is not about to make itself, so apron on, hands washed and get at it. James, you're wanted upstairs. Tim is helping too, and shouldn't you be at university, anyway? It's no good to keep putting it off.'

James disappeared out of the door. Mrs Moore and Bridie looked at one another. Bridie put Currant down on the armchair, and shrugged. 'I don't know what his plans are, but Da is glad of his help for now.'

Mr and Mrs Weare and the rest of David's family and friends were in their pews, though Estrella's weren't, of course, because they'd been killed. Bridie shut off her mind. She sat at the back with her mother, Annie and Aunt Ver, because they all had to scoot off early, to put a dollop of creamy cucumber and dill on a third of the canapés, smooth pâté on another third, and soft cheese on the remainder. While they did this, Harry and Mr Harvey would sort the champagne. This would keep the ravening hordes quiet while the photographs were taken.

Just for once, it seemed, Edward was not wearing bicycle clips as he waited for the bride. James whispered, 'Perhaps Aunt Gracie's had a word with him?'

Bridie laughed quietly as the organ struck up the wedding march. Her da was giving the bride away, and Maria and Helen, the housekeeper, had helped to make the wedding dress. Estrella looked quite beautiful as Aub walked her down the aisle to join David, who was waiting in his wheelchair. Edward had suggested the couple should sit, and a chair was arranged for Estrella. Edward sat, as well. Bridie thought that was one of the most gracious gestures she had ever known, and typical of Edward.

It was one that Dr Nicholls would have appreciated, but he was unwell, and Matron had confined him, not to his house, but to the Neave Wing, as it was his spiritual home, she had confided in Gracie, now his wife was long gone. So here he would remain, to be a bloody nuisance, Matron announced. Bridie smiled fondly. He was so lovely, but so old. Sister Newsome had stipulated that a new doctor must be found, because it was too much for the silly old fool.

Halfway through the service, the door clicked open and Potty entered, bringing with him a possible replacement for Dr Nicholls. Or so he had written to Evie, who he considered General Brampton of the Easterleigh Hall hotel army. Bridie, her mother and aunt, Annie and Mrs Moore craned round, James too. Potty directed a couple who looked to be in their late thirties, thin but neatly dressed, she in a modest felt hat, into the row in front of the Easterleigh Hall women. He waggled his fingers at them, murmuring, 'Morning, dear hearts, so sorry to be late. Trains, trains, don't let's even think of them.' They sat.

Bridie saw her mother look at Aunt Ver, and smile. That was the doctor sorted, then, Bridie assumed, grinning again.

*

After the photographs, more canapés were served, and more champagne. James took his shift at the stables, taking a plate heaped with chicken, quiche, fresh rolls, salmon, and heaven knows what, plus a bottle of wine. Bridie saw Uncle Richard take the bottle away and pour him a glass, grinning. James laughed. She heard him say, 'Worth a try.'

Uncle Richard said, 'Not while you're looking after Fanny, if you please.'

While the waitresses busied themselves, Bridie and her mam circulated, as did the rest of the family. Mrs Moore was chatting to Edward, as Bridie skirted around Lady Margaret, Penny and Sir Anthony. Lady Margaret had been invited because she and her daughter were spending a week with Sir Anthony at Searton, his estate near Washington. Aunt Ver said that at every wedding there was a cross to bear. Indeed, she thought, as she heard the wretched woman say, 'So wonderful that the Führer has gathered up more *Lebensraum*, and quite right too. He's neutralised Britain, as well. Clever ma—' She stopped as she saw Bridie. 'Hello, Bridie. Your course did you good. These canapés are an improvement on the others. Shame you didn't stay till the end.'

Bridie flushed, and moved on. She joined her mother, who was talking to Potty. 'Charming couple,' he was saying. 'Dr Gerber practised medicine until it became too – what shall we say – difficult, and he lost his patients. So here they are, in need of a calling, and in need of a home. Naturally I thought of the Neave Wing, and my heart sang when I heard dear Dr Nicholls was at last hanging up his hat.'

'Oh,' Bridie said, 'he only decided a couple of days ago. Have you a direct line to our doings?'

It was a joke, but Potty looked flustered. 'No, not at all. I can't think how I heard. Perhaps I bumped into Sir Anthony at the club.'

Evie was frowning at Bridie, her expression saying, will you *please* be quiet. She took Potty by the arm, leading him away. 'Let's have a chat, and we'll bring Matron and Sister Newsome in on it, shall we? Now is as good a time as any before Matron throws her hat over the windmill and misbehaves.'

Colonel Potter guffawed, 'That'll be a sight for sore eyes.'

Matron was already talking to the doctor. Bridie checked her watch. It would be time for her shift in an hour.

Uncle Jack was chatting to David and Estrella, who sat at one of the circular tables, and at that point Harry declared the buffet open. A swarm of bees came to mind, as the waitresses brought a selection of food to the bride and groom. Soon all the guests were taking their places, and now she saw that Tim had arrived, and her heart jolted, and then twisted as he walked to Sir Anthony. They shook hands; he kissed Lady Margaret and Penny as they waited to choose from the buffet. He looked up, and saw her watching. He waved. She made herself return it, before checking her watch again. Damn, she had another half an hour of this.

Tim looked around the room, and his mam came and talked to him, slipping her arm in his. Tim kissed her cheek, his face alight with pleasure. His father came too, then, and the men hugged. Though they had healed the breach, her own parents had not, nor the marras, because they merely nodded or waved from a distance. Silently Bridie applauded.

Tim was now nodding to Potty, who was ensconced with Sister Newsome. Potty nodded in return, briefly. Bridie saw Dr Gerber, who was sitting at the table with Potty and Matron, half rise when he saw Tim, recognition on his face, until his wife said something. He sat down immediately, his head bowed. His wife whispered to him, annoyed. Matron and Potty continued talking, or rather, Matron talked, and Potty listened.

Bridie looked from their table, to Tim. The doctor was German, she knew that much. Tim was a fascist who spent time with Nazis. Do the sums, Bridie, she told herself, and left the reception. It wasn't time for her shift, but she needed some air and something normal, so she joined James in the stall, in all her finery, wondering if Dr Gerber was a Nazi.

Fanny was calm, looking at them as though they were intruding, much as Marigold used to. There were two stools in the corner; James was sitting on one, and his lunch was on the other.

'Typical,' she said, plonking the plate on top of the newspaper on his lap.

'I'm just feeding the inner man,' he muttered, rescuing his paper. 'What are you doing here? You have another, er . . .' He checked his watch. 'Twenty-one minutes precisely.'

'I needed a break.'

He was reading about the Munich Agreement. She sat back as James folded the newspaper and handed it to her. 'Have a read, it passes the time, though she's been a tad restless. Clive looks in every half-hour, so if she starts, don't worry.' He stretched out his legs. 'I've made a decision,' he announced. 'I'm joining the Royal Air Force, and not bothering with university.'

She saw he was watching her, but what did he expect her to say? She said what she thought, 'Why? We're not at war. Peace in our time, remember.'

She waved the newspaper at him. He said, 'You don't believe that any more than I do. Because I want to be ready to do something, is why. Also, if there is no war, I was looking at the photograph of Chamberlain, with the aeroplane behind him. I think a passenger service will be the way to get around very soon, and if it is, we have land here, enough for an airfield. We could buy planes, and I could fly people to London, or even Paris.'

She was impressed, and surprised. 'It would be the best of both worlds, still at Easterleigh, but going everywhere else as well. You'll need food for the journey. I could cook it.' Fanny was becoming restless, as James had said, but that might not mean anything. However, Bridie kept an eye on her as she enthused. She forgot there was a future sometimes. 'You could fly guests to us, as part of the price of their holiday here. Or pick up the disabled – but how would we get them in the plane?'

James put up his hands in surrender. 'A ramp, I suppose. But keep quiet about it, as I need to learn the ropes first, and I might not get accepted.'

Bridie shook her head. 'Oh no, I'm not going to be the only one to know, again. It got me into enough trouble before. You tell everyone, if you don't mind.'

'What trouble is that?' Uncle Richard asked. He was standing at the entrance to the stable.

Bridie just looked at James. 'Your turn, I believe.'

She checked Fanny again, who had settled a bit, so she buried her head in the newspaper as James heaved himself off the stool and left, taking his father with him. Good luck with that, she thought, as she read about the Tory MPs who objected to the agreement, which was, they felt, nothing short of dishonourable appeasement. She was glad she was not alone in her thoughts. Part of her understood, however, because the old were so scared of war after the last one.

Fanny was restless again, looking around at her flanks, shifting her weight from one foot to the other. Bridie went to her, stroked her neck. The mare was sweating. 'Poor baby,' she murmured.

Tim said, 'And so it begins.'

She didn't turn, just wondered how long he'd been there, and now her heart was beating faster. Keeping her voice level, she said, 'Yes, Clive will be here soon.'

'I saw him, and said I'd do his check for him.'

'How dare you give him orders?'

'It wasn't an order, it was an offer, so keep your hair on, Bridie, which looks wonderful, I have to say.'

'Well don't.'

Fanny moved from one hind leg to the other.

'Alright, I won't, but let Clive have his drink, the poor beggar. Fanny seems to be progressing.'

Bridie wouldn't look at him as she stroked Fanny's neck, but the mare tossed her head.

Tim called, 'I think she wants to be alone.'

Bridie knew the feeling and left the stall, leaning on the top of the stable door next to him. 'Don't we all,' she said.

He laughed, and suddenly she was laughing too. They stood together watching the mare. He asked, 'Are you calling Bertram?'

'No, it's early yet, and I doubt she needs a vet. She's done it before and they slip out. Surely you remember?' She looked at him now, loving his high-boned cheeks, his dark eyes, the lashes that were almost longer than hers, his chestnut hair with the red glint.

He nodded, 'Of course I remember. I remember all the years, Bridie. What about the apples we

397

scrumped from Old Froggett? You got stuck up the tree, and James and I had to create a diversion.'

She wanted to laugh but couldn't, because too much time had passed, and he was who he was. She replied, 'Yes, I remember. You threw apples at him, and he called, "You little beggars, I know who you are, and if you think I'm running after you, you've another think coming. And you, Bridie, get yourself down, and try explaining that rip in your dress to your mam. That'll be punishment enough." ' She had remembered it word for word.

Tim said, 'What did your mam do?'

'Spanked me. So I wore my jodhpurs after that. I thought you said you remembered everything?'

'Well, I clearly lied.'

For a moment there was an easy silence, broken by Penny calling, 'Good heavens, this is where you are. Come along, Tim, we need to discuss our antici-pated meeting in Berlin. Mother and I so enjoyed our last trip. Don't be a spoilsport and say you're too busy again.'

Tim moved closer to Bridie, whispering, 'I want to tell you something, but I can't.'

She shook her head. 'I don't want to hear anything from you, do you understand?' She heard him leave, and smug-face's laugh.

James was watching from the path to the Neave Wing. His heart actually hurt when he heard them talk, then lifted when Penny came. But he had seen from the slump in Tim's shoulders, and the backward look, that his feelings matched Bridie's.

His father had said that he must spend time thinking carefully about the RAF. Well, he just had, and tomorrow he would see if they would accept him. He'd tell his parents of his decision, but not why. Well, not the deep reason, but how could he stay here, when he loved someone so much, and she didn't love him? The trouble was, he couldn't hate either of them. He loved them both. He always had and always would.

Chapter Twenty-Nine

Newcastle, November 1938

Sir Anthony sat at the end of the table. He had arranged a celebratory Peace Club Munich Agreement dinner in Newcastle with the usual guests. Tim thought him pale and preoccupied as Penny regaled them with her experiences of Kristallnacht, or the Night of Broken Glass in Germany, when Jewish businesses and homes were attacked and windows broken. She applauded the subsequent arrest of tens of thousands of Jewish men for the crime of being Jewish, who were then sent to concentration camps to meet up with their compatriots already in situ there. Some Jewish women were also arrested and sent to local jails; the few properties remaining in Jewish hands were confiscated. She laughed, waving her hands. 'It's just like house cleaning really.'

Sir Edgers tapped the table. 'Here, here,' he said. His wife clapped.

Tim stared at his food, unable to eat, such was his disgust.

Sir Anthony made no comment, but instead voiced

his relief at October's Munich Agreement and the hopes for peace.

Lady Margaret added, 'So clever of Herr Hitler.'

They lifted their glasses, even Tim, but he wouldn't let the wine touch his lips – though what on earth difference that made to the price of fish, he had no idea. Sir Anthony drank as though parched.

Later Tim wrote his report to Potty, including every conversation of interest Tim had with any member of the party. It made interesting reading, he was sure, especially the sections on Sir and Lady Edgers. He asked if Potty had any more information on Heine's roots, so that when he returned to Berlin, he would have a weapon if Heine ever suspected him of anything.

Tim visited Berlin again in early December, to test the ground and confirm whether Herr Bauer's initial report to Potty, following the Gerbers' escape, still remained accurate, and Tim was indeed under no suspicion.

On his arrival in Berlin, he remembered his training, checking reflections in shop windows as he passed. He jumped on and off trams, doubling back on himself. No-one was following him, and when they had the whole of the Sudeten to sort out, why would they bother about the escape of one Jewish couple? Tim relaxed an iota, but remained vigilant.

He still refused to deliver the original of the letter to Millie and Heine, explaining that he was vulnerable, that he needed the security of it. He insisted that he was repaying his obligation to Heine by carrying packages. He said, 'As long as I am safe, then so are you, Heine. Not only that, but you are now in the SD, and that is only because I am honouring my word and maintaining my promise not to reveal the letter. Take it or leave it, but if you leave it, then there are instructions for the letter to be published. Remember you are guilty by association.'

He sounded much tougher than he felt.

He then presented Heine with yet another package from Sir Anthony and changed for dinner. He had been told that Otto, Bruno and Hans were to be joining them; the three men, like Heine, were all now in the SD, the intelligence branch.

As the coffee and cognac were served, after Millie had left the room, the discussion strayed to a trip the men were taking to Austria the next day. Otto slapped Tim's arm. 'It is something that would interest you, young Tim. A trip to see our partner. Something to tell your fascist friends, to reassure them of the importance of the cause.'

Heine's eyes were cold, but he nodded, and Tim smiled. What else could either of them do in the presence of the other three SD personnel? As he lay sleepless in bed that night, Tim could imagine Potty licking his lips, while his own were dry from nervousness.

The next morning Heine, in the company of Bruno,

Hans and Otto, drove him into Austria, along snowy roads, the windscreen wipers swishing relentlessly. All four, he gathered, would be working on collating and 'obtaining' information for their department, a department that was never named. They spent a week in Vienna, building up their dossiers, while he strolled the streets, despite the cold, beneath the Nazi flags and banners already hanging from the buildings.

Tim drank morning coffee in cafés, ordering in English but listening with an increasing grasp of German to the talk all around. It was pro-German. He listened over lunch, in different restaurants each day, while waiters swanned and swayed between tables. In the evening the five of them rushed out to clubs, and while the comrades drank and ate, Tim pretended to be watching the leggy blondes in their skimpy uniforms as the men talked business: how many Jews they had listed, how many Freemasons, how many Reds, socialists, Mischlings.

At this, he thought of Avraham, and touched the mezuzah case in his pocket. Potty had said he should leave it behind – after all, if he was found with it he would be in danger. Tim wouldn't be parted from it because it enhanced his determination. Each evening, back in his hotel room, aware of bugs, he whispered as he looked in the mirror, 'Britain must have a fighting chance. To do that, we need information, and we need time.'

He would then wash, and pat his face dry. Rituals?

They all had them. Did they make a blind bit of difference? Probably not, but they kept him focused. The Nazis might say they were going to 'expand' only to the East, but he didn't believe that for a moment, neither did Potty, though some in power still did.

In the first week of January 1939, Tim expected to carry yet another package from Sir Anthony to Heine, but he delayed his trip after his da telephoned with news of James, who had been in a training crash in his RAF biplane. An anxious week followed, until the news came, via his da, that James had only broken his leg, and would be back in the air in a few months.

Tim hurried out and bought a couple of books to send to the military hospital. He also bought a couple of late Christmas gifts for his mother: soap and bath oil. For Heine he also bought soap. Well, he didn't want to spend more than he had to on them.

He travelled in the bitter January weather, set firmly on course for the lion's den, though it was a different address, an apartment closer to the centre of Berlin. Could this be a consequence of Kristallnacht? Would he find evidence of another mezuzah case? Of bloody course he would.

He wondered if they would go to the clubs. Would the SS, the SD and Uncle Tom Cobley and all be humming with escalating excitement? Would he hear more talk from Heine and his cronies about their infernal dossiers, or perhaps even, with luck, their thoughts on what they knew or surmised of the future plans of Herr Hitler, or at the very least, their department?

At the apartment, there was, of course, evidence of a removed mezuzah case on the door frame. Inside there were chandeliers capable of competing with Easterleigh Hall's. He handed over his presents. His mother opened hers, and her face fell. Tim said, 'I felt the chocolates were insufficient when I came in early December, but what do you give people who have everything?' He gestured at the room. His mother smiled. Her hair was still blonde, still done up in that ridiculous plait.

Heine was at a card table, similar to the one in their previous apartment. He had not even opened his present, but was poring over the contents of Sir Anthony's package, frowning. Tim watched as his mother burbled by his side about the difficulties of managing servants, now she had two.

'Amala's still with you, then?'

'Indeed not. It emerged her son was a Red. Can you imagine? So we have two girls from the Sudeten, but no doubt they'll find some soldier to marry, even though I chose a couple without good looks.' Tim barely listened, focusing on Heine as he compared the minutes with some handwritten papers from a dossier.

'Tim, are you listening to me?'

'Of course, Mother, but I was thinking of Fanny's foal. I didn't tell you she'd had a mare, did I? So we can breed from her.'

Heine looked up. 'We? So you are all friends?' He sounded more than curious.

Tim cursed himself, but was able to say, honestly, 'Do you really think they will be friends ever again with someone who has my politics? It was a wedding party, and Fanny went into labour. For a moment Bridie and I were together at the stall, but then it all fell apart. I don't care – why would I, when I have Penny, and Sir Anthony, and all the others? They're my family now.'

At the mention of Sir Anthony, Heine had returned to his task of checking the minutes against the other sheets.

Millie gripped Tim's wrist. 'I am your family, not anyone else.'

Heine shouted then, '*You* must remember, you foolish woman, that our family is the *Volk*, the people. They are more important than those who bore us, who parented us. It is the *Volk* that deserve our loyalty. This is what we teach our children, to look to the Führer, not their parents. If they can understand it, why can't you, especially in public, especially—' He waved his hand around. He must mean listening devices.

He was standing at the card table, and had thrown down Sir Anthony's minutes. 'Tim, you know Sir Edgers, I believe?'

Tim was alert, but made his body seem relaxed as he had trained himself to do. 'Yes, I do, but we're not exactly friends, Heine.' He leaned forward, flipping up the lid of the silver cigarette box which had come with his mother from the Gerbers' apartment. 'We've met at the Peace Club dinners and some of the fascist meetings. But we never acknowledge one another, of course, if we happen to pass. It wouldn't go down well.'

'He's still on the committee for—' Heine stopped. 'Never mind. Just— Never mind.'

He was thinking, clearly, tapping the minutes against his thumb. Tim kept his hand steady as he offered the cigarette box to his mother. She took one, as did he, before replacing the box on the table. He tapped his on the back of his hand, then reached for the lighter, also on the table. Heine was watching him. He forced himself to continue. He lit his mother's cigarette, and then his own, and replaced the lighter.

Heine asked, 'Where is the cigarette case we gave you?'

'Forgive me, I had my pocket picked, my wallet went too. I had to walk home, last summer. I didn't know how to tell you.'

Heine shrugged. 'You should have. Millie, get that red gold one from the bedroom. I don't care for it, it's too heavy.' He moved to the decanters and poured them all a Scotch. 'Go, then,' he ordered Millie, as he put her drink on the table. He sank into one of the leather armchairs. Against the far wall was a large ceramic stove which heated the room, almost too much. Millie sighed, and teetered off on her high heels. Her seams were crooked.

Heine lifted his glass towards Tim. *'Prost.'*

Tim replied, 'Cheers.' He needed to keep up the fiction of knowing no German. He sipped.

Heine said, as he took a gulp, 'You never really drink?' It was a question.

Tim laughed, as though embarrassed. 'I did, you might remember, once or twice here in Germany, and too often in Britain. It got me into trouble. It quite put me off.'

Heine looked at him over the top of his glass and gulped almost half the contents, as though that was his comment on the pathetic Britisher's answer. 'I, however, like to drink,' he said. 'Does Sir Anthony like to drink? Does he have many friends? Who are those friends? Does he get distracted? Is he showing his age?'

The questions were coming like shots, rat-a-tat. Tim played stupid, which wasn't hard because he hadn't a clue what to answer, so he tried the truth.

'Well, yes, he has friends. He's such a good man, and now he's celebrating peace, so yes, I suppose he has been, well, celebrating. But he's always the gentleman, never out of hand.'

'His friends?'

Tim shook his head, playing for time to get his head in order. 'Well, I don't know outside our own

circle. Lady Margaret, Penny, Sir and Lady Edgers –
and one or two others drink a bit.' He paused. Ah,
the Edgers. What had Potty said, something about
him being under suspicion? Yes, that was it. He said
now, 'Mark you, now I think of it, Sir Edgers tipples
for England, much more than Sir Anthony, I would
have said. His wife, well . . .' He laughed. 'He had
to take her home from one dinner party. Totally
drunk, she was, and he wasn't too far off it.'

Heine was on his feet again, hurrying to the card
table, reading the minutes, checking the handwritten
ones. He looked up, as though a problem had been
solved, and said, 'You are correct, drink does terrible
things, causes errors and unreliability.'

Millie came back into the room with the cigarette
case. 'This one?'

'How many have you?' Tim laughed.

'He was a jeweller,' Millie said.

Penny arrived with her mother two days later, and
they stayed at a smart hotel. They all met at a
restaurant, with Heine in full uniform, and Bruno
came too, at Tim's suggestion, because his wife had
died the previous year. The blonde, blue-eyed god
cast Tim into the outer darkness within minutes, and
took over Penny's amorous intentions entirely.

His mother consoled him when they arrived back
at the apartment. 'Never mind, Tim. Once she returns
to England she'll forget about him. She's worth
marrying, you know. The family has money, and

if we turn towards the West after all, you'll all be amongst the elite. It'll be such fun, and we can have Easterleigh Hall for our own. Just imagine, returning there in style. How simply wonderful.'

Heine sighed.

Tim barely listened. Potty had told him that he'd doctored the minutes of a meeting which he had left in Sir Anthony's path. He clearly hadn't realised that Sir Edgers had also sent the correct version. At least this time Heine seemed to think that Sir Anthony's were more reliable, but it only needed another agent of Heine's to rumble that Sir Edgers barely touched a drop for Tim's cover to be blown, and Sir Anthony to be put in jeopardy for forwarding misinformation.

He stared up at the chandelier, wondering what progress Potty had made in finding Heine's father's details, because they might well need something damning to wield over Heine, possibly sooner rather than later.

Chapter Thirty

Easterleigh Hall, February 1939

Easterleigh Hall hotel was beginning to earn a reputation for its haute cuisine and Bridie found herself
the star of the kitchen after a London newspaper
published a fine review. But stardom only lasted for
half an hour because then it was work as usual.

It was only Friday and Saturday that offered the
special menu, but Evie and Ver thought, in time, it
could be extended. It depended on the clientele, for
it was they who decided what Easterleigh Hall did
next, her mam told Bridie, as they set about the
luncheons. Bridie nodded. These days she listened
closely to her mam, because she recognised increasingly that she was invariably right.

'As long as we make them aware that we have
haute cuisine as an option,' she murmured, checking
the quality of the mushrooms Young Stan had forced
in the mushroom sheds.

'Bridie, absolutely. Then we assess. Now, are you
sure you don't want to come out at court? Lady
Brampton is on to your da about it again. You would
have to stay with your grandparents in London, go

to parties, meet appropriate young men. She said she'd chaperone you.'

Maudie called from the scullery, 'Don't pull that face, Bridie. It'll spoil the mushroom soup.'

Mrs Moore added from her armchair, 'And curdle the milk.'

Aunt Ver waved as she left the kitchen to do her shift behind the reception desk upstairs. 'Not to mention if the wind changes . . .'

Evie continued, through her laughter, 'Your step-grandmother points out that Penny Granville came out last year, and it really should be you, this year, given the family's standing. She's conveniently overlooking the miners on my side, and the fact that you are a cook and earn your own living.'

Clearly her facial expression was answer enough to her mam's question. Bridie decided to change the subject. 'Incidentally, Mam, I meant to tell you that Marthe and Lucy wrote to me a couple of weeks ago. They've been hunting for premises for a restaurant over the last year, and now they've found somewhere suitable and will be opening very soon, not far from the Institute.'

Evie stopped cutting up the mushrooms. 'Oh, Bridie, did they ask you to join them? You mustn't feel bound to Easterleigh Hall, pet.'

Mrs Moore muttered, 'Nonsense, she must feel bound, mustn't she, my lovely dogs? We're not having her gallivanting off again, getting up to all sorts.' She put down her knitting and pulled the dogs' ears.

Bridie smiled across at Mrs Moore, and passed more mushrooms to her mother. 'Remember not to throw away the stalks, Mam.'

Raisin yelped in his sleep. Mrs Moore said, 'Teaching your mother to suck eggs? It's she who taught you about stalks.'

'Paris?' Evie persisted.

'Not on the cards, Mam, you're stuck with me.' There was a loud groan from everyone, even Maudie and Pearl in the scullery. 'They just wanted us to spread the word to anyone we know heading for, or passing through, Paris.'

There was an uncomfortable silence. Eventually her mam said, 'Perhaps we should mention it to Tim. He seems to be on the continent rather a lot.

'I wouldn't inflict him on my friends.'

Mrs Moore tutted. 'We don't speak against him, remember, Bridie. Jack and Gracie seem to have reached an accommodation, so that is quite enough from you, madam.'

Evie was nodding, not looking at her daughter. 'Mrs Moore is right.'

Bridie rolled her eyes as her mam continued slicing mushrooms, and she did the same with the dill. Every so often she thought she'd forgotten about him, his eyes, his strong hands, his . . . She stopped herself. He was probably with smug-face at this precise moment.

Evie scooped the mushrooms into an enamel bowl, ready for the soup. But Bridie had more, and she pushed the dill to the back of the chopping board and started to flip them onto her mother's board. Evie said, 'Let's get back to the subject of your eagerly anticipated coming out.'

Bridie roared with laughter. 'Just tell her I'd rather be fluffing up a soufflé, if she doesn't mind *very* much.'

'I'll leave that pleasure to your da,' Evie muttered. 'Now, all of us in the kitchen have something for you. It's time you had a new one, for your own recipes.'

Maudie came from the scullery at that moment, with a package, beautifully wrapped in tissue paper. 'We all chipped in, bonny lass,' she said, her hair damp from the steam rising from the sink. Mrs Moore shifted Raisin from her lap and joined them at the table.

Bridie wiped her hands, and unwrapped a new recipe bible, embossed with *Bridie Brampton 1939*. It was the kitchen's way of saying that she was an equal, that she had reached the level of her mother, and Mrs Moore.

Bridie opened the book. On the first page was a message from Monsieur Allard: *For Bridie Brampton, my star pupil. Take this as your certificate.*

She could only smile at them all, because the lump in her throat prohibited all else. Maudie nudged Evie. 'We must treasure this moment, the lass is speechless.'

They all laughed. It broke the moment and Bridie was able to say, 'Thank you. Really, thank you. It's been a bit of a journey, and, well, I've made a pig's ear of it sometimes, and worried you all, but I think at eighteen I'm finally growing up.'

'Very slowly,' they all shouted in unison. The normal food preparation resumed, as the clock seemed to gallop towards luncheon, but then, Bridie thought, as the chicken stock simmered, it always did. She said, 'Don't ever think I want to be anywhere else, because I don't. We'll spread the word about the restaurant in Paris, and good luck to them, but you'd have to drag me out of here at gunpoint.'

'Has anyone taken a coffee up to James?' Mrs Moore asked.

'Harry called in a while ago for one,' Bridie said, feeling that she should have taken it up, but he still managed to make her feel guilty. His pain was too like hers for Tim.

She longed to be able to say, 'Yes, I do love you, in the same way you love me.' But she couldn't, yet neither could she bear to lose her friend.

She made another coffee and took it upstairs. James had been recovering well until he received the letter from Ian, who Bridie remembered from Paris. He had accused James of being a coward for leaving them, choosing freedom to principle. '*We wasted our time, thinking the worst, but all the time you were back with your nobs, courtesy of a bloody*

fascist, no doubt. Or was it just a Lord someone? You, a
supporter of the Republicans? Don't make me laugh.'

The worst thing was that it was the truth, and
that's what hurt him, far more than the leg, he had
told her. He had been sitting in front of his bedroom
window overlooking the garden at the rear of the
Hall at the time, his leg in plaster. She had understood, and had put her arm round him, which
seemed to make it worse, because he shrugged away
from her. But hadn't she shrugged Tim away, too?

Afterwards, James had refused to leave his room
for a whole week. Then Dr Gerber insisted, saying
that his squadron needed him, and there was no
time to sit about moping. After the Sudeten, where
would the Germans go next?

It was enough.

Today, she poked her head around the door, to
meet James' agonised face as he put his coat on,
ready to hop down the stairs for his morning walk.
'My leg itches like buggery.'

She grinned, left his coffee on the side table, then
ran back downstairs and begged a knitting needle
from Mrs Moore. She leapt back up the stairs again.
'Here, you big, strong fly-boy, have a go with this.'

She handed it to him, and as he took it, he looked
at her for a long moment, and then laughed. It was
a real laugh, and he said, 'Dear old Bridie, an answer
for everything.'

Then his face clouded again, and the emotional
pain was back. She ignored it. 'I could have thought

about it at the start, so you see, I haven't the answers. Not to anything, really.'

She left him, and flew down the stairs again and across to the Neave Wing, the paths cleared of snow. She knocked at the half-open door of the treatment room, and said, 'I do hope the plaster is coming off tomorrow, or I think he will grow fangs, Dr Gerber, and attack us all.'

'We cannot have a wolf on the prowl, Fräulein Bridie. So we take it off, the plaster, not the leg, you understand.' He put his stethoscope away in a drawer and turned to her, smiling gently.

She had asked Dr Gerber within days of his arrival where he had met Tim, but he had denied doing so and told her that Tim looked like someone he once knew, in Berlin.

She waved goodbye and headed back to the kitchen, ducking her head in.

'Chop, chop, Bridie,' her mam called.

'Slave driver,' she muttered.

'Aye, it comes easily to me,' her mam said.

Bridie said, 'I have confirmation that James' plaster is coming off tomorrow. I need to tell him.'

'Do the soup first, will you, pet?' her mam asked.

Bridie melted the butter in the pan then added the mushrooms, but as it was a normal menu on a Tuesday she left off the garlic, which would please James, as he couldn't bear the smell of it. He said it was something to do with Spain, but would not elaborate. She added salt and pepper. After a moment, when the mushrooms had softened, she added the stock and cream, and half the dill. It was better to be busy, to concentrate on cooking, instead of worrying that perhaps you should say you loved someone, because they loved you, especially if you didn't want to lose them altogether.

Mrs Moore was standing next to her, peering into the pan. 'A canny touch you have, bonny lass.'

Bridie looked around; her mam was in the cool pantry, out of earshot. She whispered, 'Ought you to love someone because they love you? If you *do* love them, in a sort of a way, but not that way, and you think you might love someone else? Well, know you do.'

Mrs Moore took the wooden spoon from her. 'Don't stir it to death, lass. Leave it to sort itself out. It is what it is, and can't be anything else.' The old lady held her hand beneath the spoon, catching the drips, as she put it onto the spare plate on the table behind them.

Bridie stared at the soup, then moved the pan onto the slow plate. Hadn't Mrs Moore heard her?

Mrs Moore was at her elbow again. 'Think on what I've just said, pet.'

Bridie wiped the surface of the stove, and silently repeated Mrs Moore's words. The furnace was burbling. It needed more coal. Mrs Moore headed to her armchair while Mr Harvey bustled down the internal corridor to the wine store. Mrs Moore sat and settled Raisin. Bridie watched them, the sense of the lovely woman's words finally falling into place, but she did wonder why Mrs Moore couldn't just have said, 'Stop worrying, and no, you can't change your feelings, and that's alright.'

She smiled at Mrs Moore, who smiled back, stroking the dachshund. 'Thank you,' Bridie said.

Mrs Moore replied, 'If you have to work out what someone means, it makes your mind work, and you arrive at a conclusion on your own.'

'You're a witch,' Bridie grinned.

Her mam came out of the cool pantry with the vegetables. 'What have you been up to now, the pair of you?'

'Nothing,' they said together.

Dr Gerber removed James' plaster cast the next day. Mrs Gerber massaged the leg and promised to do so daily. She helped him with some exercises, as she did many of those who found their way to Neave Wing. She was a trained physiotherapist, and had practised alongside her husband in Germany.

At the beginning of March, when the early thaw had cleared the snow, Bridie asked Dr and Mrs Gerber if it would be a mistake for James to walk to the beck. 'Indeed not a mistake, I think that would be a good idea, Fräulein Bridie,' Mrs Gerber said, looking tired but deliriously happy, because she was pregnant.

Bridie and James walked to the beck together, and at first the conversation between them was stilted, but almost without realising they began

419

talking, first of Ian, and then Archie. This led to the RAF, and the sergeant who had screamed that he marched like a pregnant camel. They laughed, and it was like it was when she brought him the knitting needle. As they walked along, they relaxed even more, and at last, for the first time since he had been home, they chatted easily of this and that, and laughed, and teased, and only spoke a little of the world, and nothing of love.

The next week, they galloped out the staleness of winter by racing Marigold and Terry across the countryside. This time there was no talking, just the sound of the horses breathing, the sound of their hooves, the creaking of leather, and as they turned for home, the real race began. James gave a Red Indian whoop, just as he used to, throwing back his head, laughing as he took the lead, and then slowing so that together they trotted Terry and Marigold onto the track leading to the stables.

The next day, they went on a trek with the injured – or those who were ready 'to be released into the wild', as David called it. He came too, in the double saddle, with Estrella up behind him, and Clive alongside. Young Stan, Kevin and Harry walked beside the amputees.

Finally, on 10 March, it was time James returned to base, signed off by Dr Gerber. The whole family gathered on the steps to wave. Aunt Ver hugged him, told him to be more careful from now on. She brushed an imaginary fleck from his blue uniform.

His father put his bag in the boot, and sat in the passenger seat. Uncle Jack called, 'Brave man, Richard. Your lad drives like the devil.'

He hugged James, who threatened to punch his lights out if he besmirched his driving one more time. Uncle Jack ruffled the lad's hair. Gracie shook her head, 'Leave the lad be, Jack.' She kissed him, then wiped her lipstick off his cheek.

He hugged Mrs Moore. He had confided to Bridie that each time he left, he feared it would be the last time he saw Mrs Moore, or Mr Harvey. Mr Harvey offered his hand, but he got a bear hug instead. Evie and Aub hugged him tight, and Harry and Annie too. Bridie felt a prickle of fear. It was as though he would never be home again.

He walked with Bridie to the car. She had a basket of macarons for him to share amongst his friends. He put the basket on the back seat. They looked at one another, and he hugged her closely, saying into her hair, 'You take care, bonny lass. I know you don't feel as I do, but underneath it all, I still love you like I did when we were bairns. It's the core of my life, you, Tim and me, and as long as we three still live, we'll be alright. He's the best, you know. Remember that. Look beyond the obvious. I did.'

He let her go, and said again, 'It's alright with me, Bridie, as long as we all have one another. Trust him, Bridie. He asked me to, and I do.'

They drove away.

*

James listened as his father back-seat drove through Easton, as he always did, feeling Bridie against him, longing for her, but knowing that what he had said was the truth. He said, aloud, 'I need the three of us.'

His father said, 'Watch the corner. What was that you said?'

James sighed, 'Nothing, Dad, and yes, I know it's a corner. Do you think you should join the RAF and come up in the plane with me? I might hit a cloud.'

His father braced himself for the crossroads.

'It's alright, Dad, I know there's a crossroads,' James muttered, before his father could.

He hoped that Bridie would listen to what he had just said.

He wondered what his mates would think of him having a knitting needle in his kit. But he wasn't about to leave it behind, and Mrs Moore could always find another. He needed to remember Bridie's kindness, and her laughter, and how they had found their way back to one another.

Chapter Thirty-One

On 15 March Hitler invaded and began the occupation of the rest of Czechoslovakia in contravention of the Munich Agreement, and all those at Easterleigh Hall, and throughout the country, asked, 'Does this mean war?'

On 31 March Britain issued a statement guaranteeing Poland's independence.

The first weekend after that, Tim took the sleeper down to London, in order to attend a dinner with Sir Anthony, Lady Margaret and Penny. The waiter was one of Potty's men. It was he who now added the powder to Sir Edgers' drinks on a regular basis, rendering him seemingly drunk. On this occasion it was his wife and Sir Anthony who had to take him to a taxi, through the foyer of one of the smartest hotels in London.

Penny was so outraged, this time, that she wrote the news to Bruno, with whom she was still infatuated, complaining about the lack of manners in old people today.

Potty warned Tim when they met in a café near his office the next day that, though he felt that should sort the situation for now, he might have to pull the net closed, catching a shoal of wriggling fascist informers, sooner than he had anticipated. 'Poland is guaranteed, but it is in the East, dear boy. Why on earth should Herr Hitler think we will make good our promise, rushing our troops way over there? I mean, he just has to look at our past flaccid responses.' He paused. 'Old laddie, I assume you will remain with our merry little band, for what is to come?'

Tim looked at the tea leaves at the bottom of his cup, wishing he could read them and see the world as it would be in the months and years to come. Finally he nodded. He was learning his craft, his German was almost fluent. He was good at the work, and there weren't enough people as it was. The fact that it screwed his belly up with tension and fear was neither here nor there. The fact that he lived a lie, and his extended family were ice-cold towards him, would have to be borne. But Bridie? She was the problem who tore his heart out by the roots.

The next day Bridie was preparing the menu for the day, thinking that she would use the sole from their supplier for Sole Meunière, while her mother finished the breakfasts. As they did so, they heard someone running down the steps from the garage yard. It sounded almost like James, but not quite. There was a knock at the kitchen door. Who knocked? Everyone just came in. They both looked round.

'Hello, Bridie.' It was Tim, standing in the doorway, holding the door open. 'How are you, Aunt Evie?'

He had his hat in his hand. Evie returned to watching the bacon. 'I'm fine, lad. How goes it with you?'

He didn't reply, just said, 'I'd like to talk to Bridie, only for a moment, if I may? Perhaps outside? It's not cold.'

Bridie just shook her head. He stayed in the doorway. 'I'm not going until you come. Please, Bridie, I'll stay here all day otherwise, and that will cause a draught, and Mrs Moore might get a chill, and I'd be sorry about that.'

The dogs were at his feet now, whining for a stroke, which he gave them, laughing softly.

Her mam looked across at her. 'He's got Jack's look about him, the one before his fist fights when he was a hewer in Auld Maud, so he won't go away. But it's not going to trouble her, is it, bonny lad? If it is, I'll come too.'

Bridie almost smiled, because her mam had exactly the same look on her face. Tim said quietly, 'Do you really think I'd hurt our Bridie, Aunt Evie?' He was shaking his head. He was pale, and tired. He'd lost more weight, Bridie thought.

Tim hushed the dogs now and sent them back to Mrs Moore, who waved at him and said to Bridie, 'By, go with the lad. He hasn't grown horns, not that I can see anyway, pet.'

Bridie's heart was thumping in her chest. She

longed to be with him, but it was also the last thing she wanted. 'Wait for me outside, and shut the door. You weren't born in a barn, were you?'

Looking as though she'd slapped him, he turned on his heel and shut the door, shouting, 'I'll be at the cedar tree.'

Evie stared at Bridie, then understanding dawned. 'You'd best go, and stop being rude. It doesn't solve anything and makes you sound like a three-year-old, and your feelings don't belong with a child. Go and talk it out with the lad. Love deserves that.'

Bridie looked at Mrs Moore for support, but the old cook said, 'Aye, rude as anything, I'd call that, and cowardly. Get yourself up those stairs. The sooner you get there, the sooner it'll be sorted.' The dogs were scratching at the door, wanting to be out with Tim, but Mrs Moore called them back. As Bridie left she heard her asking Evie if she'd seen her size ten knitting needle.

Bridie made herself walk up the steps, when she wanted to run to him because she had seen the love in his eyes. But it could go nowhere because of what he was. She braced her shoulders and walked through the stable yard, calling softly to Terry, who was looking out from his stall. He whinnied. 'In a moment, pet,' she said, amazed that her voice was so calm.

Tim was watching her as she headed across the grass towards him, skirting the small marquee erected a week ago for a small wedding reception next week. She held her head high. This man that she loved admired the people who had hurt Dr and Mrs Gerber. He went to those dinners of Sir Anthony's. He danced with smug-face. He wore a fascist badge, and went to their meetings. He went to Berlin, and who knew what he did there, with Penny and without her? Trust him, James had said. The boy was mad, and should know better.

Her fury was in place by the time she reached him. He looked at her. He said, 'I love you. I can't live with you thinking of me as you do.'

She shouted then, 'How can I think otherwise? You're a fascist, you're hand in glove with Heine; I hate you for it, because I want to love you back.' She ended on a high-pitched wail, longing for him to hold her, to make things better as he had always done, but how? How?

He made no move to comfort her, and had he done so, she would have beaten him back.

Instead, he stood quite still, and said, 'I don't know where to begin, really.'

She said, 'Then I will. What I feel for you is love, and I hate you for it.'

He smiled. 'So you keep saying. I understand that you hate me, loud and clear. But I also understand that you love me.' He moved now, and gripped her arms. He loomed over her, but his face was gentle, his eyes intense. 'Please trust me, Bridie. Things aren't always what they seem. There's a battle being waged, and soon we will be at war. Sometimes we have to pretend to be what we aren't. I can't say more than that. Trust me, love me as I love you.'

She almost saw the words coming from his mouth, and she couldn't understand. 'What do you mean, things aren't what they seem? You're as bad as Mrs Moore, she doesn't come straight out with things.'

'Why do you think that is?' His voice was almost a whisper, and he maintained his grip.

She remembered how Mrs Moore had said it made you think and come to a conclusion. She studied his words, which still hung in the air, somehow. In the end, she asked, 'How does Dr Gerber know you? He says he doesn't, but I don't believe him.'

He started to shake his head, then said, 'You need to trust me.'

She pulled free. 'Well, that's not good enough. You need to tell me the truth, just once, because I'm beginning to think that perhaps, yes, you are living a lie, but living it far too well. Living it in the face of great odds, and if you can do that, how can I ever trust you not to live a lie to me?' There, that was her conclusion.

He held her arms again. She could see the thoughts chasing across his face. Finally he said, 'I work for the Secret Intelligence Service, undercover in the fascist party. I have become fluent in German. This enables me to glean information from Heine and his SS and SD friends, and even from my mother. I am a trained operative. I can tell if I'm being followed. I could kill if I had to. I learned who the Nazis really are after a night in the cells, at their hands. I had been blind to them, up to that point. Yes, I was a fascist.' He repeated, 'I was a fascist. I believed it was the way forward. I was wrong. I've tried to put it right.'

She said nothing, but listened to every word, trying to put them into some sort of sense in her heart.

Tim was drawing closer. 'I brought out Dr and Mrs Gerber but no-one must know that, because there are Nazi agents here, and there are British fascists working for them. If questions are asked, they are refugees. Bridie, I need to maintain my cover. I will remain in the intelligence service because they are short of people, so my life will be secret, or if you prefer, a lie. The one thing that won't be is my enduring love for you, and everyone here.'

Bridie felt as though she was being buffeted by a turbulent wind, and couldn't grasp anything firm enough to stop the swirling thoughts.

In the end, she said, 'But you pretend so well, Tim. Perhaps you're pretending now? You must see how I can't love or trust someone like you.'

He let go of her arms. He just nodded. 'I have said all I can. I love you. I will never lie about that, but there is, and will be, crucial work to do to keep the country safe. All of us will be involved, and this will be my way. That is it, Bridie. That is the sum of it. Now, I have something to do. I will be back for your answer.'

He walked past her. He'd parked his motorbike at the bottom of the drive. She said to his back, 'I've given you my answer.'

He called back, 'I'm not accepting it.'

She watched him roar out of the drive, wanting to run after him, but wishing she'd never met him too.

Uncle Potty emerged from behind the marquee, making her jump almost out of her skin. 'You really are a silly girl. He's a good man. He helped James to return, though he knew it would put him under an obligation to that unpleasant SS officer, Heine. Great shame, really, as he'd just seen his own political leanings as a mistake and wanted to be as far from it all as anyone could. I persuaded him to return to do a double bluff, to work for his country. This he did, though he knew he could tell no-one, and would therefore jeopardise his standing in the community and his family.'

She could still hear his motorbike, as he travelled along the road. It was growing fainter. 'I gave him permission to tell his parents. I did not give him permission to tell you, but I knew he would, eventually. I did not give him permission to go where he's going, but I knew he would. I just hope he manages to work a miracle. It will save much heartache, and not his so much, this time. Of course, if you ever speak of this, I will have to kill you.'

He walked away, behind the marquee again, and Bridie thought he was teasing but she wasn't sure.

She still didn't know what to think, what to feel, because Tim was her hero again, the person who had always protected her, waited to cross the line, all of them together, the person who made her feel that she could say and do anything, and he'd still be there for her. But she hadn't been there for him.

She walked out from beneath the cedar tree, listening to his fading engine, because if he had always done that, and still professed to do so, then what the hell was she waiting for? She laughed now, lifting her head and watching the clouds racing across the sky. She was waiting for him to return, that's what. Because she knew that, quietly and in secret, she would always know the truth, and be there for him. That's what love was all about.

Tim roared up Searton's drive. It was south of Washington and half an hour from Easterleigh Hall. He had telephoned Sir Anthony early this morning, checking that he was at home. He had said, 'Come, dear Tim. I drove up last night. I have things to sort out.' He sounded so tired.

Tim parked his motorbike quite close to the front door because he wanted to return to Bridie the minute he had finished here. He drew off his leather gloves and placed them neatly on the saddle, with his leather helmet, not knowing quite what he was going to say, but he must try.

He rang the bell. Mr Dorkins, the butler, let him in. He put his hand out for Tim's goggles. He kept them. Sir Anthony came from his study, and beckoned him in.

'This is a pleasant surprise, young Tim. I have no package, if that is what you need.'

Tim entered and stood there, on the pale pink Persian rug. It was a light room, one he had never entered before. He had been here for one dinner only. He said, 'No, I do not need any packages, and neither, I feel, should you give them to me any more, Sir Anthony.'

The man's shoulders seemed to fold, and he almost staggered to one of the elegant French chairs placed either side of the fireplace. He said, as he sat and sank his head in his hands, 'It's a relief, you know. I knew it was wrong, but I simply had no choice. But that's what we traitors all say, isn't it?' His voice was muffled, and finally he raised his head, to hear Tim's answer.

'I don't know,' Tim said, which was the truth.

'And you, Tim. Why is it that you are here? I expected Potty. I knew he was something behind the scenes, but I didn't know what. But you? Yes, I see it now. You don't actually drink the toasts raised by the dreadful Lady Margaret and her equally awful daughter, or indeed, the Edgers. You listen, you say little. Ah yes, I see, I think, so tell me, Tim Forbes, what of you?'

Tim said, 'I'm not important.'

Sir Anthony half laughed. 'Do you really think so?'

Tim sat opposite him, wrapping his goggles around

his hand. 'The thing is, Sir Anthony, everyone holds you in such high esteem, but the net is going to tighten around fascists who pass information. Well, indeed, anyone who passes information, to what we consider the enemy. You have been under surveillance, and it has been noted that you have accessed files that were not in your remit. Over the last several months you have passed misinformation, placed by our intelligence service, to prove that you were indeed doing it. You are by no means alone, and we believe that you are being coerced.'

Sir Anthony shifted in his chair, looking at Tim, startled. Tim said, 'We suspect that you are being blackmailed.'

Again there was that half-laugh from Sir Anthony.

Tim didn't understand, but continued. 'People are going to be caught and interned, at the very least, if they can't be turned to work for us. I've come to you, privately, because you are such a good man, someone who has always been a supporter of peace and the disadvantaged.'

Sir Anthony said nothing, just stared down at his hands, which were clasped motionless in his lap. 'You don't understand, dear Tim Forbes,' he said. 'You are right, Herr Weber tried to blackmail me, but what is that, when all is said and done? So I refused.'

Tim shifted in his seat, staring at his goggles. Surely this man was not acting out of conviction?

Sir Anthony opened his hands helplessly. He

looked up at Tim. 'You see, my dear Tim, you travel to see your mother, of course you do. You will continue for as long as the world situation allows it. It was made clear to me that if I faltered, he'd have you arrested when you visited next, and you would be "disappeared". If I told you and you ceased to visit, he would have agents who could find you. What could I do? What can you do, now? How can we keep you safe?'

Tim felt the shock rock right through him. He felt cold, his mouth dry. He couldn't speak. All this time it was – what? – a double bluff by Heine, when he and Potty had thought they were so clever.

'So, my dear Tim, through no fault of your own, you are indeed important in this matter.'

The door opened, and Mr Dorkins announced, 'Colonel Potter for you, Sir Anthony.'

Tim spun round, because he, Tim Forbes, agent of the SIS, should not be here, but Sir Anthony rose and waited for Potty, who had stepped into the room with utter aplomb. He advanced across the carpet as though it were a cocktail party, his hand outstretched, his smile broad. Sir Anthony said, 'Dear Potty. I fear I have been a menace.' They shook hands.

'I think not. I did hear most of it, Ant, old lad. Mr Dorkins wasn't at all happy with me putting my lugs to the door, but needs must, as I said to him. Awfully naughty of me, and I do apologise, but I know you too well, Ant, old boy, to believe that you'd be stupid enough to pass important information lightly. There had to be a reason other than a bit of how's-your-father blackmail, and we just needed to confirm our German agent's findings, which you have just done. Of course, I could just have asked you, but perhaps you would not have told me?' He looked at Tim. 'Upsy daisy, young man. Time for the old ones to take a seat.'

Tim sprang to his feet and moved to one side. The chair looked too fragile to take Potty's weight, but it did, though it creaked.

'Now, let's think of a plan, dear hearts. Perhaps one does feel that an illness is imminent, Ant. So, let's pop you into a nice little nursing home with a heart attack, and then a gentle cruise in warm climes. However, sadly, you will be left with fragile health, and not up to belting across the continent to Germany, or working in the Foreign Office. What d'you think, old fella my lad?'

Tim knew his mouth hung open. Potty turned to him. 'As for you, old laddie, I do feel that a little billet-doux to the old folk in Berlin is necessary, explaining that work in the office is pressing, and you now have a lady love, so you will be seeing your ghastly mother at some stage, but you know not when. Off you go then, Tim, for dear Ant and I have many ends to tie. Incidentally, Tim, we have traced that little matter that concerns Marburg. So, we can now stick our great size nines in the door belonging to an important booted person, can we not, whenever we choose.' It wasn't a question. He was waving Tim away. 'Put the plug in the hole on your way out, dear heart.'

Tim turned to go, but Potty called him back. 'You might notice a baker's van outside, Tim, dear heart. Stop, tap on the rear doors – not for a doughnut, you understand, just to let them be on their way. I won't be needing a lift. I'm sure Ant will sort me out.' He put up his hand. 'No, no, on second thoughts, I'll see you out.'

Potty heaved his great girth from the chair, which sighed, probably with relief. Tim was hustled out of the door and Potty clapped him on the shoulder, whispering, 'We, or rather Bauer, suspected Heine's nasty little game, but we needed confirmation. One would like to imagine your mother knew nothing of it.'

He continued, 'We'll keep you in dear old Blighty, for now, at least. I doubt Herr Heine Weber would have "disappeared" you while you had the original of the letter, and certainly he won't now that we have his parental details. You are safe, Tim. Let's not, however, share that with Sir Anthony. Best all round if he thinks he was saving your life. Off on your trusty steed with you.' He shut the door firmly in Tim's face.

Tim rode back, but stopped first and tapped at the rear doors of the van plastered with the legend: 'Bread from Fred's finest flour'. A startled face appeared in the window. The man grinned when he saw Tim, and opened the door. 'We're to go, I imagine. Thanks, Tim. Interesting, I bet? Dare say he'll fill us in.'

Tim rode on, thinking how bloody much he still had to learn, just when he was thinking he was a professional and had got it all sorted. Throughout the ride to Easterleigh Hall, he tried, but failed, to rid himself of Heine's face, his voice, his devious, cold mind, and he knew Potty was wrong. Heine would have 'disappeared' him with the greatest of pleasure, but perhaps he would have waited until he had finally located the original of the letter.

He refused to even think of his mother; it was pointless. Instead he thought of poor, generous, noble Sir Anthony, who had suffered soundlessly because of him.

He didn't even bother to look for Bridie, knowing he'd have to go and knock on the kitchen door again, and haul her out and make her see that they were made for one another. What's more, he was starving, and could eat one of her lunches. His thoughts were dwelling on inanities because he could not bear to remind himself of the people his mother and her husband were, and neither could he bear to hear Bridie say, 'I hate you,' even one more time. Perhaps he would go straight to Newcastle after all.

Bridie watched from the tree as he drew up near the steps of the hotel, dismounted, and ripped off his goggles. When he removed his helmet, she was shocked at how drawn his face looked. She ran now, across the grass and the gravel. At the noise he looked up, paused, then threw his helmet down and waited, bracing himself.

She called, 'I love you. Whatever you do, whoever you are, I love you, Tim Forbes, or whoever you are today.'

He paused again, and then opened his arms.

She threw herself into them. 'I love you,' she said yet again, holding his face. 'I love you, I always have, and I always will. I will trust you till the day I die.'

He pulled her to him, and kissed her. Her hands were in his hair, pulling him down to her. She broke away, so happy she thought her heart would burst.

He said, 'Then you will trust me for millions of years, because you'll never die, Bridie Brampton. You will marry me, cook haute cuisine, have our children, and I will adore you, and tell you every truth in my life. Trust me, my love, the essence of you will remain in the world forever.'

She knew she was already home, but it felt better, much better, with Tim here too. Soon the others would see that, though they'd never know the whole truth. James would guess, though, because he was part of the three of them.

'I love you,' she said again.

Easterleigh Hall

Margaret Graham

**Her life began in the service of others.
Her future would be hers.**

When Evie Forbes starts as an assistant cook at Easterleigh Hall, she goes against her family's wishes. For ruthless Lord Brampton also owns the mine where Evie's father and brothers work and there is animosity between the two families.

But Evie is determined to better herself. And her training at the hall offers her a way out of a life below stairs.

Evie works hard and gains a valued place in the household. And her dream of running a small hotel grows ever closer.

Then war is declared and all their lives are thrown into turmoil.

arrow books

Easterleigh Hall at War

Margaret Graham

England is at war and Easterleigh Hall has been turned into a hospital for the duration of the hostilities.

With its army of volunteers and wounded servicemen, cook Evie Forbes is determined that everyone will be properly provided for, despite the threat of rationing and dwindling supplies.

All the while she waits for letters from her fiancé and beloved brother, fighting on the Western Front.

Then the worst happens – a telegram arrives with shattering news. And Evie wonders if she'll have the strength to carry on . . .

arrow books

Above Us The Sky

Milly Adams

June 1940, Waterloo Station

On one of the hottest days of the year, newly qualified teacher Phyllie Saunders is evacuated with her school to Dorset.

As she struggles to control the crowd of tearful children, she sees Sammy. Her oldest and dearest friend is on the way to join his submarine, and as he kisses her goodbye, everything changes for them.

But now that war is tearing them apart, is it too late?

Phyllie throws herself into village life, determined to protect and nurture the children in her care. But war leaves no one untouched, and Phyllie will need all the support of the community to help her through the next few years, as she waits and prays for Sammy's safe return . . .

arrow books